"IT CANNOT BE SUCH A BAD THING, FALLING IN LOVE. . . ."

"It is the worst thing." Michael tossed his head back. His eyes burned into Analisa's. "Passion steals a man's senses. It robs a woman of her strength. I have seen this to be true."

"I have never felt so strong, so filled with life, as I do at this moment," she whispered.

With a low moan he caught her against his chest. His heart beat against hers, its power steadying her. Only then did he move his lips against her hair, murmuring her name. . . .

"Analisa?" His lips brushed hers, and then rested against her forehead.

"Michael?"

"I cannot love you. _____ ____ ____ this vow to me: Pro_____

"I . . . I promise _____ said, her voice shak_____ tend that love is wo_____

PIRATE
OF MY
HEART

~

Donna Valentino

A TOPAZ BOOK

For Joe, who never says,
"Remember when you used to
have time to cook with real spices?"

TOPAZ
Published by the Penguin Group
Penguin Putnam Inc., 375 Hudson Street,
New York, New York 10014, U.S.A.
Penguin Books Ltd, 27 Wrights Lane,
London W8 5TZ, England
Penguin Books Australia Ltd, Ringwood,
Victoria, Australia
Penguin Books Canada Ltd, 10 Alcorn Avenue,
Toronto, Ontario, Canada M4V 3B2
Penguin Books (N.Z.) Ltd, 182–190 Wairau Road,
Auckland 10, New Zealand

Penguin Books Ltd, Registered Offices:
Harmondsworth, Middlesex, England

First published by Topaz, an imprint of Dutton Signet,
a member of Penguin Putnam Inc.

First Printing, January, 1998
10 9 8 7 6 5 4 3 2 1

1

The Netherlands—November 1647

Men seldom visited the Vandermann School for Company's Daughters during the day, and not at all after dark.

Certainly never at the unthinkable hour of midnight.

But there was no denying that only a strong male fist could have launched the thunderous assault on the front door that jolted Analisa Vandermann upright in her bed just as the clock tolled its twelfth stroke. There could be no doubt that the imperious voice demanding entrance belonged to the usually circumspect Director Jakob Odsvelt.

The school's budget spared little money on frivolous luxuries, such as the lighting of hallways at night. Moonlight alone illuminated Britta, Analisa's mother, as she hurried to admit the director, and then silvered her taut features when she paused briefly at Analisa's doorway. The moon bleached all color so that the anxious furrows upon Britta's forehead seemed to rise straight into her tightly braided blond hair. "I shall see what he wants, Analisa. You settle the girls."

Analisa murmured an assent as her mother sped away. Then, with a sigh, she twisted her unbound hair into a knot atop her head and tugged her much-hated nightcap into place. She dug the voluminous sleeping gown from beneath her pillow and pulled it on over her shift, fastened its buttons up to her chin, jerked at the attached capelet until it draped properly over her shoulders.

She knew that only trepidation over the director's unannounced visit had diverted Britta from noticing that Analisa had been sleeping in wanton comfort. According to Britta, Dutch ladies never approached their beds without first swathing themselves head to toe, until they resembled enormous woolen bells. Verbal lectures concerning such things had ended five years ago, when Analisa turned twenty-one and it became apparent that no decent man would ever offer for her. But though she need not worry about pleasing a husband, Analisa could not set a bad example for the girls. She never appeared before her students without looking every inch the proper Dutch matron.

Dormitories lined the hall. The doors had been cracked open despite school rules to the contrary, and from each opening poked two or three neatly braided and nightcapped heads, each girl's features avid with curiosity. Like a stable filled with inquisitive fillies, Analisa thought—exactly like it, for her students were more or less broodmares in training, though it pleased their masters to call them by the benevolent term of Company's Daughters.

She sighed, shaking her head at the futility of trying to calm her charges, and wondered at Director Odsvelt's interruption. The school sheltered girls, mostly orphans, whose reputations had to remain beyond reproach. The Dutch East India Company chose the girls, fed them, trained them, all for the express purpose of marrying those men who carried out the Company's business in far-flung places, where few white women were willing to live. Analisa could not imagine why Director Odsvelt, their most critical supervisor, flouted propriety and custom with his unannounced, late-night visit.

"Back to bed now, all of you." She urged the girls into their rooms with gentle pats and subtle pushes.

"Juffrouw Analisa, I will not be able to sleep," lisped young Lisbet.

"I will bring you warm milk," Analisa promised.

"And bring us the news as well!" cried Katje, the eldest at seventeen. "You must tell us what has caused this commotion."

"Only if you return at once to your beds—"

Clang. Clang. Clang. The unmistakable sound of the marriage parlor's bell undid all Analisa's work.

The girls surged back into the hallway. They held their collective breath and cheered when the marriage bell sounded once more in confirmation. They surrounded Analisa, clapping and giggling. Lisbet betrayed her youth by clutching at Analisa's skirts.

"Oh, Juffrouw Analisa, I . . . I am the eldest." Katje looked near to fainting from excitement, or from the sort of dread that strikes those who sense that achieving their heart's desire sometimes brings despair rather than delight. "It is my turn."

"Now, Katje, you know that just being the eldest does not mean you will be chosen for this match,' Analisa both warned and comforted.

"Yes, yes, it may be *my* turn," crowed Trudy. "I shall have a gown with lace at the throat!"

The girlish speculations filled the air, interspersed with half-muffled shrieks, nervous giggles, and one or two unladylike hops. "Remember your manners," Analisa scolded in her sternest teacherly manner. She tried to temper it with understanding, for it had been a hard task to master her own urges to shriek, giggle, and hop with excitement. "To your beds, all of you."

"Oh, but, juffrouw, we won't be able to sleep, not until we know."

"I shall return and tell you the minute my mother and Director Odsvelt decree who the new bride shall be," Analisa promised.

" 'Tis so exciting!" murmured Katje, her young features betraying hope that she might be the new bride. "It must be a very important match, for the director to come so late at night."

Analisa answered with a vague smile, but as she hurried toward the marriage parlor, she couldn't help wondering at the unseemliness of announcing a marriage in the dead of night.

Britta's unsteady hands betrayed similar unspoken concerns as she lit candles from the marriage parlor's single oil lamp. Analisa could see it was a futile effort; not even a dozen candles could pierce the parlor's midnight gloom.

"Leave off with that, Mother. I shall summon a servant to fetch logs for a fire."

"No servants." Director Odsvelt snapped the order, and then mollifying his tone, offered an explanation, which in itself was as unexpected as his presence. "No fire could blunt this room's chill in time to save me a great deal of discomfort."

Analisa bowed her head in outward acceptance of his reasoning. She had learned long ago that an apparent show of submission deflected attention away from her regrettably argumentative nature. Her lips trembled from the urge to point out to the director that his own untimely, unannounced arrival was responsible for his discomfort. A room so cavernous, so seldom used as this marriage parlor hidden deep within the Vandermann School, could retain its chill for hours. They always took care to order a fire built early on the days when a glove marriage was to be announced.

Odsvelt settled himself into a chair, his stout legs braced wide to accommodate his bulging belly. His ever-present disdain curled at the edge of his mouth, but there was a new speculative air about him as the fat pouches round his eyes narrowed to study her well-robed figure. Analisa was suddenly glad that she didn't have to kneel at the hearth and present him with a view of her bottom, equally grateful for the concealing nature of the garment she wore.

As a Vandermann woman, she should have grown accustomed by now to that sort of regard from Amsterdam's most solid citizens.

"I am in dire need of refreshment, Juffrouw Britta," said the director. Analisa sensed her mother stiffen, as she always did when called *juffrouw* and reminded of her unmarried status.

"Certainly. I shall call the maid—"

"I told you, no servants,"the director interrupted.

"I could prepare some toast and marmalade." Analisa made the offer, though she knew Odsvelt's overindulged palate would scorn such simple fare. She kept her head lowered and brushed nonexistent bits of chaff from her robe while she stifled the urge to remark that they did not keep appetizing treats on hand for chance midnight visitors.

"I would sooner starve." Odsvelt sniffed. " 'Tis such an *English* refreshment, Analisa, and I am not one of your would-be brides who must learn to pretend they enjoy foreign victuals. But, then, I suppose I must remember I am in a house known to favor all things British."

He smirked. And implicit in his smirk lay the reminder that the morally unforgiving Dutch still remembered Britta's long-ago indiscretion, still held Analisa in contempt for daring to be born.

Analisa sometimes thought things might have gone easier for Britta, and for herself, if she had been born all pink and blond like Britta, like the full-blooded Dutch girls who filled this house. Instead, the English privateer who'd seduced and deserted Britta had left his stamp all over their illegitimate daughter, and nothing could remove the stain.

Analisa had learned that no amount of lemon juice could turn chestnut-brown hair blond, or bleach a golden complexion until it resembled porcelain tinged with pink. No magic existed to transform hazel eyes into sky-blue, and no foods, no matter how prodigiously consumed, could sculpt a naturally slender body into round, soft, plump curves.

The school provided a haven for the both of them. Although Britta's family had banished her from her ancestral home, the Vandermanns had established the school with the understanding that Britta would serve as its superintendent. The arrangement suited the Dutch East India Company; by employing Britta, it pleased the Vandermann men who held high positions within the organization.

And Britta was touchingly, cringingly, *everlastingly* grateful. The responsibility fulfilled her in ways Analisa suspected no husband could match. Britta protected the Company's interests with the fierce loyalty of a lioness guarding her den. She lectured her charges with heartfelt passion on the terrible fates that could befall young ladies who strayed from the path of morality. The girls who graduated from the Vandermann School made excellent, submissive Company's Daughters.

Analisa taught the girls to read and write in English in order to make them more useful if their husbands were one of the Company employees who dealt with the British. She had learned that language when she was very young, when a Company official had suggested to Britta that Analisa might have an inborn aptitude for that difficult tongue. Britta had welcomed the opportunity to make Analisa useful to the Company. She had swayed Analisa away from the notion that the suggestion had been a not-so-subtle reminder of her illegitimacy, that the ability added another layer to her foreign demeanor and thus bound her ever more tightly to the Company.

Director Odsvelt chuckled and heaved himself from his chair with an intermittent snorting and catching of breath that contributed to his overall porcine appearance. He dug into his jacket and pulled free a wooden glove box, which he laid upon a table, unerringly placing it dead center with the familiarity of one well accustomed to the task. Britta came up beside him. The two stood staring at the glove box as though it were perfectly usual to gather at midnight merely to admire the contrast of the box's rich golden sheen against the table's age-blacked mahogany.

"I have never seen such exquisite workmanship in a glove box," Britta marveled.

"Nor have I, juffrouw. I am told it is crafted of nutmeg wood. 'Tis fitting that the female who becomes a bride with this glove shall carry the box back to its place of origin."

Analisa joined them at the table and couldn't stop herself from running a finger against the glove box's satiny finish. It felt warm, as though ten thousand days of tropical sunshine lay captured within each of its finely polished slats. She caught herself testing the air for a trace of nutmeg scent, and then shook that whimsy away. She spent much time teaching her students about the delightful climate awaiting them in the far-off Banda Islands, so it was not surprising that she should long for those warm breezes, those blue skies and sunny days, on bitter cold nights such as this.

Who would be the lucky girl to escape—no, to be chosen—this time? She had to bite her lip to keep from blurting out the question.

The director chose that very moment to open the glove box. He tilted it toward the closest candle until its contents caught the light. A rainbow of color flashed against the dark-stained walls, across the age-dulled paintings immortalizing the stern, unsmiling countenances of four generations of Vandermann men. Britta gasped. Analisa found herself stunned into immobility.

The Company men who wanted proper Dutch wives could not absent themselves from their duties for the many months required to journey to the Netherlands and present their proposals in person. Instead, prospective bridegrooms sent a glove signifying their intentions, and the tedious process of exchanging contracts commenced. Once the contracts were properly signed, a proxy marriage took place. The glove represented the absent husband, and when the bride wore it, it served as a symbol of how she would be forever bound to a man she had never met.

A marriage glove served as testament to the groom's status. The lowliest clerks, who were usually too poor for any extravagance, sent well-worn gloves bearing the stains and curled fingers attesting to hard use. Minor East India Company officials might send something soft and new, a glove fashioned expressly for that purpose, embellished with a bit of lace or a few pearls. And so it went, with the gloves of higher-ranking officials and military officers becoming ever more elaborate, but none so elegant as the rare gloves sent by the nutmeg planters, or *perkeniers.* Nobody could match the ostentatious wealth of those men who owned the rights to the nutmeg and clove plantations that provided the world's spices.

Or so Analisa had heard. No girl from the Vandermann School had ever rated such a high match.

"A planter's glove." Britta raised a shaking hand to touch her lips. A heavy silence gripped them all; Analisa understood that Britta was waiting for Director Odsvelt to contradict her. After a long wordless moment, Britta's shoulders straightened, her chin tilted infinitesimally higher. Analisa lowered her head against the excitement that surged within her at the realization that one of their Company's Daughters would be so honored.

"Which of our girls might be considered for the responsibility, Analisa?" Britta asked.

"Katje is closest to being ready, but I'm afraid she would never do." Analisa turned her mind from the glove's magnificence to the business of brides. "Katje has the unfortunate tendency to giggle during solemn proceedings, and the planters' wives must often attend official functions. Perhaps Marta."

"Yes, Marta." Britta nodded. "She possesses a calm manner and would bear up well beneath the social demands. And she is a quick learner, which is important, as we have not yet given her any medical training." Britta turned to include Odsvelt in their discussion. "Planters' wives might be called upon to tend slaves as well as house servants, and so the medical training accorded her must be more comprehensive than that given to girls who might expect to command only one or two housemaids—"

"You misunderstand, juffrouw." Director Odsvelt interrupted with an impatient wave of his hand. His throat worked, his lips tightened, and Analisa knew he found the next words difficult to say. "This glove, this proposal, is meant for Analisa."

"For me!" The comment burst forth before Analisa managed to discipline her tongue. She felt her cheeks flare with embarrassment, with something more. She bowed her head to concentrate again upon the nonexistent specks on her robe. The strong Dutch wool fluttered against her breasts as if trying to contain a

winged creature suddenly set free within the voluminous folds.

Britta sank wordlessly onto a settee.

Odsvelt withdrew a letter from the box. Its broken
seal and limp texture told Analisa that it had been
read more than once, perhaps agonized over, before
being carried to the Vandermann School. "This proposal was written by Pietr Hootendorf. Mynheer
Hootendorf is one of our most important planters."

A wordless whimper, the kind a child might make
while reaching for a doll placed high above her reach,
came from Britta.

Odsvelt paid her no mind. "Mynheer Hootendorf's
wife of many years tragically succumbed to illness. His
loss was made more difficult by Mevrouw Hootendorf's failure to produce a child. Some say he once
dreamed of founding a dynasty, and only true love
stopped him from setting his barren wife aside. He is
just now emerging from his grief and has sensibly decided to attend to the business of providing an heir
for his estate." Odsvelt cleared his throat and began
reading from the letter.

" 'No silly, simpering misses. I want a woman
grown, in her mid-twenties or a bit older, but not so
old that she can no longer carry a child. A woman
who won't wilt from the heat or burst into tears when
a servant drops a tray. Someone who can appreciate
warm tropical breezes and all the luxuries a surfeit of
money can buy, in lieu of the love and passion that
will always belong to the true wife of my heart.' "

The director's voice faltered. "I know, Analisa, that
women generally hope to find love within marriage."

Analisa let her glance travel across their dark surroundings and over the judgmental faces frowning
down from their portraits. If not for the wealth and
influence of the Vandermanns, Britta's reckless love
could have landed them in far worse straits. But the

Vandermanns had cut their daughter from the heart of the family, and Analisa had never met any of her blood kin. None would come to her rescue if she refused this loveless marriage. Not that she ever intended to need rescuing—for as long as she could remember, she'd deliberately snuffed every romantic inclination, deducing that one could not succumb to wild yearnings if one never let those yearnings take root.

"Mynheer Hootendorf's aversion to love is in accord with my own."

"Indeed?" Director Odsvelt appeared startled. "Let us go on, then." He cleared his throat and began reading again.

" 'I shall trust you to send me at once a mature woman, of excellent manners, capable of bearing many sons. I am not inclined to wait while you attend to formalities, and thus have enclosed the governor's exemption dispensing with the need to exchange contracts. Choose someone for me and send her along on the next ship.' "

Odsvelt refolded the letter along its well-worn creases. "There you have it, Analisa. Somewhat lacking in ardor, I'll admit, but an honest proposal nonetheless. Winter has gripped us early, and we are pressed for time. The *Island Treasure* is the last ship scheduled to depart this year for the Banda Islands. You will be aboard when she sails next week."

"So soon!" Britta and Analisa exclaimed as one. Odsvelt did not seem to notice that despair marked one's voice, delight, the other's.

"None of our Company's Daughters is of an age and maturity to meet Hootendorf's demands. Not a one." The director fished a handkerchief from his pocket and mopped his forehead savagely, as if he wished his anger could conjure another, more suitable prospect for Mynheer Hootendorf. "We have been more than generous to you both for many years. All of the directors concur that Analisa must do this."

The tumult of emotions raging through her released Analisa's tongue. "I am not a slave, mynheer, nor am I one of your Company's Daughters who must meekly submit to your every decree."

No, but she was illegitimate, her mother branded a whore, and both would no doubt be plying a prostitute's trade if not for the Company's willingness to let them run the school. Analisa saw the reminder tremble upon the director's lips, watched him smother it the way she had smothered retorts beyond counting. She suddenly realized that this midnight announcement, Odsvelt's scornful derision, were all meant to minimize how important it was to the Company to please Mynheer Hootendorf. For once, Analisa Vandermann might call the tune.

"Analisa?" Britta's whisper, stark with longing, pierced Analisa's heady awareness. "I never dared hope so high, for you . . . for me."

Analisa's half-formed sense of importance deflated in the face of Britta's hopefulness. She could imagine the subtle shifts in public opinion that would greet this news, the way people would absorb the Company's decree and turn it all about in their minds to make it acceptable. No longer would the epithet *harlot* be tied with the name of Britta Vandermann like *sour* was externally fixed to the word lemon. She would be Britta Vandermann, the mother of a planter's wife. No longer would the Vandermann School for Company's Daughters be treated as a second-class establishment fit only for orphans. Prominent families would beg to send their daughters to Britta, hoping for a similarly brilliant match. By accepting this marriage, Analisa could repay Britta for all her years of sacrifice.

Director Odsvelt intruded upon Analisa's thoughts, obviously anxious to sway her. "Mynheer Hootendorf is in his mid-fifties, hale and robust from all accounts, but his eagerness is understandable. Nearly eight months have passed since he sent this proposal. For a man of his age, following the usual procedure might mean the difference between siring a son and being incapable of doing so."

Analisa nodded her understanding. The Banda Islands lay thousands of miles away from the Netherlands, a difficult sea journey prone to storms, failing winds, and seaborne enemies of a human, rather than elemental, nature. It would take fourteen months or more for a round trip to exchange contracts, and another seven or eight months for Hootendorf's contracted bride to travel to the Bandas. Nearly two years, if all went well—a lifetime, perhaps, to a childless man who cherished thoughts of a dynasty while facing the age of sixty. A lifetime, perhaps, to a childless woman approaching the age of thirty who had no hope of contracting a respectable marriage in the Netherlands.

"Since contracts will not be exchanged, there must be a brief wedding ceremony conducted by the governor once you reach Banda."

"We have never sent a bride without her status being ensured with contracts. Does this hurried arrangement not mean that Mynheer Hootendorf could refuse to accept her?" Britta asked, clutching her neck worriedly.

"Well, it is true that he could." Odsvelt cleared his throat, embarrassed. "But he would not be likely to do so unless Analisa displeased him greatly. Speaking as a man, she is not unpleasant to look upon. And it is not something Mynheer Hootendorf could do upon a mere whim, as we will conduct a proxy marriage here before Analisa leaves. Although the marriage will lack the final stamp of formality, you will be Analisa

Hootendorf when you leave here. Mevrouw Analisa Hootendorf."

Analisa repeated her new name to herself. *Mevrouw Analisa Hootendorf.* Awkward on the tongue. Harsh to the ears. It might not sound so harsh when heard amidst the music of tropical breezes, not awkward at all when called out by people who would not hold her responsible for a past she could not change.

She found herself standing next to the glove box. She lifted the glove, carefully cradling it in both hands to balance its jewel-encrusted weight. Row upon row of pearls, interspersed with swirling patterns of sapphires and rubies and emeralds. Diamonds, surely, those clear stones showering rainbows from each fingertip. Other colors and other stones, the likes of which she'd never seen, including an array of milky-white ovals that flashed green and orange and blue from hidden fires buried within.

"Those are opals, Analisa," the director identified them for her. "Quite rare—small brown-skinned savages bring them to the Bandas, but refuse to say where they find them."

She stroked an opal's surface. Shimmering colors surged from the stone's heart to batter against its bland white outer shell, creating the illusion that it could explode at any moment. She felt an unexpected kinship to the stone.

But perhaps the connection should not have been unexpected. She had often told her students that their marriage gloves would be a source of comfort to them. "Imagine your husband across the sea," she'd said. "The glove is a symbol of his reaching across the thousands of miles separating you. When you wear his glove, he surrounds you with his protection and his love."

Accepting Mynheer Hootendorf's marriage glove would insulate both Analisa and her mother from the slurs, protect them from the incivility that had always been flung their way.

But Mynheer Hootendorf's letter had warned her not to expect love. The Hootendorf bride would be little more than a broodmare—but pampered, and treasured, and in no danger of developing the dangerous yearnings that had ruined her mother. A broodmare moving unrestricted beneath warm sunny skies, with no one to call her bastard, and the scent of flowers and spices perfuming her every breath.

"Can you manage without me, Mother?" Analisa asked. She would not do it if Britta displayed the slightest objection to being left, alone, to endure.

"With difficulty." A lifetime of mother love, of self-sacrifice and pride, welled in Britta's eyes. "But I will have work that I love, and to know that you . . ." She reached tentatively toward the glove.

Analisa settled it into her mother's lap. Britta rested an unsteady hand atop it, and Analisa, impulsively, laid her hand above that. The Hootendorf glove, Britta, Analisa—forming a secret pact. To reject the glove meant plodding on, enduring, an eternity of swallowing pride and knowing there was no purpose in dreaming of anything better. Accept the glove, and an aging man's dreams of a dynasty might come true, contentment might be found, respect might be assured.

"I will do it," Analisa said. "I will become the Mevrouw Pietr Hootendorf."

Director Odsvelt gave her no time to reconsider. "The proxy marriage will take place first thing in the morning. I myself will stand in for your husband."

Your husband. Analisa shivered. She wished, with a stab of desperation, that she could try on the marriage glove, but everyone knew that it brought bad luck to wear it before the marriage. It might have helped, though, to slip on the glove to see if it could banish some of the chill that unexpectedly gripped her soul.

2
~

Saldana Bay, Africa—May 1648

"Please, mevrouw, step away from the rails. Though we are at anchor, a sudden swell could pitch you straight overboard."

The captain did not add, *especially with you leaning so far over the edge in such an unladylike fashion,* but Analisa could imagine him silently finishing his warning in that manner. She lowered her head and stepped back obediently. Stripes, the ship's cat, crouched as usual at her feet, complained with a soft meow.

"Forgive me, Captain Verbeek. I have been so anticipating the sight of Africa that I let my enthusiasm overrule my good sense. Have you . . . have you reconsidered confining me for the duration of this stop?"

"Mevrouw Hootendorf, you are not confined."

"I am." She bent and caught the cat in her arms. "Stripes and I are the only creatures who have not been permitted to go ashore."

"We could not risk taking the cat ashore! She might run away."

So might I, Analisa surprised herself by thinking. *So might I.*

Verbeek gestured across the deck, which loomed

large and empty without the usual bustle of working seamen. "You have the freedom of the entire ship."

"But Africa is *there*!" She waved her hand to the shore, at least a thousand feet distant. "I can hear the workers if they shout, but I can't make out their words. Squint as I might, I can see naught but blurs and smudges."

Analisa fancied she caught a glimmer of understanding in Verbeek's eyes, though he shook his head in refusal. A lady would not beg in the face of such resistance. She whirled back to the rail, clutching at it blindly.

Would it help if she confided that only dreams of seeing wild elephants and lions had helped her survive this stage of the voyage? None of the men had suffered the stomach upheavals and matters too delicate to mention that had made her first weeks on board a misery. None seemed to miss the people left behind with the ache that gripped her still. Nor was Verbeek likely to understand that she had held on to the promise of Africa in order to retain her sanity when days stretched so dull that each one seemed to last a week, when weeks lasted months, and months loomed too long to contemplate. The seamen—Verbeek in particular—had positively relished every miserable, salt-soaked day at sea.

"I wanted you to know that I will be going ashore myself, mevrouw, with this last provisioning contingent." Verbeek sounded apologetic.

"Surely, Captain, I might accompany you."

"No. It is too dangerous."

Analisa sniffed, and then felt ashamed of displaying peevishness. The captain had been everlastingly gracious toward her, unfailingly polite, exactly the way she'd always yearned to be treated.

A starving person might crave apples; set him loose in an orchard, and he would gorge for a while. And then he would learn that many of the fruits proved to be sour, some tainted with worms, some shining and polished on the outside but soft and unpalatable within. He would soon lose his appetite for what he'd once craved.

Analisa had been fed a steady diet of respect ever since boarding the *Island Treasure.* She had dreamed her life would change, and it had, but in a manner that confined rather than liberated. She could not argue against commands couched in the most respectful terms. Impossible to refuse an order when pretty compliments blunted their sting. She had always supposed respect would free her. Instead, it tied her strength of will into knots, fashioning her into a small puppet jerking in response to the gentle tugs of its master.

She shook that inappropriate thought away. She and Britta had simply spent too much time cut off from society and had lost touch with proper female behavior. Director Odsvelt himself had often complained that the two of them displayed entirely too much independence.

"Even if I were inclined to take you ashore, I would not have time to watch over you, mevrouw. My second-in-command has returned from the Company agent with the instruction that we are to take on a rather unusual and unexpected . . . cargo."

She turned away from the shore. "Please, Captain. I honored your request to stay aboard when we made that brief provisioning stop in Lisbon. I have not felt solid earth beneath my feet for six months. There must be some quiet place where I might walk for a few moments. You need not trouble yourself—any of the crewmen will do as a companion for me. I promise not to stray an inch from any route you select." She paused. Verbeek was not swayed by her begging. A simple stating of the truth might serve her best. "Set whatever terms you like. I am quite good at following orders.'

"So I have observed, mevrouw." His gruff response conveyed disappointment, as though he were saddened rather than gladdened by her amenable nature. He glanced from her to the shore and seemed to hover at the edge of indecision, but only for a moment. He gave another regretful shake of his head. "Your health could be compromised by Africa's noxious humors. I have seen strong men die from diseases too horrible to recount."

She should bow her head, make a pretty apology. Follow the advice she had given times beyond counting to her students: *The woman must ever defer to the man's superior intellect.* Instead, she tugged at the wristband of her sleeve, then touched the edge of the high-necked collar that scraped the underside of her chin every time she swallowed. "Strong Dutch wool, Captain. Believe me when I tell you that the weave is so tight it does not permit so much as the hint of a breeze to penetrate. I am well armored against noxious humors."

She thought Verbeek might relent, then, for he had several times remarked upon her clothing's unsuitability for tropical travel. Stammering, red-faced, apologizing in advance for any offense she might take, he'd suggested that she might find the heat easier to bear if she abandoned her head covering and loosened the buttons at her neck and sleeves. Analisa had always declined with a gracious reminder that ladies did not disport themselves half-naked before a crew of seamen.

But, oh, how she had been tempted! Day after day, while sweat trickled down her back and glued her undershift to her belly, she'd fantasized ripping the itchy dark blue wool from her flesh. She'd imagined tossing the hated head covering into the sea and freeing her hair from its tightly braided crown so that the wind might dance through and drive the constant headache from her skull.

Only at night, when she'd locked herself into her windowless cabin, did she dare strip away the debilitating trappings of propriety. Sometimes she quenched her candle and knelt naked and sweating before the door, hoping a stray breeze might find its way through the narrow gap where door met frame. Night after night, her woolen bed gown and nightcap lay folded, unused, beneath her thin pillow.

Captain Verbeek, God be thanked, could not know that his passenger indulged in such wanton behavior.

Verbeek remained discouragingly set upon convincing her of all the reasons she must remain on board. "I should not care to greet Pietr Hootendorf with the news that his bride succumbed to an African fever scarcely six weeks from her new home."

The mention of her husband's name drove all further protests from Analisa's mind. She could not risk Captain Verbeek taking her husband aside to warn him that he'd saddled himself with a shrewish, complaining bride.

She had best begin tempering the distressing tendencies she'd developed, best begin quenching her vague inner dissatisfactions. Her new life would no doubt mirror the dull, constricted routine she'd found aboard ship. Pietr Hootendorf, her husband, would expect her to settle comfortably into the role of well-tended broodmare, content with her sewing, polite conversation, breakfast served invariably at dawn and dinner at dusk. He would expect a properly braided and wool-swathed broodmare in his bed, not some naked, perspiring, wild-haired wanton desperate to find some way to cool her heated flesh.

It struck her, in that brief moment of awkward silence, that she might have spent so much time mooning over Africa in order to avoid thinking of other matters. Such as whether her new husband would be handsome in the distinguished, silver-haired way of some older gentlemen, or crick-backed and damp-lipped like the worst of the disgusting, lecherous sort. Such as what she would do to occupy her time if children did not come along quickly and all her husband's household affairs were already arranged according to his habit and preference.

Nor did she want to acknowledge that after spending a lifetime hankering for respect, she'd found herself all but drowning in deferential treatment, and still she wanted to scream the same words: *Don't look at me that way. I am more than what you see. I am Analisa Vandermann.*

Analisa Vandermann *Hootendorf.* She must remember, always, to add the Hootendorf. She supposed that after she took her place at Pietr's side, she would find herself instead forgetting to insert the *Vandermann.*

She wished she had her marriage glove handy, so that she might slip it on. Yes, she should pull on her glove and then march straight down into the hold, and sit in the new carriage that had been, like herself, ordered from Amsterdam. Pietr Hootendorf's gloved and wool-swathed bride sitting in Pietr Hootendorf's glossy new carriage. Perhaps all of her inner clamoring would settle, and she would find the gratification that eluded her just now, if she immersed herself in the trappings of her good fortune.

The captain seemed to take her slight trembling as a sign of capitulation. "There now, mevrouw. I have heard that many nutmeg plantations boast safe, gentle walking paths built specially for ladies. No doubt your husband will assign a companion to you, and you can walk as much as you like when you reach your new home." Verbeek gave her shoulder an awkward pat, falsely cheerful, like an adult trying to hearten a child by promising a new plaything to replace a beloved toy ship that had sailed into a drain. "I've just thought of something that might make this more tolerable for you."

He fished around in his jacket, and then pulled free the telescope glass he often used to verify his navigator's headings. He never permitted anyone to handle the rare treasure, but he placed it now into Analisa's hand.

From such small matters were lessons learned, Analisa thought. If she'd stamped and screamed and demanded to be taken ashore, Verbeek might well have grown disgusted and ordered her locked in her cabin. For behaving like a proper lady, he'd rewarded her with the treat of using his glass, and she'd earned his approval as well. She resolved to spend the balance of this journey subduing—conquering, if she could— the disturbing wildness that stirred in her breast. She would learn to be content walking along safe, gentle paths.

And the glass did make her isolation easier to bear. She watched through it while a small wherry boat carried the captain ashore, and then she swung the glass across the dockside activity. The smudges and blurs sorted themselves into corded bales and trunks and kegs much like the cargo lining the piers when she'd left Amsterdam. Nary a lion or elephant, but a great many men swarmed everywhere, bristling with ropes and tools she could not identify. The black-skinned natives didn't appear half so savage as she'd been led to believe. The seamen had told her hair-raising tales involving the shrinking of human heads and ferocious brandishing of spears, but these Africans seemed quite industrious as they went about their work.

She might have watched them for hours, would have watched them for hours, if not for the sudden commotion that stirred the purposeful activity into chaos.

The faint dockside noises swelled into sharp alarm until the sound rolled across the water like smoke billowing from a hundred freshly fired muskets. A bell clanged to life, and its tolling speeded into desperation. Analisa swung with the glass until she could see the small brown man pulling on the bell with panicked, jerky motions. The dockside laborers abandoned their tasks and went running in response. A matching urgency shook inside her, almost as though the vibrations from their running feet shuddered through the water and straight to her heart. Her hands shook so that she feared she might drop Captain Verbeek's glass, and she knew she should set it safely away, but excitement overpowered her good sense at that moment.

"Move, move, so I can see," she muttered, frustrated when the men gathered into a clump of humanity that no telescope glass could hope to penetrate. And then she abandoned ladylike words like *move* in favor of coarse phrases she'd overheard the sailors use when they thought her sleeping in her cabin.

To her amazement, the crowd parted just as she cursed it with the most horrible phrase of all.

A knot of men remained tangled at the center of the mob. They struggled to subdue something—she could not see what it was, except for glimpsing long black hair whipping wildly in evidence of its exertions. It strength tested the might of six full-grown men. The would-be subduers hollered and strained with the effort of holding their ground against the black-haired thing thrashing in their midst.

Captain Verbeek had mentioned that the Company agent had ordered him to take on an unexpected and unusual cargo. A zebra, she thought. A zebra's fierce kicks would make it difficult to subdue; a zebra's mane and long black tail would sting the men's faces. Yes, it must be a zebra—perhaps the Company had provided this exotic creature as a wedding gift to pull Pietr Hootendorf's shiny new carriage once they unloaded it at Banda.

But then with a mighty roar, the captive broke free. Not a zebra, but a man—an exceptionally large, angry man. His fists stunned those closest to him. He bellowed his outrage as he flailed about, but it was all for naught. Another dozen men joined those who fought him. They brought their ropes into play. Nooses settled and tightened around him. Soon his hands were bound against his torso, his legs clamped so tight he might have been fitted with iron bands. Captain Verbeek supervised the roping, nodding his approval.

Despite his bonds, the prisoner struggled for quite a long time.

Stupid, for one man to stand against so many. Analisa's heart despaired, as though it understood what his heart felt with each futile surge, every hopeless twist. A silly voice in her mind whispered that there was something valiant, something admirable in his refusal to submit to their will.

Analisa gripped the glass, wishing it could somehow grant her the ability to murmur a secret into the prisoner's ear. If she could, she would tell him to give up, to cease heaving against his bonds. She would tell the prisoner that the Dutchmen of the East India Company always, always got their way.

He would have made his escape, Michael Rowland thought, if not for the neck rope choking the life out of him.

A bandy-legged bastard cackled his triumph over making the lucky throw. Michael summoned his last good lungful of air to hurl one final curse. "Misbegotten son of a jackal! I swear that you and all the seed of your loins shall find your bellies scraping the earth until you are forced to eat pig meat!"

That sent the Moslem son of a bitch scuttling away, but the pressure on Michael's air passages eased too late. Partial strangulation robbed his limbs of strength and weakened his brain so he couldn't remember the myriad insults a man needed to know in order to survive in this land of many cultures. Besides, though curses worked well enough on superstitious Africans, they would have no effect at all upon the Dutchmen who posed the most serious threat to his freedom.

With stolid, workmanlike efficiency those Dutchmen wove a web of rope around him until he stood as thoroughly netted as a sausage hung to dry from the rafter of an Italian housewife's kitchen. Perhaps he shouldn't have tried so hard to impress them with his strength. He'd have the devil of a time escaping with his arms and legs bound. He sighed as a half-dozen sailors easily lofted him to their shoulders. They marched toward the sea, and Michael imagined they all looked like a pack of gravediggers hauling a partly wrapped Egyptian mummy.

They heaved him headfirst into a wherry with a careless toss that knocked his skull against a cleat. The blow struck him nearly senseless, but he fought to remain conscious; a man who meant to escape had to go on breathing, and it took considerable effort to force the wherry's reeking air into his lungs. Sailors had cleaned fish beyond counting in that boat, and the old wood retained the smell of each one. He tried inhaling through his mouth and choked on the brackish water puddled in the bottom of the wherry..

He'd be damned if he'd die while spitting stagnant water and with the scent of fish guts filling his nose. With a groan, Michael levered his head up, though his neck had gone weak as a newly hatched nestling's. At once he realized his good fortune. Even with his arms bound to his sides and his legs laced together, he was broad enough and so long that his considerable bulk sprawled over most of the space, leaving room in the wherry for only two Dutch sailors. Just two!

Two men would pose no challenge at all—if only he could free his fists. He could overpower them and then leap into the sea, swim to freedom—if only he could swim. Better, perhaps, to toss the seamen over the side and confiscate the wherry for himself. Yes, that's what he would do.

He flexed his wrists and ankles but wasn't surprised to find the ropes taut as drawn bowstrings. Damned sailors. Knot-tying fools, the lot of them, and masterfully good at it in the bargain.

Well, he would have to get the sailors to untie him, then. A plan sprung to mind, though he didn't much relish the thought of carrying it out.

Nonetheless, he'd have to do it quickly. Each pull of the oars drew them closer to the ship he'd noticed from shore: an East Indiaman. There was no mistaking the distinctive hull, the pattern of the rigging.

As the wherry drew closer to the ship, he noticed the deck was empty save for one person. Damn, he must have bashed his head harder than he'd thought, for he would swear a dark-robed nun stood on deck, her head veil flapping in the wind while she stared at him through a telescope glass. Yes, definitely a nun, for no ordinary woman would risk heat fever by wearing so many yards of wool beneath the scorching sun.

Funny, that. He didn't think the Dutch encouraged papist vocations, and he couldn't imagine why they'd be carrying a holy sister aboard their ship. Maybe the little nun would say a prayer for his soul. He could use a prayer, for as God was his witness, things were looking a bit grim for him just then.

He couldn't think of a worse fate for one guilty of his crimes than being captured by a crew of Dutchmen and incarcerated aboard a Dutch vessel that was most likely bound for the Banda Islands. No doubt about it, he would have to escape, and he would have to act at once.

Michael thought that the best thing about having one's head bashed was that it left one less inclined to probe for flaws in a half-witted plan. The next best thing was that it left one pitifully eager to try measures that any sane-thinking man would reject.

He rolled to his left. And then he rolled to his right. And then he did it again. The wherry lurched to the side.

"Stop that, you!" One of the seamen swiveled away from his rowing and gave Michael a nasty chop on the back of the leg.

Michael swallowed the urge to kick back at the sailor—it would only serve to disrupt his rhythm. *Roll to the right. Roll to the left.* The wherry wobbled. He heard the second seaman twist in his seat, too, and the two sailors jabbered Dutch at each other so quickly that Michael's sketchy grasp of the language failed to keep up. No matter. They couldn't stop him without pinning him down, and adding their weight to his at one end of the boat would serve his purpose nearly as well as the rolling.

He felt the movement when the seamen rose into a crouch. The wherry, already overbalanced by Michael's enthusiastic rolling, dipped perilously close to capsizing. It pitched the three of them straight into the water.

A man who can't swim has no business deliberately provoking a fall into the water. Particularly when he's trussed up in the shape of a spearhead, so that he shot straight to the sea floor as if he'd been fired from a harpoon gun.

He had thought he might be able to hold his breath for two minutes. But it seemed mere seconds had passed before an agonizing pressure threatened to crush his chest, and though he knew it sapped his precious air reserves, he couldn't stop fighting against his ropes in a frantic, futile effort to flail his way back to the surface.

Strange, that while his wits flirted yet again with unconsciousness, he thought of the little nun on the deck. Perhaps concern for his immortal soul would cause her to drop her glass in favor of her rosary beads. The slim chance that she might be praying for him gave him an unexpected measure of peace, and he stopped struggling. He'd know soon enough if his idea would work.

If it didn't work, well . . . then he'd never know anything, ever again.

Analisa dropped Captain Verbeek's precious glass.

It fell straight into Saldana Bay, hitting the water with a faint splash she barely noticed over the pounding of her blood. An incessant "Please God, please God," roared through her mind.

She clutched at the rail with so much anguish that her fingernails gouged tiny half-moons in the wood. The cat, sensing her agitation, pressed its soft body against Analisa's shins. She didn't realize that she'd been holding her breath until one of the seaman broke through the water with the prisoner in tow. She gasped then, drawing a huge chestful of air, praying the prisoner did the same. The sailor began an awkward one-armed swim for the captain's wherry while holding the captive's head above water. Eager hands reached for the captive; he made no more resistance than a well-washed and wrung out bedsheet as they hauled him aboard.

A distant part of her mourned the loss of the telescope glass. She might have used it to study his chest, to see whether it rose and fell. From where she stood, he appeared discouragingly still.

The captain barked an order and one of the men sliced through the captive's bonds. Still he did not move. They tugged him, with some trouble, toward the side of the small boat until his head hung over the edge. Two seamen commenced a vigorous pounding of his unresponsive back. Just when she feared they might snap his spine, he twitched, and then began heaving. After a moment he curled into himself, coughing, choking, and then lay back, exhausted, with one arm over his face.

She hadn't been able to glimpse his face at all.

The wherries bumped up against the ship. A number of the men scrambled up the rope ladders with their customary skill, and they gathered on deck to watch, thumping each other on the backs and calling congratulations and encouragement to their shipmates. Analisa shrank away from them; their high spirits seemed somehow offensive to her.

"Leave his hands and legs free for the moment, Mr. Klopstock, so he can climb the ladder.'

"Aye, Captain." Klopstock complied, but with a frown that betrayed his doubt over the wisdom of leaving the prisoner unbound. He gave the man a shove. "Start climbing, you."

The push, the snarled order, *something* turned the prisoner from half-drowned wretch into a whirlwind of fury. He formed both hands into a battering ram, and with a frightening roar, clouted poor old Jan Klopstock alongside the head.

He should have leaped straight into the sea and swum for his freedom. Analisa would have. Instead, he went after another seaman's throat. Captain Verbeek wrenched an oar from its lock and swung it like a scythe across the captive's back, knocking him flat. Verbeek rested one foot atop the prisoner and brandished the oar in the manner of a hunter celebrating the kill of a particularly challenging quarry. The seamen laughed, some honoring their captain with a smattering of applause.

The captive stirred beneath Verbeek's booted heel. *Stay as you are,* Analisa implored him silently. But he shuddered, and when Verbeek reluctantly removed his foot, the captive slowly rose to his knees. He knelt so straight that his spine might have been fashioned from an iron pole. His uncompromising posture denied the pain that must have accompanied Verbeek's blow. He kept his head bowed. His dark hair hung in dripping black strands, shielding his face—deliberately, Analisa thought, recognizing something of her own tactics in his outwardly submissive pose.

His near-fatal dunking had left his garments plastered to his skin. His knees were braced apart, drawing his dark breeches taut against his abdomen. His shirt might have been white, but it was difficult to tell, for the thin cloth clung to his skin so tightly that his tanned flesh showed through, all sculpted and ridged with the evidence of great physical strength. At least three of his buttons had been torn away, for his shirt gapped to reveal the dark whorls of hair upon his chest.

"Let's see him put up a fight after *that* blow." Verbeek let the oar clatter to the boards. "He won't be climbing any ladders for a while. We'll haul him aboard in the sling."

They brought him aboard in the canvas-and-rope contrivance normally used to lift cattle and heavy objects, like Pietr's shiny black carriage. True to Verbeek's prediction, all fight seemed to have deserted him by the time they freed him from the sling.

He stared ahead blankly, breathing shallowly, his senses still obviously flown. He brought a hand to his head with a fearsome grimace that warned of a monstrous headache. Any man, under those circumstances, might have resembled the village idiot. This man had features so strong, his face composed of supremely masculine lines and planes, that nothing detracted from his startling handsomeness. Analisa found herself torn between drinking in the sight of him and knowing he would prefer it if she looked away from his shipboard humiliation.

He complied when a couple of men jabbed his shoulders and propelled him toward the main hatch. After a few steps he faltered, shook his head, winced, shook it again. He glanced skyward and shuddered, then swung his gaze around the ship and drew a huge, rasping breath. Something in his expression altered from bewilderment into dull despair, as if he'd just realized the finality of his captivity.

The sailors nudged him back into motion, aiming toward the gaping black hole leading to the lower decks.

They passed very close to where Analisa was standing, staring. Once more the captive's step faltered. He looked at her, straight on. His eyes, she marveled, were the color of rich ale, promising joyous intoxication. He was weak and battered, practically falling where he stood, and yet so much latent power smoldered from him that it seemed to consume the air; she found it difficult to draw breath with him standing so close. A proud intelligence burned from those remarkable eyes, telling her without words that he was a man accustomed to winning despite the odds.

Or perhaps he'd merely suffered one too many knocks to the head. He executed an awkward bow, and then fashioned a wobbly sign of the cross toward her.

"Ah, Sister Mary Telescope." He uttered the senseless address in perfect English, with a rumbling huskiness that vibrated against something low in her belly. "It appears your prayers went for naught."

Someone thumped the heel of a hand against the prisoner's back, sending him staggering forward. "Do not insult the lady with your barbarian tongue."

They prodded him down the hatch. Analisa found that her knees were quivering. It was probably the heat that drained her strength, she thought, for the atmosphere had turned so suddenly oppressive that she had to struggle against the urge to rip off her head cloth and toss it overboard.

"Do not let that rogue disturb you, mevrouw." Captain Verbeek's consolation struck her as perfunctory, given that all his attention was riveted upon the captive as he disappeared into the hold.

"Who . . . who is he?"

Verbeek spat into the bay. "Damned if I know. The wretch would not tell us his name, nor confess to anything of substance. I daresay his tongue will loosen soon enough. He will remain chained below decks without light or food until he tells us what we want to know."

"What has he done?"

" 'Tis a Company matter. You are not to give him another thought."

Chained in the dark. Those intoxicating eyes condemned to utter blackness, that raw power starved into impotence. She could not imagine what crime merited such a terrible punishment. She was not permitted to imagine it, at any rate. Anger flared in her breast, quickly quelled, lest the captain take note.

Verbeek's forehead creased with concern. "You tremble, and your skin has paled, mevrouw. I know fear can strike women senseless, but you need not worry. This ship is equipped to carry slaves between islands. That rogue cannot escape our shackles. For you it shall be as though our prisoner does not even exist."

It seemed churlish to contradict him in the face of his respectful courtesy. Analisa bowed her head.

"I shall try to hold on to my good sense, Captain."

3

~

There had been times during this journey, when the *Island Treasure* labored amid slow seas and weak winds, that Analisa had feared she might go mad from the way nature swallowed all human sound, deadened all the man-made noise and activity.

Now, as the days dragged on with everyone behaving as though they'd never manhandled a prisoner aboard, she found herself straining to hear any small sounds from below, and the ship resounded with maddening vigor. The tall masts groaned while the wind-filled sails plowed them through booming waves; amid the spitting hiss of sea spray, seamen shouted and rigging squeaked, sails snapped and wood creaked.

Sometimes, though, the normal shipboard sounds would ebb and then she'd catch the faint, muffled snatch of a man's voice, hoarse and ragged from shouting loud enough to be heard from his prison. She prowled the decks, all her attention focused upon her feet, until she sensed the sounds and vibration that she thought might pinpoint the captive's location. Sometimes she felt a steady pounding, or heard a dull thumping that played to such a relentless rhythm that she knew it had to be him.

She spent an inordinate amount of time standing

atop that spot, listening to his determined efforts to be noticed. His exertions somehow left *her* breathless, and shaken anew at remembering the taut, lean power that had radiated from the captive even as lesser men held him in bonds.

She had to know how he fared. She ached to know. But since his capture and incarceration, the lower levels had been forbidden to her and she could not slip down the hatch and investigate matters for herself. Nor did spying upon the seamen provide any clues. Their duties kept them swarming from the tips of the masts to the bowels of the ship throughout the day and night. It was impossible to tell which—if any— had been assigned to care for the captive. Verbeek had, after all, sworn that he would keep his prisoner chained without light or food until he confessed to his crimes, whatever they might be.

Oh, yes, she had to know how he fared. If only she had a friend among the sailors, she would ask, but to a man they had avoided all but the most cursory contact with her. Some of their aversion she knew stemmed from the common seamen's belief that women brought bad luck to a ship. She suspected that her status as a Company's Daughter, newly married to an influential planter, might have prompted Verbeek to warn his men against approaching her.

They had held their distance throughout the voyage. Their eyes, though, kept her company, following her when they fancied she wouldn't notice. They ignored her, and yet she felt herself pummeled by thoughts so lustful they were all but palpable. The loneliness, the hot-eyed staring, could have decimated a woman less accustomed to enduring similar treatment.

She had no friend on board save for Stripes, and the cat often disappeared for lengthy stints to keep the ship's rats and mice under control. Only the elderly Jan Klopstock, who served as the captain's personal attendant, treated her with something approaching kindness. She sometimes suspected that Klopstock would be happier pretending, like the others, that she didn't exist. His duties, which included escorting her to the captain's table for dinner each night, forced them into an uneasy companionship.

"Jan!" she called, as he scurried past her with a length of shredded sail.

"Mevrouw! 'Tis a fine day, is it not?"

"Aye." She traced the decking with her toe, summoning her nerve. Even that small delay had the ever-busy Jan edging away from her. She blurted out her concern. "The prisoner we took on board some time back—how does he fare?"

Klopstock's smile wavered and then vanished altogether. He shrugged, feigning a nonchalance that did not jibe with the nervous glance he darted toward the yawning hatch. " 'Tis black-dark below, and stinking hot."

"He is not suffering, is he?"

"Who can say?" Jan's forehead took on a sudden, sweaty sheen. "Some men relish the dark and the heat."

"Jan." Analisa reached toward him, but withdrew her hand when Jan skittered back a pace or two. "The captain threatened to starve him. Please tell me he has not carried out that threat."

"I have not taken food to the captive, mevrouw."

Analisa's vitals clenched. "Water, Jan?"

Klopstock bobbed his head rapidly. "Water, yes. Every other day, mevrouw. A full cup. Please excuse me. I must go now."

"Wait." This time she ignored his flinching and restrained him with a hand to his arm. Her throat suddenly seized up on her. A cup of water, every other day. She normally drank at least four cups every day, and she knew the hardworking seamen drank more,

liberally supplemented by draughts of gin issued by
the captain. She glanced toward the hatch. *Black-dark
and stinking hot below.* His isolation and discomfort
relieved by only one cup of water, every other day.
She had taken her last sip only an hour before, and
almost could not swallow beyond the parched agony
that had come upon her. For a moment, she felt blackness pressing in on her, felt her throat constrict. He
must feel like this all the time. She must have made
some small sound of distress, for Jan stepped closer,
peering at her with concern. "Are ye ailing,
mevrouw?"

"No." Not ailing, but neither was she feeling quite
well. "Please tell the captain I shall not be dining with
him tonight," she said impulsively.

"Then ye are ailing."

She did not know how to explain the sudden aversion she felt toward spending time in the captain's
presence, knowing he was responsible for the prisoner's suffering. Nor could she do anything to alleviate
that discomfort. She could only sympathize, perhaps
deny herself food and water for the balance of the
day. "Well, perhaps I am ill, a little. I have no
appetite."

"As ye say, mevrouw." Klopstock backed away
from her with a worried frown. Analisa wondered how
much of their conversation he would report to the
captain. She didn't care.

She went to her cabin, something she seldom did
during the day, when unremitting sunshine turned it
into a sweltering, airless box. The tiny enclosure, set
at the far end of the ship, away from the main hatch
that led to the seamen's quarters, had not been designed for passenger comfort. Rather, it was little
more than a locker normally used to secure items
known to tempt a seaman's thirst, such as the barrels

of gin that now stood stacked and roped outside the door.

Stripes followed her and then stopped rigid when Analisa opened the door and waves of heat billowed out. The cat sprang away with a reproachful yowl. She scaled the tower of gin barrels and sat with a pleased look on her feline face as the breeze ruffled through her fur.

Analisa closed herself in the stiflingly hot chamber. *Black-dark and stinking hot.* Hard as it was to believe, her cabin seemed relatively comfortable when considered in light of Klopstock's description of the prisoner's quarters. She stuffed small bits of cloth from her mending basket into every crack and gap, doing her best to eliminate the pinpoints of sunlight and wisps of fresh air that pierced the slatted wood. Though her cabin was plunged into gloom, she knew it did not match the impenetrability of the belowdecks.

The hours dragged on. She began her vigil by perching atop a small stool, trying to daydream about the life awaiting her. Each time she tried imagining her husband's face, the image of the captive intruded, and her efforts to banish the image grew less forceful as the heat seeped into her bones. Her head ached too much to think, even after she'd torn off her head covering and undid all the tight, careful braiding that kept her hair under control.

She took to her bed when the lack of light and the effort of drawing the hot, heavy air into her lungs left her too enervated to sit. She wondered with dull amazement that the captive found the energy to bellow his insults, to pound his defiance against the walls. She unfastened her high collar, baring her neck to the oppressive air, the first time she had ever done so during the day. It helped a little, and she undid the buttons at her wrists and started loosening those at her breast, intending to shrug the garment away before she realized a chained captive would not be able to remove his clothes over his shackles.

Her tongue seemed to swell to twice its normal size, and then even larger, so that while her parched throat compelled her to swallow more than usual, the dryness and clumsiness of her tongue threatened to gag her. Her eyes burned, and she realized that she had been lying there with them open, scarcely blinking. When she closed them, pinwheels of light seemed to swirl around her and carry her with them into the dark. She felt like a lost star, tumbling through the midnight velvet sky without purpose, unutterably lonely, hungering, thirsting with no hope of an end to her suffering.

All this, after but one day. Less than a day. And the prisoner had been chained belowdecks for many, many days now.

No human being should be made to suffer so. Analisa forced herself upright, ignoring the dizziness her sudden movement prompted. She had been a fool! Holding back, afraid to voice her questions for fear of sounding unladylike, when all the while a true lady would have stormed into the captain's cabin demanding an explanation for his barbaric treatment of the captive! The care of the helpless and sick fell to the lady of a household. Verbeek could not fault her for inquiring after the health of a man who had been brought aboard in her presence.

She pried free a bit of cloth from between two slats. To her surprise, a sunbeam shafted through. It seemed impossible that it could still be daylight. Verbeek ought to be sitting down to his dinner right now, and she would take him to task for indulging himself while a man suffered.

The dull throbbing in her head intensified when she pushed herself up off her bed and weakness washed through her, doing much to dim her enthusiasm for confronting the captain. She braced a hand against the wall, half tempted to tumble back into the bed, until she heard *him,* felt *him* through the timbers. *Thump. Thump.* So faint. The far-off, buried sound of metal against wood, the sound of wrist manacles thudding against seasoned oak. Her heart took up the rhythm, beating in time to the relentless pounding.

Analisa flung open her door. Outside, surprised seamen stood blinking at her while the bits of cloth she'd stuffed into the door cracks fluttered around her like snowflakes. She stormed past the men, so angry that she was halfway across the deck before she realized the shocking state she was in. The sea air kissed the skin at her neck, blessedly cool, while at the same time the sun prickled against skin never before bared. The wind lifted her hair. She hesitated for a heartbeat. Never before had she appeared before the captain with her hair undone, without her high-necked collar. But going back, putting herself in order, could mean adding interminable minutes to the prisoner's discomfort.

She drew a deep breath and hurried toward Verbeek's quarters without waiting for one of the gapejawed seaman to scurry forward and announce her.

Captain Verbeek, not expecting her, had not changed into his usual dinner attire. He glanced at her, only his raised eyebrows betraying his surprise.

"Klopstock informed me you were ill. I must say you don't look at all well. I pray there is no real cause for concern."

She shook her head and slid into her usual place.

They sat in unaccustomed silence while Klopstock ladled food onto their plates. Verbeek toyed with his portion while Jan fussed over wine and poured fresh water for both of them. Analisa could not wait; she snatched up the water goblet before the serving man had quite finished pouring and gulped down its full contents. It had been two weeks since they'd taken on fresh water in Africa, and by now it had absorbed a flat, woody taste from the barrels, but after her day of deprivation it tasted sweeter to her than any she'd ever dipped from a fast-flowing stream.

How would water taste to the prisoner, after a deprivation that had lasted far longer than hers?

She set down the goblet. Klopstock leaped to refill it. Verbeek seemed lost in thought, more unapproachable than ever on the very day when she needed his full regard. She tried to order her thoughts, thinking of the best way to approach the subject of the man suffering somewhere below them.

"I have been concerned with another's health, mynheer."

"Oh? My men seem to be in excellent condition."

He was deliberately avoiding the subject of the prisoner, she could tell. "My concerns rest upon the man who caused such a commotion while coming on board at Saldana Bay."

"Ah, our captive." Verbeek stabbed at a piece of mutton, holding it aloft and frowning at it before setting it down again. "The most stubborn, infuriating man I've ever had the misfortune of coming across." He shook his head as though angry with himself for revealing his thoughts. "I shall be glad to see the back of him when we hand him over to the authorities."

"What has he done?" she asked.

She wasn't at all certain he would tell her, and indeed he paused long enough for her to doubt that he would explain. Ultimately, he sighed. "He is the worst sort of criminal."

Disappointment knifed through her—disappointment in the prisoner for not fitting the noble mold her heat-addled mind had fashioned for him, disappointment in herself for mooning over him like some worshipful schoolgirl. "He is a murderer, then?" she asked, knowing there could be no crime more terrible than taking the life of another.

"Worse." Verbeek gathered his breath, as though admitting the full extent of the captive's atrocities pained him. "He's a pirate who does not content himself with attacking ships and stealing the usual plunder. He strikes at the very heart of the Company."

Verbeek twisted in his chair and pulled open a small drawer in his desk. He withdrew a cloth pouch, swiveled back to the table, and then poured out several oval-shaped brown lumps onto the tabletop. They were small, the size of very, very dry prunes, but closer to tan in color, and not so deeply wrinkled. "Look at these."

Analisa looked. She shrugged. "Nutmegs."

"Our belowdecks 'guest' was caught trying to smuggle these nutmegs."

Analisa's mother had often lamented that the one disadvantage of operating a school for the Dutch East India Company was that she was forced to order all her supplies through Company markets. Smugglers, she'd claimed, delivered the same spices at better prices. Smugglers, she'd said, wistfully counting out a great pile of guilders to settle the Company merchant's bill, did the budget-conscious housewife a great service.

"There are some who might say his crime is not so odious," Analisa said carefully.

Verbeek's countenance reddened. "Look at these!" He poked at the nutmegs, sending them rolling back and forth. "Can you not see how brown they are?"

The nutmegs were dusty deep tan in color—a bit darker, perhaps, than those she'd ground in the kitchen at home. "They are fresher than those we see in Amsterdam?" Analisa ventured.

Verbeek sent her a pitying glare. "Fresher? Bah. A planter's wife must know the difference between fresh

and fertile. Each and every nutmeg that leaves the
Banda Islands must be soaked in lime water, to kill
the kernel of life within. Properly limed nutmegs have
a whitish cast. These are brown! The nutmegs confiscated from that scoundrel are still fertile. *Fertile!*" He
spoke more forcefully each time he said *fertile,* as if
he thought greater volume would increase her appreciation of the terribleness of the smuggler's crime.

Analisa knew the glorious history of how the Dutch
had wrested control of the area known as the Molucca
Archipelago from the Portuguese in the previous cen-
tury. Brave and daring Company agents had ferreted
out every nutmeg tree growing in the mysterious islands of spice and cut them all down, save for the
groves on the Banda Islands. Likewise, clove trees
were restricted to the island city of Amboina. This
careful restriction on spices fattened Company coffers,
creating wealth beyond belief. The Company was not
eager to share the bounty.

Verbeek picked up one of the nutmegs, holding it
between thumb and forefinger, staring at it as if it
were a deadly dose of poison. "The Company cannot
allow just anyone to plant nutmeg trees, or the price
will come crashing down. We must deal very harshly
with this smuggler, very harshly indeed."

"Will you imprison him?"

"Good heavens, no! He has stolen fertile, life-giving
seeds from us, so we will demand the very same from
him. Before he dies, they will cut off his . . ." He
suddenly blushed furiously and snatched up his wine
goblet for a quick swallow. "Forgive me, mevrouw,
for being so indelicate. Ultimately, the man will be
taken to Fort Victoria in Amboina and the governor
shall put him to a most unpleasant death."

There flashed through Analisa's mind an image so
clear, so precise, that she caught her breath in confusion: the captive, bold and strong and filled with life,

fighting against those who needed ropes and chains to bend him to their will. All that masculine strength, those intoxicating golden brown eyes, that almost magnetic presence gone, all gone, and for what? For the sake of smuggling a few spices so someone like her mother could save a florin or two on the nutmeg she sprinkled over her stews and egg custards? It was Analisa's turn to grope for her goblet, to take a fortifying sip of wine to clear the image and the ridiculous tears that sprang up unbidden in the corners of her eyes.

She had studied her hand-copied map of the Molucca Archipelago until it nearly fell apart at the creases. Amboina, where the criminal would be maimed and executed, lay a scant hundred miles north of the Banda Islands cluster.

A swift ship like the *Island Treasure,* if blessed with favorable winds, took no time at all to sail one hundred miles. So the smuggler could be dead a day or two after she left the ship, probably dead by the time she learned her way around her husband's home, most certainly dead before she memorized the difficult native names of her husband's servants.

Analisa doubted she could ever again savor a dish flavored with nutmeg.

The aroma wafting up from her dinner plate suddenly seemed cloying. She pushed it away, lest her stomach roil.

"Disgusting, is it not?" Verbeek commiserated, misunderstanding her distress. "Men such as he threaten the very foundations of the Company, the livelihood of thousands of men and their families. I understand that your own mother owes her position to the Company."

Verbeek's comments reminded her where her loyalty belonged. The Dutch East India Company had indeed provided a safe haven for herself and her mother, and even now, she journeyed toward a new life arranged and sanctioned by the very entity this odious smuggler threatened. She should feel ashamed for allowing her loyalty to waver, and yet it stuck in her craw to condemn him.

"If they kill him at Amboina, then justice will be served," Analisa said, while inwardly crying it was too harsh a punishment.

"Justice will be appeased, but not served," Verbeek said. "This smuggler made it all the way to Africa before his crime was discovered. 'Twas only the sheerest luck that one of our agents caught him and turned him over to me. I'm afraid his moderate success indicates a viper nesting at the very heart of the Company."

A lifetime of believing that the Company had saved her from a terrible fate roused Analisa's loyalties, both to bristle at the threat that the smuggler posed and to deny that any Company employee could turn on his benefactors. "I am sure none of the Company's men are in league with this villain," she said.

"I'm afraid someone must be, mevrouw. By law, all planters must immediately bathe their harvested nutmegs in lime water. The smuggler could not have acquired so many unlimed nuts without a planter's cooperation."

Verbeek clasped his hands and leaned forward, his face suddenly alight with speculation. "If someone could pry his secrets from this villain before he is executed, why, the Company's gratitude would be unbounded. A reward, mevrouw!" Analisa involuntarily stiffened at his obvious mercenary intent, and Verbeek drew back. "The size of the, uh, reward is most certainly not, uh, the most important thing. What matters is that the Company can deal with the black-hearted scoundrel who threatens to topple a system that works very well. I have tried everything I could think of,

without success, to force him to name his con-
spirators."

"Perhaps I might try." She blurted the suggestion
with no forethought, and then sat back in her chair,
startled by the sudden anticipation surging through
her at the thought of questioning the captive.

"You?" Verbeek's astonishment at her offer
matched her own for daring to make it.

"I am half English, mynheer. I speak the language
well enough to teach it to others."

"Oh, yes. Director Odsvelt mentioned your accom-
plishments when he secured your passage. I regret to
say I had forgotten." And he did look rather disgruntled, in the manner of someone holding a securely
locked treasure box who's just learned he's torn his
house apart for no reason, because the key had been
dangling from a chain around his neck the whole time.

"It is possible this criminal does not understand
your questions. It is possible he does not realize the
seriousness of the charges against him."

"There you are wrong, mevrouw. He fought like a
cornered wolf and knows full well the extent of his
crimes. But you might be right about his not understanding my questions. Perhaps you might persuade
him to give me the information I want.'

"I am not a very persuasive person, Captain."

That brought a surprised huff of amusement from
the captain. His gaze raked over her, bold unlike any
regard he'd ever shown her, making her keenly aware
of the way her hair tumbled wantonly to her waist,
the way her collarless neckline bared her skin to her
collarbone. "Ah, mevrouw, you may not think yourself
persuasive just now, but someday, when you gain
confidence . . ." He shook his head, then rubbed his
hand over his face in a weary gesture. "I do not know
if I should permit this. And yet we have but a short
time at sea before we reach Banda Neira. Who is to

say what can happen? A pretty face, a word in a familiar language, might loosen his tongue."

The weathered lines of Verbeek's face seemed drawn in an expression of concern, his lips tilted at just the right angle to convey tremulous hope that she might lend her cooperation. But his eyes, his eyes . . . lurking within their faded blue depths, looked to be the nesting viper he spoke of, coiled and ready to strike.

For the first time in her life, she found herself dealing with a man on equal footing. She wished she'd had more practice.

It seemed as if a thousand, a million, screaming, shrieking voices possessed her mind, all urging her to spend the remainder of the voyage locked safely in her cabin. This uneasy tensing of her vitals gripped her every time she thought of the prisoner. As well it should—he was a dangerous, desperate man. She clenched her hands; they trembled even more. She lowered them to her lap and bowed her head.

"I must retract my offer, Captain. I am sorry."

"Mevrouw, no!"

She realized then how eagerly he had fallen on her offer, how wildly his hopes had surged. She had to extricate herself somehow from this mess she had made. She forcibly calmed herself and then drew on what had been until now an untapped privilege. "I doubt my husband would approve of such an activity on my part."

Verbeek expelled air as if she'd pounded his midsection with a gin tankard. But invoking the presence of Pietr Hootendorf had the desired effect. "Perhaps you are right, mevrouw. I apologize if I seemed overeager, but you did broach the subject yourself."

An uncomfortable silence followed. Analisa sat with clenched hands and bent head, peeping up through the tangles of hair that fell around her like a shield.

Verbeek fondled his chin, staring at her, seeming to assess her resolve. Musingly, he said, "The smuggler's time aboard my ship has been less than pleasant. I daresay I can add to his discomfort—that might loosen his tongue." He turned toward the door. "Klopstock!"

"Aye, Captain?" Klopstock poked his head through the door.

"The prisoner's water ration—decrease it to one cup every three days."

"We last watered him yesterday, Captain." Klopstock glanced uneasily toward Analisa.

"Then he gets his next cupful day after tomorrow," said Verbeek.

"Aye, Captain."

Analisa's throat dried. Her tentative efforts to see to the prisoner's comfort had backfired, worsening his deprivation. Her short-lived experiment had left her so thirsty that she knew she could easily swallow several more cups of water to slake the thirst that her meager deprivation had caused. Their prisoner had had no water all day, and now, because of her interference, Verbeek meant to add to his suffering. Her hand itched to reach for her water goblet. She fought the urge to lick her lips, to swallow against the sudden parched feeling.

Verbeek noticed, and he smiled.

"He has been suffering, you know," Verbeek added in a light, conversational tone. "My men, I must admit, set about him with great ferocity when he refused to divulge information. Why, now that you have introduced the subject of his well-being, it occurs to me that Company's Daughters travel with a bag of medicinals and soothing balms. You might have tended his wounds during your conversations—but I forget, you no longer wish to see to his health."

"You beat a chained man?" Analisa kept her voice low to keep her outrage from showing.

"My duty to the Company demands I stop at nothing to gain information that could prove useful. I am disappointed that your own loyalty seems lacking in that regard." Self-righteousness all but dripped from his lips. "Besides, he'll endure worse when we deliver him to Amboina. 'Tis a pity that these last weeks of his life must be passed in such wretched discomfort. Why, as you pointed out yourself, he might not even understand the nature of the charges against him. But only one who speaks his English tongue can be sure of that."

Silence again filled the room, but the nature of it had changed. Verbeek toyed with a strand of his mustache, a half smile and sidelong glance in her direction telling Analisa he expected her to capitulate. On her part, anger, and an overwhelming sense of helplessness, flooded her. She had liked Verbeek, had enjoyed his company, and now he was proving himself to be devious, cruel, and manipulative. Curse all Dutchmen! Surely no other race of men possessed such a knack for using a woman's gentle nature against her. If she wasn't careful, she would find herself destined to live her life serving as a pawn to one man or another.

"You will increase his water if I speak to him?" she asked.

"He will receive his daily ration, just like any other person aboard ship."

"You will not beat him again?"

"That, my dear mevrouw, depends on your success."

She raised her head, knowing that hatred and challenge flashed in her eyes. Verbeek seemed amused by her attitude, confident now that she'd succumbed to his blatant blackmail.

"He is a common criminal, mevrouw, and not really

worth your touching concern. Perhaps you shouldn't trouble yourself."

She could tell he had begun to enjoy toying with her. She remembered how her mother had constantly submitted her will to that of the Company directors, who delighted in tormenting her. She felt a subtle vibration beneath her feet, most likely the ship's response to wind or waves, but maybe . . . maybe the barely perceptible tremor came from the prisoner's continued defiance, his refusal to remain silent and unnoticed.

Analisa stiffened her spine. She would not spend the rest of her days bowing before men. She would not hold herself silent, hoping to avoid their disapproval.

"Take me to him," she snapped.

"Now?" Verbeek blinked, obviously startled by her command.

"Now. For years I have been told that my blood is tainted with an unfortunate impulsiveness. It would appear there is some merit to the charge." Pretending an assurance she did not feel, she rose from her chair and headed for the door.

"Er, mevrouw, it might be wise to clean him, to straighten his quarters, before, er, exposing him to a lady's delicate sensibilities. At least grant me the time to have Klopstock place a chair therein for you to sit upon."

"Now." She jerked the door open, nearly sending Verbeek's attendant tumbling to the floor. She stormed into the passageway, noting with a sidelong glance that the captain had followed and called for Klopstock to fetch a lantern and precede them down the hatch.

She had expected they would descend the narrow, iron-runged ladder-like steps into the deepest bowels of the ship, where Verbeek had told her precious nutmegs would be stored for the return journey to the

Netherlands. But they stopped at the level just below the gun deck. They made their slow way through all manner of crates, casks of salt beef, and other oilcloth-wrapped bulks toward the stalls holding a few crates of squawking chickens and the few remaining sheep from the meat stock they'd taken on in Africa. Klopstock's lantern played over the frightened beasts, who bleated and backed away from the unaccustomed light. The golden beam illuminated her husband's new carriage, carefully stored in another stall for the long voyage.

She smelled him before she saw him.

She recoiled from the stench, groping for a handkerchief. The farthest stall, still shrouded in a gloom, smelled of an infirmary, of fever and blood and untended human flesh. Verbeek claimed the lantern from Klopstock and held it aloft. Its shuttered flame did little to pierce the cryptlike darkness as Klopstock unfastened the stall gate and pulled it open. She waited for her eyes to adjust, conscious of the way her own breath rasped against her ears, the way her heart pounded against her breast and her blood thrummed through her veins.

There, in the gloom, she saw the pirate lying in a heap of soiled straw, motionless, the flutter of his chest so slight that she wasn't certain at first whether he breathed or whether the flickering lantern light played tricks upon her eyes.

Verbeek turned away when she swung an accusing stare toward him.

"Water, at once," she ordered. She crossed the few steps to the captive's side and knelt in the straw. She gathered his battered head onto her lap, heedless of the effect dried blood and crusted gore might have upon her gown. Klopstock handed her a bucket of water, foul stuff, cloudy on top, but she dipped an edge of her skirt deeply into it nonetheless, patting it softly about his forehead.

He opened his eyes at her touch.

Difficult to tell, in the dim lantern light, whether they were as gloriously golden as she remembered. He'd been clean-shaven when he'd made his valiant stand at the dock. Now, two weeks' growth of facial hair obscured the angles and planes of his face, but not so much that it hid the fresh bruises blooming along his cheekbones. He stared, unseeing and un-blinking, at the ceiling.

Had she imagined his bold shouting, his belligerent pounding, which had reverberated through the ship and into her very bones? *No,* something within her denied. No. She had not imagined those faint bellows that roused unwilling admiration within her. She had not imagined the steady, determined pounding that had lent her strength earlier, when she'd summoned the courage to confront the captain. She had yearned for too long to do a bit of yelling and pounding herself not to recognize it when she heard it.

"Bring me fresh water, something he can drink." Her words sounded thick and heavy from the effort of making it through her tight, aching throat.

It seemed an eternity, and yet no time at all, cra-dling the smuggler until Klopstock scurried back with another bucket of water. Klopstock took on the bur-den of supporting the man's head while she sought a clean spot of hem on her skirt and dipped it into the water. She dribbled the drops over the prisoner's parched, cracked lips. A small whimper escaped her when she saw how his throat worked so hard to swallow.

"Save your sympathies, mevrouw. His injuries are not that severe." Verbeek hung the lantern on a peg jutting from the wall. "I'll leave Klopstock here with you to keep watch should the rogue suddenly recover his strength and think to take you hostage. He is faking."

Faking? The thought, which should have outraged any loyal Company supporter, sent amusement surging through her. Analisa sponged the smuggler's cheek, murmuring soft, soothing words in English. Her hand trembled a bit. Having tended to young girls most of her life, she found the man's physical traits and size somewhat daunting. Women's skin felt soft and smooth, a cool covering for more softness within. The pirate's skin felt firm and warm, and nothing under it yielded at the pressure of her fingers.

He lay loose-limbed upon the fetid straw, managing somehow to look ready to spring to action. No slack-jawed, drooling gape, no flaccid, flattened flesh; nay, this man's chin tilted proudly, his arms and legs bulged with fitness. Odd, despite the sheer size of him, she felt not the slightest bit of fear at the thought of being taken hostage by him.

The captain's departure loosened Klopstock's tongue. "Believe me, mevrouw, I have obeyed the captain, but I would never have withheld this man's water for three days. I have done what I can to tend his wounds. He was hale and robust when I left him this morning. I agree with the captain—he must be feigning unconsciousness."

Analisa smiled her gratitude at Klopstock, but kept her attention on the prisoner. "You are lucky you sleep," she whispered soothingly. "They malign your character, claiming you deceive me with this show of weakness."

She dipped her hem once again in the clean water, and when she leaned forward to wipe his forehead, she caught him staring at her.

And then he winked.

4

It took Michael a moment to recognize the woman. She was the little nun he'd noticed when they'd hauled him aboard. He'd gone and winked at a nun.

She shifted her eyes away, very nunlike. And then she blushed, a delightful pinkening that began at her cheeks and led Michael's gaze naturally down, beyond her chin and throat to the rounded twin swells that merely hinted at the treasures covered by her sober dress. Not nunlike at all. He couldn't help smiling, though the movement stretched his parched lips painfully. With a sharp intake of breath, she drew back her shoulders, no doubt outraged at his leisurely appreciation of her charms.

He ought to apologize, he supposed, for allowing his gaze to feast upon a nun's bosom. Unfortunately for his soul, he wasn't feeling the least bit apologetic. It cheered him immensely to realize that the allure of an attractive woman could still drive all thoughts of misery straight from his head. There had been moments, these past weeks, when he'd wondered if he'd have the chance to revel in one more good, blood-boiling fantasy before he met his maker.

Then again, going to his death while entertaining lecherous thoughts of a holy nun might not ease his passage into heaven. With a mental sigh of regret, he shifted his gaze back to her face. He found it just as difficult to form an apology while her long lashes fluttered low against creamy, sun-gilded skin, while stray tendrils of her hair stirred in time with her quick, shallow breaths.

"Sister Mary Tele—" he rasped.

"Hush." She pressed fingers against his lips, furtively, as if she did not want the man supporting Michael's head to notice. "You should not try to speak until I give you some water. And I am not a sister."

Michael did not know what startled him more—that she spoke to him in English, or the giddy rush of delight that surged through him at learning she had not foresworn men.

And she promised him water . . . oh, dear God, water.

He had never known, never suspected, how the insistent, constant craving for water could overshadow the pain following a sound thrashing. Thirst so addled his senses that he spent the bulk of his solitary hours dreaming, not of escape, but of dousing his head in a horse trough.

The thirst shifted and altered as he looked upon her. He wanted to rip the bucket from her hands, wanted to pour its contents straight down his throat; he wanted to press hot, wet kisses against her blushing skin and then lick the moisture away. He clamped his eyes shut and clenched his fists at his sides lest he do something foolish. Even though she wasn't a nun, he rather doubted she'd sit still for such behavior, and so he lay back, forcing himself to imitate a birth-blind, slack-jawed baby bird waiting for a few drops from its mother's beak.

After a moment's hesitation, she made a rustling movement, and then cool drops trickled against his lips. He groaned low in his throat when at first it seemed the maddening method would fail. His lips and tongue behaved like sun-scorched earth, absorbing droplets of rain without turning wet. But she kept at it, and after a few moments the steady drips puddled at the back of his throat and he swallowed, near swooning with relief when the blessed moisture unstuck his passageways.

With one thirst on the verge of being slaked, the other clamored for relief. He slitted his eyes open and studied her through the tangle of his lashes. Hazel eyes, just as he'd remembered from that brief glimpse of her above deck, but with a bewitching golden cast unlike any he'd ever seen. As often as he'd thought about her during these dark days, he had not suspected that such a wealth of glorious, waist-length hair lay hidden beneath the veil she'd been wearing. It curled over her shoulders, a brown richer than sundried tobacco or melted chocolate, a brown far deeper than the goddamned nutmegs that had gotten him into this fix. Her hair's lustrous darkness served to accentuate the rose and cream hues of her skin. One shining strand curled against the pulsing hollow at the base of her throat as she leaned forward and wrung water from the cloth into his mouth.

"What is your name, madam?" Good God, he sounded like a croaking frog.

"I am to ask the questions," she said.

He quirked his brow in admiration. She'd scolded him with the authority of one who expected others to mind her orders. Unusual, in a woman. And it would have been far more effective if her blush hadn't deepened, if her hand hadn't inadvertently pressed against the delectable spot where he'd been staring, as if baring such an insignificant amount of skin to a man's regard left her quite flustered.

Whoever held his head up off the malodorous straw fired a rapid string of words at her in Dutch. She answered, her words slow and enunciated clearly enough for Michael to understand that the unseen man feared for her safety.

It cheered Michael that anyone would think him a threat under these circumstances. Truth to tell, he did feel a bit close to eruption just then, with a beautiful woman bending over him, tantalizing him with her sea-breeze freshness and her warmth. He contented himself with staring at her and listening while they babbled back and forth, and eventually Michael recognized that the man holding his head was only the captain's lackey, Klopstock, the one man on board who Michael did not actively despise.

Or at least he had not actively despised him until Klopstock heaved a reluctant sigh and said, "Ja, mevrouw."

There was a Dutch word Michael could understand. Mevrouw. Missus. Dutch wife. Curse his luck.

He had to laugh at his disappointment. As if he, chained and stinking and doomed, had any chance at all of engaging this woman's interest, whether she be nun, wife, or maid.

Klopstock gently lowered Michael's head into the straw, and then stood. Chaff drifted from his clothes as he edged toward the stall gate, shooting worried looks at the pretty little mevrouw all the while. She had to be the captain's wife. No mere passenger would be entrusted with tending a smuggler.

I am to ask the questions, she had said. No doubt her husband, the captain, had pressed her into interrogation duty. For no good reason, Michael found himself wishing that her merciful visit had been prompted by her own concern for his well-being. No matter. He'd long ago weaned himself away from reveling in a woman's concern—it came at too high a price.

She had been sent to ask him questions, so let her

ask away. She would learn nothing about him, nothing at all. He knew how to keep his words to himself.

She leaned toward his ear and her whisper was like a low, throaty caress. "What is your name?"

"Michael Rowland," he said quietly, so Klopstock could not hear. That was the extent of his sense—he'd been so overwhelmed by her soft breath, warm against his cheek, that he instantly forgot his resolve to stay silent.

She sat back on her heels and studied him soberly. "Michael Rowland." Something about the way she spoke his name caught at his heart. She said it again, but to herself, with only the movement of her lips telling him that she tested the feel of it upon her tongue. She gave a little nod, and again Michael's heart faltered, for that nod was the gesture of a woman who'd satisfied her own curiosity rather than pursuing a course dictated to her by another. She had *wanted* to know his name, more than she cared about learning the information she'd been sent to obtain.

He heard a scrabbling noise, the sound of claws against wood, and then a soft triumphant *meow* as the ship's cat balanced atop a corner post of his stall. Michael felt an absurd pleasure at being able to see the creature for the first time. The cat couldn't have come at a better moment, diverting him from dwelling on the way the little mevrouw said his name.

"Why, you're a beauty," he crooned as the cat leaped down and picked her dainty way across the floor to him. The mevrouw flushed, apparently thinking the compliment had been directed at her, and then the blush deepened when the cat hopped onto Michael's lap with the familiarity of a much-loved pet.

"Stripes knows you," she said with a hint of jealousy.

"Stripes, hmm? Not a very feminine name for such a loving miss. I'll bet the seamen named her." He scratched beneath the cat's chin, and Stripes closed her eyes in ecstasy. "She visits me often. I've wondered what she looks like." He didn't add that there had been times when the cat's comforting purrs, the warm stroke of its sleek body, had been his sole anchor to sanity. Nor did he mention that the cat sometimes brought him gifts of small, rapidly cooling carcasses that he had not yet been desperate enough to eat.

For a while, the mevrouw did nothing but stare at the cat curled comfortably in Michael's lap. Her soft breathing mingled with the usual sounds of his captivity: the purring cat, the woolly thud of one sheep butting another into the sides of its stall, the feathery whap of an angry hen defending its perch. The mevrouw started when a particularly vicious squawk came from the chicken pen, and then her eyes widened with dismay.

"Oh! Look at me, daydreaming while you still thirst." She gathered up a section of her skirt, feeling for the hem. It was splotched and dark compared to the surrounding material, and he understood why when she dipped it into the water bucket. She had been using her own garment, cloth that touched her delectable, hidden curves, to squeeze the droplets into his mouth.

He groaned and shifted in the straw. At once, Klopstock moved closer, spouting a flood of Dutch.

"If you make any movements toward me, he'll kill you." She angled her head toward the agitated lackey.

"Let him try. All of the others have given it their best," Michael said.

Her hand trembled as she squeezed the cloth and dribbled a little more water over his lips. He licked at them, and then suddenly could not bear lying before her like some cosh-cocked drunkard being nursed past his hurts. Ignoring Klopstock's frantic objections, Michael levered himself into a sitting position. His chains slithered and clanked as he braced his wrists atop his bent knee.

His back blocked the lantern beam, so that she fell completely within the shadow cast by his form. Perhaps that was why she seemed so impossibly delicate. He knew his bulk had shrunken considerably during these past weeks, and yet it seemed he dwarfed her.

She did not quail away. She studied him openly. He fancied he could feel her measuring the column of his throat, the breadth of his shoulders, the circumference of his upper arms. Comparing him to her husband, no doubt. Very well, turnabout was fair—he had any number of women he could compare her against. But damn it all, he couldn't manage to conjure the image of a single one just then, not with her looking so ripe and luscious with her lips softly parted and her eyes warm with interest, her breasts moving softly beneath the ugly dress she wore.

"Your husband must place great trust in you, to leave you here," he managed to say.

"My husband?" She paled. "Oh, no, my husband does not know whether or not to trust me. Not yet."

Again, his troublesome heart rapped an extra beat. It had been personal concern after all that brought her to him. He wanted to hear her say it. "So why did he leave you all but alone with me, if he does not trust you?"

"He cannot possibly know I am here."

"He brought you here himself."

"No, the captain brought us—oh!" Understanding dawned then. "You think I'm married to Captain Verbeek." She pressed her lips together to still the smile prompted by that notion.

"Then who?" he wondered, mentally running over the faces of the various sailors who'd come to take their shot at battering information from him. Louts and lack-wits, the lot of them, not a single one worthy of calling such a woman wife. Perhaps the ship carried a gentleman passenger who had not troubled to dirty his finery with a visit to Michael Rowland's below-decks prison.

"We are straying far from the subject at hand," she admonished. "I told you that I am to ask the questions here. My marital relations are none of your concern."

Anther rough burst of speech came from Klopstock. She cocked her head, and then shook it. "He thinks I should move away from you. He fears for my safety."

"I would not hurt you."

Her gaze flickered toward his hands, toward the lengths of chain that could so easily be wound around her supple little neck if he were so inclined.

"You give your word?" she whispered.

"Aye."

She turned her back toward him then, a gesture so brave and foolish that it wrenched his heart yet again. She spoke to Klopstock, making shooing motions with her hands. Not a man aboard this ship would dare place themselves in such a defenseless fashion within his reach, and yet she, with naught but his one-syllable vow to rely upon, left herself vulnerable to any terrible action he might choose to take.

Her trust sent strength surging through his limbs, power coursing through his veins. He gritted his teeth against the pleasure he felt. He did not want her trust. A man who accepted the trust of someone smaller, someone weaker, soon found himself trapped into making promises he might not be able to keep.

She had been arguing with Klopstock while Michael wrestled with his emotions. "I am no different than ever," she said to Klopstock. She turned, scowling, muttering a curse consisting of half Dutch, half English words, about boneheaded men who mistrusted any show of independence from a woman.

"I beg to differ, mevrouw," Michael said. "He is right."

She glared at him suspiciously. "I thought you did not speak our tongue."

"I understand some of it. I speak very little—some would say not at all."

"Well, at least you do speak. Klopstock says that before this you have done naught but make horrible grunting sounds."

Michael feigned shock. "The man has no ear for fine singing."

"Singing? Why on earth would a man in your position sing?"

He caught the chain leading to his left wrist manacle in his right hand and gave it a good pull. That simple reminder of his helplessness was enough to make him want to let loose with a good, resounding bellow of rage. "There are times when a man cannot hold himself silent. I am not partial to screaming."

"No. Screaming accomplishes nothing." She studied him with the naked sympathy of one who understands helplessness, and the folly of expending precious strength against it. "But you must admit that most captives would be begging for mercy in your place."

"I never beg."

"Nor do I."

"Then it seems we have something in common."

"We do not." She flushed. "And you have driven me off the subject once again."

"Ah, yes, we were talking about why Klopstock believes you seem changed. I would say you seem quite different from the woman I first saw when brought aboard this ship. More . . . approachable." His gaze drifted lower, toward her bare neck.

Her scowl deepened. "That is merely because I neglected to fasten my collar onto my dress before coming here."

"You should not wear such confining garments in this heat. That collar bristled about your neck like a dog's spiked collar. I wonder that your husband has not outfitted you with garments more suitable to this climate."

"I am sure my husband will provide me with proper garments when I finally meet him. Now, as to those nutmegs you were caught smuggling—"

He ignored her efforts to redirect their conversation. "What do you mean, when you finally meet him? You can't mean to say that you have never met your husband—unless you happen to be one of those glove brides I've heard about."

"Whether or not I am a glove bride is of no matter to you." She glared at him, so embarrassed and defensive that Michael knew he'd struck upon the truth.

She'd struck upon a truth as well. He had no business caring whether she was married or not, no business allowing his protective urges to kindle in her direction. It would be best for both of them, and most especially for his peace of mind, if he angered and outraged her so much that she refused to come near him again. He knew just how to do it.

"I'm not the marrying sort myself." He leaned forward and whispered softly, seductively, in her ear. "But I'm perfectly suited to introduce you to the pleasures you'll find in the marriage bed. I'm the perfect lover, mevrouw. You need never worry that I'll boast of our indiscretion. They couldn't understand me, for one, and for the other—well, my tongue will soon be permanently silenced."

He jerked back, anticipating that she might slap him—many women would. Instead, she stilled, and her features settled into the frozen, agonized expression of a woman who'd endured too many taunts, too many ribald remarks. He regretted his teasing, and felt a stab of fury at the men who had caused her such pain.

"The captain tells me you are a despicable criminal—a pirate *and* a smuggler rolled into one."

"Most pirates smuggle as well as plunder. I'm not so unusual in that respect. If you'd like, I'll show you how I differ from other men."

She tightened her lips. "It is my duty to learn who helped you steal nutmegs."

He missed the gentle cadence that had marked her voice earlier; she spoke now with the wooden expressionlessness of one merely parroting memorized phrases.

"I dislike calling you *mevrouw*. Tell me your name." It was not the sort of question he should be asking, considering that he should be seeking to place distance between them rather than bring them back to their earlier, easier company. "Tell me your name, and I'll tell you—"

"You'll give me the information the captain seeks?"

Just then, with a small spark of interest rekindling in her eyes, with a hint of warmth returning to her voice, he thought he might tell her anything. He clenched his hands into fists. "I suppose your captain thought himself very canny," he ground out, "sending you to soften my will."

She shook her head. " 'Twas my idea. At first he refused, but then relented when he ventured I might possess some persuasive charms. He shall be disappointed to learn that he was wrong."

"Damn his soul—he was not wrong."

She tilted her head, while cautious delight bloomed within her. He wondered what sort of life she'd had, to be so affected by such a grudging compliment.

"Please tell me your secrets, Michael. The captain holds a pouch of nutmegs taken from you. He says the pouch will seal your doom. He's promised to make things easier for you if you'll tell me who helped you."

Michael drew a shuddering breath and shook his head.

"Why would anyone forfeit their life for silly *nutmegs*?" she asked, not bothering to hide a hint of exasperation, a note of confusion.

"Why indeed?" he answered gruffly.

"Please tell me what the captain wants to know." She paused. "*I* want to know. He says that only a Company nutmeg planter could have helped you. It pains me to think that one of my own countrymen would risk damaging the Company's monopoly."

"A loyal little thing, aren't you?" he mocked.

"I have more reason than most to appreciate all the Company does."

He pondered that for a moment, wondering what prompted such loyalty, and wanting to shatter it as he knew it was not deserved. "The Company *is* sending you far away from your family. I suppose some might count that a blessing," he said.

" 'Tis cruel of you to taunt me with my harshest regret."

"Regret?" He thought of the endless years he'd spent dreaming of the grand adventures awaiting him, how he'd postponed his own dreams for so long, caring for his mother and siblings while his father pursued his own ambitions. "Most would rejoice in escaping a family's clinging responsibilities."

"You do indeed possess the low-natured morals of a pirate! Only a selfish, opportunistic rogue would say such a thing."

"At your service, madam," he drawled, executing a mocking little bow from the waist.

"You're impossible! I shall have to tell the captain that there is no reasoning with you."

"As you wish."

He lowered his head, studying the shackles upon his wrist. The ship's motion rocked him as if he sat in a hammock, the gentle, rhythmic creakings comfortless but familiar after all these weeks. He tried to concentrate on those sounds, to blot out the realization that Klopstock had helped her to her feet, that they were leaving, but he could not. The stall gate creaked open and then thudded closed. The lantern light receded; soon it would be black-dark again and he would be alone with the sheep, the chickens, the rats.

"Mevrouw!" he called, hating the need in his voice.

"I am here." Her assurance stroked him like a caress. He shivered from the pleasure of it.

"Will you come again?"

"I . . . I don't think I should," she said.

Mere moments ago, he had told her that he never begged. But now she was leaving. Once she was gone, the darkness would settle round him, a black so impenetrable that he could not tell whether it was night or day. He would be left alone once more with nothing but the ship's inanimate sounds and the stoic companionship of animals destined to have their throats slit for the next day's dinner. It was an isolation that would be all the harder to bear, now that she'd brightened it so briefly, now that she'd reminded him that freshness and beauty and hope still existed in the world.

"Please come again." He could hear the faint edge of desperation, and hoped she could not.

"Perhaps," she whispered.

Sometimes, usually in church, Analisa had found herself staring so intently at an object—a crucifix, or strong-burning candle—that when she glanced away, a ghostly version of the object would hover over her vision. Dark where the object had been light. Light where the object had been dark.

She must have stared thus upon Michael Rowland, for it seemed that everywhere she looked she saw his ghostly image. She stood at the ship's rail, staring out at sea, and imagined Michael's dark form sprawling atop the water. She glanced at the moon and fancied it winked, treating her to a flash of whiskey-gold when she knew naught but colorless white glowed from the moon's face.

A bell chimed softly. The ship's rigging creaked, heralding a gust of wind strong enough to fill one of the mainsails with a loud snap. "All's well," called the watchman. The air felt wondrously cool against Analisa's bare neck, and she tilted up her chin, letting the breeze swirl around her.

Michael Rowland had looked at her bare neck, almost with his first glance. After he'd winked at her.

She touched her throat, remembering the way his eyes had glittered through slitted lids, the hint of a smile curving the edges of his lips. She had hovered and bent over him while tending him, practically pushing her bosom into his face. She'd even lifted the hem of her gown knowing he was watching. No wonder he'd winked. Her bosom, though not appealing enough to bewilder the smuggler into spilling his secrets as the captain had hoped, must nonetheless have afforded Michael Rowland a welcome change from the usual scampering rats and the canvas-shrouded carriage that were all he was likely to see.

The weather was so fine that she wished she could spend the night on deck rather than retreating to the privacy of her cabin. It would surely be more comfortable than tossing upon her bed, waiting for a stray breeze to stir the sluggish air.

There would be no breezes at all in Michael's belowdecks prison.

How could a free-spirited pirate endure such confinement? He ought to be scaling the rigging, or standing at the prow of the ship with sea spray stinging his skin and the wind billowing through the sleeves of his shirt. She could just imagine the sight of him, with his hair whipping behind him and his clothes molded against the unyielding firmness of his flesh. . . .

She would get no rest that night, she knew, not if she could not enjoy a cool night without falling prey to swirling thoughts of darkness and dirty straw, of shining new carriages shrouded in canvas, and a shackled man teasing and flirting with her while well-drawn lines of humor curved from his thirst-parched lips.

She wondered if smile lines characterized her husband's face, or if his features had settled into the permanent grooves of disappointment that marked so many older men's faces.

Michael Rowland's face would never grow old, never physically bear the stamp of his feelings. *Please come again,* he had asked. He would not live long enough to develop grooves in his face, disappointed or otherwise, to mark the brief moment she'd spent in his life.

Suddenly feeling chilled, she went to her cabin. She lit her candle and shielded the flame while she studied herself in her small looking glass. Klopstock—Michael, too—had said she'd changed, seemed different. She could detect no physical difference. She longed to shout a denial, to say nothing about her had changed, but it would be a lie.

Something within her had altered. A breathless expectancy filled her, bearing down against the emptiness that had always surrounded her heart. The relentless constriction seemed eased with hope and eagerness. There had to be a logical explanation, and after some hard thinking she scrounged one: Spending time with a man who would soon die had made her own life all the sweeter.

Somehow, the logic did not ring true.

She knew she should douse the candle and go straight to bed. The sailors began their work at first light, their shouts and commotion making it impossible to sleep once they'd begun. Even without so much of a tumult, she would have to rise at dawn as well, for the cabin became intolerably hot once the sun rose.

But attempting to sleep meant closing her eyes, and closing her eyes had the unfortunate effect of sum-

moning the image of Michael Rowland. She pictured
him lying on his back, feigning unconsciousness. Sitting loose-limbed and easy, his long fingers stroking
Stripes as she lay purring on his lap. Analisa had
thought the cat as solitary and friendless as herself,
but now she had an explanation for the animal's long
absences. She sought Michael out in the dark, the way
she followed Analisa in the light. It created a strange
sort of intimacy, knowing that of all of those on board,
the cat befriended only herself and a chained prisoner.

She tried to banish that blasted prisoner from her
mind by recalling the captain's features, and then
Klopstock's, but the attempt only resulted in sharpen-
ing her awareness of how handsome and fine Michael's features were in comparison. His legs weren't
bowed like the seamen's. His hair, thick and dark as
a midnight sky, made a mockery of the ostentatious
wig Verbeek wore when dressing for dinner. Michael's
eyes beckoned her, tempting her to submerge herself
in their intoxicating golden depths. She could not recall the color of the captain's eyes, the color of Klopstock's eyes.

Odd, that a criminal's features should spring to
mind so clearly, while those loyal Company faces,
grown familiar over long months at sea, faded to a
pale blur.

Perhaps Michael Rowland's features kept intruding
because she'd cleaned his battered face, coaxed water
past his lips. Because he'd smiled when she'd touched
him, and he'd winked when no one but she could possibly see such a jaunty, devil-may-care gesture.

Dawn found her staring at the ceiling, wishing she
had been given a miniature of her husband. If only
she could look upon his solid, no-nonsense presence,
she might blot out the dark-haired, golden-eyed vision
that haunted her.

5

~

Verbeek studied Analisa through hooded eyes, every inch of him contemptuous with disbelief. "Klopstock tells me you had him squawking like a seagull. Surely he told you *something* of consequence."

Since breakfast, Verbeek had been grilling her with the intensity of a Spanish Inquisitor. He refused to accept her word that most of her conversation with Michael had concerned Analisa's own situation. Now, sitting at Verbeek's tiny dining table, with the cat winding worriedly around her ankles, surrounded by the familiar trappings of the Dutch East India Company, she found it a little hard to believe herself. Only the enforced intimacy of Michael's makeshift prison could have lulled her into so much personal conversation.

"He admitted nothing of value, mynheer, as I have already told you several times." Analisa sat rigid upon the uncomfortable stool, her spine ramrod straight, her cheeks burning with anger and mortification.

"Not even his name?"

"Nor did I tell him mine,' Analisa countered. She felt like the worst sort of traitor, and as unsure of herself as if a stranger had slipped into her skin, for she did not understand why it seemed important to deny that Michael had identified himself. She knew only that she wanted to keep his name to herself for a little while, a secret known to her alone. His name, such an innocent secret—not at all like Michael's outrageous suggestion that he teach her the delights of love before sending her off to her husband, and himself to his doom. She should have reported his rude suggestion at once and begged Verbeek to excuse her from any further contact with such an uncouth rogue.

Verbeek spat an oath, accompanied by a dismissive wave of his hand. "Pah. His name means less than nothing to me. You know the information I seek."

"He told me nothing of import."

"You will see him again this morning." Verbeek issued the order with the flat expectancy that she would obey.

A frisson of annoyance rippled through her, quickly overwhelmed by the surging thrill that whispered *you will see him again.* She stiffened her shoulders even more, praying her face did not betray her excitement.

"I will stay with you this time," Verbeek continued. "I do understand a few words of that tongue, so do not think you can conceal from me what you learn."

She felt a *thump, thump, thump* beneath her feet. Michael, pounding out his defiance against those who would smother him in the dark. The faint vibrations raised an upswell of defiance in herself, against Verbeek's autocratic order, his snide insinuations.

"Your insults are beyond bearing, Captain," she ground out.

"I beg your forgiveness." Verbeek sounded not at all apologetic. "I daresay it is my eagerness to help the Company learn the smuggler's secrets that has caused this regrettable lapse in my manners. Now, if you please, we shall confront the criminal again."

He gripped her elbow with a strength that brooked

no protest and propelled her across the deck toward the main hatch. The seamen watched, their eyes agleam with speculation. She ignored them, staring blindly ahead until a flash of silver caught her eye. Dolphins. A group of them had taken to following the *Island Treasure* of late. They frisked several hundred feet away, their smooth, glistening bodies reflecting the sunlight as they leaped through the air and delved below the waves.

To her amazement, Stripes followed them down the ladder, lightly twining herself from rung to rung.

"I did not know cats could do that!" Analisa marveled.

"She can only do it going down," Verbeek said. "Damned creature can't seem to claw her way back up. One of us will have to haul her up later. Bloody nuisance, but she's a damned good mouser and we need her down below from time to time."

The sheep and chickens greeted them as before, with anxious bleats and frantic beating of wings, and Analisa felt her heart slamming against her ribs in accord.

This time she heard him before she saw him.

Infernal racket, Klopstock had called Michael's singing. Fine singing, Michael had said. Analisa did not quite know what to call the tuneless and yet oddly rhythmic male bellowing that echoed around crates and barrels and boxes.

Verbeek flung open the stall door and held the lantern aloft. The swaying light caught Michael in the most extraordinary position. Facedown and prone, he balanced somehow upon arms bent at the elbow, his upper arms bulging at the effort of keeping his entire body taut and away from the floor, save for the very tips of his toes. He'd ceased singing the moment the light pierced the gloom. He held himself rigid in that impossible position, his muscles sweat-slicked and defined, as he stared at them through his tangled hair.

"Up, up." Verbeek motioned for Michael to rise. The emphatic gesture overcame any language difference.

Michael obeyed, slowly, never taking his eyes from the captain as he rose to his full height. His chains shifted, snaking around his arms and legs with a sinister clanking. He shook them from his limbs, letting them hang from his wrists in mute testimony of his captivity.

His head barely cleared the low ceiling, wouldn't have cleared it if he didn't keep his neck slightly bowed. She remembered her first good look at him, when they'd brought him on board. Only a fierce battering had quieted him into submission, and even then he had seemed so large, so physically overwhelming that she'd found herself unable to breathe. Yesterday he'd lain in the straw or sat upon the floor, and she'd forgotten how he overwhelmed all who stood near. She felt that same breathlessness now, as if so much male vitality, even chained, required all the air in this dark, hot hold to stoke its inner fires.

His own breath came in deep, harsh rasps, as though he'd just finished running the length of the ship, absurd in light of his confinement. With a quick jerk of his head, his hair fell away from his face. The long, tangled strands caught against the rough shirt he wore. With the movement, his gaze shifted toward her. A small smile played around his lips, almost a smirk. His gaze flickered from her to Verbeek, silently linking her to the captain. She wanted to object, wanted to tell him she was nothing like Verbeek. She wanted to tell him she'd kept the secret of his name.

Verbeek scraped his foot along a floorboard, clearing aside the scattered straws to mark a line. "He cannot reach you if you stay behind this floorboard, mevrouw." He showed her how Michael's lengthy chains were fastened to hooks bolted into the floor, and then ran upward through rings in the ceiling, with the other end bound to the manacles encircling Michael's wrists. It was a simple and yet ingenious restraint, for it gave Michael complete freedom of movement so long as he remained within the back quarter of the stall. If he tried moving toward his captors, the chains would pull him up short and hold him immobile until he stepped back again.

The captain hung his lantern from a nail meant to hold a feed bucket, and then he leaned against the stall rails, waiting for her to begin questioning the prisoner.

Michael waited, too. His hands gripped the chains near the hooks in the ceiling. The sleeves had been torn from his shirt, and so his position revealed his forearms, all sculpted and traced with ropy veins. His upper arms flexed with the motion as he leaned toward her. She wondered how often he'd gripped those chains in a more violent way, in a futile effort to wrench the stout metal from the wood. She knew he'd done so; she could see it in the hardened blisters, the calluses creasing the edges of his hands.

Both men stared at her, the expectancy radiating from each utterly different in its intensity. She licked her lips but could not swallow; her collar constricted her throat. She smoothed her hands over her skirts. The wool clung to her the way Michael's chains wrapped around his limbs.

She shifted her attention down to her feet. "Tell me about the nutmegs."

He didn't answer for a long time, long enough for her to begin suspecting that he might refuse to talk to her at all. But then with a bitter bark of a laugh, the chains jingled and he relaxed his grip upon them.

"Nutmegs. Their taste disguises rot. 'Tis not surprising you Dutch hold them in such esteem."

Despite the derisive edge to his words, his voice burst upon her hearing like nutmeg upon the tongue: initially rough, but melting into exquisite flavor, making one crave another taste.

"These nutmegs you carried were different," she forced herself to say. "They were not limed to destroy their fertility. They were brown."

"Brown. Like your hair."

She darted a quick look at Verbeek to see if the captain's grasp of English was enough to make him realize that Michael had once again diverted their conversation toward personal matters. Verbeek frowned but gave her a curt nod, granting his permission to continue.

"Not as dark as my hair," she said.

"But not all of your hair is dark, madam," said Michael. "Even in this pitiful light, I can see strands of a dozen shades, from deep chestnut to sunny gold."

Her hand went up involuntarily to the tight crown of braids she'd wound around her head. She'd worn her hair in this hated but proper fashion ever since passing from girlhood, and knew that it fitted her skull like a dark, nondescript cap. Nobody had ever remarked on her hair, other than to tell her to keep it neat and contained. Only in the privacy of her bedroom had she dared wear it unbound.

Only in her bedroom—and the first time she'd rashly stormed into this stall after demanding to see the prisoner. And he remembered, curse his eyes! His voice dropped lower, and held a hint of a smile.

"The first time you came to me, the light struck against all the gold in your hair so that you shimmered like an angel."

Verbeek burst into irritated speech, and for the first time in her memory, it took her a moment to shift from English to Dutch. "Mevrouw, I remind you that this man possesses information that will benefit the Company. I will not waste my time standing here listening to him flirt with you."

The scolding sent embarrassment surging through her. She deserved it, she thought. Her well-ordered mind seemed as erratic as those dolphins she'd noticed earlier, darting and diving and refusing to follow any predictable path. She had, of course, found herself tongue-tied before men, but always because they had infuriated her with their arrogant assumptions, or disgusted her with proof of low morals. Never had she felt this uniquely feminine sense of weakness pervading her bones, making her want to utter no more than pleading little whimpers, asking for more.

Nobody had ever flirted with her.

Michael shifted his grip higher upon the chains. His shirt seams strained, the cloth stretched across his chest. The garment rode up his abdomen and bared a good two inches of skin above his belt line. Breeches clung low on his hips. Between his breeches and his shirt, that band of skin showed, smooth save for the line of fine dark hair that seemed to divide him in half and delved low, out of her sight, below his belt.

The lantern light caught the movement of his eyes, glittering as they examined her as thoroughly as she studied him. She touched her neck and found the familiar restricting edges of her collar. Her racing heart hammered through the cloth against her fingers. She remembered how Michael had glanced at her bare neck on that first visit and she wished, suddenly, that she had not worn her collar.

"Mevrouw?" Verbeek brusquely broke the silence.

Analisa shook her head to clear her chaotic thoughts from her mind. "Those nutmegs—"

Michael's sigh interrupted her question. "You are

quite single-minded for a woman, madam. Tell me, how do you come to speak English so well?"

"It was my father's native tongue."

"Aha! I knew you could not be Dutch." He grinned as if well pleased with the knowledge, and she unaccountably found herself grinning back. Someone actually valued the blood she carried in her veins rather than despised her for what she could not change.

"No Dutchwoman would be blessed with such glorious hair," Michael said. "Such incredible eyes, such . . ." His voice drifted lower, just as his gaze dipped down her length.

The insolent, outrageous sweep of his eyes brought her body alive, feature by feature. She stood before him, properly swathed and braided, and yet a shifting in his stance, a strained heaviness in his breathing, told her that he was very aware of every inch of her that lay bound and buried beneath her outward trappings.

"Mevrouw," Verbeek chided with the impatience of a parent taking a child to task for failing to complete a chore. Analisa started, flushing guiltily for reveling in Michael's appreciation rather than scolding him for his insolence.

"Tell me about the nutmegs, Mmm . . ." She pressed her lips together to avoid speaking his name.

He noticed. A conspiratorial smile played at his lips. "Mmm . . . You give me some information about yourself first," he parried.

"You already know more about me than you should."

"I don't know what you think about when you're alone, madam. I don't know what you dream about when you sleep."

Nobody had ever wanted to know anything about her—those staid Dutch citizens had formed their rigid opinions about her while she was still in her mother's womb. Not even her husband cared what she thought or dreamed.

"Please," she whispered. "The nutmegs."

He merely tightened his jaw and stared at her, demanding more from her than anyone ever had.

"Very well. It . . . it is Wednesday." It was a useless bit of information, but she knew such matters would torment her if she were locked away in a dark prison.

"Not good enough," he said, but the way he tensed, causing his chains to slither through the rings, betrayed his interest.

"The winds are favorable. We shall reach Banda Neira in only a short while. I will depart the ship there, to join my husband." She wondered if it was only her imagination or if he really did pale and stiffen at the mention of her joining her husband.

"And what of me?"

She glanced again at Verbeek, wondering if she would be breaking his confidence by telling Michael what she knew of his fate. Verbeek nodded and her heart plummeted. She wished he had refused to allow her to go on, for she had no enthusiasm for putting Michael's fate into words. She took a deep breath.

"The ship will take on a load of the nutmegs you so cherish and then journey on to Amboina. That's where you . . ." She swallowed, remembering Verbeek's horrible prediction of Michael's fate. She could not bring herself to articulate castration and execution. "You will be given over to the governor in Amboina."

She saw in Michael's expression that he did not need her embellishments to understand what awaited him.

"Please reconsider your silence." She groped for the right words. "Unless you name your cohorts, you alone will pay the ultimate price for smuggling. The men who helped you will suffer naught. Please, tell me their names. The captain has promised to intercede for you if you cooperate."

Michael stared at her for a long while. "There is no one else, madam. I have seen to it that I am responsible only for myself."

"The captain said you could not have obtained these nutmegs without someone helping you."

He shrugged. "In the final reckoning, I must stand alone before God. I do not think He would be impressed if I come to him sniveling and whining that others are to blame for the way I lived my life. Can you understand that, madam?"

"Yes," she whispered. "Perhaps better than you can imagine."

There seemed to be nothing more to say. She had failed, utterly, to gain the information wanted by the captain. She'd learned nothing of importance, except for the heady and useless realization that someone cared about the person hidden beneath her prim and proper exterior. Someone—a rogue—*liked* the secret self she fought so hard to bury. It gave them a kinship, that they were both bound by shackles they could not break.

They stood looking at each other, illuminated only by the inadequate lantern light, beneath Verbeek's watchful eye. Her gown clung to her as if glued in place; the damnable collar threatened to choke the breath from her. She was suddenly possessed of the urge to strip it all away, the garments and all they represented.

"I am suddenly enervated by the heat, Captain," she said. She turned away from Michael, spun about, and so quickly made for the open stall door that Verbeek had no time to object before she'd gained the concealing darkness of the hold.

Verbeek was swinging the gate closed when Michael's voice rang out with one final question. "I would know your name, madam."

It had been his first question, the day before. She could not think of anyone so determined to know her identity. To the Company directors, she had been Britta's useful daughter. To the captain, she was cargo, a distraction to his crew, perhaps a tool for gaining information. To her husband, she was a female body, an unknown potential broodmare.

"I am Analisa. Analisa Vandermann." She took a few steps before remembering to add her married surname. "Hootendorf," she added in a low voice.

"Analisa," he said softly. "It suits you."

She trudged through the hold, past the doomed meat animals. She skirted the casks and kegs while scarcely being aware of her evasive movements. Verbeek would surely be furious with her; she dreaded what form his anger would take. She did not think he would try beating her, not with their journey so near its end—he would not risk turning over a new bride with half-healed bruises marring her skin.

She reached the ladder. The cat brushed her ankles, begging to be picked up, just as Verbeek had predicted she would. Analisa lifted her and the cat clung to her shoulder. Verbeek had called Stripes a bloody nuisance—he no doubt thought the same of her. Analisa stroked the cat, waiting for Verbeek's annoyance to break free.

Instead, sunlight spilled through the hatch, lighting her and Verbeek, and she found a wide smile upon the captain's face.

"Well done, mevrouw," he said. He gave her shoulder an awkward pat. "Very well done."

Verbeek did not take her to Michael the next day.

She'd spent a sleepless night. Each time she relaxed enough for sleep to steal close, her unfettered mind drifted back to those brief moments spent below deck. Michael Rowland's image played against the blackness, every detail recreated in stunning, shocking detail, from the tangled curl of his hair to the chained strength of his arms, to that distracting, compelling band of bare skin at his waist. She bolted from bed before sunup, driven by a raging headache and an even more demanding urge to . . . to . . .

To see him again.

No, it could not be. This ache within her, this burgeoning sense of anticipation, could just as easily be ascribed to the knowledge that they drew ever closer to her husband. Back at the School for Company's Daughters, the chosen brides had spent virtually every waking moment speculating on what sort of man they would meet at the end of their journeys. If visions of Michael Rowland taunted her, why, 'twas only the understandable curiosity of a woman raised with virtually no contact with men. She was quite properly concerned with wondering how she might measure up against a man, how his arms might bulge and ripple as he bent them around her, how his thighs would tighten and his belly tense when she stepped just a little closer to him.

Small wonder her head pounded and her heart raced! But Verbeek had seemed oblivious to her distress over breakfast and made no mention whatever of his prisoner. Analisa had not been able to broach the subject herself, and so she had spent a fretful day staring out at sea. Wondering. Waiting. Aching.

Stripes mewed at her feet. Analisa gathered the cat against her chest, stroking the soft black-and-gray-striped fur. The gray—her husband's hair would probably be gray, faded by time and the tropical sun. The black, the same color as Michael's, glowed rich and glossy in the bright light.

What had happened to her, that the mere act of

petting a cat would make her compare one man to another? One man she had yet to meet, another man she did not really know—but she could learn more about him, and perhaps put an end to this restlessness.

When an unsuspecting Jan Klopstock plopped himself atop a coil of rope, intent upon mending a torn bit of sail, she swooped down upon him.

"Captain Verbeek does not seem very concerned about his prisoner today," she remarked.

Klopstock grunted, as disinterested, apparently, as the captain.

"I just thought that he might be worried about the prisoner's well-being, seeing that it is so much warmer today."

"Temperature doesn't vary much, down below," Klopstock muttered.

The crusty old seaman wasn't making her conversation easy. "I . . . it's the water, Jan. The captain had promised to increase his ration, and I just want to be sure that he remembered."

"He remembered. Yon smuggler drinks and eats as well as any of us."

So she had accomplished something, at least—she'd increased Michael's comfort. Although, considering that weeks had passed since taking on supplies, he might not have noticed much of an improvement. She repressed a tiny shudder at the memory of the brackish water she'd swallowed a little earlier, at the unappetizing scent of the meat she'd forced past her nose.

"Perhaps I should go below again and check on the prisoner's injuries," Analisa said.

"He fares well enough." Klopstock's leathery features hardened into a frown. "There's no need for you to insult your ladylike sensibilities by fretting over that scum, mevrouw. 'Tis too dangerous."

"The captain showed me where to stand, so that Mi . . . the criminal . . . cannot reach me."

"There be other dangers down there in the dark, mevrouw." Klopstock spoke enigmatically, while redness bloomed beneath his permanent bronzing.

"Nevertheless, it is a lady's duty to care for the ill and infirm." Analisa could not believe her boldness in pressing an issue that so obviously roused Klopstock's disapproval.

"Yer fine as any lady I ever sailed with,' Klopstock said grudgingly. "Nobody on this ship would think less of ye if ye decided to keep to yer cabin for the rest of the journey."

"I cannot do that," she whispered. Guilt assailed her for so blatantly lying to the one man who'd showed her a little kindness. And yet she persisted, driven by an inner need to see Michael again. She could never reveal to Klopstock, nor to any other man aboard the ship, that a thrumming sense of expectancy vibrated within her, as if something wondrous waited down there in the dark with Michael Rowland.

Klopstock, obviously disgusted with her, had his attention riveted upon another comfortable-looking pile of rope while he hurriedly gathered his things together.

"Please mention my concern to the captain," she said.

He muttered something that she thought carried a grudging hint of affirmation. She clutched her hands together, knowing she could do no more. She settled against the rail, once more wondering. Waiting. Aching.

The next day, the captain took her back.

6

During the first weeks following his capture, Michael had fought bitterly against the chains that held him. It was the enforced inactivity that bothered him most. His body, accustomed to hard work and physical activity, cramped and ached from being confined to such a small space. Helped along by the debilitating heat, the lack of food, the dearth of water, he'd gradually subsided into a disbelieving kind of acceptance—his life, postponed for so long, was all over before it really began. In such a frame of mind, the days had passed, endless in some respects, all too quick in others, but endurable.

And then she had come. Analisa.

If only she were truly a nun, or some sour-faced scold. Why did she have to be a beautiful, vital female trembling on the edge of great discovery? She reminded him of the way he'd once been, biding time, fulfilling the expectations of others, until it was turn to run free. Her innocence and simmering vibrancy called to his blood. She made him so aware of himself as a man that his tenuous acceptance of his lot dissolved, leaving him edgy and aroused.

The hours in the dark stretched longer than ever before; his dreams returned to haunt him with all he would never experience. At times he wished she would never return, and at others he thought he would tumble into the abyss of madness if he could not see her again.

And so he threw himself with renewed determination into the limbering and stretching exercises. He practiced the Indian chants he'd learned from Stalking Dog in Virginia, even though the plaintive, soaring sounds evoked memories of a wild freedom he might never know again.

He tried to empty his mind of all thought, but always he listened, waiting for the slightest sound from the sheep and chickens penned next to him. Better than any guard dogs, they always bleated and squawked when someone came through the hatch, whether it was the cook coming to choose one of them for dinner or a couple of gin-hearted sailors bent for his prison, intent upon a little practice work with their fists.

When at last he heard the clucks and the clatter of cloven feet, he knew she was coming. He did not know how he could tell, but his pulse quickened. She was coming. He clambered to his feet. His pride demanded he be standing when she saw him.

She looked more beautiful than he remembered, more alluring than he'd dreamed. Her creamy skin, lit by the lantern, glowed luminously lovely against her drab gown. Countless washings with seawater had rendered it some indefinable color, so that Analisa's hazel eyes and the lush rose of her lips seemed all the more brilliant.

Captain Son of a Bitch stood behind her. He held the lantern high, his eyes narrowed with malevolent intent while he judged Michael's reaction to Analisa's presence. The wily old dog knew exactly what he was doing, doling out moments with her the way an opium den operator stoked the pipes of his addicts. Michael knew he ought to thwart the captain, retreat to his bed in the straw and turn his face to the wall, refusing to talk to her. He was hungry enough for the sight of her to refuse that notion out of hand; he still held on to enough remnants of his pride that he thought he might be able to taunt the captain right beneath his nose and get away with it.

For instance, he could tell Analisa that he was ever so aware of how she looked, and yet reveal nothing of how he dwelled incessantly and replayed every moment of their visits in his mind once she was gone.

"I used half my drinking water to wash my hair so I'd look nice for you," he teased. "And there you are, wearing the same dress once again."

His observation stung her pride. She curled her fists into the folds of her skirt. The unconscious motion pulled the voluminous garment tight against her belly, lending it a shapeliness that no dressmaker could contrive with fancy darts and stitches. Analisa alone was responsible for those curves.

"I do not plan my wardrobe around you," she said.

"You'll be dressing to please a man soon enough, when you join your husband. Your maid ought to be practicing."

"I do not have maid."

"Then your chaperone ought to be advising you."

"I am traveling alone."

Although he was no expert on social proprieties, it struck him as odd that a beautiful young woman would be consigned to spend months at sea alone. He'd always thought the custom of attaching a maid or elderly female chaperone to a beautiful young woman to be a complete waste of time and effort. Men could not resist drinking in the sight of a lovely woman, no matter who stood next to her. Some inborn male impulse forced a man to speculate on the charms hidden beneath the most staid garments. And yet, hearing that Analisa traveled without the flimsy barrier of female companionship roused an equally male outrage at the thought that other men would be looking at her and daydreaming.

"If you were my woman," he lowered his voice, "I would surround you with a virtual cadre of cross-armed hags to keep the men at bay."

"There is no need. I am married and thus beyond men's attentions."

"That is the statement of an innocent, Analisa. Your husband ought to know better and should have provided for you."

"There was no time. Few women could prepare for a trip of such duration with but a week's notice. And since good servants are so difficult to come by in Amsterdam, but plentiful in my new home, the Company directors deemed it a waste to send a servant with me. Matters simply developed too quickly."

"What if you don't like the way he looks?"

"My preferences are of no import."

"No? Then what of his—what if he doesn't like you?"

He'd meant only to tease, but she swayed a little, and he knew she feared that very thing. "It would not be a simple matter to cast me aside," she said. "I spoke vows during the proxy ceremony."

"Then you are only half a bride, because your husband refused to wait, and the Company skimped." He could tell by the way she lifted her chin the tiniest fraction that he'd hit upon a truth that left her feeling uncomfortable. "He must be overcome with passion for you."

Most women would have ended the conversation there. Analisa darted another quick glance toward the glowering captain. "Passion has nothing to do with my marriage." She said it with such quiet dignity that Michael regretted teasing her over the matter. "I hope that Pietr and I might find ourselves compatible, nothing more."

"Analisa, if you were my bride, I would demand a great deal more than simple compatibility."

For one quick, unguarded moment, pleasure lit her face. One moment it was there, setting her trembling and blushing, the most entrancing smile tipping the corners of her lips. And the next moment it was gone, her face smoothed of all emotion. People did not naturally have that ability—'twas something that had to be learned, and practiced often, for the sole purpose of concealing deep feelings, be they pleasure or pain. A street urchin, perhaps, who had to feign innocence when caught at pickpocketing. A wife of many years, mayhap, who learns her husband has been unfaithful.

It seemed an odd skill for a new bride to possess—or was it? She traveled without a maid, with no luxurious wardrobe, aboard a ship more suited to cargo than passengers. Perhaps she knew she was journeying toward a tight-fisted husband and thought it best to conceal her disappointment beneath an outward veneer of acceptance. Perhaps her staunch defense of that pitiable wreck of a dress was designed to hide a lack of confidence.

"What do you know of what you would or would not demand of a wife?" She looked cross, but he could tell it was pretense; he could read her uncertainty, her vulnerability, in her every line. "You have told me yourself that you are not the marrying sort."

Her uncertainty could well stem from his earlier remark that her husband might not like her, might repudiate her on sight. Impossible. The lucky fool would be more apt to kick his heels together with delight upon seeing her.

"Do not worry, Analisa," he said. "He will find you delightful."

"Do you think so?" Such naked hope illuminated

her that he wanted to bask in its glow, wanted it to be for him and not some unknown nutmeg planter who ordered wives the way bored housewives ordered bolts of cloth. "I will look better for him," she went on, oblivious to his emotions. "I have one other dress."

"Wear it for me. Tomorrow."

"Oh, I couldn't—it is my wedding dress! I did not even wear it during the proxy ceremony. I will not put it on until I meet Pietr face-to-face and we speak our final vows before the governor. My husband should be the first man to see it."

"It would not matter what you wore if you came to me as a bride. You would be so quickly divested of any garment that—"

With a frantic look at Verbeek, she stepped back a pace, and Michael clapped his mouth shut. He knew he'd overstepped the bounds of polite conversation. Overstepped, hell—he'd trampled the bounds right into the ground. But there was something about thinking of Analisa saving her best gown for a man who hadn't cared enough to provide for her comfort that fair rankled Michael's sense of righteousness.

Verbeek burst into angry dialogue. Analisa answered him, touching her dress, so Michael understood she was explaining their conversation to the captain. The captain issued a quick order, cast her a look of utter disgust, and stomped out into the darkness of the hold.

"The captain," she said quietly, "said that before he comes back I am to explain to you that it is traditional for the Company to send its Daughters off with only two dresses. You see, some girls are destined to be married to clerks and have no need for more than two dresses. Wealthy men like my husband can afford to give their wives as many dresses as they need."

"The Company knows how to watch its pennies," Michael remarked.

"The Company watches everything, which is why you must account for those nutmegs you smuggled. The captain expects me to give him a full explanation upon his return."

Nutmegs. Michael was sick unto death of nutmegs. The smell of them was so embedded in the ship's timbers that the odor imbued every breath he drew. The cloying scent was a fitting reminder for a man who'd sworn to abandon good deeds, only to get caught in the performance of the largest good deed of his life. He'd spent countless hours in this hellhole reliving that moment when he'd accepted the small bundle of nutmegs and stuffed them carelessly into his shirt. His only thought then had been for the starving colonists who so desperately needed a cash crop to survive. He should have stuck to his plan to think only of himself. He sighed.

"I would rather talk about your dresses, Analisa."

"I refuse to do that."

"Very well. I shall have to content myself with thinking about them, then."

"Men do not think about such silly trifles."

"You are quite correct. We tend to think about the lovely form buried beneath all those yards of silky, soft fabrics. So when you leave here, you will go with the knowledge that I will be alone here in the dark, thinking about your . . . dresses."

"You are impossible!"

"And you are delectable."

"You should spend your time praying and repenting your sins, preparing yourself to . . ." Her voice trailed away. Her eyes widened with horror of the words she had not spoken.

"Preparing myself to die?" He finished the sentence

for her, and then gave a little laugh. "I much prefer thinking about you."

"I will leave this instant if you continue talking about me."

The threat sent dread curling through him. At once it became harder to breathe, as if the ever-present darkness closed around him, a living death. He shuddered, and prayed Analisa had not noticed how he dreaded being plunged back into the dark. "Very well. Let us talk about your husband, instead. What will you say when you first meet him?"

"Why, I—I haven't decided yet," she stammered.

"I'll bet you haven't given your husband a single thought since meeting me," he teased her in his best roguish manner, but watching her blush and quiver in silent acknowledgment thrilled him to his very core.

"That is not true! I think about my husband all the time."

She clasped her hands together, but not before he noticed the way they trembled. She was lying; he would stake what remained of his life on it. Absurd, learning that a woman he could never possess did not think about a man he would never meet could send his spirits soaring so high.

"Will you curtsy before him? You may practice before me, if you like."

She sent him a withering glare. "I do not curtsy before criminals. Besides, you would no doubt find my practicing exceedingly dull."

"Not if you shuck off that god-awful collar. I surely hope your wedding dress bares more of your charms. A man who's bought himself a new wife probably wants to get an eyeful of what his wealth has paid for when she bows low before him."

"He did not buy me," she ground out. "He saved me."

"From what?"

He thought for a moment that she would not answer. "If not for his marriage offer, I would be destined to spend all my days turning spirited little girls into proper ladies."

"Just as someone has done to you, hmm?"

"Nobody has done anything to me!"

"What a pity. I thought I'd detected a little fire and spirit beneath that ever-so-proper facade. I prefer my women with a bit of spirit."

"I am not your woman, and your preferences only prove what an unrefined criminal you are, for all true gentlemen prefer meek, submissive wives."

"Is that so? Well, as I said, I'm not the marrying sort." He studied her for a moment, considering whether she might flay into him if he told her that her own teacher had done a miserable job of stifling her. He could sense her spirit quivering, barely contained. He could almost feel her fire, ready to burst into flame. He had not lied when he'd said he was not the marrying sort, but, dear God, a woman like this, so vibrant, so smoldering and waiting to be brought to passionate life, could go far in changing his mind.

Dangerous ground. His well-honed sense of self-preservation cried its warning. He scrambled back to safety.

"So you're a teacher of young girls?" She gave a curt nod. He laughed. "I might have known. You stand there scolding me with such authority that I cringe in dread of having my knuckles rapped."

"Your shocking conversation proves some teacher ought to have taken the stick to you a long time ago, Mi—!"

He noticed how, even though the captain had moved beyond earshot, she held back from saying his name. Part of him craved to hear it from her lips. Part of him savored the knowledge that she must not have revealed his identity. Her silence warmed something inside him, the way spring sunshine coaxed seeds into life.

Dangerous ground. Better by far to remain unaffected. Why, she might merely be a bubbleheaded female who'd forgotten his name.

"I'm sorry to refuse your offer of a paddling, Analisa. Not my sort of pleasure at all. Your new husband might like it, though, if you stood over him every night while brandishing a stick."

She seemed perplexed by his reference to male peccadilloes. "I do not expect my husband to demand any such thing. He is far too old and wise to play pranks with sticks. I don't expect any of his demands to be unbearable, considering what he offers in return."

"And what is that? His money? The role of mistress over a huge swarm of servants?"

"Respectability."

She spoke the word with a lingering caress, the way a woman whispers the name of her lover.

"No man will dare leer at me, no woman stick her nose in the air as I pass by." She shook her head as if dispelling a daydream, and then found her teacher's voice again. "I don't expect you to understand. You have done nothing with your life but make a mess of it—sneaking round the world, plundering others' property, caring naught for what anyone thinks of what you do or worrying how what you do affects others."

Her criticism stung. "Perhaps I have had my fill of worrying about others."

"Oh, yes, those onerous family responsibilities you say I should be happy to be rid of." She gave a contemptuous little sniff. He supposed he could not blame her. He'd vowed long ago to bury all traces of the man who'd spent too many years putting others ahead of himself, too much of his energies caring for those more helpless. He'd deliberately fashioned himself into the unrepentant, devil-may-care rogue standing before her. It should have thrilled him to know how thoroughly he'd succeeded in remolding himself. Instead, he felt an odd ache to realize that she might have liked the old Michael Rowland better than the chained adventurer standing before her.

The captain returned, barking questions at Analisa that she answered with a simple negative shake of her head. He battered her with a flurry of Dutch. She glanced down, summoning a deep breath, and when she looked up at him again, he could tell that Verbeek had embarrassed her.

"I fear my captain tires of this pointless conversation. We must return to the topic of nutmegs."

"I have no interest in nutmegs. I am far more interested in knowing why you are willing to sacrifice yourself for the sake of respectability. I assure you it is a highly overrated state of affairs."

"You are impossible! And it goes to prove that you have no care for anyone but yourself, or you would help me instead of trying to make me doubt the wisdom of the course I've chosen."

"One day you will think of this conversation and realize I did my best to help you, Analisa."

"Then I suppose it is fortunate for me that you will no longer be around to remind me that you told me so," she retorted. And then her eyes widened with remorse.

"Ah, there you are, spirited little spitfire," Michael murmured.

"Come, mevrouw." The captain caught Analisa at the elbow and propelled her out of the stall before either of them could say good-bye.

The darkness closed in. The scent of nutmegs thickened until it clogged Michael's every breath.

He lay back upon his straw, gasping and sweating. He tried counting the passing minutes, but lost track again and again. He knew hours were passing by the changes in his body—the building thirst, the gnawing emptiness in his stomach.

At last Klopstock appeared with a bucket of water and a pan of food, and Michael realized a full day had passed since Analisa's visit. He drank half the water beneath Klopstock's watchful eye, setting the balance aside to use for washing later. Klopstock motioned for him to stop.

"No need to save it. Captain says I'm to give you separate washing water. Mevrouw requested it to be so."

So she'd noticed that flippant comment he'd sent her way, about reserving some of his precious water to keep himself clean. Michael's throat tightened with gratitude. He could not understand why Klopstock seemed so uncomfortable as he hefted a second bucket of water. And then he understood when the seaman flung it straight at him, dousing him from head to toe in raw seawater.

The hours stretched, endless and interminable, until Klopstock visited him again. He varied his performance of the day before by drenching him with seawater first before passing along his food and drinking water, and Michael knew another day had passed.

He was not fool enough to waste the food or water, but once he'd finished drinking, once he'd eaten, he could not stop himself from bellowing his rage. He stood there dripping and called her name again and again, sending the few remaining meat animals into fits of confusion. When his throat was scraped raw, he caught up the water bucket and battered it against the wall until the iron bindings snapped and the closely fitted slats fell apart.

She did not return the next day, either.

By the fourth day, he realized she would never come again.

*   *   *

Analisa. Analisa. Come to me, Analisa. . . .

Analisa tossed restlessly on her bed, caught in that netherworld between dreaming and wakefulness. *Analisa. Come to me . . .* The call was so faint that she could barely decipher her name, and yet she could hear the raw huskiness of that male voice, could feel the rich rumbling. A pounding commenced, demanding, compelling, urging her to come. . . .

She sat bolt upright, startled that her heart should pound so loudly—but, no, it truly was someone pounding, at her door. She wrapped her bedsheet around her and opened the door a crack. Klopstock stood outside.

"Captain says you must take breakfast early today, mevrouw. Storm's brewing."

Food held no appeal, not with her nerves all ajangle from her dream. "Please give the captain my regrets, Jan. I am not hungry just now, and perhaps it is best I do not eat if we're in for rough seas."

"Aye, mevrouw." He took his leave.

She put a hand to her head and let the bedsheet drop to the floor. She had lied to Jan Klopstock when she'd said she wasn't hungry—a nameless, empty ache gnawed away at her, demanding to be filled.

And she knew just who to blame for this. Michael Rowland.

He was impossible. He was an arrogant, uncouth rogue. No—she could despise a rogue, dismiss a rogue out of hand. She could not seem to banish thoughts of Michael Rowland. He had to be a spawn of the devil, alluring and enticing and altogether too appealing for a man who insulted her and pried into her inmost secrets right beneath the eye of a captain of the Dutch East India Company. Well, she was glad, glad, glad that Verbeek seemed to have abandoned his plan for getting her to pry Michael's secrets away from him.

She needed time to herself, anyway. Michael's outrageous questions had roused all sorts of uncertainties within her. She ought to be preparing herself for meeting her husband. Michael's reminder that Pietr could reject her had caused a curl of apprehension in the pit of her stomach. For all these months she had played the part of Mevrouw Hootendorf, tried so hard to submerge herself in that role, without success. Perhaps knowing that the contracts had not been exchanged, that the formal vows had yet to be spoken, had somehow kept her from believing it was true. If only another glove bride—or even a lady's maid—had accompanied her, she might have someone to confide in, someone who might confess that she, too, had trouble feeling married in her heart.

But Pietr Hootendorf had not cared to wait for contracts to be exchanged so that the marriage would be irrevocable. He had not granted his new wife the time to make arrangements for companionship; the Company had not thought enough of her to provide a maid. . . .

Curse Michael Rowland for planting those thoughts in her head!

And those weren't the only remnants of their conversations that haunted her. *Perhaps I have had my fill of worrying about others,* he had said—and yet he refused to implicate anyone else, holding his tongue to safeguard his accomplices. Those questions that so annoyed her stemmed from legitimate concerns that ought to have been raised by people who claimed to care about her: the Company directors, her new husband, her own mother. Somewhere behind Michael Rowland's teasing, flirtatious facade dwelled a man who worried about people, who cared what happened to them.

So why had he turned pirate?

Did he really care about her? And so what if he did?

Questions without answers. She dug her hand through her hair to massage her scalp against the headache raging there. Stripes, doing her feline imitation, groomed her fur.

Analisa tickled the soft pads under Stripes's upturned paw. "I don't need some doomed criminal fretting over me and telling me what to do," she told the cat. "I have always relied upon myself. I don't need anyone else."

The cat trilled softly, and then arched an inquisitive paw toward a hairpin that had fallen. Analisa rescued the hairpin. "You'd choke if you tried to eat this, but it's your nature to be curious, isn't it? I'm not curious, not at all." But she knew it was a lie even as she spoke it. She was curious about many things, but not the least bit about the man who was her husband. In fact, her lack of anticipation bordered on apathy.

Perhaps she could stoke it by trying different arrangements for her hair, or primping her good gown. Maybe she should take Michael's suggestion and practice a pretty speech to impress the man who would control the rest of her life. For some reason the idea that she should practice called to mind the way Michael's eyes lit with appreciation each time he'd seen her, when she'd made absolutely no effort to prepare for their meetings.

Pound, pound, pound. No, not her headache—it was her door again. Once more she wrapped herself in the bedsheet and yanked open the door. "What!"

Poor Klopstock cringed away from her unaccustomed rage. He rolled his eyes toward the empty sea over his shoulder. "Just thought you'd like to know, mevrouw, that our lookout spotted signs. Banda Neira's less than a week's sail away. Thought it might comfort you to know we're so close to the end, in case things get a mite rough during the storm."

Remorse flooded her as the bent little man scurried away. The heightened wind had drowned out the celebratory sounds that were so obvious now that her door was open. The sailors were cheering the news, clanging the ship's bell and twirling each other about in a scampering dance. Even the Captain seemed to have shaken his near-constant bad temper and stood smiling at the revelers.

She slammed her door shut, a heavy dull thud, like the sound of the *Island Treasure*'s guns. She leaned back against the door, feeling as empty and gasping for breath as if the ship's guns had shot a hole through her belly.

She heard a sound like a soft whisper. She strained to hear it, wondering if it was Michael calling for her from belowdecks. But, no, it was just the rain, falling as Klopstock had forewarned, pattering against her door.

She stared at her bed longingly, wanting nothing more than to climb back into it and pull the covers over her head, leaving her alone with her thoughts. But rain could not be wasted. She tugged her gown over her head, and then glanced at her collar. She decided it would take too long to fasten it just then. She got the length of clean sail that she kept on hand specifically for rainstorms and went out into the wet. Stripes followed only so far before settling herself neatly at the threshold, staring disdainfully at the wet decking.

Chuckling at the cat's good sense, Analisa tied one end of her sailcloth to a nail pounded into the outside wall of her cabin and tucked the other end into the rope that secured a stack of barrels. She propped a bucket to catch the rainwater and angled the sail toward it. Rainwater was doubly precious now, since the water they had taken on in Africa had turned so brackish. Her throat worked, anticipating a drink of fresh cool water.

Michael had never had a cup of rainwater throughout this journey.

Why did every ordinary thought lead her back to him? No sensible person would dwell so much over that stubborn, bullheaded criminal. Let him carry his secrets to his grave, if that was his desire.

He'd be in his grave soon enough. The realization filled her with a dread melancholy. She stiffened her impulses against it. Melancholy was a sin, and so she should do some small penance—perhaps don the collar.

She returned to her room and sought out the offending collar and buttoned it to her neckline. After so many months at sea, so many washings, it had gone all floppy, but was no less constricting. She tried to pinch it into some semblance of its former starchiness, and then shrugged. What did it matter? Once she arrived on Banda Neira, she'd never wear the collar again. As soon as her new home came into sight, she'd change into her wedding gown and pitch her old dress and collar straight into the sea, never giving the garments or this ship or any of the people on board, particularly an infuriating nutmeg smuggler, a second thought.

A timid knock sounded once again at her door.

Klopstock's worried face peered up at her when she inched open the door. He scooted back, as if he feared she might wallop him. "Mevrouw, the captain asks you to keep to this cabin. It looks like we're in store for a bit of a blow."

Beyond the sheltering wall of gin barrels, the wind howled, and rain pelted the ship. Suddenly the *Island Treasure* pitched, sending Klopstock staggering and Analisa grabbing for support. "Don't worry—I'll stay inside," she screamed, but the wind snatched up her words and she doubted Klopstock could hear them. He had worries enough. She watched him wind a length of rope around his waist before he lowered his head and forged his way through the wind and the sea spray toward the rest of the sailors, who worked frantically to secure the ship against the storm.

Analisa closed herself into the cabin, shivering from the sudden drop in temperature and the wet spots where rain had splattered her. She couldn't see Stripes—perhaps the cat had darted away to one of her mysterious, safe hiding places. Perhaps she'd streaked for the hatch and the dark safety of the lower decks . . . and Michael.

Without the cat's company, the cabin seemed gloomier than ever. Analisa lit a candle, and when that did little to make things more cheerful, she lit her lantern. She remembered her rainwater bucket then, and almost abandoned it to the storm, but a brief lull in the wind gave her the courage to open the door and snatch the bucket inside.

She treated herself to a cupful, and it went down her throat every bit as cool and delicious as she'd imagined. She started to dip her cup again, but her hand stilled. All she could think of was Michael, down there in the dark, not knowing that they were within a few days of landfall, that this storm was pitching the ship about like a straw upon the waves.

As if to make light of her worries, the wind calmed again. The *Island Treasure* shuddered into stillness, but the air was punctuated by the frantic shouts of seamen. She peeked out of her door and saw all the men clustered aft, some in the rigging, some standing below and staring up. She wondered if a mast had been compromised in the wind—whatever, their attention was all directed there. Nobody watched her cabin.

The auxiliary hatch. It yawned open a scant dozen

yards from her door. The fastening had been left un-battened in case any of them had to take refuge below in the storm. It would be a simple matter for her to slip unnoticed into the dark void.

For what? To give Michael a drink of water, she thought virtuously. To say her good-byes, she ac-knowledged as the truth.

It would be poisonously difficult to negotiate the ladder while holding a lantern and the water bucket. But a few seconds of experimentation convinced her that she could grip the bucket handle and the lantern handle together in one hand, leaving her other hand free to hold on to the ladder rails.

The wind picked up again, not quite as fierce, but with a low-pitched whine that promised worse to come.

She was across the deck and down the hatch before she had time to change her mind.

She leaned against the wall for a moment after descending the ladder. Her limbs quaked, partly from the effort it had taken to hold on while the ship pitched and tossed, and partly from the realization that her impulsive behavior could get her into real trouble. If the captain should see her, he'd feel obliged to report to Pietr that his proper Company's Daughter wife had been caught sneaking belowdecks to visit a criminal.

If she had the least bit of sense, she'd scamper right back up that ladder and lock herself in her cabin. She looked upward, toward respectability, and knew she had turned as helpless as the cat to climb up that ladder. Rain misted over her face. Rain. The bucket of water dragged against her arm, reminding her that she stood only yards away from a man who hadn't tasted fresh water in weeks. She glanced once more toward the open hatch, and then moved away from it, deeper into the dark.

The storm sounds echoed down the hatch and grew ever more muted as she made her way through the cargo hold, until she could not hear the wind and rain at all, only the pounding of her heart. The sailors had lashed the cargo in place with strong, sure knots so that the ropes creaked a bit but nothing moved. She walked stiffly through the towering stacks, holding herself rigid for balance. The crates and bales stood still as mountains, so it was not fear of being crushed that made her pulse race.

Her lantern beam arced across the animal stalls. The one remaining sheep had backed itself into a corner, staring out at her with dull resignation, its legs braced against the ship's motion. The chicken crates stood empty save for one bird that still clung to a perch, flapping its wings for balance. The hen turned its head to follow the light and then voiced its displeasure with muted squawks.

The sounds must have alerted Michael to her presence. His voice rasped out into the darkness. "Get the hell out of here. You've had your fun for the day."

He had obviously mistaken her for one of the sailors. She shifted her grip on the water pail and tightened her hold on the lantern. The beam danced wildly through the darkness, evidence of the trembling that had seized her upon hearing him. Something more than the real fear brought on by her risky behavior caused her to shake so—it was the simple thrill of knowing she would soon see him again, talk to him again.

" 'Tis only me," she called quietly. "Analisa."

At first she thought he had not heard her, that the indignant chicken and close-packed cargo had muffled her voice. But a moment later, she heard the clinking of his chains, the rustling of boot leather scraping at straw.

"Stay away."

The gruff order caused something to twist inside her. She had never imagined he might not want her company. The secret soft part inside herself that she always tried to protect by hiding away screamed at her to return to the safety above deck rather than risk her pride, risk her very future, by seeing him again. Her arm ached from holding the heavy bucket. The instincts that had served her so well for so long urged her to run for the safety of her cabin. She could so easily relieve her physical and mental discomforts—Michael could not.

"I brought water," she called to him. "Rainwater. It is icy cold and fresh."

A long silence greeted the announcement of her treat, a silence heavy with wanting. She fancied she could sense his throat working, his tongue savoring the taste of cold, clean, sweet water.

"Go away. I don't want it."

"Nonsense." By then she'd reached his stall and swung open the gate. He moved quickly away, withdrawing to the deep shadows at the back of his stall.

She held the lantern high, puzzled and hurt by his rejection. He jerked his head away from the swinging beam, but not quickly enough to avoid it. She had no free hand to stifle her scream.

It looked as if Michael suffered from frostbite.

He crouched, as if trying to minimize what the light revealed. A dull white film coated every visible bit of his skin. His black hair looked gray beneath it. His beard appeared to be frozen against his jaw. His eyebrows bristled white at the tips. His clothes hung in brittle, frosted folds, the way clean laundry stiffens when hung out to dry beneath winter's frigid sun.

She stared in horrified disbelief, watching as a bead of sweat formed upon his forehead and trickled down his cheek, into his beard and through to his neck. It left a little skin-colored runnel in its wake. She felt dampness spring up on her own upper lips and thoughtlessly touched her tongue to it, finding the salty taste of sweat.

And then she understood. Captain Verbeek, boasting of going beyond his word by giving the prisoner daily baths—he'd been dousing Michael Rowland with water from the sea. Salt water, which sucked the life from one's skin and crusted one's clothing with an itching, harsh residue once it dried.

Raw, rough patches edged Michael's neck where his shirt collar had rubbed—reddened and inflamed. She could only guess at the pain and stinging that must accompany the dousing, how his very own sweat would melt the dried salt and double the stinging of his wounds.

He turned his head to the side. His jaw tightened and lifted. It shamed him for her to see him like this. She understood with the experience of one who could not shed the image forced upon her by others more powerful.

She paused long enough to hang the lantern on its usual nail. And then, giving no thought to her safety, to the fact that Michael could easily overpower her once she moved into his grasp, she ran straight to him, tearing the collar away from her neck as she ran.

The light, though it barely pierced the darkness, blinded Michael for a brief, merciful moment, so he could not see how Analisa reacted to this evidence of his latest humiliation. And so he sensed, rather than saw, her quick crossing of the usually unbreachable space between them. He blinked, then found her kneeling before him.

She dipped her collar into her bucket of rainwater, then pressed it, dripping and cool, against his forehead.

Again, she did it again, that wondrously fresh water sluicing through his second skin of salt. He closed his eyes, shuddering at the sensation.

"Yes, close your eyes," she cautioned. "The water might run into your eyes and sting."

"You care about me," he whispered, only half teasing.

She grew very still for a moment. "What I feel for

you is compassion, nothing more, the way I'd spare a kind thought for a blind donkey trotting off to the knackers, or a toothless dog who starves while stronger beasts shove him away from his food."

She made her little speech with the practiced air of one who had given the matter much thought, as if she had spent many hours working this out in her own mind.

"Ah, you lump me together with the noble, hard-working donkey and that most loyal of creatures, the dog. I see you hold a high opinion of me, Analisa."

"Cease your braying and whining and close your eyes," she snapped back at him.

"Yes, teacher," he said, grinning.

She wiped at his eyelids, her touch as light as a butterfly's. He could feel her fingers through the cloth, more firmly when she passed over his cheeks, molding cloth against the bones and hollows of his face. He opened his eyes then and watched her, entranced by the studious pucker of her brow as she bunched the cloth and scrubbed at his beard. She paused, and dipped the cloth again, and spread it thin, and met his stare.

"I'll just do . . . I'll just do your mouth now," she said, her voice scarcely above a whisper, her gaze skipping away.

Only a single thickness of cloth kept her bare fingertips from touching his lips.

Dear God, he could feel her warmth through the cloth. Unbidden, his lips parted and a rush of breath escaped when she traced his upper lip.

She swallowed. He did, too. Cool water trickled past his lips and down his throat, doing little to ease a dryness that had nothing to do with a thirst for water.

She dipped the collar and pressed it against his mouth again. Wet, the cloth seemed no barrier, might as well not even have existed. Her fingertip pulsed against his lower lip; his lip swelled and throbbed in accord. Swelled and throbbed in accord with another, even more sensitive part of his anatomy, which had lain dormant and disinterested until she had come and reminded him what it felt like to be a man, even if it be only for a span of days.

She dipped her free hand into the bucket, tilted her head back, and opened her mouth to catch water from her hand. A few droplets missed and trickled down the smooth column of her throat, leaving wet, glistening trails just begging for some thirsty man to come along and lick his fill.

Even had he not been chained, Michael could not have freed himself from staring.

She blushed when she caught his gaze riveted upon her. "I wanted to make certain the water had not grown too salty from my dipping the collar into it."

Michael hadn't noticed, didn't care, how the water tasted. Only a thorough immersion in an ice-slivered pond could cool and quench the hot thirst raging through him now.

He tried to cool his passions, tried to regain his ability to think. Damn that wily Dutch captain! He might well have sent her here, telling her to splash about with the water in the hopes she would succeed at seducing the information from him. She had but to glance toward his breeches to see how well her antics were succeeding. He shifted into a crouch so his knees could create concealing shadows from the lantern's glare.

His movement startled her. He watched her expressive face shift as she realized her vulnerability. Her pulse leapt in her throat and she dropped her collar into the bucket. She slid backward, away from him. Acting on its own, his hand reached toward her, his throat worked, an inarticulate sound struggled free. The sound trapped her in place and she stared with the helpless fascination of a treed raccoon, her hazel eyes wide and luminous in the dim light, her breath coming in short, quick gasps that stretched the cloth over her breasts.

He lowered his hand. He swallowed his impulse to ask her to come back to him.

"I must go," she whispered. She gestured toward the bucket, the slight tremor in her arm matching that in her voice. "I only meant to bring you some water, and to tell you that we are caught in a storm."

He glanced into the bucket and spotted her collar floating on the water. He ought to remind her not to forget it.

She edged farther away. When her backside met the edge of the stall, she rose and reached for the lantern.

"Stay." He hated the taint of pleading in his voice. "There's nothing you can do above during a storm."

"I can pray for you, Michael Rowland."

She walked toward the yawning stall gate, which creaked back and forth each time the ship heaved. She stopped it in an open position and looked back at him over her shoulder, uncertain, as if unused to being permitted to have her say, but determined to have it this once. "Even after I am certain you are dead, I shall ask God to be lenient toward one who gave his life for such a witless cause."

"Then my soul is surely saved," he drawled, falling back on mockery to disguise how it affected him, to hear her promise to pray for him once he was dead. "Analisa." The name sounded in his mind, lovely and soothing and perfectly suited to her. He closed his eyes, his heart thudding against his ribs, his lips throbbing with the remembered feel of her fingers pressing against their fullness. "Be off with you, then. I don't want you to stay anyway."

Womanlike, she turned contrary at his dismissal of her. She hung the lantern back upon its nail. She clasped her hands, looking as if she meant to launch into praying for him then and there, and then pressed the resulting fist against her lips. But only for a moment, for the ship shifted and she had to grab hold of the stall rails to stay on her feet. Her eyes, wide and troubled, seemed to pierce straight through his casual facade.

"Talk to me, Michael. Not the things the captain asked me to learn—tell me something about yourself. Please."

She wanted to know something about *him,* about Michael Rowland the man, not Michael Rowland the smuggler. He felt an odd little twist in his vitals at the thought.

"Come closer if you want to talk," he said. She shook her head. "You must," he insisted. When she shook her head again, he lurched forward and fished her collar out of the bucket. He let it dangle from his hand, and the ship's lurching sent it waving back and forth.

"My collar!" she shrieked. Her voice cracked as she pleaded, "I must have it back or they will know I visited you without the captain's permission."

Michael bunched it in his fist, intending to toss it to her, but then his hand stilled. These Dutch were a treacherous lot. Unlikely as it appeared, it was just possible that the captain had rigged this little act, casting Analisa into the role of nervous, flustered wife, in order to break Michael's silence.

She stared at him, quivering. Analisa. Biting her lip, her color flaring and fading, her breath coming in quick, short gasps. No, she had not come to betray him.

She had promised to pray for him.

"I would like it as a keepsake," he said. "As you so helpfully pointed out, I will not have need of it for long, and no one will know I have it."

"Yes, they will."

She swiveled her head wildly, and then pulling herself hand over hand, she dragged herself to the farthest edge of his stall, where a canvas-wrapped hulk loomed over the rails. She tugged at a rope until she freed a corner of the canvas. She hooked her fingers beneath it and pulled until she revealed a spoked wheel.

"Look here, Michael. This is why you must hand over my collar. My husband ordered this all the way from Amsterdam. They'll unload it when we reach Banda Neira. They'll have to move you to make room for the unloading, and they'll find the collar. You have nowhere to hide it."

She freed more canvas. A lacquered expanse gleamed ebony in the lantern light. She teased another section of canvas free, until Michael could make out the shape of a door, embellished with brass handle and hinges, and an ornate crest featuring the letter *H*.

"That's a carriage," Michael said, stunned. A carriage. Her arrogant son of a bitch of a husband had ordered a carriage.

He couldn't help it; he laughed.

"Humph!" She drew herself up, projecting prim and proper wifely outrage at his mockery of her husband's carriage. "You might not be so amused once I tell you that I at first thought *you* were a zebra, meant to draw this carriage as a wedding gift for me."

The notion of a zebra drawing a carriage anywhere, let alone within the Banda Islands, made Michael choke even more with laughter. "Without a wild zebra, I fear you'll have no chance at all to enjoy a wedding drive," he managed to gasp.

"You . . . you do not think my husband will want to drive with me?" She suddenly looked very young and unsure of herself.

Something in Michael's gut twisted, stifling his merriment.

"Your husband should know better than to import that monstrosity to the Bandas."

"It looks like a very nice carriage to me."

"I can see he has told you nothing at all about the place where you'll be living."

"How could he? There was no time for letters to be exchanged. I know next to nothing about him. He knows even less about me—he does not yet even know my name." Her voice caught at the end of her admission, as if it both embarrassed and frightened her.

All Michael could think was, *I knew her name before her husband.*

He slowly stood. His left leg cramped and he grimaced, stretching it out before him while he kneaded his thigh with rough fingers to still the spasms. The pain mattered not—he knew her name and her husband did not, and that little bit of intimacy made him want to shout with triumph. "Nobody owns a carriage on the Bandas, Analisa. There are no horses, no cattle. Every inch of space is given over to the growing of nutmegs."

"Surely they have *some* livestock." As if on cue, the sheep bleated. She lowered her voice as if she sought to protect the sheep from hearing what she said. "I am quite fond of mutton."

"No sheep. A few pigs, perhaps, but only if your husband's fabulously wealthy. You'll never eat fresh beef again, nor drink milk or eat soft cheeses. There's no room spared for flowers or grass or hay, no barns, no roads."

"But there must be roads! I . . . my temperament often compels me to take long solitary walks, and Captain Verbeek promised me that I would find pleasant walking trails."

"He can only mean the paths that wind through the nutmeg trees, barely wide enough for the harvesters, who balance two nutmeg baskets across their necks, yoked like oxen. You might not be allowed to walk these trails unescorted. You will never ride on horseback or travel by carriage to visit your friends. A carriage for the Bandas is naught but . . . an abomination."

An abomination. A rich man's sick delight in fetching a useless, costly bauble from halfway around the world just to impress upon others his power and wealth. Judging by the quality of the carriage, the skill of the artist who'd painted the crest, Pietr Hootendorf had commissioned this carriage years earlier. He'd put more thought and effort into obtaining a useless hunk of wood and metal than he had in ordering a flesh-and-blood wife.

Analisa's hand rested against the carriage as if she'd hoped to draw strength from its presence. Her hand dropped now, lifeless and drained, and Michael understood that she'd just realized the same thing for herself. With trembling fingers, she tucked the canvas back into its rope bindings.

"Help me escape, Analisa." He spoke without thinking, articulating the fantasy that plagued him day and night. "Set me free and we shall escape this ship together."

A soft, sad smile played at the edges of her lips.

"I am married, Michael."

"You have never met the man you call husband."

"But the vows were said."

"You said them. He did not. You admitted yourself that final vows must be spoken."

"Before God, and in front of witnesses, I became Pietr Hootendorf's proxy bride. In my mind, I know I am married."

"But what of your heart, Analisa? What does your heart say to you?"

"It says I owe Pietr Hootendorf more than you can ever imagine. Soon, I will become his wife in every sense of the word, the wife of a very important and influential man."

"So it is his wealth that makes you so loyal."

"I suppose I should not expect you to understand. You are a criminal. Even if . . . even if I had the slightest interest in setting you free, I could never run off with you without thoroughly humiliating my husband. He would set the law upon us."

He hated to admit the logic behind her refusal. At the same time, her reasoning restored a bit of his pride. He had been begging her for one thing or another throughout this little visit, and she had granted him nothing. It soothed something inside to think that her refusals stemmed from a fear for his safety rather than a preference for her rich old husband.

"Set me free. I'll make my way alone."

"I cannot betray the Company. I owe my very life to it. My mother's livelihood rests completely in Company hands." Tears shimmered in her eyes.

Please don't cry. He wondered what she would do if he tried to gather her in his arms and console her past those tears while he pressed her slim length against his surging flesh. He closed his eyes, willing the impulse away.

"Please give me my collar, Michael."

"Find and destroy the nutmeg pouch Verbeek holds against me. He can prove nothing without evidence."

"You are no different than all the others. You pretend to like me, but really want to use me." She said it with the dull despair of one who had found herself pressed into unpleasant duties far too often.

He wanted to shout a denial, to demand that she admit she had misjudged his character—but he could not. Truly, he *had* been trying to manipulate her. When he'd vowed to change his life, to think of himself before worrying about others, he had never imagined that that decision would put him in a position where he would try to take advantage of a frightened young female who found herself caught between two bad situations. He could not let her see how this affected him.

"I have never denied being a rogue," he said, striving for the easy bantering he'd used with her before. "The rogue's code of dishonor demands I obtain some sort of favor from you before returning your collar."

She took him seriously. She caught her lower lip between her teeth and worried it a little. "I cannot set you free, and I cannot search Captain Verbeek's quarters for that nutmeg pouch!" She steepled her hands and held her fingers, trembling, against her lips. "I . . . what if I promise to write to your loved ones and tell them what happened to you? I wouldn't tell them that you'd become a despicable criminal, of course, only that you'd . . . died." She swallowed hard, her color flaring again, and looked toward Pietr's carriage. "I know you said you were glad to be rid of your family, but I would want to know what happened to you—if you were . . . someone I loved."

He laughed to cover the odd sensation that swept through him at her words. "I fear there might not be anyone left to worry about me after all this time."

"Surely there's someone," she insisted. "My mother always told me Englishmen could claim relatives in nearly every corner of the country."

"I'm not an Englishman, not anymore. Two years ago I left the British navy and became a colonist. A Virginian, to be precise." A thrill of pride ran through him even as he prayed she wouldn't share his secret with the captain. God knows few enough colonists were still alive when he'd left Virginia for this ill-fated quest. They'd not thank him if a Dutch warship sailed into Chesapeake Bay to finish off what savages and starvation had begun.

"A colonist! Oh, I have yearned to learn more about the colonies. But . . . but—you are a pirate."

"By necessity, Analisa, though I must admit the assignment well suited my nature."

Her fears and tears and collar all seemed to be forgotten as she moved toward him. Avid interest, equal to his own, vibrated from her. "A pirate and a colonist. Tell me, did you propose to plant a nutmeg grove with those seeds you'd smuggled?"

Her quick leap of logic impressed him; her obvious interest in a topic that sent most women shivering with loathing lulled him into admitting the truth about his mission. "The Virginia climate is temperate but we've had little success in establishing a cash crop. I'd served a tour on Run Island. I think nutmegs could thrive in Virginia, and my old navy friends on Run Island agreed to help. They got the nutmegs; I was to take them to Virginia. I failed this once, but I mean to try again."

He took heart from the vow, even though cold iron encircled his wrists and ankles. She said nothing, though the very air seemed to chill with her disbelief.

"Michael, please, my collar," she reminded him gently.

He held it up and shook his hand until the cloth flapped wetly, and then he tucked the collar into his shirt. She made a small sound of despair.

"You can claim it with a kiss," he said.

Analisa had often watched the sailors as they sat upon the floor, tending their netting. None of them took up as much space as Michael Rowland. His legs seemed ridiculously long, even with one bent at the knee and the foot of the other tracing patterns against the floor.

They seemed overly tempered, too, so that the tiny motions of his foot sent huge clumps of muscle and sinew bunching beneath his breeches.

He slouched against the wall, his posture revealing a torso long and equally muscled. His shoulders were pressed against the wall, otherwise they would certainly look a normal width rather than as if they would dwarf any two sailors'. He'd clasped his hands over his stomach, as if daring her to pry them apart and fish her collar from his shirt.

"One little kiss," he drawled, his eyes glittering mischievously through lowered lids. Amber eyes, lion's eyes, he reminded her of a jungle cat, all supple and feigning nonchalance but ready to pounce the moment its prey got within reach.

"No gentleman would request such a thing." Analisa ignored the fluttering in her breast.

"Ah, but I am a rogue, not a gentleman. I am a doomed man, Analisa. Doomed. Is one little kiss so much to ask?"

Why, it was just as the captain had complained— Michael was flirting with her! She had always warned her girls that flirting led to kissing, and then kissing led to other, unmentionable, activities between men and women. She had never suspected that a little flirting could be so . . . pleasurable. It almost made up for the pulse-pounding terrors she had endured in sneaking down here like this.

Perhaps a little kissing was equally enjoyable.

She studied Michael's mouth, remembering how she'd wiped the salt from him, the way his warmth and heartbeat had passed through the cloth to her fingers. He caught her staring and his teasing smile transformed itself into something more—not the "sweet dreams" sort of pucker her mother used to blow toward her as a child, but a sensual shifting that promised to mold his lips to the shape of her own, to capture hers with a heated, pulsing pressure she would feel straight to her toes.

She realized suddenly that he was offering her a choice. She could kiss him or not as she pleased. It might be the last time in her life she could enjoy that particular decision, for once she was Pietr's wife, her kisses would be his upon demand. She would have no say in the matter.

Michael winked.

Laughter bubbled to her lips. "Just one, then," she capitulated, marveling that she managed to sound like a practiced miss accustomed to favoring her swains with flirtatious kisses and not a wife who remained unkissed and untouched after six long lonely months of marriage.

He stood slowly, careful as a horse trainer who approached an untamed filly, knowing that any sudden movement could spook his quarry into running away. He crooked his finger and beckoned her to come closer.

"Aye." She answered his silent command, and then took one step, two, and then more until she could no longer see his face without bending her neck. She stared at his shoulder, feeling the heat of him warm the space between them. Though he'd tucked most of his hair behind his ears, one hank of it had escaped when he bent his head. It lay against his neck, still damp from the water she'd washed him with, the soft, dark ends stirring from her breath.

"My lips are up here," he said.

"Aye." It surprised her to realize that she had been able to feel the vibrations in his voice. She tilted her head and looked up at him. "I must state a rule, though. You must not try to wrap your arms around me."

"No arms," he agreed. "Unless you want them."

"Oh, I won't."

With his head bent over hers, their lips nearly collided as they spoke. She laughed weakly, feeling her face heat with sudden embarrassment. She longed to run—he couldn't follow without his chains pulling him up short. But soon, soon, she would meet her husband, Pietr. Pietr was an experienced man, who would no doubt be comparing Analisa's kisses to those of the dead wife he mourned. Perhaps she should welcome Michael's demand as an opportunity to hone a skill she did not possess. Perhaps she could pretend to be kissing Pietr.

Michael's eyes flamed into hers, hot and intent, golden and glittering with a fire that drove all thoughts of practicing for Pietr straight from Analisa's mind.

This would be Michael's kiss. Michael's alone.

She leaned forward a little. Rose on her toes. Obeyed an irrational impulse to close her eyes and lift her chin even higher. She stood poised like a ship's figurehead until Michael growled something unintelligible and lowered his mouth to hers.

A torrent of heat and unsteadiness shot through her so that she had no choice but to lean even closer and brace her hands against the broad planes of his chest. His lips burned against hers, so hot, so firm, and yet softer than anything she'd ever imagined, pulsating, insistent, drawing forth an echoing sensation from some secret place that dwelled low within.

She wanted his arms around her, wanted to feel surrounded by him so badly that she whimpered. The sound roused a groaning gasp from him. Her eyes flew open; her lips parted from his with the reluctance of tulip bulbs being separated for transplanting.

"Analisa?" His eyes burned into hers, naked with want and desire, his voice a husky pleasure that stirred that newly awakened place within her.

Transplanted tulips bulbs . . . Michael from the colo-

nies to Amboina and certain death; she transplanted
to Banda and Pietr.

Pietr. The mere echo of his name in her mind
drowned her fancies as thoroughly as if the captain
had treated her to one of those saltwater baths.

"My—my collar," she stammered, stepping back.

The light in his eyes dimmed, the lids lowering like
shutters. "In my shirt."

She couldn't look at him, couldn't face the ragged
need his voice so clearly conveyed. She reached a tentative hand toward his waist, tried plucking at the fabric, but the shirt was too tautly stretched to let her
collar simply fall free. She slid her hand into the gap
between his shirt and his skin.

Her knees weakened at the hot smoothness of his
skin, at the way he shivered at her touch. Of its own
accord, her other hand joined the first, her fingertips
brushing over crisp curling hairs to rest upon the muscled expanse guarding his heart. Its strong, steady beat
seemed to falter beneath her touch. For the first time
in her life, she felt the glorious power of a female who
knows she is desired, desired for herself and not for
the sanctioned purpose of begetting children or fulfilling a marriage contract. Desire, simple and raw desire.

The way she desired him.

She shivered with the realization. His body, young
and taut and bursting with masculinity, roused hers to
a quivering mass of need. But it was the essence of
him, the teasing facade that hid a man of depth and
character, that compelled her most.

"Hold me, Michael," she whispered.

One mighty arm circled her waist. With his other
hand, he cradled her head as gently as a father with
a newborn babe and pressed her reverently against
his chest. His breath rasped against her ear, his heart
drummed an ancient, addictive rhythm. The ship
lurched and he held her even tighter. His chains

clinked and slithered with his movements. They wound around her as well as him, holding them both prisoner to this raging desire that stormed wilder in the dark hold of the ship than the rainstorm battering the outside.

He murmured something against her hair and then he kissed her again. He tilted her head back to run lips and tongue over her neck. He cupped her bottom, lifting her against him until she felt him hard and insistent against her most private parts, with naught but her gown and his breeches separating them.

He bent and laid her upon his straw. They stared at each other, breathing hard. He drew back a little; she whimpered in denial. He reached for the neckline of her dress, his fingers toying with the buttons there. The chain leading from his wrist lay within the valley of her breasts and curved over her waist; she tossed impatiently, the chain was too insubstantial, it was insufficient, she wanted something more, something heavier and hotter and more pliant weighing her down. She wanted Michael, his skin against hers, his body pressing against hers.

She raised her hand. It trembled wildly but did her bidding and joined Michael's at her neckline. She fumbled ineffectually at the buttons, at the ribbon tying her shift. With a low growl of triumph, he tended to those jobs himself, and soon her breasts lay bare to his hungry gaze.

"You are even more beautiful than I imagined." His whisper blew across her skin, hot and yet rousing shivers within her. His lips trailed from her neck to her breasts, and lower, and somehow with his hands and his lips he nudged the bodice of her gown and her light chemise away until she lay beneath him, bared to the waist. She wanted him bare, too. Her hands worked frantically at his shirt, pulling it open and then down until she realized she could not remove it past the chains at his wrists. He shrugged it back into place but let the front gape open and she traced the hard ropy muscles of his abdomen, the curling hair that swirled from his breastbone to his heart. And still it wasn't enough.

"Michael?" She half whispered, half whimpered his name in an entreaty.

"You are mine," he said. "Mine. Forever. All of you." He made astonishingly short work of her gown and shift, even divesting her of her shoes and stockings. "All of you," he murmured again. His lips claimed her everywhere, marking her as his from her toes to the soles of her feet, up her legs and in places where not even her mother had told her a man might want to kiss her. He turned her into a quivering, shaking mass of need, and when she thought she might never manage another coherent thought, he stopped.

He stopped with his hand cupping her womanhood, with his long fingers teasing the most exquisite sensations from her, with his tongue working against the nipple of her right breast.

"This is yours to give, Analisa." She felt his finger move inside her, felt it come up against the barrier nature had fashioned to provide a woman with her most precious gift. "God knows how I will manage it, but if you tell me to stop, I will."

He shook with a need that equaled or perhaps surpassed her own. He faced imminent death, and he knew it, and it was unlikely that his magnificent body would ever know or give such pleasure again. And still he offered her a choice.

At that moment, Analisa knew that all her husband's wealth and power could not equal Michael's gift to her. She had but one gift its equal to offer in return, the one thing that was hers and hers alone to bestow where she willed.

"I do not want you to stop, Michael."

He moved between her legs then. "Wrap yourself around me, Analisa," he murmured against her ear. "Hold me while I love you."

She obeyed, wanting more than anything to get so close to him that she might burrow into his very flesh. Instead, he did that to her. Her eyes flew open at the shock when she felt him hot and huge and hard at her softest places, and then she abandoned herself to the sensation when he moved inside her, when her body stretched and clung and proved to them both that she had been born to fit with this man. The pain seemed a small price to pay, and soon enough it was gone.

He tried to be careful with her, she could tell, she could feel the tension gripping his massive shoulders, feel the tautness of his belly against hers. But the ship and the storm fought against his tenuous control. The wind and rain pounded against the ship, and it seemed like the perfect accompaniment to the storm raging inside her. She heard the muted rumble of thunder just as she lost herself in an explosive wave of passion and Michael shouted his own release.

He would not let go of her. She did not mind, even though his wrist manacles dug into the tender flesh of her back. She wished wildly that there could be some permanent mark of this night, but knew that she would look to the world the same as she always had.

Michael wrapped her hair around his fist. His chains slid over her skin, binding her to him, and yet she had never felt more free. He pulled back gently until her throat was exposed. He began with kisses there, and then . . . then the whole wondrous, dizzying thing happened all over again.

She did not know how much time had passed when she realized the ship had gone quiet, that they no longer had to brace their feet against the stall rails to keep from sliding back and forth across the floor.

"The storm is over." She felt for her clothes in the

straw, and drew first her shift and then her gown over her head. "I must go."

He stared at her, his eyes bleak. The air between them seethed, their desire not at all abated.

"Yes, you must go. And you must never come back alone. You risk too much."

She nodded her understanding and acceptance of his advice, though some small part of her rebelled. What would it be like, she wondered, to be so loved by a man that he dared her to risk everything for the sake of his love?

"My collar, Michael."

He was lying on it. He shifted his hips and raised himself high enough for her to pull it free. It held his heat and carried an elusive scent of him. She held it against her cheek as she backed away, savoring its warmth, feeling still surrounded by him.

"I must go," she said again. The words fell hollow and inadequate from lips still longing for his.

"Go—and for both our sakes, do not return," he called, low and husky, as she plunged him once again into darkness.

8

~

Someone had battened the hatch. Though Analisa pushed and strained at it, she could not force it open. Defeated, she backed down the ladder and huddled against the wall, so that whoever opened the hatch would see her at once. She was trapped, and she would have to face the consequences. If she pretended to welcome a rescue, it might divert the captain away from looking for the secrets she truly was hiding.

The lantern burned all its oil and guttered out with a smoky sizzle. She spent dark miserable hours shivering, torn between wanting to go back to Michael and knowing she must sit there and wait to be discovered. Being caught with Michael's arms wrapped around her would bring disaster down upon them both.

Besides, he had told her to stay away.

He'd meant it for her own good, she knew, but there was still an uncertain, deep-rooted bud inside of her that wondered if there was more to it than that. He was a man who scorned tender feelings, who claimed caring what happened to others only left one vulnerable to pain. If he truly believed those things, he might not want her to come back to him.

With such thoughts to torment her, the hatch popped open far sooner than she would have expected. It made her realize how many hours she must have spent in Michael's embrace, hours that had flown past like minutes. She sat there blinking up at the sunlight flooding down.

"Here she be, Captain, 'neath the auxiliary hatch!" bellowed the seaman who'd opened the hatch.

Soon the opening was ringed with seamen's curious faces. A moment later, Captain Verbeek shouldered them aside and made his agile way down the ladder. Klopstock followed at once, and then one or two others.

"We were sick with fear for you, mevrouw." Verbeek stood rigid, his fists clenched, looking more furious than concerned. "We thought you had been washed overboard during the storm."

She bit her lip. She had been worried only about herself and Michael, about the disgrace she would bring down on her own head, about the punishment that would befall Michael. She'd never given a thought to the panic the captain must have felt when he searched her cabin and found his passenger gone.

Stripes squirmed through the ring of men and made her sinuous way down the ladder. With a delighted trill, she rubbed up against Analisa's leg.

"I am sorry for causing you worry, Captain. I grew frightened during the storm. I could not find Stripes and thought she might have sought shelter below deck. And then it seemed so much safer down here. . . ." She was babbling. She bit her lip to still the breathless rush of words.

"I ordered you to keep to your cabin. Klopstock tells me he delivered the order."

"He did. I am sorry," she whispered.

"We called for you. I myself shouted your name down this hatch not three hours ago."

"I must have been trying to find my way to the main hatch. I . . . I was lost for a time amidships, and . . . and I was crying too hard to hear you, mynheer."

"Let me look at you." He gripped her by the chin and lifted her face to the sunlight. His lips tightened into a grim line. "Your skin is quite reddened, mevrouw. Your lips are swollen."

And she knew exactly how she'd gotten that way. Heat surged, worsening her flushed complexion, at the memory of the way Michael's bearded face had rasped against her own softer skin, the way his demanding lips had claimed hers again and again.

"It is from the crying, Captain. I am not a woman who cries prettily. And as for my lips, well, I spent most of the night biting them between my teeth to keep from screaming."

He made a little grunt of disbelief but let go his grip. She lowered her head. To her horror, she saw bits of straw clinging to the hem of her skirt. Only two places on board—the meat animal pens and Michael's prison—were bedded with straw. If the captain noticed, he would know where she'd been. She clutched her hands into fists to stifle the frantic urge she felt to shake her skirts clean, knowing the motion would only draw Verbeek's attention to what she did not want him to see.

"Klopstock, go see how the prisoner fared through the storm and report back to me in my quarters."

"Aye, Captain."

He dispatched the other seamen on errands, as well, until it was only the two of them standing there, and then he looked pointedly at the straw clinging to her hem.

"You understand my concern, mevrouw. You were handed over to me in a certain . . . healthy condition. I have done my best to see you remained . . . healthy . . .

throughout this journey. I would hate to have to report to your husband that you suffered any ill effects while under my care." Verbeek's expression grew increasingly mottled.

"My health has never been more robust, mynheer."

"Perhaps you do not understand. Sometimes a person succumbs to a . . . fever that leaves one less of a woman than she used to be."

She had not been a woman at all until last night, but she did not think it wise to mention her awakening to the captain.

"I would not appreciate being held accountable if your husband should find himself displeased with your . . . condition, mevrouw."

"My husband should have no expectations of my condition. If he is displeased, he has no one to blame but himself. Or me."

Verbeek studied her. Disapproval and suspicion radiated from him almost visibly. Eventually he sighed. "Very well. Keep to your cabin for the balance of the journey, mevrouw."

"You are confining me?"

"Only for a brief time. We are little more than one hundred nautical miles from Banda Neira."

"How long will it take us to sail so far?"

"A day, perhaps a little more, depending as always on the winds. They have calmed considerably since the storm."

"Only a day? Then . . . then I suppose you will want me to interrogate the prisoner once more?"

It was the worst possible thing she could have asked, the last possible thing that should have been on her mind at that moment. Oddly enough, Verbeek seemed to welcome her introduction of the subject.

"Pressing you into such onerous duty was a serious error on my part. I regret it mightily, and only wish I could be relieved of the responsibility of admitting my mistake to your husband."

She understood. Verbeek suspected she'd been ruined, and he took the blame squarely upon his shoulders for encouraging her to talk to Michael.

"Then we have both made mistakes, Captain. My husband need never know that you exposed me to a dangerous criminal—or that I was so frightened that I spent a night away from my cabin."

"We must learn from our mistakes. As of this moment, the belowdecks are off limits to you, mevrouw. For any reason."

"Yes, mynheer."

She would have kept to her cabin even if Verbeek had not issued the order, for a subtle change had taken place among the crewmen. Where before they had studiously ignored her, or were careful to keep their lustful yearnings to themselves, they now followed her progress to her cabin with eyes that told her they knew exactly what she'd been up to the night before.

Nobody accused her of consorting with a criminal. Nobody pointed a finger and called her a criminal's whore. And yet she felt their judgment in the air when she walked toward her cabin, and felt it again when she whirled about and caught two men looking at her and snickering.

She felt their almost palpable antagonism. Someone—the captain, Klopstock, someone—must have speculated on how she'd spent the night, and the crew had obviously chosen to believe it. They stared boldly, some sneering their contempt, others raking their gazes over her, insulting, absent of any respect.

Men had been looking at her like this for all her life, without cause, speculating that she might follow in the footsteps of her mother. She had always held her head high, proud of her virtue in the face of their disbelief. And now she understood how her mother had managed to hold on to her pride during those long years, for if she had given herself to Analisa's father with the same joy and delight that Analisa had given herself to Michael, then neither of them had cause for shame or regret.

She closed herself in her cabin, feeling as if she had gained sanctuary.

The heat, always oppressive, seemed doubly so now that she could not walk on deck. She stripped down to her shift, and still she sweated—and still she shivered. She pleated a fold of her shift. The thin, sheer cloth was scarcely any covering at all for flesh that ached to be stroked. She suddenly understood her mother's insistence that proper ladies spent their days and went to their beds gowned in voluminous yards of wool. All her cravings had raged out of control the minute Michael Rowland started teasing her buttons loose, and by the time he'd stripped her to her skin, she'd been a writhing, gasping wanton. And she didn't regret one single minute of it, no matter how many suspicions and contemptuous leers were sent her way.

But Pietr would learn, all too soon, that what Verbeek had euphemistically called Analisa's good health had been well and truly compromised. Her maidenhead was gone, and even though it had been hers to give, she might well be called upon to explain its disappearance.

The trouble was, every time she tried to think about her husband, about what she would say to him, her thoughts would stray back to the night before. Back to Michael.

Maybe it was because these were the clothes she had worn for him, the way her wedding gown was to be saved for Pietr. Perhaps garbing herself in the costume of Pietr Hootendorf's wife would align her thoughts in the proper direction. She stripped the shift off over her head.

She pulled her wedding gown free of its muslin dust cover. She held it to her breast for a moment, oddly reluctant to put it on, and then without bothering with underthings or petticoats, pulled the gown into place, buttoning it up tight. The silk settled over her bare limbs, cool against her breasts and belly, which were still heated from Michael's touch. . . .

This wasn't working. The gown alone wasn't enough to smother the spirit Michael had awakened within her.

She knelt, careful of the silk, before her trunk. She opened the lid to reveal her marriage glove box nestled atop her meager store of undergarments. She withdrew the heavy, jeweled glove and pulled it over her hand. Just as a knight donned armor before facing his foes, she clad herself in the raiment of Mevrouw Pietr Hootendorf to confront her conscience.

It wasn't much of a battle. Her conscience was merrily unrepentant. *You aren't really married yet,* it whispered. *You did nothing wrong.*

She climbed carefully into her bed and smoothed the gown against herself, hoping it wouldn't wrinkle too badly. She curved her gloved hand over her waist. The glove weighed heavy. She could feel the prongs poke through the cloth of her wedding gown. She wedged her other arm beneath the glove to prevent damage to the silk and then closed her eyes. Every night for the rest of her life, she would lie like this in her bed, waiting for her husband to come to her, as helpless to escape him as Michael was to flee this ship.

Her thoughts fired a certain panic rather than acceptance. Though dressed and rehearsed for the role, she still didn't feel like Pietr's wife. More like a corpse. Except the dead felt no pain. She would be better off dead than knowing she was a faithless wife who had fallen in love with a desperate criminal.

"I am in love with Michael Rowland," she said aloud.

Saying the words, saying his name, roused something soft and yearning within her. Her legs trembled. Her hands shook. It took all her force of will to remain in the bed, clad in her marriage glove and wedding dress, when she longed to fling off the trappings of Mevrouw Pietr Hootendorf and run to Michael, do as he asked, set him free, and escape with him.

"I love him," she said again, hearing the awe in her own voice. Now that she'd admitted it, she realized she must have loved him from the first, when he'd passed her on deck and she could scarcely breathe. And all this time, though he was the prisoner, she was the one who'd felt captivated each time she saw him. When he kissed her, when he loved her, it was as though all the forces of nature leaped to life within her. Apart from him, she was dry and dead inside.

No wonder she trembled now, like an empty cocoon quivering in the wind. Trembling and empty, the way the rest of her life would be without him.

She had one more day. One hundred miles. And then she would speak her final vows and begin her new life as the respectably married Mevrouw Pietr Hootendorf. Until then, she could be Analisa Vandermann, beloved of Michael Rowland.

She had to see him, be with him, once more.

More men than usual were posted on lookout, but all were remarkably intent upon studying the sea. Analisa slipped behind them unnoticed, down the auxiliary hatch. She had dared take only a candle, which she lit with her small flint once she was well away from the ladder. She would prefer not to light it at all, for the risk she ran was so great, but she knew she could not manage to find her way through the dark. She would draw more attention bashing and crashing her way through the cargo than would the tiny pool of light glimmering from one candle.

Michael stirred when she neared his cell, and the soft clinking of his chains marked his movements as he prepared himself to meet what came. She could sense his alertness, the sudden tension in the air, and wished she could dispel it, but dared not speak until she was nearly upon him.

" 'Tis only me," she called. She leaned over the edge of the stall and held the candle near her chin so its weak glow would illuminate her face.

"Analisa!" He reacted with surprise and a quickly stifled grin. She might not have noticed it if she had not been so attuned to him. Though he tried to hide it, there was joy in his greeting. Nobody had ever responded to her mere presence with joy. She suspected that for the rest of her life she would remember, and crave to bask in it again.

"Oh, Michael, I love . . . the way you say my name." She blushed, realizing she'd nearly blurted out the secret of her love for him in such an unceremonious fashion. They had so little of everything—time, luxury, pleasure—that each moment must be savored to the fullest. "Until now, only whining schoolgirls and overbearing men have ever called to me."

"Mayhap I should have taken an overbearing stance with you, for you have not paid any heed to my warning. You should not have risked coming here."

The candle wavered, its flame threatened by the sudden trembling of her hand. She had been so anxious to see him again that she had ignored her inner doubts that he might have truly meant it when he'd told her to stay away. Hurt, she was ready to flee, when his gruff words stopped her. "Even so, I am glad you have come. I worried about you, Analisa. I am happy to see that you were not caught last night."

She bit her lip. She didn't think it would be a lie to simply not offer an explanation. And she knew that if she told him she had been caught, that Verbeek had forbidden her to see him again, he would urge her away at all speed.

"I had to tell you . . ." She swallowed. She had not realized, until it came time to form the words, how difficult they would be to say. "I had to tell you that we shall reach Banda in another day."

"Ah. I assumed we were close."

He sounded so unconcerned that she might have told him the price of an apple, rather than announced the limit of the time they would have together. She moved closer to him and caught his face in the light, caught the utter bleakness that dulled his eyes and darkened his expression, and she knew his casualness was but a pose.

"I don't think I can bear it, Michael."

"You can. You can bear anything. You are strong."

I am strong, she agreed silently. For so long, she had forcibly subdued her inner strength, buried it deep until she wondered how it had survived at all. Only Michael recognized her strength as something good and fine, only Michael urged her to hold her head high and proud.

The candle, so essential for light, frustrated her with the need to hold on to it, when she wanted her hands free to touch Michael. She cast about for a handy place to wedge the candle, and lit upon the shrouded carriage. Pietr's carriage. Carriages came equipped with lantern holders, she knew. She seized upon the task of uncovering that part of the carriage, postponing for a time the moment when she made her admission that she loved him.

The cuplike holder was too wide to hold the candle

upright, so it rested askew. Melted wax dripped down the polished side of the carriage, leaving a hot, glistening trail that hardened into wax tears. She stroked one, feeling it warm and lumpy beneath her fingertip, and then whirled about to face Michael.

"I came to tell you that I love you."

Michael's hands tightened around the chains, his knuckles so whitened that she wondered why the iron links did not snap beneath their force.

"Love is for fools."

"I agree. No woman could be more foolish than I." She moved closer to him, conscious of the way her silk skirts caressed her bare legs, the way the bodice slid against her turgid nipples.

"You have not worn that gown before." Michael tore his gaze from the clinging silk to meet hers head-on. "You have but two gowns, you said. Your other was your wedding gown—this gown. For your husband's eyes only, you said."

She forced herself to meet his gaze steadily, while waves of heat surged through her, while her skin tingled and warmed. "I told you I would wear this gown when I spoke my true vows, Michael. I make this vow to you now: I will always love you."

To her dismay, Michael gave a short barking laugh of disbelief. "You do not know what you say."

"I am not a child—especially after last night. I understand full well what I am saying to you."

"Do you?" She took an involuntary step backward, startled by the ferocity of his challenge. "You have bargained to wed a man you have never met. And now you say you—" He stopped short, his throat visibly tightening, as if he could not bring himself to say the word *love*. "Now you offer yourself to me."

"I have nothing of value to offer, except myself."

"You could set me free."

"I cannot!" Her heart lurched. Within its pulsating

depths warred her newborn love for him against her lifelong loyalty to the Company. "And even if I could, what purpose would it serve? You cannot overpower all the men on this ship. We are far at sea, and from what I saw when you were captured, I know you are not a fish that could swim for days until you reach shore."

"You forget that I know this part of the world, Analisa. If we are as close as you say to the Bandas, then we will very soon be traveling through hundreds of tiny islets. Some are so small that they flood with each day's tides. Others keep their heads above water, at least enough to sprout a few blades of grass or the occasional tree."

"That must be why the captain posted so many lookouts."

"Aye, to watch for obstructions in the water—but also to keep a sharp eye for pirates."

"Pirates!"

"Pirates. My comrades, Analisa. They prey mercilessly upon your slow, heavy Dutch ships, and then slip like eels on their small boats into the safety of the island passages. I could do the same. I could slip from the rear of the ship while the men concentrate on the course ahead and—"

"You do not want me," she whispered.

His chains slithered through the ceiling loops as he dropped to his knees. His mighty shoulders bowed, his head hung low while candlelight glimmered against the hair curling over his shoulders.

"God help me, I want you more than life itself. Were you to sever my chains right now, I would stay your willing prisoner with naught but your touch to bind me to you."

With a small cry, she ran to him and knelt in the straw before him. She raised a tentative hand to his shoulder. He did not flinch away, as she'd feared he might, but shuddered, and leaned heavily into her touch. His pulse throbbed against hers.

"It cannot be such a bad thing, falling in love," she said.

"It is the worst thing." He tossed his head back, flinging his hair away. His eyes burned into hers, all hot and dark with the wanting he claimed to deplore. "Passion steals a man's senses. It robs a woman of her strength. I have seen this to be true."

"I have never felt so strong, so filled with life, as I do at this moment," she whispered.

With a low moan he caught her against his chest and crushed her within his embrace. His heart beat against hers, its power steadying her. Only then did he move his lips against her hair, murmuring her name. She lifted her chin, letting her hair fall away until her neck and throat lay bare for the heated kisses he trailed along her hungry flesh.

His hands molded her to him, running possessively from knees to waist, and then upward to cup her breasts. He fell back into the straw, pulling her atop him while he continued his long, delicious kisses. She writhed against him in an agony of wanting to be closer, closer, and whimpered with pleasure when at last he rolled her over, pressing her into the warm straw with his full weight delightfully heavy upon her.

"Analisa?" His lips brushed hers, and then rested against her forehead.

"Michael?"

"I cannot love you. You cannot love me. Make *this* vow to me: Promise me you won't love me."

"I . . . I promise to try. But for tonight," she said, her voice shaking oddly, "couldn't we pretend that love is wondrous?"

"Yes, Analisa, for tonight we can love as no others have loved before."

At that moment he plunged into her, and her prom-

ises melted into his name, and she called it again and
again as he brought her the full measure of the exquisite pleasure she had only tasted the night before.

The candle guttered low, its fitful light casting them
in dancing shadows. Analisa could not stop touching
him, though she was replete. She ran her fingertips
through the whorls of hair crowning his chest. He
sighed with pleasure, and then something changed. A
subtle tension firmed his flesh and he drew in a great
breath, in the manner of someone girding himself for
an unpleasant task.

"You deserve a soft bed and silk, not a rough
wooden floor strewn with straw."

"It does not matter, Michael." For no good reason
she felt frightened, and her fear heightened when he
placed a silencing finger against her lips.

"It is the nature of lovers to be so caught up in their
desires that they would do anything for each other. I
warned you that such is the way of passion."

"Yes. I would do anything you ask." She imagined
she knew what he wanted; she felt the evidence hot
and hard against her hip. She closed her eyes and
could not hold back a small whimper of anticipation.
"I might be inclined to grant such a favor."

"No, Analisa, I am not so honorable as that. You'd
best cover yourself now." He drew away from her and
groped about in the straw until he found her gown.
He tossed it to her and then shrugged his shirt back
into place. His chains clanked with every movement
and her fears returned with each metallic clink. In his
determination to clothe their nakedness, she sensed
the same desperation with which she'd garbed herself
in her wedding gown. She clutched the gown against
her breasts, too numb to attempt dressing.

"Michael—what do you want?"

His eyes burned into hers. "Set me free, Analisa. Do not let them kill me."

She could not let him be killed, not while the taste of him rested sweet on her lips, while her skin still tingled from the feel of his weight against hers, while her most secret places still throbbed and moistened from the sensations he roused. She had held his male splendor in her arms, thrilled to his surging strength, gloried in his unbridled masculinity. To think of so much vigor gone, wiped from the earth in the cruelest possible way, all over a few sweet-smelling spices . . . impossible.

"Captain Verbeek keeps his keys clipped to his belt at all times. I don't think I could get hold of an ax, either, and even if I could, the noise of breaking the chains would ring through the ship."

"A strong knife would suffice. I could use the blade to pry open a link near my wrists, close enough so that the added weight would not hamper my swimming."

"You cannot swim. I saw you floundering in the water that day they caught you."

"Better drowned than unmanned."

She shivered at the reminder of the punishment the Dutch would inflict upon him and knew she could not deny him. "I know where they keep a very heavy knife handy in case a broken rope or sail requires quick severing. If we are quick about it, I might be able to fetch the knife and have it restored to its usual place, then take to my cabin, awaiting the outcry that will announce you have been discovered missing."

"Not exactly."

She tilted her head at him, confused.

"The captain will know someone helped me. He will be relentless in seeking out who's responsible. The best course is to hand him my accomplice—but to make it appear as though you helped me against your will."

"You are saying you *want* the captain to realize that I am the one who set you free?" It seemed such a stunning betrayal that numbness gripped her entire body.

"It is the only way to assure your safety. The only part of the plan that eludes me is fashioning some reasonable excuse for you coming down here on your own."

Stripes chose that moment to saunter toward them, her tail twitching a greeting.

"That's it!" cried Michael, all signs of passion gone now that he'd clicked the last piece of this puzzle into place. "You must tell the captain you were looking for your cat. When you came near to me, I told you she'd gotten herself hopelessly tangled in all that canvas wrapped around your husband's carriage. Too late, you realized it was a lie. You must tell Verbeek that I overpowered you when you innocently sought to free your beloved pet."

She thought of the suspicions Verbeek already held about her and how he'd forbidden her to come below-decks. She wished now that she'd told Michael the truth about it. "He would never believe me."

"He would have little choice if he finds you gagged and trussed like a Christmas goose."

"Gagged?" she whispered.

"With my shirt tied between your teeth."

"Trussed?"

"With that cursed collar of yours wound about your wrists and ankles. Your captain might suspect you had a hand in my escape, but if he found you bound and gagged he would have to give you the benefit of the doubt. However, if you were wandering about free as you please, you would be in collusion with a criminal, and Verbeek might be compelled to turn you over to the law for punishment."

"You have given this much thought, Michael."

"I had little else to think about, and many hours to fill."

So had she—but her thoughts had run along a decidedly different course. She had been all but wallowing in the sensual haze of her memories, the awe-inspiring realization that she'd fallen in love. He had been plotting a way to use her for his escape.

She felt dazed and sickened, like the school dolt who had to be clouted a dozen times before learning her lesson. Michael had told her time and again that he scorned responsibility. Her mother had spent a lifetime warning her about men exactly like Michael Rowland. And what had Analisa done? The minute she'd found such a man, she repeated her mother's mistakes, compounded a hundredfold.

I cannot love you, he had said. *You cannot love me.*

Michael Rowland would not provide for her the way the Company always had. He would not give her his name, or the life of respectability offered by Pietr Hootendorf. She had spent all her life dreaming she might one day find something magical, something extraordinary, that would make her life perfect. There was no such magical thing—only duty and responsibility, with respect its only reward.

"You said we could escape together," she whispered. "But you never intended to take me with you."

He hesitated for only the merest moment. "No."

It would be best if she were bound, she realized, because even with him confirming his lie with his own lips, she might yield to the temptation to follow him, to dive into the sea and take her chances among the uninhabited scraps of land, among the pirates. And how fitting that the cloth keeping her away from him, keeping her on the prim and proper path, would be that wretched collar that represented everything stifling and strangling about her life.

He stared at her, his chin tilted in the manner of

one who halfway expects a blow to the jaw, his eyes wary and warring between hopefulness and agony. She could not deny him. She did not trust her voice to hold steady, so she said nothing as she tugged her gown into place, as she fastened the buttons. She brushed the clinging straw from the silk and twisted her hair firmly behind her ears. She collected the candle stub from its holder and tucked the canvas back into place, hiding the trailing tears of wax. She felt her own tears, unshed, harden inside her.

"Will you be back?"

It hurt, that he'd felt the need to put his doubts into words. "Aye," she answered in a breathy, weak sigh.

"With a knife."

She nodded, curtly, and left.

He was right about love, she thought as she made her way blindly to her cabin. It weakened a woman.

And, she thought, remembering the bleak despair that held him rigid as he watched her walk away, it did not do much for a man, either.

9
〜

Michael had not realized, until Analisa slipped through the stall gate once more, that he'd been taking half breaths and holding on to his chains so tightly that his fingers had gone numb, all for fear that she might never return.

He wouldn't have blamed her if she'd stayed away. It would have been easier that way, for her.

Perhaps for himself, as well.

He watched her approach him. He didn't see a knife.

"You changed your dress. And bound up your hair."

She answered with a careless shrug, but he understood the significance behind her changing her silk wedding gown for the familiar, enveloping wool dress, and the taming of her glorious hair into tight braids, wrapped around her head. The candlelight illuminated her; she looked ghostly pale, all color drained from her cheeks and lips, her eyes dull and so dark that it seemed her very spirit had deserted her. The transformation was more startling than garments and hair arrangement could account for—the knowledge that she was letting her passion overrule her principles radiated from her with every step.

"Now you see for yourself," he said. "Love makes us do things we know are not right, no matter the personal cost. I wish I could have spared you this, Analisa. I wish—"

"You need not belabor the point," she cut in. "You made your feelings and your ultimate goal clear from the beginning."

Yes, he'd told her he did not believe in love, or the self-sacrifice that accompanied it. And yet he asked self-sacrifice from her. After years of carefully guarding his tongue around women, he'd let passion blur his resolve and rashly made promises he could not keep. "I said some things that other day that might have led you to expect—"

Again, she interrupted before he could fully explain. "Rest easy, Michael, that I never took anything you said very seriously. I hope you did not put great weight into my words, either. I would never run away with you, not even if you begged."

He supposed she said it to save her pride; even so, it rocked him to the core, that she should be so willing to set him free and see him go off without being tempted to join him.

"You have given me so much, Analisa. I dislike leaving with the debt between us so one-sided."

"The problem with you, Michael Rowland, is that you have an overactive conscience for a criminal. It worries you that you have harmed me in some way. I assure you that you have not."

"I see. You have emerged unscathed from your encounter with a callous, selfish lout."

"Exactly so."

She stopped so close that he caught the scent of his loving upon her. His body burned once again into hot, throbbing need.

"Did you bring the knife?" His voice had gone all gritty.

"Of course." She had been clutching it within a fold of her gown. "Here."

She thrust the tool into his hands and then simply stood there, so innocent and trusting. His fingers curled around the shaft, and all the tender emotions he dared not articulate manifested themselves in fury. He lashed out at her.

"You should know better than to give a desperate man a knife and just stand there, waiting for him to make up his mind about what he intends to do with it."

She cocked her head and stared at him curiously. "Do you intend to gut me with it?"

"I could."

She lifted her chin, baring inches of soft, vulnerable flesh. "Cut my throat, perhaps?"

"I might."

"You would not."

"You cannot be sure."

"I am sure."

His anger diminished with each utterance of her complete faith and trust in him.

"I could slice through your neck and hang your head from a nail," he continued with a good deal less enthusiasm.

"You would not hurt me, Michael." She drew a shaky breath. "Not physically."

Implicit in her trust was the knowledge that he had already shattered her true vulnerabilities. He knew she would never again trust a man so easily, give herself so freely.

"If you were half the rogue you claim to be, you would kill me. You admitted your guilt to me and told me what you planned to do with those nutmegs. It can't be wise for you to leave a witness."

Witness. Merely thinking the word had the unpleasant effect of conjuring the image of Analisa surrounded by furious Dutch officials determined to get the truth from her in one manner or another.

"You must promise me," he said urgently, "that you will never, ever reveal your true role in this escape."

Her eyes flickered with a spark of something— anger, perhaps—and a faint, humorless smile curled her lips. "Do not fear, Michael. I have many years of experience in keeping my thoughts to myself. I won't betray you."

"My neck is not the only one I worry about, Ana- lisa. You do not understand the depths men might sink to in order to obtain the information they want from a woman." And, God help him, he could not bring himself to point them out to her. The images alone suffused him with impotent wrath. "I will be long gone, far beyond any ability to help you." Good God, if he kept this up, he'd talk himself right out of escaping.

"You see, a trace of honor *does* lurk, despite your claims to the contrary." She looked at him, all smiling and misty-eyed.

Honor? He gave a little snort of derision. He would have to live with the knowledge that he alone was responsible for placing her in such an untenable situa- tion. And he would have to face his conscience every night, knowing that he did nothing to sway her from this dangerous course.

"No, Analisa. I am not honorable. If I were, I would turn the knife upon myself rather than put you at risk, but I cannot do it." His whole body shook, and self- loathing threatened to drown his spirit, but he could not take his own life to spare her the ordeal that was sure to follow. If he were able to kill himself, he would have done it long ago by hanging himself with his chains. Analisa offered him his only chance to save his worthless skin, and though it sickened him to real- ize the extent of his selfishness, the urge to live was so strong that it left him incapable of doing the honorable, noble thing.

The knife fit snugly into his hand, suffusing him with the urge to flay it about, smashing everything in his path in a effort to ease some of the frustration within him. Only her earlier, astute observation that a loud banging might draw curious sailors stayed his arm. His gaze swung toward the carriage that had been his cell mate for these past weeks, and another image formed to taunt him—that of Analisa sitting within its polished ebony walls while the shadowy figure of her unknown husband sat across from her, drinking in every detail of the precious treasure that was his.

"If I dared risk the noise," he grated, "I would hoist this knife high and drive it again and again into that shining hulk until nothing but splinters remained."

"Why?"

"Because I know your husband means to keep your beauty to himself by concealing you within its walls."

God's blood, but he'd done it again! She must think him a witless oaf, to be babbling on one hand about prizing his freedom so highly, and on the other admitting to jealousy.

But she had not noticed. "You think I am beautiful?" she whispered.

"Oh, Analisa—how could you doubt it?"

Angry with himself, he dropped into a crouch before he could begin hacking away at the carriage, put one foot as close to his left wrist as he could, and then drove the point of the knife into a link near his hand. He tried prying the link apart, but he did not have enough purchase to hold the chain in place.

Analisa saw his struggle. Without his asking, she stood on the chain until a deft twist of the blade popped a link. He switched hands, and working together wordlessly, they freed him from that restraint, and his ankle chains as well.

He stood. There was no difference in the way his neck had to tilt to avoid banging into the ceiling, and no change in position from where he stood, but with every beat of his heart he knew he was free. Free.

"Tie me up," she said. "And then be off with you."

His chains had been severed, and yet he stood as immobile as a nose-ringed bull, paralyzed by the lurching of his heart, the tiny whispering voice that said *She wants you gone.*

"Hurry," she said, accompanied by a soft push, the sort of angry nudge a tenderhearted child might use when returning a beloved pet to the wild. He took two great strides, his whole body tingling with the thrill of unfettered movement. The two steps carried him beyond the plank that had always before marked the limit of his movement. He stood there, looking into the blackness of the hold, that murky pit that had surrounded and isolated him for weeks. It now promised freedom—he need only step out of the candle's small circle of light and let the gloom swallow him.

And then he turned and pulled Analisa into his arms. He would hold her one time as a free man, with no chains between them.

"Thank you," he whispered against her crown. It seemed so inadequate, and for once he wished for a greater skill with words. He did not know how he could make her understand that his gratitude held so many layers. Her early kindness had restored some of his faith in humanity. Her beauty had fired passions that had long lain dormant. Her love had suffused him with pride and restored confidence in a man who had every reason to retreat into a cowering shell. Over all of that, her valiant, selfless willingness to set him free reminded him that sometimes miracles can occur.

She trembled in his arms, but he could scarcely feel it above the shuddering in his own limbs. No embrace could feel so bittersweet as this final leave-taking. He

pressed her as close as he could, memorizing the way
her curves fit against his angles and planes, the way
her softness nestled his hardness. He yearned to kiss her,
to taste her sweetness once more, but knew he would
not be able to rein in his passions. He settled for
brushing his lips against her braids, inhaling her subtle
fragrance. The dangling chains clinked from his wrists
as he traced the line of her chin with one finger, trailing it to the pulse at the base of her throat, where her
heartbeat fluttered through the tight-woven cloth like
a wild thing trapped against its will.

"I'm sorry," he rasped, apologizing for a dozen
wounds that he'd inflicted that did not bleed.

"Finish this and go," she cried in a heartsick whisper. "Go, before I ask you to stay." She had begun
fumbling at the fastening of her collar when he stilled
her hand.

"Let me do it. The captain might believe you more
easily if it appeared you put up a fight." He tore the
collar away, ripping the neckline. With a startled gasp,
she clutched at the gaping cloth, holding it modestly
in place, but he said, "No, Analisa. You must let me
tie you."

He helped her sit in the most comfortable position
possible, with her back braced against the wall and
her legs stretched cleanly before her. His will fought
him at every step; it seemed so against his nature to
be tying her, to be binding her, when she had risked
so much to set him free. And yet he could think of
no better way to protect her, to shield her from blame.

He could not bear looking at her when he'd
finished.

His gaze flicked toward the hated carriage. He could
not bear looking at that, either. Best to just go. Leaving her without any parting words would be the cruel,
selfish act of a rogue—but then he'd spent the best
part of his adult life striving toward roguedom. He'd

never imagined it would exact such a high cost. He quelled his attacks of conscience, telling himself they were merely highly inconvenient reminders of the troubles a man might let himself get into if he let his love for a woman overrule his need for self-preservation. Love had a damned seductive way of making a man want to give up everything.

"I left an empty water cask wedged in a rope coil near the lee rail," she said. "It would hold you afloat until you reach an island."

"Aye." He acknowledged this additional gift with a curt nod.

"You said you would gag me with your shirt."

"I . . . I cannot do it." He didn't think he could touch her without doing something, anything, to shake her out of her polite, distant mood and restore her to the quivering, sensual woman writhing beneath him. "My shirt is fearsome rank."

"I am intimate with your scent, Michael. I can endure it."

He remembered how he'd held on to her collar when he'd thought he would never see her again, wanting that awful scrap of cloth as a keepsake. Cloth that had touched her skin, that carried a trace of her essence. Despite her brave words, her denial of any interest in him, she wanted his shirt for the same reason. He would stake his life on it.

He shook his head.

"You'd best gag me, or they'll wonder why I didn't scream," she pointed out.

"Aye. You're right about that."

It was the sheerest torture to watch her part her lips for him and not claim her mouth with his own. It was pulsating agony to brush his fingers against her skin and her hair without pausing for a lingering caress, to feel her breath warm his chest when he leaned close to tie the gag and not press his bare flesh to her lips. But he could not make his trussing of her into erotic play, no matter how he might want it, no matter how her pulse and breathing called to him to do so. At the end of it, he found himself knuckling a tear away from her cheek, only to have another trickle into its track and flow down to soak the gag he made of his shirt.

He might as well have tied a sleeve between his own teeth, for his throat had seized up and he could say nothing. And so he turned and plunged into the darkness, leaving her behind in the prison that was meant to be his.

His eyes, so accustomed to the dark, had no trouble adjusting to the gloom in the hold. His muscles, kept fit by his incessant exercising, worked with supple ease as he scaled the ladder and stole across the deck. He kept a sharp eye out for sentries. They were, as Analisa said, completely preoccupied with steering a course through these treacherous waters.

Still, he did not risk making any sound as he scanned the waters for an island. One loomed a few hundred yards away, an indistinct and insubstantial-looking hump crouching above the water. The tenuous safety it promised might as well have been a hundred miles away for a man who could not swim, and he swallowed against the fear that gripped him by the throat.

And then he remembered that she'd said she'd left him an empty water cask. He found it in a coil of rope near the lee rail, just as she'd promised. He tucked the cask beneath his arm and then levered himself onto the rail, and then jumped feet first into the sea, holding himself tight and refusing to flail around, knowing that any undue splashing would bring the sentries running to see what was responsible for the noise. The cool water engulfed him, but the buoyant cask brought him back to the surface. He hunched over it, kicking his feet softly, careful to keep them below the water's surface, as he paddled along in silence, away from the *Island Treasure* and the woman he loved.

Michael was gone. Just like that, he was gone.

The women in her line must be doomed to love men who deserted them. Analisa wondered if her mother had experienced this aching feeling of loss, this dull sense of betrayal, when she watched Analisa's father sail away, never to return. Analisa didn't even have the questionable privilege of watching Michael's departure. One minute he'd been standing before her; the next he'd slipped beyond the flickering candlelight and disappeared into the cargo hold. Gone.

She strained her ears, but could hear no commotion from above, no sharp splash of water that might herald his leap from the ship. Nothing. He was gone as thoroughly as if she'd imagined his presence.

But her body still remembered his weight, her innermost places still throbbed with a sweet tenderness where he had taken the most secret, precious gift she had to offer. A gift she had given gladly, willingly, knowing it could never be undone.

Analisa closed her eyes and leaned her head back against the ship's wall. If she had it all to do again . . . she would do it again.

Tears seeped from her closed lids. Soon, all physical reminders of his possession would diminish. She would heal. She would forget his unique, compelling scent, she would not remember exactly the pleasant rasp of his beard against her cheek; she would not recapture the exquisite thrill of his mouth closing over her breast. She would have only memories, memories that grew dimmer with each passing day.

She brought her knees up and pressed her forehead against them. She didn't know how long she had sat that way when she felt the soft brush of her cat against

her shins. With soft, trilling sounds, Stripes rubbed her
head against Analisa and then pawed at her thigh,
demanding access to Analisa's lap.

She shifted her position and the cat hopped up,
purring, to knead Analisa's belly with soft paws. Analisa settled back against the wall, and the cat obligingly
curled itself into a comfortable ball, looking nothing
like a desperate animal in need of rescue.

Michael had been careful, when he tied her, that
the knots did not cut into her wrists or pull her arms
uncomfortably tight. It wouldn't have mattered. She
felt so numb that she doubted she would have noticed.
The purring cat on her lap ought to have made her
feel warm; it didn't. She felt nothing but great waves
of cold, impossible in the sweltering confines of the
ship. Nonetheless, she shivered and felt numb, as if
she'd been abandoned naked upon the tundra. She
doubted she would ever feel warm again.

10

~

"**M**ein Gott! Mevrouw, what has happened to you? Where is the prisoner?"

Klopstock dropped the water pail he carried and gaped at Analisa, taking in the gag, her bound limbs, and the snoozing cat. He swiveled his gaze to follow the severed chains lying near her feet. Almost comically, he swung his lantern in an arc and squinted into the shadows, as if expecting to find Michael Rowland crouching in a corner like a good prisoner.

Analisa struggled against her bonds, whimpering a little for effect, though she wasn't certain Klopstock could hear her through the gag. The cat shifted on her lap, meowing its displeasure at being disturbed, and then curled itself back into sleep.

Klopstock shook his head and then moved toward her. He reached out to work her hands free, and then let his hands hover uncertainly. "No, mevrouw, I'd best bring the captain down to see this before I set you free. I am sorry."

Verbeek's fury was awesome. He stormed into the area with the force of a swirling hurricane, his face mottled with rage, his entire being quivering with violence. Analisa shivered back into the wall, realizing for the first time how precarious her position was. Michael's warning to be sure not to reveal her true part in his escape came back to her, and she realized that he had anticipated this reaction from Verbeek.

"What is the meaning of this?" he thundered.

Analisa stared up at him mutely; even if she had not been gagged, she would have been too frightened to respond.

Verbeek carried his own lantern, and its light, combined with Klopstock's, flooded this small dismal space as never before. The stall, without Michael's presence, no longer seemed a precious haven enclosing the two of them against the world. The light revealed it in all its stark ugliness and shed new light upon her behavior.

Oh, God, what had she done? Her sins were far worse than any her mother had ever committed. Her mother had merely loved unwisely and shouldered the consequences herself. Analisa, on the other hand, had allowed her passion for a forbidden man to jeopardize the formalization of an honest marriage. Even if Pietr was willing to speak formal vows after hearing of her escapades, she had robbed him of her virginity. She had allowed her soft heart to release a dangerous criminal, a man whose actions threatened the very foundation of the Company that provided the livelihood for thousands upon thousands of good, upright Dutch citizens, her own mother included.

"I will have answers from you, mevrouw!" Verbeek roared.

"Mayhap if I untied her, Captain, she might be able to speak." Klopstock ventured close to Analisa, and Verbeek waved him on with a curt slash of his hand, the same motion a butcher might use to sever the throat of a suckling pig. Or a long-ago chieftain might use to sever the throat of a human sacrifice.

Klopstock released her bonds so easily that Analisa feared Verbeek might notice how insecurely she'd been bound. But he was pacing the deck in a fearsome rage, kicking at the straw that had once formed Michael's bed, cursing in languages she could not understand. Only when Klopstock had her entirely free and had helped her to her feet did Verbeek whirl about and fix her with his white-hot rage.

"Well?" he demanded. "What are you doing in my prisoner's place?"

Stripes obligingly sat at her feet, lifting a paw and licking at it delicately. Analisa had only to point from the animal to the carriage, and repeat the story Michael had concocted about trying to free the cat with the knife, but the words clogged in her throat. She wanted to cry—from the pain of losing the man she loved, from the realization of how badly she'd bungled things. She had always despised sniveling women, always held a somewhat superior attitude toward them, believing that her own strong-minded determination was by far more desirable. Damn Michael Rowland for stealing that from her!

Anger usually made her feel strong. Now, though, the weight of so many emotions weakened her, turning her knees to jelly and causing her voice to quiver. "He . . . the cat . . . his name is Michael Rowland . . ." she began, and then burst into tears.

Amazingly, she could have done nothing that would have served her better. Though the captain's face was cross with annoyance, his fury subsided somewhat. He was obviously accustomed to bursts of tears from weak-willed, ineffectual women.

Klopstock clumsily patted her shoulder.

"There, there, mevrouw. That scoundrel tricked you, didn't he?"

Gulping back her tears, Analisa nodded. It wasn't truly a lie.

"Now, you must tell the captain exactly what happened." Klopstock curved his arm around her shoul-

ders and led her over to Pietr's carriage. She rested
her weight against the ebony lacquer, her hand brushing over the trailing wax that marred its side. Oh, if
she had not been a faithless wife, she might have
drawn strength from this reminder of her husband.
Instead, its stolid support mocked her with the evidence of what she had cast aside for the sake of a
few moments' passion. Respectability, the hope for an
agreeable marriage, all had been sacrificed for Michael
Rowland's love.

Somehow, between the shudders of self-loathing
that shook her, she managed to squeak out a bare
explanation along the lines that she and Michael had
concocted.

At the end of it, she subsided into a helpless huddle.
When she risked peeking upward at Verbeek to gauge
his reaction to her story, she quivered with alarm. He
frowned at her with a skepticism so broad that it
marked every inch of him.

"I do not believe a word of your story, mevrouw."
He was so angry that his voice shook.

"What . . . what reason would I have to lie?"

"To save your pretty neck," he snarled. He pushed
away from her in disgust and resumed his pacing.
"What I cannot fathom is how that scoundrel wormed
his way into your sympathies. You were guarded
every moment!"

For some reason, his refusal to believe her lie
strengthened her will. She stiffened, drawing strength
from the return of her spirit. "Exactly so, Captain. I
am grievously insulted that you doubt my loyalties."

"Your husband shall hear of this, mevrouw. You
may count on it." Verbeek raked his glance over her
insultingly; all trace of respect and decorum fled in
the face of his anger. He looked at her as if he somehow knew that Michael Rowland's seed still lay warm
beneath her belly. His lip curled in a sneer. "I will

take it upon myself to explain to Mynheer Hootendorf the role his wife played in losing a man wanted by the Company. I will leave it to him to determine your punishment."

He flicked his hand, indicating that Klopstock was to follow him. They left Klopstock's lantern to help her find her way alone through the cargo hold, but nobody waited to assist her up the ladder, nobody acknowledged her presence when she emerged through the hatch, blinking against the sunlight.

She was left alone, more of an outcast than she had ever been back in Amsterdam. She had nothing but her memories for company, nothing but her thoughts to occupy her mind. The specter of Pietr Hootendorf loomed ever larger in her conscience. She had cheated him. She had to live with that knowledge, as well as the growing realization of how thoroughly dependent she would be upon a man who would truly have every reason to despise her.

She kept to her windowless cabin, curled upon her bed, while she yearned above all else to stand on deck peering out to sea, striving for some glimpse of an island, a bobbing water keg, that might indicate Michael still lived. She sweated in the heat, the cabin's rough walls isolating her more thoroughly than she'd been within the School for Company's Daughters. There, at least, she'd had a role to fulfill, a modicum of respect from the girls she trained. Most importantly, she'd had hope—hope that one day society would learn how wrong they were about her, that one day she would be welcome.

Now, she had no hope. She could not make even the weakest protest about the way Verbeek had treated her, for he was right to do so. She had no defense, for she was guilty. She could not admit her part in Michael's escape, or she might well die as a traitor.

She pulled on her marriage glove, as she told herself that perhaps she was wrong, perhaps she could still hope. She could have run off after Michael, but she'd done the honorable thing. She'd stayed, ready to honor the bargain she'd made to wed Pietr Hootendorf. If he accepted her after this, she would strive to make him the best possible wife.

A curious blankness overtook her mind when she tried to imagine what her role might demand.

From outside, a seaman's voice pierced her mindless reverie. "Land ho!"

Footsteps pounded past her door. She heard the squeal of winches, the creak of ropes, as the sailors began furling sails. She heaved herself from her bed, so anxious to see and touch land after so many months at sea that she didn't care anymore about her status as a pariah. And it didn't matter, anyway. The sailors were so occupied with their duties that they had no attention to spare on her.

The *Island Treasure*'s working sails bulged, sending the ship surging onward, past tiny bumps in the sea that looked like whales or dolphins from a distance but proved to be miniature islands rising from the depths. The ten thousand islands of the East Indies— here they were, just as Michael had promised. Dozens of them. Hundreds of them, some so small the ship's wake engulfed them, others capable of supporting a scrawny tree or two. Some lay so close together it seemed not even a rowboat could squeeze between them. She swallowed, her throat full with the relief of knowing that Michael could have survived his escape after all.

Captain Verbeek stood at the prow, watchful, barking orders to his navigator. Seamen called out, and another row of sails got cranked up into the rigging, slowing the ship. Analisa caught at the rail for balance as the ship bucked against the change in momentum. Hazy blurs loomed in the distance, dark, crowned with a vibrant green not seen for many, many months . . . the Banda Islands, taking form as the ship plowed onward, slower, and slower still as more sails were rolled away from the wind.

"Sun Gate ahoy!" shouted the lookout. Verbeek gestured, shouting more orders. The ship turned majestically, assuming a course that would let it drift through a chasm between two treacherous-looking cliffs that rose high and sheer and yet were somehow impossibly dotted with close-clinging trees. The men's voices, the creaking rigging, the ship's wake all echoed from the cliffs, so that when they glided free of the passage and entered Banda Neira harbor, the air seemed curiously flat, the sounds dissipating in the brilliant, blinding blue sky.

Her first glimpse of Banda Neira roused a surprising wave of homesickness within Analisa. Warehouses crowded the waterfront. The close-massed, pastel-tinted houses rising immediately behind the warehouses had all been built in true Dutch style with no regard for this climate. She looked upon Banda Neira and thought for a moment that the ship had somehow gotten turned about, that they were instead approaching a shoreline in Amsterdam.

And yet the curiously familiar sight seemed skewed. Strange tropical trees waved in the wind, their long feathery fronds brushing against the warehouses and homes. A massive volcano towered behind, casting its shadow over it all. She had seen the volcano in drawings and taught her young charges that it provided an ever-present threat of eruption. *Gunung Api*, they called it, the Fire Mountain. It rose high, crowned by ominous yellowish, soot-darkened clouds attesting to the fiery cauldron boiling within its bowels.

Instead of Amsterdam's sedate, businesslike atmosphere, Banda Neira burst with vibrant life, resounding from the rhythmic thumping of countless drums, the sharp whistling of pipes carved from bamboo. Narrow yellow and red and blue boats, rocking back and forth against arched braces curving from their sides and manned by double rows of near-naked, smiling brown men, shot from shore to welcome and ride escort alongside the *Island Treasure.*

A mighty splash heralded the drop of the ship's anchor. A sudden lurching tested their balance as the ship's forward momentum fought against the dragging weight.

Verbeek called a greeting in a strange tongue to the nearby colorful boats. With the ease of long practice, he climbed down a rope ladder and leaped, taking a seat of honor at the forefront of one of the slim crafts that kept pace with the ship's lagging speed. The boat darted away, paddled in a most extraordinary manner by men equipped with only one oar apiece.

Analisa knew the landing procedure—she'd explained it often enough to the young brides she'd sent on ahead of her. She knew the captain merely went ahead to report that the ship carried no plague. She'd lost her affection for the captain, but still it left her feeling unsettled to watch his familiar, authoritative figure absorbed into the groups of people and stacks of cargo lining the dock, leaving his ship surrounded by strange men in strange little boats, with hundreds of strange faces turned in their direction.

Pietr Hootendorf no doubt stood upon that dock right now, might even be one of the strange faces watching the captain alight from his little boat.

She knew it would be hours yet before she could disembark. The Company agent would first come aboard with a scribe to make lists of everything the ship carried before anyone, save the captain, would be allowed to step ashore. She had much to do in the intervening time, but she felt a curious reluctance to return to her cabin and begin packing away her reminders of her time aboard ship, and begin the primping to prepare for the first meeting with her husband.

Young girls stood waving flowers at them. At some hidden signal, their voices rose in song, their slim, delicate forms performing an intricate dance, their movements sending their gauzy, bright-colored gowns and shining, blue-black hair swirling about them.

A row of odd-looking boats, similar to those escorting the *Island Treasure* but sporting sun-shielding canopies, bobbed at the water's edge. The ship drifted gently past them, bereft of wind in her sails, hampered by the dragging anchor, coming to rest with a shuddering, creaking groan while still a hundred feet or more from shore. Crowds of people surged forward to the waterline.

Analisa searched the noisy throng, trying to guess which of the older men might be Pietr. One portly gentleman, obviously prosperous, looked kind, with a broad smile creasing his face. Another aged fellow sat like an Egyptian pharaoh in a railed sedan chair held off the ground by six sweating men, his querulous manner evident by the way he flicked his riding crop indiscriminately about. Please, God, she prayed, let my husband be the smiling man—not the one in the chair.

A man, his muted blue tunic and breeches somehow marking him as a servant, separated himself from the crowd and bowed his head toward Captain Verbeek. He gestured toward the ship and the captain gave a curt nod. The man ducked his head, made a motion for the captain to follow him, and turned into the crowd.

Analisa caught her breath, feeling her blood thunder through her veins. They walked without pausing past the smiling, portly, kind-looking man. She bit against a knuckle as the servant led the captain toward the miserable-seeming one in the sedan chair, and nearly fainted with relief when they continued past him without a moment's hesitation.

The crowd parted before them, a sudden hush descending over the dockside clamor. A man clad in black and gunmetal gray stepped from behind a tower of nutmeg baskets. Tall, as tall as Michael. His head was crowned with a mass of hair the color of iron, the color of the wisps of steam smoldering from Fire Mountain. He moved with a lithe agility not often seen among men of his age.

Pietr Hootendorf. There could be no doubt.

He stood taller by several inches than the captain. The two men exchanged matching stiff bows, and then Pietr turned to say something to the servant, who cringed and fawned in the manner of a dog eager to please its master before melting away into the crowd. Verbeek rubbed his hand over his face, and then pointed out toward the ship, straight at Analisa.

It was impossible to hear what they said from this distance, especially over the babble that had resumed. Verbeek gesticulated wildly from the ship to the nutmeg baskets, and Analisa knew with sinking certainty that he was telling Pietr of his suspicions about her role in helping Michael escape.

Pietr's head swiveled to follow Verbeek's pointing finger. For a timeless, impossible moment, Analisa felt as though her husband's hard, dark stare locked onto her own, boring into her through the intervening distance. Impossible. Impossible. And yet she could not move, could not blink, could not draw breath until he broke the tenuous connection by turning to the captain with a spoken word.

She gulped in a great draught of air, trying to calm herself. She was suddenly grateful for the hours it would take before she would have to meet Pietr Hootendorf face-to-face.

But, to her horror, she saw the blue-garbed servant work free of the crowd and beckon toward one of the canopied boats that bobbed in the water. Within moments, the boat drifted close. The servant splashed into the water and caught a rope tossed from someone within the boat. He returned to shore, towing the boat behind him. Before she could do more than blink a few times, hoping to clear that sight from her eyes, Verbeek and Pietr had forged through the crowd toward the boat. They hopped over the sides and settled themselves beneath the canopy. The servant pushed them back into the sea, and then pulled himself aboard. Oars bristled from the little boat, and it lunged toward the *Island Treasure*.

Dear God.

Her heart commenced a panicky pounding. A buzz began between her ears, drowning out all ability to think. She ought to race for her cabin, ought to change into her wedding gown, don her marriage glove, do whatever primping possible before meeting the man who'd bargained to wed her. Instead, she stood motionless as a goose who'd stood so long upon a frozen lake that its feet had adhered to the ice.

She watched, mute and numb, while the little boat drew closer. It seemed to arrive before she had time to take a breath, and yet her whole life replayed itself in that brief space of time, taunting her with all the mistakes she'd made, all the hopes that died aborning because of her wanton behavior.

A seaman tossed a rope over the ship's rail. The servant snagged it and used it to lever the small boat against the side of the ship, near the rope ladder. Pietr leaped to his feet and scaled it at once, quick and agile as a panther. He jumped lightly onto the deck and cast an assessing gaze over the ship. Analisa imagined he must be judging the working seamen, calculating the value of the cargo. And then his gaze found her.

He studied her for the merest fraction of a heartbeat, just long enough for one corner of his mouth to curl with a sneering dismissal. His attention flicked away.

The captain and the servant tumbled onto the deck. They stood back, breathlessly watching and waiting while Pietr scanned the deck again, studying, seeking. His gaze snapped back to her, and his eyes widened with dismay as he took in her wind-tousled hair, her sun-darkened skin. He fired a question toward the captain, who answered with a smirking amusement that caused Pietr's complexion to mottle.

He walked toward her, but the natural grace she had noted in his movements had altered. The unwifely thought sprang to her mind that Pietr approached her the way a guard dog might advance stiff-legged to warn off an intruder.

She swallowed. after so many months of trying to imagine what he might look like, she had to admit he matched none of her expectations. No pouching stomach. No bald head. No double chin to hint at a fondness for the pleasures of food or drink. There was a controlled energy about him, almost the equal of Michael's, that spoke of many years of preparing for what he wanted. But Pietr also projected the assurance of one who'd spent many more years holding on to it. She had not even imagined that such men existed, and now she'd met two in the space of a few weeks.

"I am Pietr Hootendorf," he said. "*You* are my wife?"

The horror in his voice, the undisguised disappointment in his expression, roused every self-doubt Analisa had tried so hard to quell.

"I . . . I am Analisa."

After a brief, scowling pause, he inclined his head slightly, accepting her name, and she had the uncomfortable feeling that he would have ordered her to change her name if it had not pleased him.

Just then the wind lifted, sending a strand of her dark hair stinging against her sunburned cheek and molding the limp folds of her gown against a frame grown too thin.

"Good God," he ground out between clenched teeth. "Brown hair and skin and eyes. They might as well have given me leave to marry a native doxy." He turned his head away as if the very sight of her caused him pain. "Where is your marriage glove?"

His disappointment in her was so obvious that she felt no surprise that his first concern was for his admittedly expensive token, without sparing a single question for her own state of health. "Safely locked away in my trunk."

He nodded, looking her up and down, his attention pausing at her hips. She wondered wildly if he was judging their suitability for childbearing.

"Verbeek tells me you are headstrong, and he holds you responsible for some shameful behavior."

Relief welled within her—she could answer him safely enough without lying. She lifted her chin and glared at the captain. "I am ashamed of nothing." Verbeek snorted his disbelief, and she squared her shoulders to face Pietr straight on. "I will understand if you wish to reject me." As she spoke, she realized she meant it. Oh, to be so suddenly set free. . . . Her skin heated at the impropriety of such a thought.

"Fear not," Pietr said, mistaking her leaping excitement for worry. "You'll learn to curb those troublesome impulses."

His prediction chilled her to the core.

"I will admit that so many years of ordering students about has left me headstrong. Your letter, mynheer, asking for this glove match, specified a woman of strength and intelligence. Director Odsvelt himself chose me for you, for he believes I possess those qualities."

"Strength and intelligence are important when breeding horses. Men require other attributes in a wife."

Attributes that she lacked. She could virtually hear his unspoken words ringing in the pure, cool air. She attempted to justify his insult by telling herself that she had annoyed and perhaps threatened Pietr by bringing the director's name into their conversation. Pietr's ramrod-straight posture had taken on an added rigidity. His lips tightened, whitening a little around the edges. He reminded her of the volcano, all smoldering fury, and she knew that their marriage had gotten off to the worst possible start.

"The governor waits on shore to greet you and bleat a few words over our heads. Then I will take you home."

So, despite his disappointment with her, he meant to formalize their vows. She should have simply nodded and moved obediently toward the dangling ladder. Instead, she betrayed her headstrong nature, clinging wildly to her final moments of freedom. "The Company agent has not been here. Nobody is to leave the ship until he inspects—"

"The agent will not question my command," said Pietr, very softly. "Neither should you."

"But . . . my things," she protested, worsening matters.

"My man shall see to them." Pietr's eyes flashed. "I must remember that you are not a wife of many years, who understands the meanings implicit in my commands. This first meeting between us is not going well, Analisa."

"Will you beat her, mynheer?" asked Verbeek eagerly.

This brought a bark of humorless laughter from her husband. "No, my good man. There are better ways to tame a headstrong wife."

"I am not an animal, to be tamed," Analisa spoke impulsively.

Her defiance drew Pietr's regard, and for the first time, she fancied she saw a spark of interest flare in his eyes. He inspected her again, grimacing a little as his regard quickly shifted away from her hair and face. He lingered beyond the bounds of propriety at where she curved from hips to breasts. He then gave a brief nod, such as an auction patron might make after discovering that the goods he'd purchased bore some defect, but were not beyond salvaging.

"You will give me many spirited sons," he said, drawing gasps from both the captain and Analisa with his outrageous, improper remark. "Now, come along and pay close attention when the governor orders you to obey me in all things. And then I will take you home."

11

You will bear many spirited sons for me. Pietr's comment swirled through Analisa's mind, benumbing it, making it almost impossible for her to do more than respond with an occasional murmur or nod of the head while Governor Hoon spoke some words from a book, binding her forever to Pietr Hootendorf.

Her frozen calm held her silent as well while her husband acted as tour guide for their brief journey from Banda Neira to the nearby island of Lonthar. Pietr pointed to the quick, darting, jewellike flashes beneath the water and told her they were tiny fishes, unlike anything known to the Netherlands. A verdant green haze covered the distant islands. "Nutmeg trees," he boasted. "No other trees produce leaves exactly that color."

The canopied boat they rode in, so light and quick that two natives armed with but one oar apiece could skim over the glorious blue water, was called a *prahu*, Pietr told her. The five Banda Islands were so close together that traveling between one and another took no more than thirty minutes by *prahu*. Lonthar, their island, boasted the largest number of nutmeg plantations, called *perken*. Those who owned the rights to the plantations were called *perkenier*, and Pietr was one of only thirty-four on Lonthar, one of the exalted few who ruled these small islands like sultans of old.

He told her all those things and more while the dark-skinned oarsmen paddled through surroundings so vivid and vibrant that only a blind woman could fail to be awed by the beauty. She strove to appear properly appreciative, to keep a bright smile on her face, while she clenched her teeth so tightly together she feared they might crack. She had to do this to keep them from chattering. *You will bear many spirited sons for me,* he'd said, just after her impertinent announcement that she was not an animal. *You will bear many spirited sons for me*—he'd taken her moment of defiance to remind her not so subtly that she had bargained to become his broodmare. Even worse, his statement, so filled with possessive glee, taunted her with the inevitability of submitting to this man in bed, of allowing him to claim that which her heart cried belonged to Michael alone.

But Michael was gone. He had left her without saying good-bye, left her without looking back or expressing any regret, just as he had warned he would do. She would never, ever see him again.

Her mother had opted for a life of spinsterhood. She had endured the shame of bearing and raising an illegitimate child all alone, rather than contract a marriage to cover her sins of lust. How many nights had Analisa cried herself to sleep, wondering why her mother had done this? Now she knew. If it were within her power, she would return to her cabin on the *Island Treasure* and head straight back to Amsterdam. She and her mother could continue running the school together, safe and content in each other's company, two of a kind in more ways than Analisa ever suspected.

Except Pietr would never let her go. She knew that. The Company had bent its rules for him; the governor had become involved. Pietr could not now admit that he was displeased with the result of so much effort.

But displeased he was. Each time he glanced her way, he frowned and shook his head ever so slightly before turning and pretending great interest in sights he lived with every day. After a few moments, he took to resting his gaze on her breasts, along the curve of her waist, at the swell of her hips, as if hoping to convince himself that she was a woman capable of bearing the sons he so desired.

No, he would not set her free. He had waited nearly a year and a half for a wife—a long, tedious time while his marriage glove journeyed to Amsterdam, more long months while his new bride traveled to his side. A man of his age could not afford to fritter away so much time with nothing to show for it. He might despair of her headstrong ways, of her physical appearance, but he had admitted he desired her bold traits in his sons. He would never let her go.

Ahead, a small dock jutted from a veritable jungle of swaying, fragrant trees. She could not shake the sensation that once she stepped into that mass of greenery, all trace of Analisa Vandermann would disappear. That realization gave her the courage—or the desperation—to make one stab at freedom.

"Pietr, I assure you, I will understand completely if you wish to turn this boat about and return me to Banda Neira. If you have given your heart to a native woman, perhaps you would rather marry her."

He snapped a short oath. "You are ignorant, Analisa. *Some* Dutch men might dally with native women, but not I. And any man foolish enough to consider marrying one would soon find himself condemned to a public whipping and possible confiscation of his holdings. No sensible man would be willing to pay such a price for indulging in their dubious charms."

"You speak of those women with scorn in your voice," she murmured, taken aback.

"And well I should. Their intelligence is below average, and with their dark hair and dark eyes they remind me of little better than cows."

She huddled lower in her seat.

"Ironic, is it not," he said, filling the silence, "that the Company should expend so much effort in discouraging its men from consorting with those women, and then send to me one who embodies their very attributes. How my colleagues will snicker! Well, I am nothing if not a loyal Company man. Considering all that the Company has done for me, I daresay I can become accustomed to what they have sent my way this time."

Their *prahu* bumped up against the dock. The trees stretched cool shadows, the nutmeg trees that had made Pietr so fabulously wealthy, the trees that formed the foundation for the Dutch East India Company's profits. Those trees were the Company's gift to Pietr, just as she was. One gift he treasured; one he despised.

Only one man had ever thought her beautiful, thought her intelligent and resourceful, and even Michael Rowland preferred those trees and the fruit they bore over her. He had risked his life to steal seed from those nutmeg trees, to carry them across the sea to the wild new land he called home. He didn't want her that way.

She resolutely shook all thoughts of him away. It wouldn't do to pine over a man who'd warned her from the first that he did not believe in love. It wouldn't do to take her first steps into her new home, with her new husband at her side, while her heart ached for another man.

"Up with you, now," Pietr said once the servant had roped the *prahu* to the dock. Her husband helped her from her bench and gripped her elbow to steady her. "Take care—'tis a big step from here to the dock."

His hold upon her was steady and unwavering, rock-solid. He stood beside her, his legs slightly braced for balance in the softly rocking *prahu*. He handed her over to a servant who stood atop the dock. The servant pulled at her hand, but as Pietr had warned, the step between the boat and dock was too great to take easily.

Pietr chuckled. "Up you go." He boosted her with a hand clamped soundly to her bottom. The shock of his touch upon such an intimate part of her body propelled her upward with a little shriek, which she tried to stifle. A wife could not complain over such a liberty taken by her husband, especially when it was so obvious that he had not relished the touch. She glanced back over her shoulder and caught him rubbing his palm against his breeches as if eager to remove the feel of her from his skin.

Captain Verbeek had promised her that the plantation would offer well-tended paths for walking. One such path snaked from the dock through the trees which looked like they were laden with large, ripening apricots. Doves cooed in the branches, fluttering about as they passed beneath. One particularly agitated bird burst into flight, causing a round, blush-tinged fruit to drop to the ground. It split neatly in half, and almost at once, another dove plummeted from a branch and snatched the seed from the fruit's middle. Pietr kicked at the bird, sending it fluttering away, and muttered an oath.

"Hans," he said to the servant, "I ordered the men to beat these scavengers out of the branches this morning."

"We have, mynheer. Twice."

"Do it again."

"Yes, mynheer."

"Why must they drive the doves from the trees?" Analisa asked.

"They are thieves," Pietr spat. "They gorge themselves upon the nutmeg seeds." He toed the fallen fruit while juices oozed from its gaping, empty middle.

So, this was a nutmeg. Its golden flesh oozed juice like a ripe peach awaiting a dollop of cream. Analisa felt a sudden kinship with the nutmeg fruit—it with its hollow core, she with the emptiness where her heart used to be.

"This will go against me when the Company agent tallies my harvest," Pietr said.

"How so?"

"The agents estimate the potential harvest at the beginning of each season. They grant some leeway, but never enough to cover all the seeds those damned birds steal."

"I had not realized they kept such close watch upon the nutmegs."

He cocked a brow in amusement. "How else would they assure themselves that we planters do not personally line our pockets with profits that should go into Company coffers?" he asked. "A planter whose harvest falls short can be forced to pay heavy fines, even when scavengers cause the shortage."

She remembered Verbeek's suspicion that a planter had to be in collusion with smugglers. If so, the planter was surely a foolish man, considering how the Company kept such close watch on the harvest.

"Why take such a risk? I thought all planters were immensely wealthy."

Annoyance and dissatisfaction flickered over his features. She bit her lip. Her comment must have struck him as mercenary and calculating, and she would deserve a rebuke.

But it seemed that Company policy, and not she, was responsible for his discontent.

"Some would say a man never has wealth enough," he said. "Some begrudge a man's successes without taking into account how hard he works to succeed. I assure you I dislike having a Company lackey totting my harvest and telling me how much profit I am permitted to make."

"I suppose that so closely monitoring the harvest aids in keeping down smuggling as well." She was glad to have something to talk about, anything to empty her mind of *You will bear many spirited sons for me.*

Pietr's interest sharpened at once, and she belatedly realized that broaching the subject of smuggling undoubtedly raised the specter of the escaped pirate Michael Rowland in his mind. "What do you know of smuggling?"

All at once she was sick of their excruciating politeness, the wall of reserve between them that she knew had been erected by whatever accusations Verbeek had made against her. Perhaps if she cleared the air between them, if she could somehow convince Pietr that she meant to devote herself to becoming the good wife he desired, this awkwardness between them would ease. Perhaps, if she felt more comfortable with him, she might begin to feel some anticipation about taking her place as his wife.

"Pietr, I know the captain has accused me of aiding that smuggler in his escape. We carried him on board. He was the topic of discussion, day after day. I learned many things about smuggling, but could not understand why it was such a great puzzle as to how that criminal might have gotten his hands on fertile nutmegs. Now I understand how difficult it must have been, since you have explained to me that the Company monitors the harvest so closely. It makes sense of the captain's suspicions that a planter must have been involved in the scheme."

Pietr's face whitened. "Nonsense," he hissed through tightened lips. "Such suspicions must never be allowed to circulate. Any planter engaged in smuggling would be arrested. He would be publicly ridiculed, his *perken* confiscated, and worse—he would be forced to work for three years as a slave."

It seemed all her good intentions were doomed to backfire. She merely wanted to express an interest in his business, and she'd succeeded instead at casting slurs against his peers. He was furiously angry and she could not blame him.

Before she could think of something to say that might smooth things over, they turned a bend in the path and came face-to-face with her new home.

"Oh, my," she gasped.

She had expected a low-slung, thick-walled structure built to withstand tropical heat, not this three-story gambrel-roofed Dutch mansion that loomed incongruously in the midst of an East Indian jungle.

"I built it to please my wife," Pietr said with gruff pride. "I fashioned it after the vanBiesbrouck mansion, which Hilde had always admired. I had always dreamed that one day a dozen such mansions would grace this island, so many that it would be known as Hootendorf Island rather than Lonthar."

"It is lovely," Analisa whispered. *Hilde.* His first wife had been named Hilde.

He paused, his gaze softening as he studied his home's facade. "I have a crew of servants who do nothing but paint and replace rotted fretwork. In this climate, the dark colors deteriorate within months. The servants grumble. They dislike working at anything more difficult than tending nutmegs."

She thought he might be offering her a way of making this home her own, of testing her ability to pacify bored servants. "Perhaps painting with a different shade of—" she began.

"Hilde chose those colors herself. I will not allow anything about this house to be changed."

"Of course not." She swallowed, and looked at the house again. Such a familiar design should have been a welcoming and comforting sight. Instead, Hilde's house projected a sinister air. The sun reflected off its many windows, as if some malevolent force within repelled all light, all signs of life. Involuntarily, Analisa shivered.

Pietr escorted her up the broad stairs, and through the wide front door. Despite the brilliant sunshine, the interior was dim. All of the windows were covered with dark shades; Analisa subsided with relief to find such an innocent reason to explain why the windows had appeared so black and empty from the outside. The murky gloom was deepened with dark walls, heavy furniture, and intricately patterned carpets that stretched over dark mahogany floors.

A massive portrait of a woman hung over a mantel, where a fire flickered incongruously in the grate. The late morning air already shimmered with heat; the fire made it near impossible to draw a comfortable breath.

"My wife followed Dutch custom," said Pietr, nodding toward the fire. "We light the fireplaces each morning to banish the chill."

"I see," she whispered.

"That is my wife, Hilde," he nodded again, this time toward the portrait, as though Analisa had any doubt of whom it portrayed. "I have many such memories of her hung throughout this house. They are to remain."

"Of course."

Analisa lowered her eyes, but studied the portrait covertly through her lashes. Hilde Hootendorf stared back imperturbably, secure in her position as Analisa never could be. Hilde was everything Analisa wasn't—

small and curvy and pink-and-white, with thick golden braids wrapped around her head, pure-blooded Dutch to the core. Pietr stared at the portrait with a longing that made Analisa wish to leave him alone with his desires. Hilde seemed to stare back at him, beckoning with a half smile that rivaled the Italian masterpiece, Mona Lisa.

Pietr's trancelike pose before this altar to Hilde's memory snapped the last thread of tenuous hope within Analisa. She had given her heart to Michael, and he had never looked at her that way. Pietr would never look at her that way, either. All of a sudden, she simply didn't care anymore. Let Hilde continue to rule Pietr's heart and home—it didn't matter. Nothing mattered. The years stretched endlessly before her, imminently respectable but devoid of joy.

It seemed fitting. She was a mere husk of a woman now that her heart had been unwisely given. She would spend the remainder of her days wandering about in this tomb of a house, this memorial to another woman. She could grieve for Michael; Pietr could grieve for his lost love.

"I am a bit fatigued," she whispered. "If I could rest for a while . . ."

"Of course!" His attention dragged over to her and then drifted at once back to the portrait. She caught a hint of mingled regret and anticipation as he sighed at his Hilde before turning back to his new wife. "You will no doubt find this climate enervating. The other planters tell me their wives often take to their beds during the hottest parts of the day. Hilde, of course, was not prone to such weakness."

Analisa had never been a slug-a-bed and could have assured Pietr that she equaled his Hilde in that regard, but she nodded anyway. The more she could sleep, the less she would have to think and feel.

"A few hours' sleep should set me right," she said.

"Then perhaps you will dine with me this evening?"

"Of course."

"Has the sea journey left you utterly exhausted?"

It seemed a rather belated and halfhearted inquiry into the state of her health, the cursory curiosity one polite stranger might show for another. She quelled the memory of how Michael had noticed every nuance of her appearance, how he could tell with uncanny certainty whether she fared well or not.

She shook her head, dispelling thoughts of Michael as well as Pietr's shallow concern. "I had so little to do aboard ship that I grew very indolent. I've never been so well-rested in my life."

"I suppose there's no reason to put it off, then." Pietr crossed his arms and threw a glance back at the portrait. Apology and sorrow furrowed his brow briefly, and then he shook it away and turned back to Analisa. "We might as well dispense with the business of consummating our marriage tonight."

12

~

Seven hours of staring blankly at the netting covering her bed had robbed Analisa of whatever vitality she possessed. Seven hours of lying in the bed she knew Pietr would visit all too soon, through the door that was now discreetly shut, but which she knew opened from his adjoining room.

"You must begin dressing for dinner," advised the Bandanese serving girl who tugged the mosquito netting away, jerking Analisa from her torpor.

Pietr had likened her to a native girl. She assessed the young woman standing before her: dark hair, brown skin, brown eyes, and yet nothing like Analisa—she did not understand how Pietr could look upon her and confuse her with a native. His revulsion had to stem from another cause.

"What is your name?" Analisa asked.

The girl paused, surprise stamped across her exotically lovely features. "The first mevrouw called me Gerte."

Analisa studied the maid. Her chocolate-brown eyes were slightly tip-tilted at the edges, her skin the shade of cream-lightened coffee. Lustrous black hair had been fashioned into a single heavy braid. Despite her name, she looked less Dutch than Analisa.

"Gerte is not your real name, is it?"

"No, mevrouw."

Analisa waited expectantly, but the little maid tightened her lips.

"I would like to know your real name."

"Mynheer would not approve. We females are all Gerte; our men are all Hans."

Analisa laid a hand upon the girl's arm. "Here, in my room, you shall be . . ."

"Tali," blurted the girl. She shot Analisa a conspiratorial smile, and then busied herself with removing Analisa's wrinkled wedding gown from its muslin dust cover. Tali's delicate brows arched in amazement when she shook the silken folds and sent a few bits of straw wafting into the air. Analisa swallowed against the sudden fullness in her throat, remembering how those straws had gotten worked into the material.

"Perhaps you would choose another gown for tonight, mevrouw?"

"I have no other gowns."

"There are many gowns, belonging to the first mevrouw."

"No! I shall wear this one."

So Pietr had not disposed of Hilde's old clothing. Analisa wondered if he expected her to wear the deceased woman's clothes the way he expected her to blend seamlessly into the deceased woman's house. She might have no choice in the matter, she realized. Her shipboard gown was little better than tatters after so many months at sea. Her silk wedding gown would not hold up for long under the strain of daily wear. If Pietr refused to supply her with new garments, she would be forced to wear Hilde's leavings.

Soon another maid joined them, and after a brief flurry of denials and evasions, Analisa learned that her name was Maru.

"She is well trained in the first mevrouw's ways,

particularly in the arrangement of hair," Tali assured
Analisa earnestly. Maru tsked agitatedly over Analisa's unruly hair while Tali clucked over the wedding
gown. They looked so distressed when they finished
primping and tugging that she felt sorry for them, until
she realized that it was not their efforts that dismayed
them, but her personal features.

"We have done our best, but still you look nothing
like the first mevrouw," whimpered Maru.

Paradoxically, nothing could have been said at that
moment to cheer her more. Analisa studied herself in
the mirror; her hair had been so tightly braided and
bound that her facial skin was pulled back somewhat,
lending her a rather startled, wide-eyed look. No
proper pink-and-blond Dutch maiden, but a dark-
haired, hazel-eyed wanton with lips too red and cheeks
colored with trepidation. The maids twisted their
hands, and she knew she ought to say something to
reassure them.

"I am delighted with your efforts. Now, I believe it
is time for dinner."

Pietr rose from the table when the maids escorted
her into the dining room. His glance flickered over
her in the manner she was coming to expect, skipping
quickly past her face to pause at her breasts, her waist,
her hips. The maids still seemed agitated over their
failure to transform her into Hilde's image, and she
wondered now whether Pietr's deliberate concentration upon her torso was his way of ignoring the reality
that the wrong face existed above the woman's body
he meant to use to sire his sons.

Well, let him look where he pleased. It didn't matter
to her whether he liked her face or not. He'd be
forced to look at it eventually, especially while they
were eating, when the only features he required in a
wife would be hidden beneath the table.

She took a moment to study him. He was impeccably dressed in the loose, flowing tunic and pantaloons of a prosperous Dutch burgher. His iron-gray hair lay hidden beneath the curls of a shoulder-length black wig. A snowy white collar draped over his shoulders in a blindingly brilliant match to his white stockings. Golden tassels adorned his knees, complimented by the golden rosettes decorating highly polished open-sided shoes. A broad-brimmed hat hung over the knob of his chair.

Her wedding gown seemed dowdy and hopelessly inadequate for the fine life Pietr obviously led. And to think of how carefully she had guarded it, how she'd tended it throughout the journey to make sure it didn't suffer from the damp, the salt spray, the hungry rodents and insects. She was suddenly fiercely glad that she had worn it once for Michael, that she had watched his eyes kindle in appreciation of the way she'd looked in it, how he'd marveled over the way its color lent added sparkle to her eyes.

"Has Dutch fashion changed so much that men clothe their wives in rags?" Pietr asked.

"This is my wedding gown," she defended her garment, which she knew had strained Britta's resources. "I have never owned anything of finer quality or cut."

"Truly?" He seemed amazed. "I shudder to think of the ordinary evening wear you must have brought with you."

"I brought no evening wear, Pietr. Only this gown and the one I wore aboard ship." His lips tightened, his shoulders stiffened, and she realized that he'd somehow taken this information as a slur, that his wife had been so ill provided for. And then he relaxed.

"Ah, yes, I had forgotten about that quaint custom of outfitting the Company's Daughters with only the barest necessities. I imagine that the accountant who developed that scheme was well rewarded. No doubt it's saved the Company thousands of guilders." He chuckled. "It is of no importance. Extraordinary men such as myself have the financial means to clothe our women as we please."

"I did not mean to be a financial burden upon you, Pietr."

"I said it is of no matter. I cannot have my wife going about looking as you do now."

Michael had loved the way she looked in this gown. His whole being had surged into a man's unique display of appreciation. He had told her she looked beautiful. He had made her *feel* beautiful.

Standing beneath Hilde Hootendorf's portrait, with her husband studying the dining table and the arrangement of plates and utensils with more interest than he'd shown toward her, his new wife, she felt . . . inadequate.

"Do not fret," Pietr said. "You shall have new clothes tomorrow."

"The . . . the clothing that has been . . . stored?" She could think of no other way he could garb her so swiftly.

"No!" He barked the denial. And then he gave himself a physical shake. "It requires a great deal of effort to keep my Hilde's things from disintegrating in this climate, but I cannot bear to discard them. Nor could I bear to see another female attempt to fill her clothes."

It was an insult, something of a rejection, and yet she felt grateful.

"I shall send a servant to market in the morning to purchase native garments for you. Hilde wore a sari on occasion, and claimed it was quite comfortable. Such things will suffice for a day or so until proper Dutch clothing can be made."

She nodded her acceptance as he led her to the dining chair, and then she found herself fascinated by the bewildering array of small plates and silverware spread around the standard place setting. The moment they were both seated, a servant clapped his hands and a parade of scurrying waiters appeared, each bearing a steaming, fragrant dish.

In the center of the table, they placed a typical Dutch meal of sausage, boiled cabbage, and beet soup. Radiating outward from these were a host of colorful dishes, none of which she recognized.

"Ordinarily, you could ask the servants for any beverage," said Pietr. "Hilde enjoyed a weak decoction of water and lemon with a hint of sugarcane. But for tonight I have ordered something special for you, the same as what I am drinking." He lifted a cup of steaming brew. "Nutmeg tea, made at great effort from the essential oils of nutmeg and mace. Only planters can afford to indulge. It is an acquired taste, but its unique properties should serve us well during the chore facing us tonight."

We might as well dispense with the business of consummating our marriage tonight, he had decreed. "What . . . what special properties does this tea possess?" she whispered.

"A rather unique sort of inebriation." He smiled and took a hearty swallow of his tea. "Insensibility, if one overindulges. Have you heard why sea captains are so careful to carry stores of gin and arrack on board ship when transporting cargoes of nutmeg?"

She had watched Captain Verbeek dole out daily measures of gin, thinking it a kindness meant to offer men a taste of home. "The men joked that the unofficial Dutch motto is, 'We must drink gin or die.' "

"True enough. But the Company knows that men deprived of gin will all too readily turn to nutmeg tea and drink up the Company's entire profit. I have heard tales of mutiny at sea, with the crews ignoring their chores so they might devote every minute to pressing the essential oils from the nutmeg and then consuming so much of the tea that they sail into home port with empty cargo holds."

Pietr seemed little affected by the beverage, save for an increased volubility. She ventured a sip. The taste of nutmeg burst upon her tongue, pleasant at first, but then growing too strong. She grimaced.

"As I said, it is an acquired taste. And this," he gestured toward the myriad dishes, "we call *rijsttafel.* Rice table. I daresay you've not partaken of it before."

"No, I have not."

"Of course, we *perkeniers* hold to the old ways and insist upon traditional meals served up in true Dutch fashion." He inclined his head toward the familiar foods at the center of the table. "Hilde, though she was most traditional, convinced me to broaden my palate to include *rijsttafel.* I am quite pleased that she did."

"I too will strive to find new dishes to please you, Pietr."

"You will not. Over the years, Hilde developed a fourteen-day menu that suits my digestion admirably and yet does not grow tiresome. I see no reason to alter it."

"As you wish."

He sipped his nutmeg tea, totally oblivious to her distress. Each mention of the late, sainted Hilde seemed to paint Analisa into a deeper corner, from which she might never venture. She stared at her nutmeg tea, and then snatched it up and drank it in a gulp despite its near-scalding warmth. Inebriation and insensibility suddenly seemed very appealing.

"This is rice," he said, pointing to the strangest dish, a mound of sticky-looking, whitish-colored grain. "They do not eat rice back home in the Netherlands, but 'tis a staple food here on the islands. I've grown quite fond of it. Spread a bit over your plate."

Analisa obeyed while a servant refilled her teacup. The pasty, unappealing glob of rice did not tempt her appetite, so she lifted the nutmeg tea to her lips again and again.

"Now, choose from among the side dishes. As a rule, the golden and brown-colored ones are meats, the oranges and reds fruits, the others vegetables. Go on, heap it right atop the rice, a little here and a little there. The foods are all highly seasoned and you will welcome the rice's moderating effect."

She ladled some brown-sauced chunks over her rice and warily inhaled the rich scent wafting from her plate. So many spices—she and her mother had not used such a liberal hand with seasonings unless the meat had turned. Then again, nothing could taste worse than the last few meals served aboard the *Island Treasure,* after the ship's cook had been reduced to serving up scrapings from the bottom of rancid, un-spiced meat barrels.

Following Pietr's example, she chose a wide, shal-low, spoonlike utensil which easily scooped up a mouthful of the crumbly, aromatic rice mixture. To her delight, a world of flavor blossomed upon her tongue.

"Why, it is delicious!" she marveled.

Pietr nodded, approving her reaction. "Depending upon which side dish you choose, each mouthful is like eating a new meal."

Their conversation lagged, then, with each drifting into silence broken only by the soft chink of silver against china, the muffled thump of teacups lifted and then set down atop the damask-covered table. Analisa lost count of the number of times her cup was refilled. Consuming so much tea filled her stomach. Despite the food's savory appeal, her appetite failed and she managed to taste only a few things. To keep Pietr from remarking on it, she forced herself to raise the spoon again and again. But even though she levered only a grain or two of sauced rice, the spoon seemed to grow heavier and heavier, turning her arms numb with the effort. She'd never expended so much effort to complete such a simple task.

"Your afternoon rest does not seem to have restored your strength, Analisa," Peter remarked. "I hope you are not sickly by nature."

"Oh, no, I assure you that I am usually quite robust." She could not fathom the curious heaviness of her limbs, the almost overwhelming urge she felt to rest her head upon the table and fall into a sound sleep. Unless it was the tea—but Pietr had swallowed much more than she while remaining unaffected. "It must be the heat. I am not accustomed to it." It was a blatant lie. Her airy room had been infinitely more comfortable than her stiflingly hot shipboard cabin, and a servant had stood near her bed throughout those long hours of her abortive attempts to sleep, waving large fronds of some type that served to circulate the air even more.

Pietr merely nodded, surprising her by not commenting that one who had just sailed the tropical seas ought to be well accustomed to the heat. He looked at her face, and for once his regard lingered. She tried to fix an amiable smile upon her lips, but her muscles refused to cooperate. She tried looking back at him with some semblance of interest and devotion, but felt bleary-eyed and unable to focus.

"I will have two servants stand over us with fans tonight," he said. "Afterwards."

Afterwards. He kept his hand at the small of her back as he guided her up the stairs and back to her room. She found herself embarrassingly needful of his assistance. Whether from dread or from the promised effects of the nutmeg tea, all strength seemed to have deserted her legs.

He steered her into her room and then left her swaying near the foot of the bed while the two anxious maids hurried in to make her ready for him. Remembering their unhappiness over her wedding gown, she assumed her shapeless woolen bed gown would send them into fits of despair, but they seemed delighted with it.

"Just like the first mevrouw's," rhapsodized Tali.

Analisa endured the tugs upon her hair as Maru loosened her braiding. It would be convenient to have Maru's service in the morning, when her hair would be a tangled mess. To her surprise, Maru quickly rebraided her hair and fastened it into a tight crown.

"Just like the first mevrouw," she said, with a pat that Analisa fancied carried a hint of sympathy.

Tali discreetly placed a damp washcloth and folded towel upon the bedside table.

They hurried from the room, as if they'd been given a set amount of time to spend with her and no more. Seconds later a soft knock sounded at the door separating her room from Pietr's, and then her husband stepped through it. He tested her own door into the hallway, and then he turned the key, locking them together.

His gaze swept over her, taking in the voluminous gown, her bound hair. "You look better so." His words sounded garbled, as if they came from a great distance, through water. He bent over the lantern and extinguished its light. Moonlight streamed through the windows. Her eyes did not seem to be working properly. She was blinded by the change in illumination for a few heartbeats, and when her eyes adjusted, she found Pietr standing scant inches away from her. She had not heard him move, so perhaps her ears were not functioning, either.

"Perhaps you should keep these few buttons unfastened until you become accustomed to the heat." His fingers moved with quick, sure precision along the short row of buttons that ran from her chinline to her breastbone. He parted the resulting flaps with familiarity, and tugged loose the ribbons of her undershift with the ease of long practice. He must have undressed his precious Hilde every night, Analisa thought with dull distraction as she stood there and waited for him to strip her bare. Instead, he turned his attention to his own garments.

The moon bathed the room with silver and shadows. He shrugged free of his clothes and stood before her, lean and fit, and with the darkness hiding the silver in his hair, he might have been twenty years younger. He was an admirable specimen of a man, and a woman who had not known the magnificence of Michael Rowland's body might have found Pietr's exciting.

Her lack of interest bothered him not at all. He guided her to the bed. He stood back and waited patiently while she dragged her leaden limbs onto the bed, while she settled her head carefully upon the pillow and tugged her woolen gown demurely into place. She ran a mental inventory: hair bound; breasts, waist, hips, thoroughly swathed in stout Dutch wool. Her mother would have approved.

She remembered how Michael had dispensed with every shred of cloth, how he'd delighted in freeing every inch of her skin and savored her from head to toe. She tensed, knowing that Pietr, too, would surely strip her gown from her and bare all to his curious eyes.

"Are you a virgin, Analisa?"

Her heart slammed against her ribs as she shook her head. It was the one question she had dreaded more than any other, and he would ask it when her wits were deadened. *Be wary,* her mind warned, but no reassuring glimmer of sense answered that it would.

"Your request for a wife specified a woman of mature years. It did not specify a virgin."

"Nor did I agree to take a harlot to wife. Have you entertained many lovers?"

"Only one."

Mortification should have held her tongue silent, but she found herself savoring those words again. *Only one.* A sweet lassitude had overtaken her from head to toe, so that thoughts of the man evoked by those words quivered through her the way musical peals vibrated a bell. She closed her eyes and at once her head began spinning. The nutmeg tea. The promised inebriation. She pressed her head back into the pillow and prayed for the insensibility to follow.

"So you left your lover pining away for you in Amsterdam?"

"No. He is not a Dutchman—"

One tiny, sentient part of her mind screamed a warning, but too late. She had revealed too much. She struggled to open her eyes and found Pietr staring down at her. The moonlight cast strange shadows against his face—or perhaps it was the nutmeg tea playing havoc with her senses, for surely he could not be smiling and looking pleased at her revelation.

"I know how well the Company guards its Daughters, Analisa. You would not have had an opportunity for dalliance in Amsterdam. So I must assume you indulged in a shipboard romance, my headstrong bride. Tell me, was he vigorous?"

"Most . . . most vigorous." Curse her truthful tongue, but she could not keep it still.

"Did you dally with Verbeek?"

"No!"

Pietr chuckled. "Now I understand the good captain's antagonism toward you. He no doubt resented that you bestowed your favors upon one of his underlings."

She stared at him, praying he would not ask her to name her lover, for the effects of the tea had turned her tongue treacherous beyond belief and she was not at all certain she could withhold anything from Pietr just then.

God must have heard her prayers, for Pietr treated her to an indulgent shake of his head. "Well, no need to fret over it. Hilde came virgin to me and I have no need of another. In truth, I am relieved that I need not spend time cosseting you through a deflowering."

It did not seem possible that he would let her off so easily. She braced herself for an angry outburst, but he merely stood there staring down at her. She supposed most women would feel insulted to find that their new husbands cared so little, but she felt only a vast relief that the issue of her virginity would not be flung in her face again and again over the coming years.

He placed a finger beneath her chin and tilted her face upward, forcing her to look into his eyes. "I know everything is strange to you. If you need more time to become accustomed to this place . . . to me . . . I will not force you. I can wait."

His kindness nearly undid her. He had from the beginning been honest about his intentions, promising nothing more than a passionless marriage contracted for the purpose of creating children. Once, that prospect had beckoned her with the brightness of a thousand stars. It was not Pietr's fault that she had come to regret the bargain she made. He should not be made to feel she spurned all he had offered, should not be made to force his contracted bride to uphold her end of the bargain.

Besides, she had to stop dwelling on those forbidden hours spent in Michael's arms. She had not known she was capable of such passion before his lips and body woke her to pleasure. She was Pietr's wife. She should find joy in his embrace, should look forward to beginning their new life together.

"You will not have to force me. I married you willingly, and expected . . . this . . . to be part of the bargain." She attempted to smile, to lend a shred of satisfaction to her voice, hoping he might be tricked into believing she welcomed his attentions. She willed strength into her arms, willed herself to hold them up, offering an embrace. "I am your wife."

He studied her trembling arms and sighed. "I would rather you not play false with me, Analisa. You must understand the nature of a man. Give him a bed, a woman, and sufficient darkness, and most times his body will perform as nature intended. Ladies need not pretend to enjoy it."

She let her arms drop. He did not mind that she was experienced. He did not expect a false show of passion. She should have been filled with relief. Instead, she felt as if a great weight pressed down upon her, crushing the spirit Michael had set free.

Pietr settled beside her. He kissed her, a perfunctory brushing of his lips against her forehead, then for a moment on her mouth. His lips were dry, firm. He briefly cupped one breast and then the other through the ever-so-proper folds of her nightgown, the way, she thought, a farmer might judge the milk-making capacity of a new heifer. He rubbed his palm over the heavy wool covering her stomach, and then lower, smoothing the folds against her skin all the way to her ankles.

Michael had done all these things to her, and she'd been far more than a numb-muscled, disinterested observer. Michael's touch had driven her wild, turning her into a naked, moaning creature, quivering and wet and aching for possession. How could it be so different—unless she had done it all wrong with Michael? Pietr was not physically displeasing. He attempted to be kind, in his own heavy-handed, Hilde-obsessed fashion.

But Pietr was not Michael. Her mind, benumbed by the effects of the nutmeg tea, kept repeating it over and over: *He is not Michael.*

She turned her head against the pillow.

Pietr heaved a sigh.

And then she felt her consciousness desert her. Just for an instant. She wanted to sob with frustration when she felt herself come quickly to awareness again. Her insensibility had not lasted long enough to draw Pietr's attention, for when she forced her eyes open, she caught him staring down at his lap, shaking his head, his shoulders rigid with fury.

"—I had hoped this would not happen, since I have not indulged for so long, but it appears I will require a few moments alone to ready myself." He seemed to be in the middle of explaining something. She wasn't sure whether his voice was actually slurred, or if her inebriated ears were merely having difficulty in understanding him. "It is not always easy at my age, especially when my lusts are not adequately fired. When I return, I want you to be ready to receive me instantly."

Her consciousness winked out again. When it drifted back, her despair at its return was so great that she let out a small whimper. Pietr loomed over her, shaking her into wakefulness. She did not know how long he'd been doing so, and it frightened her a little, to think she could have grown so numb that she could not remember being touched. Pietr noticed at once the return of her senses.

"Listen, now. I want you to fold your gown to here, no further." He used the side of his hand to draw an invisible line across her thighs. "I will return in a few moments."

Blackness engulfed her once more. When it lifted, she dazedly tried to remember what Pietr had ordered her to do—something about folding her gown. She plucked ineffectually at the stout Dutch wool. A faint creaking and a strange groaning sound, coming from Pietr's room, registered in her ears. Her husband, making himself ready for her. She could not imagine what he might be doing.

And she was supposed to be doing something, too—something involving her gown. Oh, yes, she was to fold it up to her thighs. She passed out once when she'd worked the heavy cloth to midcalf, and then blacked out again, for a little longer, when the hem reached her knees. The sounds coming from Pietr's room were growing louder, and then she heard the thump of his feet hitting the floor, the sound of his hand upon the door. *Be ready to receive me instantly,* he had instructed. She managed to curl her fingers into the folds and drag her hem a few inches higher when she felt her essential spark dim once again, with a finality that promised the insensibility she craved.

But this period of nothingness did not last, either, though she could not tell how much time had passed when her eyelids once again fluttered open. The tranquilizing effects of the nutmeg tea deserted her with her next breath.

Pietr, naked and sweating in the moonlight, stood alongside the bed. Arms crossed, he stared through the window. His manhood lay in a limp curl atop the juncture of his thighs, but a bitter sneer distorted Pietr's features, as though he had gained no pleasure from indulging his lusts.

And he must have indulged himself. Why else would the hem she had struggled to raise to her thighs now be tucked snugly around her ankles? She remembered her fingers being wound in the woolen folds of her gown; now they lay covered by a damp washcloth and crumpled towel. She could not recall adjusting her garment on her own, or using the washcloth and towel.

Nor could she remember Pietr touching her in any way.

Each time she'd loved with Michael, her body had tingled and surged with an afterglow that lasted for hours. She remembered the rasp of his beard against her skin, the way her breasts throbbed at his touch, the clenching and moistening and joyous release of her most secret places. Now she felt . . . nothing. Hair bound, well-swathed in wool, dry and untouched . . . nothing.

The nutmeg tea could have left her numb. Or perhaps she felt so lifeless and inert because marital sex was just as the old women whispered—a bothersome and boring business, with nothing in it for the woman. Or, perhaps, by some God-sent miracle, Pietr's distaste for her had made it impossible for him to claim what was his by law.

One simply could not ask one's new husband, "Pardon me, but did we just couple for the first time?" She imagined that a man whose wife had confessed she'd recently embraced a vigorous lover might be offended to learn that his wife had no memory of her husband's possession. Small wonder Pietr looked so angry and frustrated. In taking her tonight, he had been reminded how recently she'd lost her virginity, and despite his apparent acceptance of her ruined state, it must have bothered him more than he'd expected.

But surely a woman would feel *something,* some evidence that her body had been used. Maybe . . . maybe nothing had happened. She could not stop the small moan of relief that erupted at the thought.

Pietr swiveled his head toward her the minute she made the sound, and then dashed her hopes.

"I will not tolerate you reminding me how I lost control this evening. You will do your best to forget that distasteful scene, because you are mine now," he whispered in a vicious snarl. "Mine."

He snatched the washcloth and towel from her and stormed from her room. She lay awake for many hours, wishing her mind could grow as numb and unfeeling as the rest of her body.

He expected very little of her, Pietr explained the next morning. "You will take all morning and evening meals with me so we might converse, for I crave the sound of Dutch unsullied by native cant."

"I will, of course, assume charge of the housekeeping," Analisa remarked, idly stirring a stick of sugarcane through her lemon and water.

"You will not. I am well served by the procedures instituted by Hilde and do not wish to endure any upheavals in the routine. Besides, you are to conserve all your strength and focus all your attention on motherhood. I am told the physical demands take an exceeding toll on women newly transported from the Netherlands to this clime."

She thought of the sometimes overwhelming busyness of her old life, the heavy responsibilities she'd juggled and shared with her mother. There were times when she would have welcomed a respite, but now, threatened with unremitting indolence, she thought she might go mad.

"So I will converse with you morning and evening, and . . . entertain you at night," she whispered, scarcely able to believe her life had been reduced to this.

"Only when necessary, for that last." Pietr's face flushed a dull red. For the first time since meeting him, she thought he looked uncertain. "I have been thinking about what happened last night, Analisa."

"You . . . you told me to forget it."

"As though any woman could! I can only assume that sordid excuse for a wedding night was as embarrassing for you as it was for me."

She understood his agitation now. One thing she had learned about Pietr was his absolute abhorrence of any display of passion or emotion. He had told her that he would not tolerate being reminded of how he'd lost control with her. She bit back hysterical laughter, wondering what he might think if she admitted that she remembered nothing, that even now her body felt as empty and untouched as it had since last claimed by Michael. "I am sorry you found exercising your rights to be such an unpleasant chore, Pietr."

"Exercising my rights . . ." His flush deepened, and then drained away as he bolted upright in his chair. His eyes narrowed upon her. "The nutmeg tea truly dulled your wits last night, eh?" At her reluctant nod, he leaned back, and a most curious smile hovered at the edges of his mouth.

"Perhaps it was for the best," he murmured.

"Yes, perhaps it was."

She could not understand the barely restrained mirth that seemed to grip him. He chuckled and then rearranged his posture, and all the confidence that she'd thought he'd misplaced seemed to flow back into him.

"I am sorry," she said.

"And so you should be. Why, my new wife cannot recall whether I failed her or performed like a veritable stallion, with a most impressive demonstration of my manly power."

"I will pay better attention tonight," she whispered.

He looked at her and visibly shuddered. "I think not. You revealed your most intimate secrets to me last night, Analisa, and I have every reason to hope you might already be nurturing a child between those bony hips of yours. We need not attempt to repeat last night's unpleasant business until your body proves you have not quickened.''

There were in his remarks the sort of contemptuous insults that one part of her mind told her meant that he would never, ever grow fond of her. She didn't care, for another part of her mind seized upon *We need not repeat last night's unpleasant business.* He would not be coming to her bed that night, or the next night, or any other night, providing her womb had turned fruitful.

She clasped her hands against her belly and began to pray.

13

~

"Ahoy! You in the tree! Dutch or English! Dutch or English?" The hail rang out across the water in both languages.

Michael slitted his eyes open the narrowest measure, and still enough light pierced through the feathery tree fronds and the shield of his lashes to make him wince. Two days of peering out across the sun-glazed sea had all but blinded him, and so he was not certain at first that the cheerful boatman waving to him from a narrow little skiff was real or a wishful manifestation of his overstrained vision.

"Ahoy!" he croaked with a weak flap of his hand. "British."

The boatman's grin widened, and Michael knew that if he'd claimed Dutch citizenship, he'd soon have found himself staring once more at an empty sea.

"You taking holiday, British sir, or you need a ride somewheres?"

"I wouldn't mind a ride."

"For a price."

"Get me to Run Island, and someone will pay."

The boatman nodded his acceptance of their bargain and dug his paddle into the water, piloting toward shore.

Michael made the first infinitesimal shift in his position and grimaced from the agony shafting through his muscles. A man's body wasn't designed for roosting in trees like a pigeon, and yet he'd wedged himself into the broadest, highest crook soon after splashing ashore. The better to spot rescue, he'd figured. Besides, high tides flooded his tiny sanctuary, strong enough to sweep a strong swimmer out to sea, and he'd be damned if he'd die drowning. And so he'd sat there all but immobile, all but blinded by the sun, thirsting despite an ocean full of water lapping at the edges of his miniature haven.

Confined, unable to see, thirsty—hell, he might as well have stayed in his prison aboard the *Island Treasure*. At least there he'd had food and water . . . and so much more.

Analisa. He'd had Analisa.

He was glad, then, that his muscles screeched their protests. He could concentrate on physical pain rather than the heavy agony that weighed against his heart. He worked himself out of the tree and sloshed through the shallow water to the waiting skiff. He collapsed into the small craft behind his rescuer, finding the narrow board bench no more comfortable than his tree branch. The boatman handed him a flask. Michael took a quick swallow. Whiskey. Water would have been better, but whiskey was just what he craved at the moment. He swallowed some more and at once it worked its quick, mind-numbing magic.

He handed back the flask. "Thank you."

The boatman shrugged away his gratitude. "You, British sir—you want to go to Run, eh? Big reward for me."

No, Michael truly wanted to go to Lonthar, to see for himself that Analisa was safe, that the Dutch hadn't exacted punishment upon her for helping him escape. He wanted to gain the measure of the man she'd married, to make sure he was worthy of such a precious treasure, to judge how he'd reacted to learning his new bride was no longer a virgin.

"Run Island," Michael agreed aloud. "Someone there will pay you for my passage."

"Your woman, eh? She be glad I fetch you down from that tree, and pay big reward, eh?"

The aching muscles, the sudden light-headedness brought on by the whiskey, weren't enough to dampen the pain that surged at knowing Analisa now belonged to another. "I don't have a woman."

"Too bad, British sir," the boatman said with a sympathetic grunt. He turned his back to Michael and began plying his oar. The boat shot over the water as if carried by an invisible wave. "Nice to come home to a woman; I like very much. My woman, she sees me and is like a hundred candles light up inside her. Me, too, when I see her, I guess," he called over his shoulder.

The boatman invited Michael's confidence without coming right out and asking, but Michael ignored the hint. He'd spent too many years convincing himself that finding a woman waiting at home was a shackle, and not a pleasure. Analisa had shone for him, her whole being would flare with warmth and welcome when the meager light she carried brought his features into focus for her. At that moment, he envied this smiling brown man and his incandescently welcoming wife with every fiber of his being.

There wasn't even anything special about the boatman to make a woman ignite into life. He had a Bandanese native's sun-bronzed complexion, but some European influence had sharpened his features. His hair was not raven-black, but a dark, deep brown. He must be *sirani*, the half-blooded offspring of a native woman and a white man—Portuguese, British, Dutch—whoever held power over her at the time.

"Are you Sirani?" Michael asked.

"Aye. Three-quarters Banda," he qualified proudly.

"Pirate?"

The boatman looked back over his shoulder again and grinned. Michael grinned back.

The Dutch, determined to control every nutmeg, every clove, that left these islands, had ruthlessly exterminated the native Bandanese, hoping to eradicate their legitimate claims to the land. The few who lived were enslaved, forced to work the plantations they once owned. A tiny number managed to escape altogether and fled to the most isolated islets or the desolate areas beyond *Gunung Api*. They banded with the outcast sirani, filling each other's heads with tales of the riches that should have been theirs.

They exacted their revenge upon those who'd stolen their heritage by sabotaging the spice production wherever they could, and by becoming pirates of the most indolent sort—superior boatsmen plying tiny, swift craft, who hid themselves between the numerous small islands and attacked without notice. Once they crippled a ship, they were nearly impossible to catch, for their small, agile boats quickly vanished into the tortuous waterways where no larger, armed ship could travel.

"You want a woman, British sir? I know ladies, very nice, very lonely."

"No ladies." Michael closed his eyes and shuddered, because he did want one lady, very much. "Too much trouble."

"No trouble, these ladies. Only delight. You come to the door, they smile, very happy to see you. You love once or twice, eh, and they go away. No trouble— you forget all about them."

"It doesn't always work that way."

Michael's response caused the boatman to miss a beat in his rhythmic paddling. The sudden loss of momentum sent water slapping against the side of the skiff. It sprayed over them, and then he shrugged and bent over the oar again.

It was just his luck, Michael figured, that of all the pirates skulking about Banda's ten thousand islands, he'd get rescued by one more interested in selling the services of whores than seeking out Dutch ships to plunder. Just when he least wanted to think about women, he was trapped in a boat with a man bent upon reminding him of all the delights and pleasures a woman offered a man.

Once, he would have eagerly accepted the man's offer. Delight and pleasure were all he'd ever wanted—no more. Not love. He had spent too many years watching his always-pregnant mother pine while his father, a navy seaman, was off serving the king. He'd witnessed the physical and emotional tolls the long separations took upon his father; he'd listened to his younger siblings cry when hunger struck their bellies and he, a boy himself, had not been able to work hard enough or long enough to keep then well fed.

He'd watched, and learned, as his mother's acceptance of his father's long absences shifted into resentment. She accused her husband of selfishness, ignoring the very real fact that they needed his inadequate navy wages to survive. His father's reluctant leave-taking transformed into a bolting for relief from a clinging wife and a brood of demanding, clutching children. It had fallen to Michael to keep the family together. He'd sacrificed his youth to do it—and late at night, when exhaustion weighed down his limbs and pinned him to his bed and forced him to listen to his mother's tears, his brothers' hungry whimpers, he'd dreamed of the day when he might take to the sea himself and escape all those terrifying responsibilities.

Yes, delight and pleasure were enough for him. He'd never asked to have a woman's whole being light from within just because he smiled at her. Not to have her place her full trust in him, to rest her hand against his heart and know she took reassurance from its strong and steady beat. That sort of love stifled a man; it could not possibly be recompense enough to come home every night to see that luminous smile, to feel that touch upon his breast.

So why, all of a sudden, did close-guarded freedom strike him as shallow and empty? What man could ask for more than he'd lived through these past weeks: the pulse-pounding thrill of smuggling nutmegs past the noses of the Dutch; the soul-deadening agony of getting caught; the alternating hope and despair of being held captive, knowing he was to die, praying for a miracle . . . and then finding that miracle. And even these past two days, clinging to a tree for survival, finding himself rescued by a pirate, and knowing the adventures were about to begin anew.

He ought to be savoring those tumultuous moments. Instead, he could think of nothing but Analisa. Wishing that he were the man who would walk through the door and find her smiling for him. Wishing that he were the man who would share her bed that night, who would feel her arms wrap round his shoulders, feel her breath against his hair, feel her quivering beneath him, from deep inside, where she could not control the tremors coursing through her. Such were the pleasures of love.

He had willingly forsworn those pleasures for the freedom of not saddling himself with worry for a woman's welfare, a family's needs. Now he found himself suffering all the worst fates of love, with none of its pleasures and delights.

These realizations made gloomy company during the lengthy trip. When they finally came upon Run Island, the sun had shifted a little lower, casting Run in a sunset haze of orange and gold. The warm colors

softened the island's harsh contours. Run was a survival outpost, nothing more. The small island was Brit-
ain's only toehold in the East Indies. Soldiers posted
there expected—and received—few comforts.

Pirate craft docking at Run was nothing out of the
ordinary, so Michael's arrival caused no commotion.
He spotted a water bucket; scorning the dipper, he
held the bucket aloft and drank deeply, while most of
the water sluiced over his sunburned face. He shook
himself like a dog, the water spraying from his hair.
He promised his rescuer that he would return soon
with something to pay him for his troubles, and then
he stepped into the ramshackle hut that served as the
commanding officer's headquarters.

Captain Richard Ellington was playing cards with
one of his soldiers. He glanced up from his hand and
whitened, staring at Michael as if he'd seen a ghost.

"You can't have gone to Virginia and come back
already," he protested. "You must have abandoned
the mission."

"Not willingly. They caught me in Africa and hauled
me back here on a Dutch ship." Michael made light
of his capture and subsequent incarceration aboard
the *Island Treasure.*

Richard goggled at him. "They caught you with fertile nutmegs? How did you talk your way out of
that one?"

"I didn't. I escaped."

"Nobody escapes the Dutch."

"I had help." Michael turned away, swallowing
against the gorge that rose at recalling how he'd managed that escape.

Richard shook his head, half admiringly, half in disbelief. "You know they'll come here first thing, looking for you."

"I know."

"So you'll leave at once."

"I should." There was no mistaking his hesitation, his reluctance to leave this tenuous sanctuary. Richard looked all but bursting with more questions. Michael waved a forestalling hand and inclined his head infinitesimally toward Richard's gaping card partner. "I owe the fellow outside something for his trouble."

"I have a few Dutch guilders." Richard pulled the coins from the pouch at his waist and gave them to his soldier to deliver to the boatman. Once they were alone, Richard beckoned Michael to sit.

"You can't stay here," Richard said.

"I know. My presence puts all of you in danger."

"I'm not just worried about us—I'm worried about you as well. How long did they hold you before you escaped?"

Michael shook his head. "I don't know—six or seven weeks."

Richard's face creased with sympathy. Without asking he poured Michael some water, as if he knew how many hours Michael had spent thirsting. "You'd break if they caught you again."

"I wouldn't."

"You don't think so? Let me tell you, their fury at you must be boundless. If you fall into their clutches again, they'll show no mercy. Death is certain, but you'll pay the price before you die. I've heard tales of the tortures they employ. You'll betray us before they're done with you."

"Then they'll have learned little of value. Good God, Richard, these islands aren't exactly teeming with Englishmen. They surely suspect I came from here."

"Too true." Richard gave a humorless chuckle. "They'll want to know who supplied you with the fertile nutmeg seed."

"Well, unless they put *you* to the rack, they'll fail there as well. You never entrusted me with our benefactor's name. They can torture me till I die and I won't be able to tell them."

Richard stared at him sadly. "You know something they'll value highly. You can name a traitor in their midst—you can give them the name of the person who helped you escape."

"Never," Michael shot back immediately. "I would never betray her."

"Her?"

"That's a closed subject."

"Very well, but consider this—deep in the night, when the pain grows beyond bearing and some cruel Dutchman is staring you in the eyes and promising you an end to the agony in exchange for one small piece of information, can you trust yourself to withhold her name? I have seen men far more honorable than you break beneath a skilled torturer's hands, heard them babble every secret thought and deed they'd committed since birth."

Richard's warning struck Michael like a blow. There had been times, aboard the *Island Treasure,* when thirst and hunger had so weakened his body and spirit that he would have promised anything for relief. Fortunately for him, Verbeek and his minions had lacked the persistence of true interrogators. He would not be so lucky if he should get caught again.

With self-loathing, he realized Richard spoke the truth. He might betray Analisa. His inclination to save his own hide had already reared its unstoppable head, when he'd compromised her in order to make his escape.

"You're right. I should leave here at once."

Richard nodded. "Good. Your timing couldn't be better—I'm going home at last. We're sending the *Glorious Elizabeth* home in two weeks. They'll search her from stem to stern before they let her pass through Banda Neira Bay, but we'll manage to hide you somewhere in the hold. We've smuggled people out before, behind false walls. It's dark and damned hot, but only temporary."

Michael shuddered, but he quelled the aversion that sprang up at imagining himself back in the suffocating belly of a sailing ship.

But two weeks . . . two weeks before leaving this part of the earth forever . . .

"Is it safe to wait so long?"

"We have little choice. We have already approached them to request permission to pass through Banda Neira Bay, and have placed orders for provisions. They'll suspect something if we try to move up the schedule."

"Maybe I'd better take myself off somewhere, in case they come looking for me."

Richard nodded. "I'll send you over to the Grove."

The Grove was their ambitious name for the tiny secluded island where the British were secretly establishing their own nutmeg groves. The young trees had years to grow before reaching production—providing they survived. If a Dutch patrol happened to spot the saplings, they'd hack every one of them to the ground.

"You can stay with the caretaker," Richard went on. "He has adequate stores—"

Michael interrupted him. He had two weeks. *Two weeks.* "I don't want to go to the grove. I want to go—I *must* go—to Lonthar."

The name hung in the air between them. Lonthar, the largest of the Banda Islands, where Pietr Hootendorf ruled his private plantation and his new bride.

"Lonthar? We're not welcome there under the best of conditions. Lonthar is out of the question. Those crazy *perkeniers* would shoot on sight if we dared send a British vessel to their shores."

"No doubt." Michael took a deep breath. "And her

husband would be at the forefront of the pack. He has more reason that most to wish me dead."

"Her husband—you escaped with the help of a *planter's* wife?" Richard alternated between incredulity and concentration as he worked with the scanty clues Michael had provided. The truth dawned on him with horror, rather than satisfaction. "Good God, it's Hootendorf's new bride. All of Banda's been abuzz, waiting for her arrival. You sweet-talked Hootendorf's new bride into helping you."

"Her name is Analisa." He could not bear hearing her called only *Hootendorf's new bride*. Unfortunately, in saying her name, there sprang up within him a longing so bittersweet that he could no longer hold back from talking about her. At least with Richard he was on fairly safe ground. He had no better friend on Run Island, knew no man he could trust more.

"I sweet-talked her into doing more than helping me. I must see with my own eyes that she hasn't suffered any consequences for . . . helping me."

"You're a dead man," Richard said flatly. "You couldn't have picked a worse enemy. Hootendorf fancies himself the next thing to a king. He's relentless when it comes to getting what he wants."

"All the more reason I have to go there." Sick dread curled in Michael's gut at the thought of Analisa suffering at the hands of a man who could make Richard Ellington blanch at the mere mention of his name. "It's odd, how a man's heart can demand the very thing that might rend it in two. She wants so little from life—to please her husband, to be accepted by the other Dutch women as a respectable matron. I must see with my own eyes that she's well and happy, even if it tears my heart in two to see her so."

Richard shook his head with the firm denial of a senior officer accustomed to having his orders obeyed. "No, Michael. I forbid it." When Michael moved to argue, Richard stood and held up a forestalling hand. "You're not thinking with your head, my friend. I am ordering you to confine yourself to the Grove until the *Glorious Elizabeth* sails."

Michael knew Richard was right, but he couldn't help protesting. "I have to see her once before I go. Just a glimpse." It was a lie; he would never be satisfied with a mere glimpse.

Richard crossed his arms and heaved a sigh. "I've already made my intentions clear, Michael. You'll have to content yourself with catching sight of her from on board ship. Half the islands turn out to watch us take on provisions. Hootendorf's sure to join the throng. You might catch a glimpse of her then. Give me your word on this, or I'll clap you in irons myself."

"No irons." The very notion set the scabs round his ankles and wrists to throbbing. But . . .

Two weeks, and *maybe* he'd catch a glimpse of her through a tiny peephole poked in the side of a ship. He wanted to shout against the enforced eternity of waiting, against being handed such a minuscule chance. "I must see her."

"Damn it all, Rowland, you sound like a man in love. I don't like it."

"Nor do I." Sweat sprang to Michael's brow, but the earth didn't collapse, the sky didn't fall in. He loved Analisa. Refusing to say so aloud did not shield him from all the heartache that came from being separated from her.

"I'll not hide on board ship, Richard. I'll wear my old uniform and take my place as one of your officers. I'll go ashore with you and the rest of the crew. I'll be standing at attention and looking them straight in the eye while they search the ship."

"Blast you, Rowland—that does make a bizarre kind of sense." Richard began pacing, muttering the advantages to Michael's suggestion. "They'll be expecting us to hide you aboard ship. With luck, they'll never suspect that one of my officers is really an escaped smuggler."

Michael held his breath while Richard rubbed his chin, weighing the consequences. His heart sank when Richard shook his head. "No. It's too risky. If you're recognized in full regalia, then they'll have all the proof they need to declare war against us and drive us off of Run."

"The captain who held me prisoner meant to sail for Amboina at once. The ship and crew will be long gone before we sail into Banda Neira Bay. There will be only one person on all the Bandas who could recognize me. She would not betray me."

"You're putting your trust in a woman?' Richard's lip curled in a sneer. "What happened to the Michael Rowland who left here three months ago, swearing no woman was trustworthy or worth risking his life for?"

"He's still here." Michael thumped his chest, though his conscience called him a liar. "I merely feel . . . an obligation. The Dutch would never expect me to show up right on their doorstep. They'll be looking for a wild, filthy escaped smuggler, not a well-trimmed and immaculate British officer. I won't be caught."

Richard hesitated, and Michael knew he could get his way with but the slightest edge weighing the balance in his favor. "If they recognize me, Richard, shoot me at once. It will resolve your dilemma, and as God is my witness, I don't think I could endure being captured again. I would rather die than risk betraying her."

Richard remained silent for a very long time, so long that Michael feared he might deny him after all. But at last his friend and officer shook his head in defeat. "It's your neck, not mine. Now get out of here."

But just as Michael reached the door, Richard

stopped him. "She must be a remarkable woman, Rowland."

"Aye," said Michael. "That she is."

Two weeks of idleness left Analisa ready to scream. She had nothing—nothing—to do. The household hummed along quite efficiently, powered by a vast army of slaves and servants, all following the procedures developed long ago by the first mevrouw.

It was the first mevrouw who still ran the house and ruled Pietr's heart. Portraits of Hilde Hootendorf hung in each room, and the servants scurried in fright when in range of Hilde's never-blinking stare. No task was left undone, no matter left unattended. Analisa felt like a long-term guest, taking meals and conversing with Pietr while his wistful attention rested upon the portrait of his lost pink-and-blond Dutch beauty.

Only at night, in the dark, did Analisa escape Hilde's eternally watching eye.

In the dark, alone, with her husband's absence proving his disinterest, she felt no guilt over allowing her mind to dwell on thoughts of Michael Rowland. She worried about whether he'd survived. If he'd made it to Run Island and his friends had truly been able to smuggle him out of the area. She did not know what would be worse—to never be certain of what had happened to him, or to know that he had made good on his escape and was even now sailing toward his beloved Virginia, where a new life awaited him, a life that would never include her.

She wondered if Michael ever thought of her, if his nights were plagued with memories so vivid that his body remembered every touch, every stroke, every whisper.

She longed for a child, and not just to evade Pietr's return to her bed. If she bore a child now, there would be a chance it had been conceived when her body had been alive and welcoming, when Michael's embrace had made her heart sing. Strange, how she could recall each exquisite moment spent in Michael's arms, how deep in her soul she still felt she belonged to him and him alone, as though Pietr's possession had never occurred. She could not help nurturing the hope that nothing had happened on her nightmarish wedding night.

But surely Pietr would not have abandoned her bed without consummating the marriage. He would not have regretted losing control, or kept himself celibate to await the results of a coupling that her body denied having experienced. In the absence of any physical proof that a mating had occurred, she racked her mind for other clues. What had he said? *You have revealed your most intimate secrets to me, Analisa.* Yes, a man who'd made himself free with a woman's body might speak thus—but so might a man who'd listened to his inebriated new wife babble about taking a vigorous lover mere days before solemnizing her wedding vows. Pietr had paid such close attention to everything she'd said that night, shrewdly interpreting her most evasive comments. Since then, he'd monopolized the mealtime conversations, as if he'd already decided that she would have nothing of interest to say to him.

Except for one morning, earlier in the week. She'd taken breakfast with him as usual, and said something that amused him into an unfamiliar chuckle. He'd looked at her, then, really looked at her. She'd stood in a wash of bright sunlight streaming through a window, a light so bright that she knew it blinded him to everything else in the room save for the sight of her. The first mevrouw's portrait would have been invisible behind the glare. Pietr had stared at Analisa with the stunned pleasure of a man who'd taken a taste of a strange food and found it unexpectedly quite to his liking.

Since that morning, she'd caught his gaze on her more often than before, caught him staring at her, looking so bewildered and . . . and *hungry* that she wondered what had wrought the change. But she didn't care enough to ask.

Pietr worked very hard for a man in such an important position, which probably accounted for his startling physical condition. He seemed to enjoy having her listen to his plans for his plantation, and so she paid close attention while he described his activities, while he outlined the plans he had to expand the business for his sons. During this past week, he'd taken to leaving a little later in the morning; he arrived home for dinner a little earlier. Analisa supposed that she ought to feel grateful that her husband was altering his schedule so she need not spend so many hours alone, but she could not work up any enthusiasm for greeting him. She felt just as lonely—perhaps even more lonely—when Pietr sat there staring at her breasts, her waist, her hips, than when she was by herself, dreaming of Michael.

She wrote to her mother every day, compiling a collection of brief paragraphs remarking on her new home, the plantation, the weather. She kept her comments cheerful and vague, for she knew she lacked the skill to convey how different the reality was from what they taught their young charges to expect. Her urge to confess her doubts, her heartache, was tempered by knowing Pietr read these daily missives. She missed her mother greatly as she chose her careful phrases. She ached for Britta's company, for her hard-won wisdom, and sometimes did not think she could endure waiting eighteen months or more for an answer to her letters.

"What did she do all day?" Analisa finally asked Tali, after two weeks had passed and she thought she might rather join the slaves at flushing doves from the nutmeg trees than spend another indolent day in the mansion.

"What did who do, mevrouw?"

"Hilde. The first mevrouw. It couldn't have taken her twenty years to organize the household and develop that fourteen-day menu plan."

"Ah." Tali looked uncomfortable. "She sewed."

"Sewed?" Sewing was not one of Analisa's favorite chores, but it might help pass the time. "Pietr told me we have staff who tend to the sewing and mending."

"Yes. First mevrouw, she did Dutchwoman's sewing."

"Dutchwoman's sewing?"

"I will show you. We must get the key from Maru."

Maru objected until Analisa pointed out that she, and not Maru, was mistress of this house and had the right to visit any room she pleased. With great reluctance, Maru led Analisa and Tali down a dim hallway, to a door that had been locked every time Analisa had explored that area of the house.

Maru inched open the door and stepped back with a worried scowl. Analisa peeked past the doorframe, and could not understand Maru's agitation. It was a small room in comparison to those in the rest of the house, no more than twelve feet square. Shelves lined the walls from floor to ceiling, and piled upon the shelves were stacks of folded cloth.

They had all been white at sometime, Analisa realized, but the years had discolored them to varying degrees. Those piled closest to the door had a yellow cast, hinting that they'd been folded, stacked, and left untouched for many years. The yellow tinge paled until those stacked farthest away were as pure white as clouds.

"The first mevrouw's sewing." Tali gestured toward the stacks.

Analisa pulled one yellowed cloth from the bottom

of the closest stack and let it tumble open. A cascade of vibrant color seemed to explode from the cloth as it unfurled against her, as though Hilde Hootendorf had captured a wildflower garden in silken thread.

"It's beautiful," Analisa whispered. "I have never seen such skillful embroidery." She thought of the many portraits of Hilde displayed throughout the house and wondered why Pietr had not framed some of these exquisite handiworks to remind him of his beloved wife's skills. "Why does Pietr not display some of this?"

"There is too much," Maru said with an eloquent shrug of her shoulder. "Now, let us close the room, mevrouw."

"Not just yet." Analisa stepped farther into the room. A glance around the shelves proved the simple truth of Maru's statement. The sheer number of folded cloths was overwhelming. She carefully refolded the one she'd examined and went to the farthest stack, selecting the folded cloth at the top. Hilde's last work. A needlewoman of such vast talents could only have improved over the years.

Analisa shook the white cloth open, and almost dropped it.

It was impossible to determine what pattern Hilde had been attempting to create. The stitches hopped aimlessly over the cloth, like bird tracks against snow. Holes pocked the finely woven fabric, holes that came from stabbing a needle repeatedly in the same place, and small brownish red dots sprayed outward from those holes.

A horrible suffocation gripped Analisa's chest. Agony seemed to bleed from that desperate needlework into her hands.

"Was the first mevrouw very ill when she did this?" Analisa whispered.

"No, the first mevrouw was never sick. Sometimes

she very angry. Sometimes she very sad. Sometimes she very, very tired of Dutchwoman's sewing and nothing else."

"She did nothing else?"

"Mynheer would not permit it. It was for her as it is for you, mevrouw. Mynheer says wife's duty is for children. Mynheer says she sews while she waits for child."

Analisa's tepid antagonism toward the woman who had preceded her vanished like fog beneath the morning sun. She could so easily imagine the young, beautiful Hilde coming to this home as a new bride, filled with dreams and enthusiasm, developing a working schedule and fourteen-day menu for her husband. Waiting, month after endless month, for her womb to quicken, with nothing left to her except this endless, pointless embroidery, until she was so blinded by heartache and despair that she couldn't control the threads, that she blindly stabbed her needle into the cloth, into her own flesh, regretting her wasted life.

Pietr found them. His lips were tight, whitened with rage, when he saw what Analisa held.

"You have no need to visit this room again," he grated hoarsely.

"No. I won't." Analisa carefully folded the hideous parody of embroidery and placed it reverently atop its stack. She stepped into the hallway and waited while her husband locked the door. She pasted a pleasant smile upon her face and tried to appear amiable, pretending it was the most common thing in the world to be banished from a room in her own home.

"You are home early, Pietr."

"The British are sailing into port at Banda Neira to take on provisions and pass inspection before they can traverse the bay. It is always an entertaining sight. I had thought to take you there, to watch, and perhaps meet some of our fellow planters under less trying circumstances than a formal gathering, but now I do not know. Perhaps you had best remain here in seclusion."

He wanted to punish her for her explorations, she could tell. A good wife would bow her head and meekly accept his decree, but her spirit would not permit it. It raged anew—she'd done nothing wrong! And she was so bored! A trip to Banda Neira would relieve some of the tedium. . . .

No. She had to be honest with herself. She might hear news of Michael on Banda Neira, especially if the British were landing. The past endless weeks dropped away and it was as though she had just moments ago heard Michael's rich-timbered voice saying her name, heard his husky whispers against her ear. Longing welled within her. Michael was British. She would be seeing men who dressed as Michael dressed. Men who spoke as Michael spoke. One of the British soldiers might know Michael. One of them might have heard from him, might have learned whether he'd survived his escape and was now safely on his way to his beloved Virginia Colony.

Pietr's ill-concealed hostility had discouraged her from attempting any display of affection, but her desperation was so great that she could not still her hand when it darted out and rested upon his forearm, just below the elbow joint. She knew he hated any show of emotion, but she could not keep her voice from quivering her need, could not keep the longing from her features.

"Please, Pietr. It would please me greatly to go to Banda Neira."

He meant to refuse. She could tell by the way his lips tightened and his jaw raised fractionally. But then his eyes fell to where her hand rested against his arm, and she felt a tremor course through him. He could not seem to tear his gaze away from the sight of her flesh touching his, and she realized that she had never before willingly touched him for any reason.

"Very well," he grated hoarsely, his eyes riveted upon her flesh against his. "If it would please you, we shall go."

14

~

Pietr dispatched a servant at once to make arrangements for their arrival on Banda Neira, and then Analisa proceeded to make herself ready for this venture into transplanted Dutch society.

She had been dreading the inevitable introductions. She knew what to expect: avid eyes watching her, instantly assessing her clothes, her movements, her appearance. These gleanings would be balanced against whatever rumors swirled about her, whether spread by Captain Verbeek or Pietr's own terse remarks. She would soon be meeting the people who would be her friends, her social peers, for the rest of her life, and they would approach her with opinions fully formed, while she had no knowledge of them at all. Not even Pietr's promise of a carnivallike atmosphere, or her excitement over having something to do, outweighed her trepidation.

Tali helped her dress in one of her new gowns, one Pietr had ordered without consulting her. She could not fault his choice. It was cut along classic Dutch lines and enveloped her from toes to chin, and came with a headcloth in matching color. Despite its bulk, the native fabric wasn't nearly as stifling as her old woolen gown had been. Pietr's choice of color was remarkably flattering—it was a pale coral that suited her coloring quite well. He must have happened upon the color by chance. To have chosen it deliberately, with her hair and eyes and skin tone in mind, would have required a greater appreciation for her looks than he had ever shown.

When she presented herself, ready to leave, Pietr stared at her for quite a long time, until she grew uncomfortable with the way his gaze rested on her feminine parts.

"You will not shame me before my colleagues," he eventually said with an approving nod, and then they embarked upon a *prahu* for the short journey to Banda Neira.

He talked throughout the entire thirty-minute trip, telling her the names of people she might expect to meet.

"I'm dreadful at remembering names, Pietr," she murmured.

"Your memory might not be so dreadful if you focused your attention on me, where it belongs, rather than bouncing about like a half-trained puppy. Anyone chancing to see you would think you've already grown bored with my company."

His reprimand startled her. She didn't think he cared much about whether she paid attention to him or not, but as she studied him covertly, she realized he was looking rather disgruntled. She sent him a tentative smile, which only made him frown, and she sighed inwardly. Married two weeks, and this husband of hers was growing less understandable rather than more.

Banda Neira reached out to welcome them while they were still hundreds of yards from shore. The scent of spices, wafting from the slatted warehouses, perfumed every breath. The peal of children singing, the ping of tiny cymbals, the thump of leather drums reverberated through the air.

The servant Pietr had sent on ahead stood at the edge of the crowd massed at the shore. He craned his neck, watching for them. Their oarsmen called out greetings and the servant ran to meet them while motioning toward another fellow, who hitched up the rails of a large, well-sprung cart over his shoulder and raced after the servant. The cartman joined in to help Pietr and Analisa disembark from their *prahu,* and then he gestured toward his cart. He scurried backward, bowing to them repeatedly as he urged them to follow.

"We are to ride in this?" Analisa asked when Pietr stopped at the cart.

"Only the lower classes walk on Banda Neira. Not the Hootendorfs."

The cart hauler looked so slim and slight standing there between the shafts of his big-wheeled cart. He did not look capable of pulling the cart once it was laden with her weight and Pietr's. "What of the carriage you had shipped in from Amsterdam? I saw it on board ship."

"All in good time, Analisa. Now, hop aboard."

She hesitated.

"Analisa." Pietr spoke her name with such deadly precision that she knew her brief pause had annoyed him. She meekly climbed aboard, and was at once proved a softhearted fool. The cartman heaved the poles against his hips and started running easily, plunging them deep into the crowds surging toward the docks. She soon realized that all those afoot had sun-browned or oriental features, while everyone being pulled in carts similar to theirs was white. Fellow Dutch men and women. Her new neighbors.

"I had not realized there would be such a diversity of people here," she remarked to postpone the moment when she must concentrate on her own countrymen. "I thought only Dutch and Bandanese lived here."

"There are few native Bandanese left, and they are hopeless when it comes to work outside the nutmeg groves. They're content to live the most indolent lives—they claim one coconut tree can support a family of four for a year and they will not bestir themselves to do more. So we import workers from many lands. The Chinese make the best house servants, and Japanese the best mercenaries."

"Mercenaries? Why on earth would you require mercenaries?"

He chose to ignore her question. He jutted his chin toward a small gathering of people surrounding a pole driven deep into the dirt, and when he spoke, his voice was heavy with sympathy. "There's a poor Chinese fellow now."

Poor Chinese *fellow*? It looked to Analisa as if the gentleman in question was very much in charge of his small gathering. With incomprehensible shouts and strong hand motions, he ordered two younger men to tie a weeping, straining woman to the pole.

"What has she done to deserve such treatment?" Analisa asked.

"Nothing. He most likely is ready to return to his homeland." At Analisa's questioning look, Pietr continued. "The Chinese workers take island wives. When they return to their homeland, they have no need of those wives or any female children they might have borne them. They take only their sons back to China with them."

The cruelty rocked her. So did the shaking of her long-held beliefs. Marriage was supposed to be a haven, a shelter where a woman could depend upon her husband, not fear that he might casually abandon her and steal her children away from her. And yet all the Dutch, even Pietr, seemed quite accepting of such barbarous behavior.

"He's tying her to that pole for her own good. In this way, she can watch as her husband and sons leave, but she will be unable to hurl herself into the water. She would, you know. These island women are regrettably impulsive. Not so long ago, one man failed to restrain his wife. She plunged into the sea to swim after her husband and four sons. Her body washed ashore a few days later."

All around them, an air of festivity prevailed. People laughed and called to one another. Children raced through the throngs, their high-pitched squeals conveying their excitement. Groups of young girls crowded the shore, waving out to sea where a large vessel could be seen disgorging men into small *prahus*. Analisa squinted a little to make out the name of the ship: *Glorious Elizabeth*. Such an English name . . . it could only be an English ship. Her pulse quickened.

The sweet music and dancing that had heralded the *Island Treasure*'s arrival floated out to greet this new-coming ship, music created by beautiful young girls who might one day find themselves tied to a pole, weeping their anguish while the man they loved, the children they loved, sailed far away, never to return. Unconsciously, Analisa's hand strayed to splay protectively over her belly. If she ever bore a child . . . when she bore a child . . . she could not bear to have it torn from her arms.

Pietr noticed where her hand rested and a faint smile curled his lip. "You would be surprised to know what even the proudest man would do for sons," he said.

She wondered if he meant it as a warning, as a reminder of how thoroughly under his control she was. As all women were. It seemed it didn't matter whether one lived in the center of Dutch civilization, or halfway around the world on scented islands lush with tropical pleasures, a woman's life was a man's to control.

Their cart pulled up next to a canvas-shrouded bulk. A servant stepped forward and pulled the canvas free, revealing Pietr's carriage. A quick look confirmed that it was the only such conveyance along the waterfront. "We will sit within, Analisa," Pietr said, smug satisfaction oozing from him.

Analisa felt all eyes upon them as they changed vehicles. Pietr handed her into the carriage; she could see the way his eyes shifted to learn whether others noticed the fine conveyance. He didn't seem to think it the least bit odd that they would sit within a stifling hot, enclosed carriage, with no horses between the shafts, with no space for such a large vehicle to move about. Michael had called a carriage for the Bandas an abomination. Now she understood why.

The first *prahus* carrying the British sailors from their ship hit the shore. Dockworkers ran to meet them, catching the ropes thrown to them by those in the small boats and hauling the boats ashore so those within could step out onto solid earth rather than slog through the shallow water.

Nobody but Analisa seemed affected by the continued anguish pouring from the Chinese man's wife. Nobody else's eyes seemed to be struggling against sympathetic, and empathetic, tears. Everyone strained to watch the Englishmen disembarking from the *prahus* onto shore. A good two dozen of them made up this official delegation, ranging from minor shipboard officers to British commanders in full regalia.

With the tied woman's sobs echoing in her ears, Analisa stared hungrily at the Englishmen, wishing she might get closer, wishing she weren't enclosed by the carriage's walls, for then she might be able to hear them speak. She leaned forward, poking her head through the window, wishing so hard that she might hear something, anything, about Michael. An involuntary, wistful sigh escaped her.

At once, Pietr's hand clamped around her elbow like a vise.

"You will conduct yourself properly, madam," he ordered tersely.

She blinked at him in bewilderment. "But I didn't do—"

"You are gazing at those British swine as if they were saviors come to rescue you," he spat. " 'Tis bad enough that the islands are abuzz with rumors of your weakness regarding that smuggler. I will not tolerate you consorting with these men."

His words were like hammer blows. While she'd been idling away the time at the plantation, all of Dutch society on the islands had been speculating upon her true role in Michael's escape. And Pietr had not told her anything about it, had kept her secluded—so she might rest and regain her strength, he'd said, never hinting that his new wife was the subject of whispers and innuendo.

She was aware now as she hadn't been before of how the numerous man-drawn carts were all clustered near one end of the bustling waterfront while their carriage sat in solitary splendor. How could she not have noticed that nobody approached, demanding an introduction to the new Mevrouw Hootendorf? If all the Dutch women were even a quarter as bored as she was, the arrival of a new white woman should have sparked numerous invitations, as well as dozens of courteous welcoming calls. She'd been so immured in her sadness over losing Michael, so absorbed in nursing her aching heart, that she'd been oblivious to how thoroughly ostracized she'd been.

She'd come halfway around the world to escape ostracism. She'd married a man she could never love, and consigned herself to spending the rest of her life far away from her mother and everything familiar, all for the sake of starting fresh. It was worse here than it ever had been in Holland. At least there she'd had her position with the school, she'd had her work, she'd had some little bit of hope that one day something unexpectedly wonderful might happen to give meaning to her barren, pointless existence.

Something wonderful *had* happened—she had found Michael. Unfortunately, she had found him at the worst possible time, under the worst possible circumstances.

Michael had wanted her, Analisa Vandermann, without caring a whit about her history or worrying about the opinions others held of her. Nobody had ever wanted her like that; nobody ever would again. She missed him with a blinding, grinding ache that threatened to kill her just then.

The throng of incoming British approached them. Her wounded spirit, seeking a refuge, searched the men as they came near. She fancied that one tall officer shared Michael's height. One broad-shouldered fellow reminded her of his strength. Another walked with an easy-limbed grace, the way she'd always imagined Michael might walk, if she'd ever been able to watch him move about unhampered by chains. One man hovered near the rear, his head bent as he fiddled with a piece of rope. His hair gleamed as blue-black as Michael's had in the sunshine on that first day she'd seen him hauled aboard as a prisoner.

And then the man looked up. His eyes, the color of cool ale on a hot day, met hers across the intervening distance.

He smiled at her.

She was suddenly glad of the death grip Pietr had upon her poor elbow, for if he had not been holding her upright she might have melted into a puddle of gibbering mush when that British sailor smiled at her.

And then he winked.

Michael.

Impossible.

It had been more than two weeks since Michael's escape. By now he was either dead or safely away, hundreds of miles away, well out of the reach of Dutch justice—he couldn't have survived his plunge into the sea only to be risking his life to come here, where Fort Belgica loomed ominously in the background and a full battalion of well-armed Dutch soldiers massed in front of it, watching the British with hostile, suspicious eyes.

She sat paralyzed, barely breathing. She reminded herself of all the scathing mockeries she had heard over the years about her British father, how British seamen were known rogues. No doubt they spent half their days smiling, winking at women, risking their lives. Michael Rowland wasn't the only one who might do such a thing. But her body would not accede to the greater power of her mind. Her body thrummed with awareness, her pulse raced and her skin tingled, demanding she move closer to the stranger. Something of her distress must have communicated itself to Pietr, for he loosened his hold on her and bent over with true concern.

"Analisa? What is it—is the heat too overpowering?"

She wanted to answer her husband, reassure him that she was fine, but she feared opening her mouth would cause her teeth to chatter, and she wasn't at all sure that she could form a coherent sentence.

She simply shook her head and did her best to avert her eyes from the man who held her in thrall, but she could not tear her gaze away from Michael Rowland as he strode, tall and strong and free, straight into the shadow of the Dutch stronghold.

It was all Michael could do to keep his place among the British officers. Every muscle in his body quivered with the need to race to Analisa and snatch her away from that grim, possessive bastard who hovered over her like a hawk standing guard over a recent kill.

The man was besotted with her, any fool could see that. Michael had been searching the crowd ever since the *Glorious Elizabeth* had drawn close to shore, and he'd spotted Analisa long before she'd seen him. Her husband—and with that proprietary air he could be no other—couldn't keep his eyes from her. All the while she'd been staring about with the wide-eyed delight of a child taken on its first trip to a circus, Hootendorf had been drinking in the sight of his lovely bride looking so cool and pretty beneath the hot East Indian sun. And then he'd stuffed her into that hideous, useless monstrosity of a carriage, where nobody but he could even look at her.

But she was able to look out, through the large window, and Michael was able to see inside. He knew it the moment she saw him. Her glance locked with his with the explosive effect of fire igniting gunpowder. Unfortunately, her husband had noticed it, too, and now he sat there glowering unhappily from Analisa toward the melee of men. Michael supposed that the only good fortune was that Pietr could not possibly know which of them had so captivated his bride's interest. With great reluctance, and even greater effort, he forced himself to look away from her and concentrate instead on melting into the crowd unnoticed while the ship's officers settled their tiresome business.

Well, he had accomplished what he had set out to do—he had proven to himself that she had survived her ordeal. She was obviously being cosseted by a man who doted on her. He should return to the ship with all speed and hide himself belowdecks until they sailed back out onto the open sea.

Instead, he made the fatal mistake of looking at Analisa again, and this time Pietr Hootendorf intercepted the gaze.

The stiff, proper Dutchman stiffened and postured even more, wrapping his arm around Analisa, who sat still as a doll. There was a faint sneer to Hootendorf's expression, as if to tell Michael without words that this woman belonged to him and he would tolerate no interference.

Not that Michael could interfere. Not that Hootendorf could possibly know his identity, nor—if Analisa had kept her secrets—could the Dutchman know how much Michael had stolen from him. But there was unmistakable challenge in Hootendorf's stance, an angry male animal marking its territory, and threatening anyone who dared trespass with punishment beyond measure.

Feeling like the worst sort of coward, Michael looked away.

He and his fellow soldiers stood for an interminable time while Richard and his senior officers parlayed with the Dutch officials. The wait was made unbearable by the heat and the difficulty of keeping his eyes from wandering back to the only thing he wanted to see—Analisa. At long last, the delegation of Dutch officers dispersed. Some stalked back to the fort, their swords clanking at their sides. Others went to a wherry and struck out for the *Glorious Elizabeth*. The British officers, their faces red from the heat and from unmistakable anger, erupted with rage once the Dutch were out of earshot.

"They won't let us pass through the bay for three days," Richard announced.

The men surrounding Michael exploded with denials. He stood silent and ramrod still, paralyzed with delight. Three days! He might see her again and again.

"Why can't we go on, sir?" whined a deckhand.

"That bloody damned deGroot is visiting from Java. He wants to report back to the Company firsthand on how Governor Hoon keeps us under control."

This roused another outburst of male outrage. "We ain't under no Dutch control! Show 'em, Captain—just sail on out, swift as you please. They'll not catch our old *Glory Bess.*"

Richard, the voice of reason, tried to calm men who yearned for home. "They won't revictual us until after deGroot satisfies his curiosity and makes his bloody damned report."

"Sodding bastards! They know we don't produce enough food on Run Island to revictual a ship."

"Pirates would sell us enough food to reach Africa. We don't need these damned spice men."

"They'd run us down at sea. Without a safe conduct from them, we'd be fair game in Dutch-controlled waters. No, we're trapped here for another three days." Richard paused, and then offered them a treat. "They've invited us all to the fancy dress ball that Hoon's throwing in deGroot's honor."

"Fancy dress ball? You mean music, Captain? Dancing and women?"

"Aye."

The sailors' grumbles diminished somewhat. "I guess they expect us to just show up like a lot of trained monkeys," complained one halfheartedly. Excitement vibrated from them as they plodded over to their small boats and stood talking in small groups, waiting for permission to return to the *Glorious Elizabeth.*

Richard edged nearer to Michael, and spoke from the side of his mouth. "Well, have you satisfied your curiosity?"

"Aye."

'Governor Hoon asked about you right off, and of course I denied having seen or heard from you in months. I also assured him that we British would never harbor a renegade officer who'd turned pirate against our good Dutch friends."

"Did he believe you?"

Richard's smile flashed. "Not a word. I suspect he fabricated this three-day delay to give his soldiers time to thoroughly search the ship and Run, looking for you while you shade yourself in his fort's shadow. I hate to admit it, but this ridiculous plan of yours succeeded. We'll reboard once they give us the all-clear, and then you are not to leave the ship again under any circumstances."

Only a fool would ignore an order that had been issued with the best intentions. Only a fool—or a man in love.

"Nay, Richard. We've been invited to a party. I mean to attend."

"Are you insane? I can see Hootendorf and his wife right now. You got that glimpse you claimed you wanted. Now, use your head, man!"

The necessity of speaking in whispers meant their voices did not carry, but Michael knew that if anyone chanced to glance their way, Richard's red-faced exasperation would wave a warning flag.

"It's not enough. She looks pale, as if she's not feeling well."

"Perhaps you did old Hootendorf a favor and got her breeding. I know a man or two who will collect on hefty bets if that comes about."

"What do you mean?"

"Hell, man, don't take offense. I mean no insult to your lady. These pious Dutchmen take any native girl they fancy, scattering half-breeds throughout these islands. None of them carries Hootendorf's features, though. There was a little whore who visited us on Run a while back who claimed Hootendorf was impotent. Can't credit that, not with him going to all that trouble over a wife, but you have to admit it's strange, considering how his first wife never gave him a child."

Richard's casual comments struck Michael like a hammer blow to the gut. Analisa, with child . . . and with every likelihood that that child had been sired by *him*.

He'd deliberately squelched any worries that he might have impregnated her, telling himself that the few times they'd spent together hadn't been enough, that they'd both been weakened by months at sea.

She might be carrying his child.

The idea filled him with a quiet joy unlike anything he'd ever known. All of his disavowals of love had led to naught. How had he ever thought himself capable of running off, leaving so much responsibility behind, without it forever haunting him? The answer was simple enough—he'd never found himself in love before. All those people he'd despised for succumbing to love's lure had known the truth—the joys far outweighed the sacrifice. And no matter that he'd deliberately avoided acknowledging his love out loud, for love had wrapped gentle fingers round his heart, and the only way to dislodge them was to die.

Michael joined the men waiting at the boats. To his left, Analisa sat with her husband, motionless, and to his right, the *Glorious Elizabeth* rode the waves, offering safety and sanctuary to any man wise enough to stay within her walls.

Analisa would certainly attend the ball. He would be there, too.

By the time they'd returned to Lonthar, and Analisa had changed gowns and presented herself for dinner, she had convinced herself that the man she'd seen on

Banda Neira could not possibly have been Michael Rowland.

The wild surge of emotions that had pounded through her, only to be tamped down, had left her feeling listless. It came home in full force that she would never, ever see him again. She'd merely caught herself acting like some of the pathetic old people who'd been the object of whispers back in Amsterdam, men and women whose spouses or loved ones had died. They studied every passing face in the futile hope that a mistake had been made, that the one they'd lost wasn't truly gone and would come striding down the street one day, bold as you please, smiling from ear to ear as if they'd played a huge joke on the world.

Smiling . . . and winking. She swallowed against the tightness in her throat.

"I am surprised that our little journey has left you so exhausted, Analisa," Pietr said, breaking into her thoughts.

"I . . . I've become so accustomed to the quiet and cooling breezes here at home that the crowded dock was somewhat overwhelming."

She gave herself a mental shake. On the one hand, she'd woven more lies of late than she had in her entire life, and on the other, they were weak, half-hearted things. She would have to either come up with better excuses than the weather for her continued list-lessness, or she'd better overcome that listlessness al-together. She could not spend the rest of her days pining over what was essentially a shipboard romance. It wasn't fair to Pietr; it wasn't fair to herself.

"I thought there might be another reason for your lethargy," said Pietr.

She stiffened, wondering if she'd somehow betrayed her yearning for another man.

"You have been here for almost three weeks now,

and your maid tells me you have not bled." Pietr continued selecting his *rijsttafel* items calmly, as if discussing a woman's most intimate functions were a suitable topic of conversation at the dinner table. "Tell me, when did you experience your last courses aboard ship?"

Astonishment held her silent. For so many nights she had prayed she carried a child, and yet she had never bothered to add up the days.

"I . . . I don't remember," she equivocated, though her brain worked frantically. Considering what a dreary and predictable business it was, especially on board ship, she remembered exactly when she'd endured her courses: three weeks before landing at Banda Neira. In all, then, almost six weeks had passed since her last flux, and she had never in her life missed it by more than a day.

She might be with child. At that very moment, Michael Rowland's child might be growing in her womb.

Of course, she had to acknowledge the possibility that it could be Pietr Hootendorf's child. One stubborn part of her still clung to the hope that Pietr had never consummated their marriage, but the logical part of her mind had to dismiss that hope. Pietr would not be so obviously pleased by the prospect of her pregnancy if he had not sown his own seed within her. But, oh, dear God, there was definitely the possibility that she carried Michael's child! Such joy surged through her that she lowered her fork to the table lest she drop it in her excitement.

She ought to admit the truth to Pietr at once, and yet something inside compelled her to silence. She wanted a few moments, a little while, to nurture this wondrous possibility, to revel in the thought that she might bear the child of the man she loved. Ever after, she would have this child as a reminder of the passion and happiness that had been hers for such a very brief time.

She understood then why her mother had struggled so hard to keep her babe at her side, to raise her illegitimate daughter herself rather than hide her mistake and go on with her life. Analisa wished she could do that—she wished she could run away with her black-haired, golden-eyed baby. Every minute spent watching it grow would be a delight, knowing Michael had fathered her child.

Unbidden came the memory of the Chinese man tying his native woman to the pole so she could not swim after her children.

She'd forgotten for a moment all about Pietr and his obsession for a son.

No matter who actually sired her child, Pietr Hootendorf would be its acknowledged father, in name and in the eyes of the law.

"I see this possibility does not fill you with delight as it does me," Pietr commented. "Today, at the bay, you seemed truly happy for a moment, and I hoped you might be settling in here." His glance strayed over her shoulder to the portrait of Hilde, and Analisa knew how he must be regretting that it had not been his beloved first wife who sat across from him, presenting him with such a possibility.

The tiny spark of independence that had always dwelled within her flared, as did a glimmer of understanding. She'd learned today that she would always search every face in the hope she might see Michael again. She knew she would always love him, no matter that her life went on in this dull, unsatisfying way. Pietr's attitude toward her was understandable under those terms. He had merely been a little wiser than she, knowing from the beginning that they would never find love with each other. "I know you could never care about me, or any child I give you, as strongly as if it were Hilde who bore your first child."

"You cannot possibly understand how my devotion to Hilde differs from my feelings for you." This innocuous admission for some reason left him agitated. He pushed away his dinner plate and whirled around in his chair, as if he could not bear the sight of Analisa sitting where Hilde should be, with Analisa alive and speaking and possibly pregnant while his first wife's presence was reduced to fading paints against age-cracked canvas. He pressed his hand against his forehead and quivered. "I do not understand my feelings very well myself."

He left her. After a moment she, too, pushed her meal away untasted.

Maru was brushing her hair that night and had not yet bound it into its usual nighttime crown of braids when Pietr came to her room.

"Go," he said, flicking his hand at Maru. Tali appeared at the door at once, ready to turn the covers and draw the drapes. He motioned her away as well.

Analisa had not yet buttoned her nightgown completely and it gapped open to her breasts. She clutched the garment together, conscious of the way her well-brushed hair floated around her, over her shoulders and down her back to her waist. Pietr had never seen her in such disarray, and it seemed from the way he closed his eyes and shuddered that he found her loose appearance somewhat distasteful.

She felt like shuddering away from him as well. If she were truly pregnant, she had fulfilled her duties in that regard. She'd been anxiously anticipating a few moments alone, to merely sit with her fingers pressed to her womb, dreaming of carrying Michael's child.

"I did not think you would come to me again," she whispered. "Not until I provided . . . proof . . . that I am not with child."

"I meant only to look in and ask whether you have reckoned the days yet."

"No, I—" Guilt smote her over her continuing reluctance to share her conviction with him. Had it been Michael standing across from her, her joy would have been unbounded.

"I want . . ." Pietr's hand twitched, as if he ached to reach out toward her but held himself back by force of will alone. He cleared his throat. "I hope you have not been disobeying my orders by leaving your hair unbound at night. I will not be able to tolerate the sight of it when the time comes to resume my duty."

His reminder of the power he held over her sent revulsion coursing through her. "Maru was just ready to rebraid my hair when you entered the room."

This time his hand did move, in a long stroking motion against the air, an unconscious imitation of a man who enjoyed twining a woman's hair through his fingers. The motion was at odds with the scowl that overtook his features. "I will send her back to tend to it at once."

It seemed she'd scarcely fallen into an exhausted sleep when the rising sun woke her. The muted sound of meal preparation floated up from the kitchens at the rear of the house. She wondered at her maids' continued absence—Pietr expected Analisa's presence at breakfast, and Tali and Maru had standing instructions to arrive early enough to dress her and make her ready.

But neither maid appeared, and Analisa rebelliously stayed abed. She did not enjoy those early morning breakfasts at all well enough to bestir herself. She lolled in bed, wondering at this unusual change of routine, until well past the time when she knew Pietr would be gone, seeing to his work in the nutmeg groves.

Hunger pangs finally rousted her. She did not

bother calling Tali to help her into her dress, nor did she require Maru, for not one tendril of her hair had escaped its nighttime coil.

She wandered into the breakfast room. It seemed different without Pietr's commanding presence. But its emptiness was not the only odd thing—fruit and juice still graced the sideboard. Pietr ordinarily did not tolerate uneaten food cluttering the tables after his meal had been finished. He knew she preferred a light breakfast of fruit, and he must have left orders to keep it on hand for her. She ought to feel grateful, she supposed—but then he was probably only concerned because of the child she might carry. A pregnant broodmare required the proper nourishment.

She plopped herself tiredly into the closest chair, wondering why she felt unsettled about the room. She had so often wished she might enjoy a solitary breakfast amid its sunny prettiness. It took her a moment of idly studying the walls to realize why the room felt so different.

Hilde's portrait had been removed.

15

The morning of the Governor's Ball dawned with the usual splendor. Analisa blinked herself awake, and found both Tali and Maru standing at the foot of her bed, their arms loaded down with the gown and undergarments Pietr had provided her for this special occasion.

Still a little sleepy, she smiled lazily at their eagerness. "You two must be even more excited than I for some break in the routine," she said around a huge yawn. "It's too early to dress for the ball. Put that away until later and bring one of my usual day gowns."

"No, mevrouw. Mynheer says you are to prepare yourself in these clothes at once. You have been summoned to the fort. You must arrive there hours before the other guests."

"We have been summoned? But why?'

"Only you have been summoned, mevrouw." Maru looked very unhappy. "No woman has been summoned to the fort, ever, in all these years. Mynheer is most displeased. He clouted the governor's messenger straight across the jaw."

Analisa jolted upright, clutching her light cover to her breast, certain that her heavy bed gown wasn't enough to conceal the sudden pounding of her heart. She could think of only one reason her presence should be demanded at the fort: That man who'd captured her attention was indeed Michael Rowland. He'd been discovered, and they wanted her to identify him.

"Mynheer will go with you," Tali soothed, misunderstanding Analisa's flaring panic.

She sat limp and unresponsive as a rag doll during the hours it took them to arrange her hair and garb her in the luxurious new garments. She sipped at some juice, but declined their offer to bring her a light breakfast, knowing she could never manage to swallow a single bite of solid food.

Pietr stood rigid with white-lipped fury at the base of the stairs when at last she joined him.

"This is an unpardonable insult," he grated. "I have told them again and again that you played no part in that damned pirate's escape. Now they insist you personally inspect that wretched lot of Englishmen to see whether he might be hiding among them."

Relief washed through her, nearly buckling her knees. They had not discovered Michael, dead or alive. And then dread seized her. It was one thing to fail to report him to the authorities; it was quite another to look him in the face and deny that he was the man who'd tried to break the Company's monopoly. She gripped the banister for support.

Pietr noticed. "Goddamn them! You see how this affects you, and at such a time. I swear, if my heir suffers from this, they will all pay the price. Go back to your room, Analisa. I will tell them you are too delicate to be subjected to this."

"No. No, Pietr, I am fine." She straightened her spine. Refusing to cooperate would only deepen the officials' suspicions that they held the right man within their grasp. She had to appear before them, had to let them parade the entire British contingent in front of her, and swear that none of those men was the smuggler she'd seen on board the *Island Treasure.* Only then would Michael be permitted to go free. "It is my duty to do as the Company asks."

And, she would see him again. She would come face-to-face with him once more. Somehow, she would have to strengthen herself so she would not betray him. She would have to maintain a calm, strong voice. She could not melt into a quivering ball of desire. She would have to stare straight at him, study every beloved feature as if she'd never seen it before, and watch him walk away.

She began praying for the strength.

Their *prahu* sped toward Banda Neira with Pietr still fuming his outrage. She welcomed his anger, for it relieved her of the need to make conversation with him.

They were greeted with a parody of social propriety, with the governor himself greeting them effusively. He escorted them into his private office as if their visit were an unexpected pleasure rather than a command performance. A hovering servant offered a tray of refreshments. Analisa declined with a little shake of her head, knowing she would never be able to swallow in this room, where so many reminders of Dutch violence lined the walls. Sabers were displayed in racks. A harquebus, and several smaller Italian guns, hung from brackets. All of these weapons of death could be brought to play against a notorious smuggler.

Pietr snatched a brimming tankard of gin and quaffed fully half of it without pausing for breath. He slammed the tankard down upon Governor Hoon's desk. "You did not call us here simply to sample your liquor."

"No, I did not." The governor leaned back in his chair and steepled his fingers below his chin. "I cannot blame you for getting angry with me, Pietr, but I ask your indulgence. Perhaps if I explain our dilemma, you will forgive my overbearing behavior in ordering you here."

Pietr, slightly mollified, settled back into his own chair. Analisa had noticed this about him before, that any pandering to his vanity seemed to satisfy some need within him, seemed to blunt the edge of the anger that always leached from him like scent from a nutmeg.

"We have used Mynheer deGroot's presence to detain the British on our island for several days. During that time we have examined their ship so thoroughly that I swear not a single flea has escaped our notice. We have taken advantage of their presence here to thoroughly search that miserable Run Island. We have not turned up a trace of the smuggler who escaped from the *Island Treasure.* It is possible he melted back into the ranks of pirates who plague our seas, but one of my men raised the interesting possibility that the rogue might be passing himself off as one of the British officers. Since the *Island Treasure* and its crew have sailed off, your wife is the only person on Banda Neira who could recognize him. All we ask is that she look at those men and tell us if the smuggler is hiding among them."

The conversation continued between the two men while Analisa sat silent between them. They never glanced her way, never asked if she was willing to perform the simple task. Their total lack of concern for her feelings somehow shed light on a truth that she had barely acknowledged—neither Pietr nor the Company cared a whit about Analisa Vandermann, the person, only for what she could do for them.

It didn't matter to them that in all respects she was a loyal Dutch citizen, a respectable married woman, soon to be a mother. It rocked her—for so many years, she'd striven toward these ideals, only to learn that they meant less than nothing to anyone other than herself. All her life she'd yearned for validation from other people, for the approval of others. That approval and validation was but a fleeting thing, easily taken away with but the slightest indiscretion, the barest hint of impropriety, no matter whether she was guilty or not.

All of a sudden, she hated the Company. And she despised the life she had once craved.

Too late, she realized that she had always had it within herself to make herself happy. She had never needed anyone's approval.

The damned Dutch had kept them standing for hours inside the stockade. "You are not prisoners," stated the officer keeping watch over them when Richard protested for the tenth time. "You are merely awaiting an inspection."

Michael knew what that meant, and guilt ate at him for subjecting his fellow men to this scrutiny. Paradoxically, they did not seem to mind—they seemed to find it hilarious that they tweaked Dutch noses by keeping their knowledge about him a secret. Somehow, too, word had leaked out about his passion for Analisa, and more than one man had sidled up to him, promising to do what he could to steal a moment or two for Michael to spend with her.

At long last the double doors from the governor's office slammed open. The governor came out, followed by two of his aides—and Analisa. Her husband hovered behind with a tight grip on her elbow.

Michael closed his eyes.

The Dutch aides harangued the British into lining up, single file. Michael found himself smack in the middle of the queue. One by one, each man stepped up to Analisa. As Michael drew closer to the front of the line, he could hear her low murmurs.

"No, I have not seen this man before."

"Next!" barked an aide.

And then another man would step forward. Doing England proud, each executed a stiff, proper bow, and then spun on his heel, presenting Analisa with first a view of his back, then his side, then full front. And each time she would murmur, "No, he is not the man I saw on board ship." Or, "No, this man is not the criminal you seek." She never shifted her eyes away from the subject standing immediately in front of her, never glanced along the line to see who might be coming next. Her comments were flat, emotionless. She rejected each man the way a housewife might cast aside overripe apples at a market stall.

His slow progress toward her gave him plenty of time to worry that she might betray him, to make plans for bolting from the stockade if she should point a finger and shriek, "There he is!" Instead, his heart seemed disinclined to nurture that possibility. He spent every moment studying her.

She was well and expensively clothed. Her gown was the exact shade of blush that tinged the apricotlike nutmeg fruits. A matching apricot-blush headdress covered her hair, except for a scant inch or two of tightly bound braid that peeped from the edge just above her forehead. Nobody could possibly know what a wealth of silken beauty would spring forth when she set her hair free. He swallowed a surge of jealousy when he realized that Pietr Hootendorf probably availed himself of that pleasure every single night, probably stood there now secure in the knowledge that no man but he knew what exquisite treasures lay hidden beneath the folds of apricot-blush silk.

But Michael had seen her first. All of her. Michael had loosened the heavy curls and let them drift over his bare flesh, had run his fingers through its silken mass and inhaled its rain-sweet fragrance. His hands had stroked her flesh and learned her innermost secrets. Hootendorf could have enclosed her within a nutmeg crate, with only her head sticking out, and still Michael would know what he concealed.

And he was glad that he'd lost so much flesh during his captivity, flesh he had not yet regained, for his uniform hung loosely upon him and concealed the evidence of what his intimate memories had done to him.

And then it was his turn.

He looked straight at her, but she had fixed her gaze at some point over his shoulder, so that those standing alongside and watching her every move would think that she met his eyes. He executed his bow and swiveled, wondering what she thought of him now that she had her first good look at him in daylight. He turned back, and had to forcibly keep his arms at his sides, he longed so badly to pull her into them.

Her gaze flickered over his hair, shorn short, his face, shaved smooth—his weak attempts at a disguise. She dwelled a little longer at his cheeks and lips. He remembered the way she'd washed the salt from his face, the way her fingers had trembled against his lips.

And then, for a heart-lurching moment, her eyes met his. He did not know what his betrayed, but within hers he read a hunger to match his own, an agony that told him she found this moment as bittersweet as he did.

Now. If she intended to betray him, she would have to do so now.

"This man is not a criminal," she whispered, and he did not know whether the other men caught the slight variance in her denial. He bowed again and stepped smartly away into the group who'd already passed their tests.

He stood among his fellows and wondered that his body did not explode from the emotions warring within. She had not betrayed him. Her silence—nay, her outright lie—told him that she loved him still.

Or did she? Her failure to identify him could be completely selfish. If they clapped him in chains, if they tortured him, he might admit the truth about their being lovers. She could not risk it, not if she valued her marriage.

Her voice broke a little as she absolved yet another Englishman, and her gaze shifted toward him, quick and fleeting as a butterfly. At once he knew he'd done her a disservice by crediting her with self-preservationist motives. She loved him and sought to protect him, and only a man who loved her as much as he would notice the agony etched across her features, the force of will holding her upright.

"No, he is not the criminal you seek."

The procession continued. Far from growing fidgety at the prolonged delay, Michael savored every moment. He stood there, cross-armed and sour-countenanced as the rest of his fellow Englishmen, to hide his pleasure in being able to spend every minute staring straight at her, knowing nobody would remark on it. All of them, every woman-starved lout, stared at her—she was incredibly lovely despite her restrictive garments, her hideously bound hair. It would have seemed suspicious if he had not watched the proceedings.

As he'd told Richard, she looked paler than she had aboard ship, but he could not be certain. She had come to him in candlelight, with the soft golden glow caressing her skin and lighting her eyes. She had spent many hours on deck, she'd told him, letting herself develop an unladylike tan. The tan would have faded by now, if she'd not kept up her hours in the sun.

Her gown did almost as masterful a job of hiding

her figure as the shapeless thing she'd worn on ship. The apricot-blush silk concealed her lush swells and curves, but he had spent so many hours reliving every touch, retracing every curve, that they were burned into his memory and she might as well have stood naked before him.

He was ashamed of himself suddenly. He was staring at her lustfully, the way she'd said men had always stared at her. It gave him pause. She had not betrayed him; he could not betray her. Regardless of how he felt, she had found some measure of contentment in her new life. Her husband stood at her side. The Dutch officials treated her with courtesy and respect. She had achieved her heart's desire, that which she had spent so many months journeying to find. He could not do anything that would jeopardize these things for her.

Eventually, every Englishman had been inspected and passed by Analisa. She wilted a little, and Pietr Hootendorf stepped closer, lending his strength. The Dutch governor, looking annoyed and embarrassed, stepped forward to address the collection of Englishmen.

"I thank you for your cooperation, gentlemen. And I repeat my invitation—you are all welcome at my Governor's Ball this evening. I trust you will not have found this day's events too taxing. There will be dancing—and I dare hope that Mevrouw Hootendorf will permit one or two of you to take a turn with her."

The Englishmen roared their approval; Hootendorf pursed his mouth as if he were sucking a lemon. Michael met Analisa's startled glance and saw that she had not realized the British would be attending that evening's ball. Sheer joy radiated from her for the space of a heartbeat, followed at once by the familiar pale blankness he'd seen her use when she wanted to conceal her feelings. Only someone fearful of having her weaknesses turned against her developed that skill.

She had not felt the need to do this with him. Only with the Dutch.

He inclined his head just the barest measure, not certain at all that she saw it. But in his mind it was an acknowledgment of the night to come, and his acceptance of a challenge.

He meant to make her come alive once more before she buried her soul deep within the prim and proper folds of the Mevrouw Hootendorf. For a few moments, she would dance with him, she would burn with the fires that flared for him, only him.

16

~

She was already there when he and his fellow officers marched into the ballroom.

"She's a looker, all right." A seaman by the name
of Nelson nudged Michael in the ribs. "I wouldn't
mind a stint in the brig myself, if she was my jailer."

Michael silenced him with an icy glare. "There are
worse fates than beheading and castration, Nelson.
Keep nattering, and you'll learn what they are."

"Aye, sir." Nelson faded back into the group.

Michael gave Nelson no further thought. His attention riveted on Analisa as if she were a candle flame
and he a light-starved moth. She stood at Hootendorf's
side, amid a group of others whose stiff posture and
brittle smiles marked them as strangers to each other.
Unfriendly strangers, judging by the puckered expres-
sions upon the other women and the carefully averted
and yet occasionally lewd glances the men shot Analisa's way. His fists clenched; he yearned to pummel
every one of them to a pulp, but at the same time he
could not fault them for appreciating her beauty. She
looked lovelier than ever, with the light from a thousand candles dancing over her skin and her hair.

Richard appeared at his side, holding glasses of

water. "Here you go, Rowland. I don't think you ought to be trifling with spirits tonight, hmm?"

Michael snatched up the glass and gulped it down. He would have done the same with whiskey, so he appreciated Richard's wisdom.

"Seems like we're not the only lot the Dutch rounded up to impress old deGroot," Richard mused. He inclined his head toward a far corner, where a group of Spaniards stood, slugging back goblets of red wine while glowering unhappily at the Dutch. Spain clung as tenaciously to the islands of Timor and Tenate as the British clung to Run Island, and were equally as dependent upon the Dutch for provisions and safe passage through East Indian waters. "A rather strained gathering, wouldn't you say?" Richard asked.

"It suits my mood."

"No doubt. There's so much tension sizzling from you, I daresay the cook could fry my morning eggs on your back."

"There's so much antagonism flying between the Dutch and everyone else that I doubt anyone notices."

"Lucky for you that it's so. Otherwise, I'd order you back to the ship at once. Pull yourself together, man. You promised me you'd get through this evening without calling attention to yourself."

Michael fought for control. As always, Richard was right. A man with sense would have stayed behind on the *Glorious Elizabeth,* secure in the knowledge that come morning he'd make his escape. Instead, he stood here burning for Analisa with a fever pitch that threatened to burst into full flame.

He did not know how many others had noticed his intensity, but Analisa was aware of him. He was as certain of it as he was of his own tingling skin. She stood the tiniest bit straighter. Her voice had an added edge of huskiness when she spoke. She kept her eyes modestly lowered for the most part, but on occasion they slanted his way, and a barely perceptible tremor would set the folds of her skirts to vibrating.

Something within himself was vibrating as well. He stood there amid the stiff, formal gathering and yearned to undo the buttons down her back, part her gown, and stroke his hands over every lush, warm inch of her.

She darted a surreptitious glance at him, then blushed, as if she'd read his mind.

He did not know how he would endure this punishment that he had forced upon himself.

But endure it he did, all through the interminable reception. He forced refreshments down his throat without tasting anything. At virtually every moment, his good sense reminded him that he ought to remove himself from the crowd, ought to return to the safety of the *Glorious Elizabeth* and let this night go on without him. For all his life he had wished to turn his back on responsibility, and here he was, risking his freedom, his very life, for the sake of looking at a woman he loved but could never again possess.

When it came time to go in to dinner, he found his torture increased a hundredfold.

The governor approached Hootendorf and executed a curt little nod. "Once more, mynheer, I would impose upon your wife."

Hootendorf stiffened as if the governor had dealt him a deadly insult. "She has been plagued enough. How many times do you intend to rub my nose in your suspicions that she helped that smuggler escape?"

A strained hush fell over the crowd. Analisa paled. Michael's gut clenched when he realized how terrible this must have been for her. He wanted to hate Hootendorf for claiming the woman Michael loved, but he had to admire the man for standing up for his bride, when it obviously put him at odds with the rest of his compatriots.

The governor gave a weak little laugh. "No insult intended, mynheer. It is her facility with the English tongue that I seek to borrow for a brief time. Mynheer deGroot, our distinguished guest, is anxious to sharpen his command of the language. He asks that Mevrouw Hootendorf sit with him and help him converse with some of the British officers."

Hootendorf eased his stance a little, but Analisa wilted.

And Michael rejoiced.

She had dared to pray for one more opportunity to drink in the sight of him. One more chance to hear his voice, thrill to his laughter, melt at the warmth in his eyes. Of all the prayers in her life that had gone unanswered, God had chosen to bless this one beyond all hope—after a bit of comically confused milling, the British officers seated themselves, and Michael settled into the chair right next to her at the dinner table.

She had so often dreamed, at night and during the day, of what she might say to him if she ever had the chance for a moment alone with him again. She found herself tongue-tied, unable to speak at all.

And he—well, he obviously had no problem. He settled back lazily in his chair, with his hands resting lightly against his thighs, his eyes half closed in the manner of a dozing panther planning its next strike.

"Your husband rivals *Gunung Api* with all his glowering and smoldering," Michael remarked.

"*Gunung Api*, he is the smoldering volcano!" Mynheer deGroot cried happily. He glanced around to see whether the others had noticed how he'd understood some of the English words.

"Excellent, mynheer," Analisa said, grasping for the comfort of her teacher's role.

Pietr did indeed present as forbidding a face as the churning volcano. She felt him watching her every move, judging her every word, even though she knew he could not understand her when she spoke in English.

And he was not the only one. It seemed that virtually everyone's attention was focused upon her at these very moments when she yearned for nothing more than a quiet place to embrace her joy that Michael lived, to revel in the delight of having him so close once more. But she was the new white woman, Pietr Hootendorf's new bride, notorious for the suspicions swirling about her, and now so shockingly honored by being placed directly across from the governor and Mynheer deGroot that it roused no little jealousy among the other Dutch, who were always striving for notice.

She deliberately concentrated her attention on the gentleman to her right, a Captain Richard Ellington. It was not an obvious slur upon Michael, for Captain Ellington outranked him. And yet she was so conscious of the man she loved that she feared any moment the sensations racing through her might send her swooning.

And he would not be ignored.

"You are radiant, mevrouw," Michael said. "I suppose it is the glow of a new bride."

"I am indeed a woman in love, sir," she whispered.

"I envy the lucky man his good fortune."

"Do you? I did not think you believed in love."

"Fancy you recalling I said that. I wonder, do you remember everything else with equal clarity?"

Mynheer deGroot, obviously having a difficult time following their mumbled, rapid-fire discourse, leaned forward with the quizzical look of one desperately trying to understand something. "Fancy?" he queried. "Clarity?"

"My apologies, mynheer, for speaking so quickly." Analisa slanted Michael a furious look. "I must remind these men to speak a little slower, and a bit louder, so everyone can understand and enjoy their conversation."

"Oh, I am enjoying this, Analisa," Michael murmured. "That little spot of color on your cheeks—I had despaired of seeing it again. I thought you might have dipped your head in wet plaster to present such a pale, frozen countenance to the world."

He was shameless and provocative. He sipped from her water glass and set it down in such a way that if she ever picked it up and drank from it, her lips would touch the same place as his.

"Why are you doing this?" she whispered.

"Because I cannot bear to see you so stiff and proper. I know the fires that burn within you, Analisa. Before I leave, I want to see you glow, so I know you are happy."

"I am very happy."

"Prove it. Smile."

"Smile! Smile." Mynheer deGroot grinned broadly, and crooked both of his index fingers toward his lips.

Michael grinned back at deGroot as though the two of them were the best of friends. "Do you think fabric can sin?"

"What an absurd question!"

"Not really. For example, if the folds of your skirt rest against my breeches, do the silk and wool commit some heinous sin of fornication right beneath the eyes of all these good citizens?" He paused while she shifted her leg, noting with horror that he'd trapped the edge of her gown beneath his thigh. "You look a trifle heated, mevrouw. Have a little water."

All she could think of was the way his lips and tongue had branded her glass. She took a sip, swallowed water she didn't want while hoping to catch an elusive taste of *him*. She touched her tongue to her lips to catch a droplet and he inhaled quickly, raspily.

"Consider moisture, mevrouw," he murmured. "I drink water, you drink water. It replenishes the vital forces within our bodies so we might call upon it to cool our skin, to slake our every thirst."

"Everyone drinks the water." Mynheer deGroot nodded sagely.

Analisa took a bit of her capon, hoping that chewing might stop her teeth from chattering.

"Everyone eats the fowl," Michael answered, skewering a portion of roasted capon with his fork and raising it in salute to the dignitary from Java. He caught the meat with his tongue and drew it into his mouth. He matched his chewing motions to hers; when she swallowed, he swallowed. Their bodies acted in accord in this most mundane of functions, as they had in the most joyous union.

In some ways, it was the most interminable night of her life, stretching her nerves to a thrumming, twanging state, leaving them in danger of snapping from the strain of acting the proper Dutch wife while not betraying her secret lover. In other ways, the time raced past with such speed that she wanted to beg it to slow, so she might pile up more precious moments with Michael that she could draw out and savor later. Moments that would have to last her a lifetime.

At length the governor stood, signaling an end to the meal. "If you gentlemen will join me in the rear parlor, we will raise a toast to Mynheer deGroot. I will leave the ladies in my wife's capable hands."

Captain Ellington and Michael shot to their feet and stood politely behind their chairs until most of the men had filed along behind the governor. She stared down at her plate, wondering if Pietr had noticed how little she'd eaten. He would remark on her lack of appetite. He would not be pleased; he would remind her that the babe likely growing in her womb required nourishment.

Soon, only she and the four other Dutch women remained at the long table. The governor's wife, Mevrouw Hoon, broke the uneasy silence that gripped them all.

"Mevrouw Hootendorf?" After a long moment, she repeated herself, more sharply. "Mevrouw Hootendorf!"

Analisa started. "Forgive me, Mevrouw Hoon. I am so newly wed that I have not yet begun to recognize myself as Mevrouw Hootendorf." Heat flared across her face—how could she have been so stupid? Because her thoughts weren't on this small gathering of women, but on the tall, lithe-moving man who'd disappeared into the rear parlor. Instead of worrying over how to make a good impression upon these women, who would comprise her narrow social circle for the rest of her life, all she could think about was that soon, in less than an hour, the ladies would join the men and she would see Michael again.

The youngest of the other women, who introduced herself as Mevrouw vanHelmer, tittered in sympathy. "You will become accustomed soon enough, Mevrouw Hootendorf. Your husband will see to it."

"I am Gerda Goenstedt," offered another. She gestured around the table, encompassing them all. "We have been wondering about you."

"We are surprised that Pietr has not formally introduced you to society," said Mevrouw Hoon. " 'Tis not like him—he is usually so eager to act the host."

"He was eager when Hilde was his wife," spat the oldest woman, Mevrouw Pedersveldt. "Perhaps he has good reason to keep this one hidden away."

"Marta!" The three Dutch ladies gaped at her.

"Marta me all you like. Hilde Hootendorf must be turning in her grave to see how this one has made a fool of her husband."

"I have done nothing disrespectful toward my husband," Analisa protested, knowing she had already made an enemy.

"Bah. Simpering and flirting with those British dogs!"

"Marta," chided Mevrouw Hoon. "The governor and Mynheer deGroot asked the mevrouw to entertain them. You cannot hold such a thing against her."

"I have eyes as well as ears, mevrouw," snapped back Marta. She leaned into the back of her chair, her arms crossed over her breasts, her expression daring any of them to ask her what she had seen, what she had heard.

"I . . . I am sorry. Please excuse me. I do not feel well." Analisa, despising herself for being a coward, pushed herself away from the table and raced out of the room.

She followed the hint of coolness wafting through the hallway until she stood near a window. She breathed deep of the sea-swept night air. Her breath rasped against her ears, but not loudly enough to completely drown out the shrill female voices arguing from the room she'd left. It sounded as though the three kindest ones had grouped against Mevrouw Pedersveldt, which would not endear Analisa to her.

Somehow she would have to make amends with those women. And she would, someday. Not today. For now, she cared only that Michael was right down the hallway, and after this night, she would really, truly never see him again.

The first strains of the orchestra tuning up penetrated her thoughts. Well, perhaps orchestra was too kind a description—a motley collection of servants and slaves, equipped with pipes and drums and other native instruments, labored beneath Mynheer Hoon's enthusiastically waving arms.

Pietr came looking for her. He burst from the dining room where she should have been, looking furious and frantic all at once. When he saw her standing alone by the window, his shoulders slumped with relief. She felt sick to realize that her husband had not trusted he would find her alone. And he was right to doubt her.

"Come, Analisa," he said. "With so few women present, you will be expected to dance."

"With you?" she whispered.

"I do not dance, not anymore."

Dancing was a joyful exercise to be performed only with Hilde, she supposed. Dutifully, she followed him down the hallway. Mynheer deGroot stepped forward to claim her for the first dance.

A blurred flurry of Dutch officers followed. She danced with them all, pretending to pay attention to their token compliments, smiling when they attempted jokes, nodding when they told her how much they missed their wives, their mothers, their sweethearts, their friends back home.

She was surprised when Captain Ellington crooked his arm toward her next, and then she remembered that the governor had promised the Englishmen that she might dance with a few of them. The captain guided her sedately around the perimeter of the ballroom, and then handed her over to the next-highest-ranking British soldier. He, too, limited himself to one turn around the floor before handing her over to another.

And then, when she'd finished with him, she felt the light touch of a hand against her elbow. A surge of raw pleasure shot straight into her heart, and she knew Michael's flesh touched hers before she turned and saw his face.

He bowed, and held wide his arms. She stepped close, feeling his heat mingle with hers through the circumspect six inches that separated their bellies.

It was heaven. She wanted to die then, with the feel of his arms around her and the scent of him filling every breath she took. He seemed likewise inclined, drawing her the merest fraction closer than any before him had done, but not so close that anyone could notice. She could feel the tension trembling through him.

She stiffened a little, fearing that he might return to the relentless bantering of the dinner table, but he seemed content to hold her in his arms, to match his breath to hers. And so they did not speak at all. They did absolutely nothing to betray what they meant to each other, but somehow it still must have been evident, for Pietr chose a moment when they were but halfway through their sedate course around the room and broke in on them.

"My wife is tired."

She pressed her fingers to her lips before her protest could come forth. It would be sheer folly to object to Pietr's decree. She could not explain that her eyes had been half closed, her expression no doubt dreamy, because of the heady pleasures of dancing in Michael Rowland's arms. No, best to meekly nod, bow her head, step away from Michael with Pietr's hand firm at her elbow.

" 'Twas a pleasure, mevrouw," Michael said, his voice suspiciously husky, as he gave a half bow from the waist and courteously stepped back.

She stood with Pietr along the sidelines, resentful of the gaiety surrounding her. Michael stood not far away, sipping his drink, pretending to watch the dancing, but she knew he wasn't paying any more attention to the couples twirling about the floor than she was.

After a little while, some of the Dutchmen approached, asking if she might return to the dancing. Pietr rebuffed them, one after the other, and when a contingent of determined-looking Englishmen approached, he drew a big breath.

"I suppose my wife shall have no rest unless I make the announcement," he said to Governor Hoon.

She froze, knowing what he meant to say, praying that he wouldn't.

"What do you have to tell us, Pietr?"

Her husband curled his arm around Analisa's shoulder and drew her against him. He straightened proudly, his chin jutting toward the ceiling. "Only that my new bride should not be tiring herself with dancing, now that she might have another's health beside her own to consider."

The few women were all dancing, so there were none to chide Pietr over the unsuitability of his announcement in mixed company, but even so, jaws gaped, and there were a few startled, disbelieving gasps. One man nudged another with his elbow while his brows rose to his hairline. The men surrounding them appeared stunned by Pietr's announcement. Only Mynheer deGroot brightened. "Do you mean you're about to become a father at long last, Pietr?" he blared in his loud way.

"Perhaps. It is far too soon to be certain, as she has been with me for less than a month, but I don't mind telling you I have every reason to hold high hopes."

It wasn't too soon to be certain, not anymore. But she realized that pretending so suited Pietr, making it seem certain her pregnancy could only have come about after her arrival in Banda. While the men recovered from their surprise to "oh ho!" and nudge Pietr with their elbows, and exchange manly winks, Analisa wanted to die. Such news should come from her lips, not Pietr's. It didn't even matter to her that pregnancy was not discussed in polite society, only that Michael should not hear from Pietr that she was to bear a child.

And he had heard. When she dared risk a glance in his direction, she caught him staring white-faced at her, rigid and agonized. He understood enough of the Dutch tongue to know what had been said. She did not know what she could say to him even if she did have an opportunity. She did not know whose child she carried.

Even if she were utterly certain that it was Michael's, what good would it do to admit it? Pietr, who dreamed of founding a dynasty, of transforming Lonthar into Hootendorf Island, would fight any attempt to credit another man with siring his first child.

Visions of the woman tied to the pole while her husband and sons sailed away assailed her. Not only that, but Michael would be doomed. He would be revealed as the smuggler who had dared defile a Company's Daughter, a woman pledged in marriage to a loyal Company planter. His death would be a foregone conclusion.

He had told her that he would not leave until he saw her glow, until she smiled and convinced him she was happy. She closed her eyes for a moment, summoning the image of herself cradling Michael's child. A smile bloomed upon her with no effort whatsoever.

"I am very happy," she said to the men surrounding her. "Very, very happy."

17

~

Richard beckoned Michael toward the quiet hallway. His face was a blank mask, betraying nothing, which warned Michael that he would not like the outcome of this interview.

"You are finished, as of this moment, with mooning over Mevrouw Hootendorf."

"You are the only man here who knows me well enough to tell that I'm mooning," Michael shot back. Hearing his passion, his love, reduced to such status infuriated him.

Richard sighed and shook his head. "Of all the women in this world, you would pick the wife of the one man we cannot afford to antagonize."

"Hootendorf? Surely he does not provide you with food and goods."

Richard lifted his head, a soldier's motion, as if he needed to pinpoint every potential enemy in the room. He lowered his voice and spoke, scarcely moving his lips. "I had hoped there would be no need to tell you this, but it seems there's no stopping you unless you know what is at stake. Hootendorf's *our* man."

"Your man?" Knowing he sounded like a dolt, but unable to fathom where Richard was headed, Michael shook his head in bewilderment.

"He's our contact, Michael. He's the one who provides us with the nutmegs for our grove, the nutmegs we gave you to pirate out of here."

The implications hit him at once. Hootendorf had provided the forbidden fruit for Michael's ill-fated journey, the very journey that had led him to Analisa! God must be holding His sides from laughing at the irony.

And then with a sudden slamming of his heart, he realized that Analisa could be in danger. Hootendorf played a dangerous game. Small wonder he'd looked so sour while Analisa studied the British seamen—he must have been sick with dread that she would point out the smuggler, fearing that the smuggler would implicate Hootendorf in exchange for leniency. Perhaps Analisa had saved her own life by not identifying him.

"Why would he take such an incredible risk? The Dutch are ruthless with those who seek to cheat them or crack their monopoly."

"Aye. But who can say what motivates Hootendorf? Everyone whispers about him. He fancies himself a notch above mortal men, and God pity anyone who threatens his sense of superiority. It's laughable, in a way, because all of those *perkeniers* descend from rogues and outlaws. Nobody can predict how they will behave, which is why the Dutch keep such a tight leash on them."

"If that tight leash should begin to strangle Hootendorf, it will choke the life from Analisa as well."

Richard shrugged. "She is his wife, Michael. She must pay the consequences if her marriage puts her in jeopardy."

"But you do not understand. She contracted this marriage believing it to be of the utmost respectability." Pain shafted through him at the memory of how Analisa desired respectability above everything—even above the love they shared—and how Hootendorf's clandestine activities could rob her of the only thing she ever craved. "I must warn her. She must be prepared if something happens."

"You cannot risk—"

Michael interrupted Richard with a graphic curse. "I will do this, Richard. And then I will leave quietly, without implicating a single Englishman. But do not attempt to dissuade me from seeing her one more time, to warn her, or I swear I will confess everything and bring the Dutch straight to your doorstep."

She looked lovelier than ever, and so fragile and delicate that Michael wanted to enfold her in his arms and protect her against anything and everything that threatened her.

Threatened her, and perhaps the babe she carried in her womb. The very thought sent shivers through him. How foolish he had been to think that deliberately refusing to acknowledge love would protect his heart. Instead, it had made everything worse. If he'd admitted the depth of his feelings for her, he might have wooed her away from this deadly course of becoming Hootendorf's wife in truth as well as in name. If he'd declared himself, he might have convinced her to come along with him—instead, he'd walked away, forcing himself to believe she'd been little more than a mere dalliance, all so he could indulge childhood dreams of freedom and adventure.

His foolishness compounded his suffering a hundredfold, a thousandfold. For now he felt no lessening of responsibility; indeed he experienced a hammering sense of impotence. He was helpless to protect her from the forces massing against her, helpless to shelter her from the pain that could soon come her way. And his own careless self-indulgence had put him in this position of impotence. He had only himself to blame.

Hootendorf hovered at her side, vigilant as a hawk.

He had stopped her from dancing and now obviously had no intention of allowing her to mingle with the other guests.

And so Michael approached her.

He walked toward her, feeling his heart grow fuller with every step he took, and he wondered how he could have ever been so foolish as to believe he could live the rest of his life without seeing her again.

She stared at him worriedly, her skin turning pale, and such fright darkened her eyes that he nearly faltered in his resolve. But the knowledge that she did not know about her husband's treachery kept him on course. His pulse pounded with the frustration of knowing he was causing her anguish, and yet he had to smile and pretend to be unaware of it, could not speak out the reassuring words that he longed to say, at least until he had satisfied the meaningless, two-faced rules of society.

He gave a bow from his waist and kept his eyes locked upon hers the whole while. "Madam."

"Mr. Rowland." Her formal acknowledgment, stiff with trepidation, gouged at his heart.

Hootendorf glowered next to her. Michael tore his hungry gaze from Analisa and directed his attention to the man he despised, pasting a false smile upon his face.

He shifted into his execrable Dutch. "Mynheer, I beg your indulgence. After so many months of hearing nothing but ourselves, my friends and I crave the sound of our native tongue coming from a woman's lips. Would you grant permission for your wife to speak to us?"

"No."

Hootendorf's flat refusal sent rage coursing through Michael. His fist curled into a ball, and it was only with the greatest effort that he held back from planting his fist right in the middle of the older man's self-righteous face.

And then, to his amazement, his friend Richard stepped up and addressed Hootendorf in nearly flawless Dutch.

"Oh, come, old man, don't be so selfish. My fellows are leaving tomorrow and heading back to their wives and sweethearts. They need a healthy dose of female company just now to remind them how to behave in front of a proper lady."

"There are some here who would not accord my wife that status."

Analisa jerked infinitesimally at the deliberate insult. Richard's composure shifted briefly, and Michael was consumed with a rage so violent that everything altered, as though a red haze bathed the room.

"There are other women here," Hootendorf added.

"Aye, but none who can speak our language, mynheer. And besides, I had hoped to claim your attention for myself, to discuss a matter of mutual concern. Of course, I suppose my men and I could cultivate another relationship, but it would take so much time and end up less profitable to all concerned, wouldn't you say?"

Richard's veiled reference to the relationship between the British and Hootendorf would have gone unnoticed if Richard had not admitted to Michael that Hootendorf was the source of their illicit nutmegs. Hootendorf drew in a deep breath, and held it long enough that Michael knew he was considering jeopardizing their scheme, but then he relented. Michael wondered anew at Hootendorf's reasons for breaking the Company's most sacred law, but he didn't really care about that matter, only that he would soon have Analisa away from her husband's watchful eye.

"Perhaps a tour of the gardens, with all my men," Richard suggested. "The mevrouw could point out

how the flora transported from Holland thrive alongside the native plants."

"Do your sailors intend to take up gardening upon
leaving the sea?" Hootendorf inquired dryly.

"Don't have a shred of interest in it," Richard answered with broad cheer. "I daresay your wife will
feel as if she's shepherding a batch of schoolboys on
an outing."

Hootendorf gave his curt approval, and Michael
bowed from the waist once more, lifting Analisa's
hand in his.

His touch nearly undid her. She had followed the
conversation with mingled disbelief and excitement,
praying on one hand that Pietr would consent and on
the other that he wouldn't. The compromise of sending her into the gardens with Michael and a chaperon
contingent of British officers promised bittersweet
agony.

Michael very properly placed her hand atop his
forearm and led her toward the garden.

Every eye in the place was upon them. She caught
her new female acquaintances whispering behind their
hands, a few of the men watching with interest. But
then the band struck up a lively tune and the women
were claimed for dancing and the men found other
things to occupy them. All except for the British naval
officers who formed a solid wall behind her and Michael as they left the ballroom.

Michael turned, murmured a few low instructions,
and the men behind them shifted into a broad semicir-
cle. They commenced talking very loudly, laughing,
taking an inordinate interest in the moon-bathed
flowers.

"I want to kiss you," Michael said, his voice shaking
with emotion.

"No! That sort of thing is finished between us," she
exclaimed, even while her heart soared at the thought,

while her lips tingled with the need to feel his pressed against them.

"I love you, Analisa."

She wished she were deaf so that she would not have to hear these words that her soul ached to hear. Now, when it was too late for them, he made this admission.

"You love me, too," he added. "I know it. I can feel it. I can see it in your eyes when you look at me."

"What if I do?" she cried. Behind them, Michael's fellow officers created such a rowdy disturbance that nobody within the house could possibly hear the intimate conversation going on between them. Paradoxically, their presence and the noise they created sealed her and Michael into a tiny cocoon of privacy, a poignant privacy, where they could see and hear and ache but could not touch.

"You are carrying a child."

"I am sorry you had to hear it that way."

"It is mine. It is *ours!*"

"I don't know." She trembled. "You need not concern yourself. I know you wanted nothing less."

He paled and ran a shaking hand over his face. "I have come to believe that I never knew what I wanted, until now."

"It might well be Pietr's babe," she whispered.

He stared at her with such anguish that she wished she could call back the words. She longed to tell him that he had made her so thoroughly his that her body repudiated all memory of her husband's touch. "What did you expect, Michael? That I would refuse Pietr because of what had happened between us aboard ship?"

"He forced you."

"Nay. I accepted him willingly. He is my husband. I always knew he would claim me as his wife, and I always knew what my duties would be. I am his by right of law."

"Are you? Did you give him your heart, Analisa?"

"No. That still belongs to you."

"Then come away with me. Right now. Richard will keep Hootendorf occupied for an hour or more. We can steal away."

"He would never let me go."

"I will keep you safe from him."

"But you can never change the fact that I am his wife. My child would be branded a bastard. I know too well how such a mark stigmatizes a person. I cannot let that happen to my child."

"I will claim the child as my own."

"But we could never marry. And the child belongs to Pietr by law." Visions of the woman tied to the pole swam through her head. "He would hunt us down to the ends of the earth and use every means at his disposal to take the child away from us. Already I love my child with all my heart. I would sooner die than be separated from my baby."

He drew a shuddering breath and shook his head. "You present me with arguments I cannot counter, Analisa. I could never ask you to choose our child over me. I love you both too much."

"Oh, Michael." She felt the tears welling in her eyes. "And even if I did go with you, we would be doomed, can't you see it? These islands, these waters, belong to the Dutch. We could not hope to escape. If they learned you fathered my babe, then they would know that you were the nutmeg smuggler I helped to escape. They would steal my babe from my arms and hang you from the closest tree. Pietr would have sole control over our child—and who knows how he might vent his rage? He is such a powerful man. His influence stretches clear back to Amsterdam, where he can ruin my mother as well. Oh, Michael, if it were only you and me then I would come with you without hesitation. But now there is the babe, and my mother, and I cannot take the risk."

"You take a risk by staying, Analisa."

"I know this match has not brought me the respect I sought, but there is little risk if I stay with Pietr."

"You are wrong. You run a terrible risk by staying. I had hoped I would not have to tell you this—your husband is as guilty as I when it comes to undermining your precious Company."

"What do you mean?"

"The nutmegs I smuggled came from your husband's *perken*, Analisa. Pietr Hootendorf is engaged in smuggling right beneath the Company's nose."

"Impossible! Why, he bristled with outrage when I merely mentioned the notion that some planter had to be involved in the scheme."

"He can bristle like a hedgehog, but it doesn't change the fact that he's guilty. And if the company should discover his role, he'd be tried as a traitor. As his wife, you will suffer along with him—as will our child."

"So you mean to expose him, then?"

"Only if you want me to. I can see you are unhappy. I know you do not love him. I can free you from him."

"You cannot expose him without revealing your own role in the smuggling. They would toss you in jail as well. I will be branded the unfaithful wife of a traitor, and our child the offspring of either a criminal or a traitor."

"No! I would never admit to our having loved one another, Analisa. Nobody would know that there was the slightest chance this child belonged to anyone but Pietr."

"But I would lose you. Don't you understand, Michael? I can live with the life I've chosen. I could not live knowing that I was responsible for your death. So long as you walk this earth, I can remember our love and dream of how it was between us. I cannot let you sacrifice yourself merely to free me from a bargain I made of my own free will."

She leaned against him, reveling in the forbidden feel of him pressed against her, knowing she was making a spectacle of herself in front of his men, but not caring. She would claim this final branding, savor the heat of him that penetrated his garments and through her own. "Don't you see, Michael, that loving you has been a priceless treasure I never hoped to experience? Nothing can take my memories away from me. Nothing. But now you must go. Flee this place and make a life for yourself."

"Do what you have done, in other words."

"Yes. You might find some measure of contentment."

"Will you?"

She gazed into his eyes, understanding his bleak heartbreak. "I might have your child to hold in my arms."

"And he will call Pietr Hootendorf Father."

"But I will tell him tales of a daring pirate who risked his life for the sake of adventure."

"It is what I have always wanted, but hearing it from your lips makes it seem a bleak, purposeless existence."

She could not answer—she had tried so many times to tell him this, to no avail. She gathered her skirts in her hands and broke through the concealing wall of men and returned to the ballroom, past the staring eyes to stand alongside the tall, silent figure of her husband.

It all boiled down to this—she feared *he* might die. She consigned herself and their child to a life of grief so that he, Michael Rowland, might pursue his adolescent dreams of carefree adventure.

No man could despise himself more than Michael did.

And no man could rejoice less in attaining his heart's desire. The freedom he'd craved for so long felt like an endless ocean of emptiness, where he would wallow for a solitary eternity. The responsibility he'd shunned for so long now beckoned with the allure of a siren. He could imagine no sweeter pleasure than working hard all day for the privilege of coming home to watch Analisa suckle their babe.

Analisa thought memories would be enough to see her through—she was wrong. No memory could compensate for the vast aching emptiness that awaited them both. She thought she might enjoy imagining him wending his carefree adventurous way through life, when he would more likely find himself mired in a drunken, self-indulgent stupor for the best part of that life. No, without Analisa he had no life.

And though she might pretend that memories were enough for her, he knew she had no life, either. Her very existence was under Pietr Hootendorf's control. He determined what she wore, what she ate, how she spent every hour of the day. Michael's beloved, spirited, vital beauty—stifled beneath the respectability she craved. She had no weapon to break herself free. Except for the one Michael could give her.

He and he alone could find the proof that would implicate Pietr Hootendorf in smuggling activities. He could give the proof to her to use as she saw fit, if and when the need arose. He could set her free.

Even if he died doing it.

18

~

While Maru brushed out her hair, Analisa stared at herself in the mirror. Or she supposed it was herself—that wild-eyed, pallid wraith of a woman who stared back at her. She felt on the edge of a mental collapse, and she looked the part. The day had been a continual drain on her strength, a constant strain on her nerves.

Seeing Michael, talking to him, dancing in his arms, all had been a blessing as well as a torture. She had never thought to see him again, had inured herself to a lifetime of pining for him. To have him in her arms for such a brief time, only to be reminded that on the morrow he would sail away, never to return, ripped through the tenuous mending she'd begun on her heart.

Pietr stepped into her room, and a raw hunger, a potent longing, emanated from him. Her heart sank. Though he had never looked at her with lust, it was there now, in his eyes and stance, and she understood the meaning of the bulge in his breeches. Seeing her dancing in the arms of other men must have roused his possessive nature. Oh, God, not tonight. She could not bear it. She could not endure Pietr's embrace when her whole being still tingled from Michael's touch, while her body still craved the weight of his against hers.

"I am sorry," she moaned, a miserable whisper. "I feel so ill tonight."

He tightened his jaw the merest fraction, and she knew his pride would not permit him to acknowledge that she had just refused him.

"You do look rather distraught. I must say I am not surprised. I should have put a stop to your dancing well before I did."

His skill at manipulating the situation from embarrassment to logical explanation both impressed and depressed her. She would never be able to outthink this man. "A good night's sleep should set me right."

Yes, if she had the night to gather the shredded tatters of her heart together, she might present some semblance of normalcy by morning. By morning, Michael would be gone from Banda Neira. She need no longer live with the sick dread that he might have died during his escape, or entertain the passing fancy that he might have survived and would stop to see her once before he went on his way. He'd done that, and now he would be gone. She could put all thoughts of him behind her and begin her life anew.

"I will instruct your maid to bring you something soothing to drink," Pietr said.

"Nutmeg tea," Analisa requested impulsively. On this night, she craved numbness to overtake her.

Maru's hands faltered a bit, but she kept brushing until Pietr left. Once the door closed behind him, the brush clattered to the floor.

"What's wrong?" Analisa asked.

"That nutmeg tea, bad for mevrouw," Maru muttered.

"Pietr drinks it every evening," Analisa defended her decision, while silently acknowledging that Maru was right.

Maru sniffed contemptuously. "All men like nutmeg tea. Men all the same, mevrouw, no matter if they mynheer or Banda. Drink the nutmeg tea, get silly same as rum. See things that are not there."

"No, Maru—when you drink the tea, you see and feel nothing."

"Drink too much and feel like dead, but drink a little and see much. Flowers, maybe. Beautiful birds. Feeling like you can fly with birds."

Maybe a flower-scented, free-flying hallucination would suit her purposes as well as insensibility. A sweet, soaring dream to wipe all memories of Michael Rowland straight from her mind.

And so she gulped down all the tea contained in the small pot brought by Tali, two cups perhaps, far less than she'd swallowed on her wedding night. Her mind remained depressingly clear, but she recognized effects within her body. Warmth radiated from the tea settled in her stomach, so that her skin dewed despite the pleasant tropical night. Another cup of tea might be enough to push her into insensibility, but she had no more.

She could not lie abed beneath the cloying folds of mosquito netting, and so she went to the windows. There was always a breeze from the sea, and at night it carried extra coolness. She fumbled at the pins binding her braids to her crown and undid all Maru's careful work. She raked her fingers through the loosened braids until her hair floated free around her shoulders, down to her hips. She lifted her face into the wind and felt the moon caressing her skin. It wasn't enough. She undid her buttons, every one, until her bed gown gapped open. The breeze teased past the open seams and swirled around her, cool and delicious.

She stared out over the sea. If the nutmeg tea could indeed grant her the sensation of flying like a bird, she knew exactly where she would go—across the water, to Michael.

She made it easy for him. When Michael approached the vast mansion, he'd been daunted by the challenge of finding her room among so many. He'd stood beneath the shade trees, watching, trying to guess. He saw Pietr Hootendorf's silhouette through a second-floor window. He was sitting in a chair reading, judging by his posture. Eventually he doused the lantern light and all was still, and Michael's vitals clenched to think that Pietr might have turned from his book to Analisa.

And then she'd appeared, two windows away, obviously in another room. Hers had not been lit by Hootendorf's light. The wind lifted her hair and caused her voluminous bed gown to billow around her until it looked as if she might be lifted into the air. Now he knew which room was hers. Though he trembled with eagerness to go to her, he knew that Hootendorf had just settled into his bed and might awaken at the slightest noise.

He hunkered down in the deepest shadows, prepared to wait.

He touched his shirt and felt the folded cloth he'd tucked inside—cloth he'd filched from Hootendorf's packaging hut that bore the same unique weaving as the cloth that had enwrapped the nutmegs he'd tried pirating away. He knew that weaving was as distinctive as handwriting. All Analisa had to do was convince the Dutch to compare her husband's cloth stock against the nutmeg pouch that had been confiscated from him.

Even better, a hefty handful of Richard's coins and two hours spent asking questions along the waterfront had bought him two names. One, a disreputable fisherman whose loyalty went to the highest bidder—for a price, he remembered and confirmed that he sometimes carried fertile nutmegs from Mynheer Pietr Hootendorf to pirate hands. For another handful of silver, he'd be willing to repeat his story to Governor Hoon.

The second name belonged to a full-blooded Bandanese native who worked as a slave on this very plantation, which once belonged to his family. He despised all the Dutch, but Hootendorf more than most, and was ready to provide dates and quantities of Hootendorf's illicit shipments to the British at Run.

The second informant had also chillingly echoed Richard Ellington's suspicions that Pietr Hootendorf might not be the father of Analisa's child. "No *sirani* children cursed with Hootendorf's ugly looks," the informant had chortled, and then sobered. "One slave girl, very pretty, she say another planter tease Hootendorf to give her away if he not want her for himself. Hootendorf lock her in secret cabin, keep her in bed for a week for no reason. She tells everyone, because she very pretty, no man ever put her in bed for no reason before. People laugh at story, and girl, she disappear. No girl ever talk about Hootendorf again."

Michael had fathered Analisa's baby. He would stake his life on it.

The wind molded Analisa's gown against her belly, and then lifted it away. His woman. His child. His woman, who dreamed of respectability, of a fine life where she could hold her head high, where her child might grow strong and happy with no taint surrounding its birth. Michael could not give her such a life.

He kept watch over Analisa until she withdrew, a long time later, into her room. And then he watched over the slumbering house a little while longer, judging the way the moonlight struck the walls. The tree closest to Analisa's room was unfortunately cast in full light, but the house stood still and silent. Hootendorf was so secure in his island enclave that he must not have found it necessary to post guards, as many of the *perkenier* did—or perhaps knowing that he himself was responsible for any nutmegs mysteriously disappearing from his groves made it seem a ridiculous precaution.

Michael ran, crouching, to the tree, and skinned up it with a dexterity that would have done any mast-climbing sailor proud. Edging along the likeliest limb was a chancier prospect, but not half so risky as the leap from branch to windowsill. The chasm to be crossed loomed greater than it had from below, but he had to risk it. The worst that could happen was that he'd fall, and his body wouldn't make that much noise thudding to the ground.

Actually, it made more noise slamming into the open window. He couldn't prevent a little *oof* from escaping when the wooden windowsill caught him right in the belly, and his feet with their damned hard leather boots smacked smartly against the side of the house. He dangled there like a worm caught on a fishhook for a few minutes, struggling to get his wind back.

There was no sound from the room. His arrival could not possibly have gone unnoticed, save by the soundest sleeper. But perhaps Analisa did sleep like the dead—he had no way of knowing. It was just one of the many wondrous discoveries a man could make about a woman if she truly belonged to him each and every day and night of their lives.

He gathered himself, and using his arms as levers, rolled headfirst into the room.

He lay there a moment, letting his eyes become accustomed to the gloom, trying to quiet his breathing so he could listen for sounds of life in the room. Nothing. Cautiously, he rose into a crouch, balancing one hand flat against the floor. Still nothing.

A bed, shrouded in netting, stood at the far wall.

He went to it. The sheer netting enveloped the bed like a cloud, and deep within he could see her slumbering form. Alone. He parted the netting. She looked like an angel asleep amid billowing pillows and frothy white bedclothes. Save for the creamy, luscious flesh bared by her open bed gown. She breathed so softly, so quietly, that it was no wonder he hadn't heard her.

He braced his weight upon one knee. The bed shifted and she turned slightly toward him. The movement sent half of her gown spilling away from her shoulder, revealing one perfect, rose-crested breast.

He meant to kiss her forehead to waken her gently, he honestly meant to do no more, but the feel of her flesh against his lips was as addictive as the first drops of water she'd ever trickled into his mouth. He craved more. His lips traveled down, over the peak of her nose, to claim her lips. He meant to do no more, honestly, but when she let free a breathy sigh and moved into his kiss, his hands somehow ignored his mind's command to stay still and delved into the inviting opening of her unbuttoned gown. One hand curled around her side, the other unerringly found her breast. She murmured, a feminine sound of pleasure that tore loose the last remaining shreds of sense that he had. He pulled her to him, hard, his lips drinking hers, his tongue seeking hers, his flesh straining to burst through his garments to find the warm, silky texture of her. He trailed through the valley of her breasts, tasting every inch of her along the way, until he found the smooth, firm flesh of her belly. He let his lips rest there a moment, thinking of his babe nestled within her silken depths. 'Twas torture to think so—he retraced his path until her mouth was his again.

Her eyelids dragged open and widened. Her lips, too, drawing away from his with exquisite slowness.

"Oh, my!" she whispered. "I thought it would make me fly like a bird."

"Shhh." He pressed a gentle finger against her lips. "What are you talking about, Analisa? Are you not well?"

"Michael?"

She jerked away as she whispered his name, and her eyes widened ever more. All traces of her slumbering dreaminess vanished, to be replaced by a horror so profound that it rocked Michael to his core.

She glanced down at herself, saw his hand cupping her breast, and even in the dim moonlight he could see her flesh redden with embarrassment.

"No!" She strained away from him. "I spoke the final vows! I cannot do this, even in an hallucination!"

"Analisa!" She was growing increasingly agitated, and he saw nothing to do but clamp his hand over her mouth until she settled down. "This is no hallucination, Analisa. 'Tis me, Michael. Calm yourself, or you'll wake your husband."

She stiffened and shook her head wildly, nearly dislodging his hand. He pulled her up tight against his chest. "Please, stop thrashing. I am no hallucination, beloved. Can you not feel my heart beating against your ear? Can you not feel my breath stirring your hair?"

She quivered and tensed for a long moment, and then he felt her flesh ease beneath his hand, felt her tentative nod brush against his breast.

He let his weight carry the both of them back down onto the bed, into the billowing luxury of her pillows. For one breathless, exquisite moment, she returned his kiss, her flesh swelled to his touch, and then she pushed him away.

"No. This is wrong. Please, Michael, get out of my husband's bed."

He did. Nothing she said could have driven him away from her faster. He stood there trembling with the realization of what he'd come within a hairbreadth of doing—nearly cuckolding another man in his own bed, so swept up by passion that all sense had leaked from his head.

She came up behind him. He felt her touch, light against the back of his neck and then brushing across his shoulders, as if she meant to memorize their width. And then to his amazement, her arms curved around his waist and she pressed herself against his back. He could feel her tears, hot and wet, through his shirt.

"You must leave at once."

"I brought something for you. For the babe."

He did not know if she noticed how he choked over those words. He did not want to break her embrace, but the cloth had to be fished from his shirt, and he had to see her face-to-face to make sure she understood the importance of what he was giving her.

"Guard this secret with your life," he warned. "This cloth matches the nutmeg pouch I carried when they caught me."

"Captain Verbeek turned that pouch over to the governor," said Analisa.

"Excellent. Then Hoon can match the two."

"Match it? And why?"

He stroked her hair and held her closer. He was about to shatter many of her illusions, and he did not know how to ease the pain. "I tried to tell you this before, Analisa, but your husband provided the nutmegs for smuggling. He is a traitor to the Company."

She shuddered away from him. "No! You lie!"

He had to quiet her, and so he drew her back against his chest. "I do not say this to hurt you, beloved. I must leave in the morning with the *Glorious*

Elizabeth. I cannot be here to protect you or the babe if something terrible happens, but this knowledge could give you strength."

"No. I don't want to know."

"You must know these things, to protect yourself against being sucked into the quagmire along with him, if he is ever discovered."

He told her the names of his informants, told her how to find them, and made her repeat everything twice so she would remember.

"I must leave now."

"Yes. But . . ." She looked up at him, and all her emotions were there upon her face for him to see. She loved him. She did not want him to go. And yet they both knew he could not stay. "Will you hold me, just for a minute, before you go?"

"Aye." He wrapped one arm around her, and his other hand brushed the open bed gown down off one shoulder. He ran his fingers over the smooth line of her shoulder, down her arm, and then stroked his hand against the curve of her waist. In silent accord they sank to the edge of the bed. They sat there, holding each other, nothing more, listening to each other's heartbeats, their warmth mingling one final time.

The door to Pietr's room eased open.

"Analisa? The creaking of your bed wakened me. If you are truly unwell, I will—"

Pietr Hootendorf stepped into the room. Analisa and Michael sat welded together by moonlight. His lips were pressed against the top of her head, his hand plunged into her open gown. Her hair tumbled wild and free around them both, but not concealing enough to hide the tip of her naked breast peeping through the silken strands.

Moving faster than Michael would have expected from a man of his age, Pietr feinted back into his room, then burst once more through the door.

Moonlight gleamed from the foot-long shaft of the knife he clutched in his fist.

"Pietr, no!"

Analisa whirled free of Michael's arms. Heedless of her own safety, she planted herself between her husband and the man she loved. Her movements sent her hair swirling, sent the bed gown slipping off her other shoulder. She stood naked to the waist, the cloud of her hair her only covering.

The moonlight was not kind to her husband. His lean features, in the stark light and shadows, took on the aspect of a near-skeletal corpse. His eyes burned dark with fury and hatred.

"Pietr, no," he mimicked. "No, what, Analisa? No, this is not as it seems? No, you do not understand what you see? Bah."

"It is not innocent, but I swear to you, we did nothing to cause you dishonor. I swear it."

He waved the knife threateningly, and she took a step back. Michael's arm came around her, and before she could object, he shifted her to his side, protecting her with his body. Pietr's knife came up against Michael's breastbone. She felt the minute flinch, the barely perceptible shiver, that told her the tip of the knife had pierced Michael's skin. Pietr's bleak black eyes swept over Michael's face and then kindled with recognition.

"You," he growled. "I remarked you all evening. You could scarce keep your hands off her, with myself and all the island watching you dance attendance. You might as well have taken her on the floor, in front of everyone, and saved yourself the trouble of coming here."

"Pietr, please," she whispered. "We did nothing. We . . . touched. It was wrong, but we did not—"

He turned his head to fix that malevolent glare upon

her. "Whore," he spat. He let loose a string of such foul profanities that she could not believe they came from his ordinarily circumspect lips. "Spreading your legs for him after but a few hours' acquaintance."

Michael growled low in his throat. She felt him tense, preparatory to a lunge, and she dug her fingers into his arm.

"No, Michael, let him say what he pleases about me. It doesn't matter."

To her amazement, she realized it truly didn't matter what Pietr thought of her. For all her life, people had been believing the worst of her, no matter how hard she tried to change their opinions. She knew the truth. She knew that she had clung as best she could to her marriage vows, despite soul-crushing temptation. She did not need Pietr to acknowledge her tenuous hold on her chastity; she did not need his approval of her behavior.

She had never needed it. She had but to search her own soul and decide whether she could live with what she read there. And she could. Dear God, she could.

"I cannot let this pass, Analisa. You are not at fault here, and he must know."

"No, Michael." Sick with dread, she knew what he meant to do—and he did it.

"I am no stranger to Analisa. I used your bride cruelly, Hootendorf. I seduced her on board that ship, while she was lonely and bereft and had no defenses against my tender assault."

"On board ship?" Stunned, Pietr let the knife waver.

"Aye. I knew that only she could help me escape certain death, and I used every wile, every bit of experience I had with women to play upon her sympathies. She never had a chance."

"That is not true!" She lifted her chin. Her eyes met Michael's for one brief, liquid caress. She parted her lips, ready to admit that it had been she who sought him out. Michael forestalled her. He placed his hand over the one she still had resting on his arm, and he squeezed so tightly that she caught her breath. "Shhh," he breathed, so low that to Pietr it must have sounded like a mere outrush of breath.

"You see—even now she cannot admit how thoroughly I foxed her."

"Do you mistake me for a fool? You are the smuggler! She did help you escape!" Pietr roared. He slashed the knife toward Analisa. "You knew who he was all the time. You deliberately lied and said he was not among the British!"

"She did not know it was me, not until a moment ago. She never saw me in the light of day, nor did she see me without a wild mane of hair and beard to rival that of Moses." Michael's words rang through the room, absolving her of so much that she did not deserve.

"On board ship," Pietr repeated with dull resignation. He stared toward her, the familiar speculation traveling from her breasts to her waist to her hips. His eyes smoldered anew at the sight of Michael's arm wrapped around her waist, his hand splayed protectively over her belly. "The babe," Pietr grated hoarsely. "So it was you, and not a Dutchman who might share some common features . . ."

"She is your wife, Hootendorf. Nobody will question that the child is yours—providing you do nothing foolish to discredit her."

Pietr could not believe such a wild tale, could not accept the outright admission that her child might have been fathered by Michael—and yet it seemed that he wanted to, very badly. A tiny shred of hope kindled in his expression, and rather than feeling relieved, it made her ache with pity for him.

Pietr stepped back. Without taking his eyes from

them, he yanked the netting down from over her bed and flung it at Analisa. "Use one end of this to tie his hands behind his back. Tightly. And then give the other end to me. And you—" He waved the knife at Michael before bringing it to rest just below Analisa's shoulder blade. "This gets plunged straight into her heart if you try to act the hero."

"I'll kill you if you hurt her," Michael rasped.

"She is mine. I can do with her what I will."

"She will never be yours. Not the part of her that matters."

"I have all of her that I want."

"Then you're more of a fool than I."

Analisa hurriedly knotted the netting. She could not bear listening to them snarl over her like wolves snapping at each other over a fresh-killed deer.

She handed the end of Michael's bindings over to Pietr. "What will you do with us now?"

"Get into the bed."

Stricken, she could not move. Surely he did not mean to prove his possession of her by taking what was his by right of law right beneath Michael's watchful eye. Michael drew a ragged breath, no doubt thinking the same, and she felt the air sizzle with his fury.

"By God," he roared, "this flimsy binding will not stop me from killing you if you treat her with so much disrespect."

"Get into the bed, Analisa," Pietr repeated. His lip curled with triumph. "I don't need to take her in front of you to prove she's mine. I'm merely going to lock her into this room. I'll lock you elsewhere until I can send for the authorities. And you can sit there stewing, wondering what I might be doing with her."

He drove Michael from the room at knifepoint. He never looked back at her. She cowered on her bed, shivering, while the lock snicked into place.

19

$\sim$

The sky lightened, first with a band of pewter-gray, and then one the color of ash, and then shimmering strips of gold and orange and white inched up over the horizon.

Analisa leaned from her window until her body instinctively clenched for balance. The household began its usual stirring. The scent of woodsmoke curled through the air, announcing that the cook had stoked the kitchen fires. Hens squawked their indignation as quick hands filched eggs from beneath their sleep-warmed, feathered bellies. A boy stumbled through the yard, yawning and scratching his belly, dragging a basket meant for collecting fresh fruit from the mango and orange trees.

There was no sound, no outcry, nothing to hint at what Pietr had done with Michael.

She left the window and paced the confines of her room, tested the locked door a dozen times, a hundred times. She even rattled the knob of the door connecting her room to Pietr's. He did not answer her entreaties, though she begged for his mercy until she went hoarse.

The sun was high in the sky when at last she heard a quick tap at the door. She whirled about in time to see unfamiliar brown hands deposit a breakfast tray upon her floor, and then the door closed and the lock clicked into place once more.

She had no appetite, no thirst, save for information about Michael. But she was conscious as never before of the babe she carried in her womb. Michael's shouldering of all blame had somehow blunted Pietr's immediate wrath, but she knew it was the child more than herself that had granted her this temporary respite from punishment. She must nurture her babe, treasure that tiny life, not only for the sake of saving her own life, but for the possibility of keeping some spark of Michael Rowland alive as well. She had no doubt he would die now—either Pietr would kill him, or he would turn him over to the Dutch to finish the job.

She glanced toward her bed. She supposed she ought to feel righteous, knowing she'd upheld her wedding vows, but some part of her regretted that she'd pushed Michael away the night before.

She judged it was nearly noon when Tali, her eyes red-rimmed and puffy, was passed through the door in much the same manner as Analisa's breakfast tray.

"I am to make you ready for walking, mevrouw," she mumbled.

Analisa gripped her maid's hands. "Tell me—what has Pietr done?"

"I am not permitted to speak to you, mevrouw. Only to make you ready."

Tali did not share Maru's skill with the Dutch way of arranging hair, and so she gathered Analisa's hair into one long braid that snaked down her back, native style. She pulled Analisa's wedding gown from her wardrobe.

"No, Tali—choose another. Any other," Analisa said.

"Mynheer said you are to wear this one."

Pietr met her in the hall. He stood straight and forbidding and dismissed Tali with a curt shake of his head. When the servant had gone, he motioned toward a small table, and Analisa saw her glove box resting atop it. "Put that on," he said.

She lifted the glittering glove and slipped her hand into it. It felt cold and heavy, even as glorious colored fires sparked from the jewels and embraced her and Pietr both within its rainbow shower.

"Come with me." He took Analisa by the elbow, a punishing hold. She could not help comparing his touch to the night before, when the merest brush of Michael's fingers against that very place had sent her heart surging with joy.

Pietr guided her out of the house and then down one of the paths winding through the nutmeg groves. Analisa's arm went numb from his hold on her. The doves fluttered in the trees, and their beating wings, coupled with the soft sea breezes, stirred the heady scent of nutmeg through the air. They passed through the cool, fragrant grove in utter silence, and then came upon a small rocky promontory looking out over the sea. Overhead the sun shone in brilliant gold, the sky a blue so pure that it almost hurt one's eyes to stare at it. Analisa thought no shade of blue could be more beautiful until she looked out over the sea and saw its crystal azure depths crowned with the white froth of the tide.

Paradise.

She stood there, in the midst of lush, fragrant beauty, and wondered whether her husband meant to push her off the cliff into the sea.

But Pietr's rage had altered, shifted into something dark and wretched. A sickly pallor whitened his tan, throwing every age line and wrinkle into prominence. Instead of looking far younger than his years, he stood with the stooped bent of an old, old man.

She had done this to him.

"You knew him." Pietr's observation rang with confidence. "Do not lie to me. You knew who he was all along."

There seemed little point in lying, not when she was so bad at it and not when he had obviously already made up his mind about what to believe.

"Aye. I recognized him that day when we sat in the carriage, when we watched the British come ashore seeking victuals."

Pietr flinched. "I saw you come alive then, Analisa, in a way that you've never done in my presence. You were like a flower, blossoming like a rose opening its velvet petals to the sun."

"I did not think my happiness mattered to you."

"God knows I never meant it to, but . . ." His words trailed away, and he caught her by the shoulders, his hands trembling with something like panic. "Look around you. All of this is mine, *mine*. By your marriage to me, it becomes yours as well. Our children will thrive and prosper amid beauty and luxury that most people cannot even dream about. Why, when I give you so much, can you not come to life for *me*?"

She could not answer him, for there was no answer that would satisfy the naked craving that radiated from him. Images raced through her mind—her wanton, glorious passion with Michael against the couplings she dreaded enduring with Pietr. Michael had only to glance her way to send her trembling and flowing with desire; she had never felt a shred of desire for Pietr, never would.

"I know what it is," he broke into her silence. "I erred in my treatment of you from the beginning. I thought to hold you distant, to hold my heart true to Hilde. I will change, Analisa. I swear it. Tell me what I must do."

"Set him free."

Something died in him. The uncertain eagerness shining in his eyes shifted into fury. He had humbled himself to her, and she'd rejected his offer. She'd devastated the pride of a vindictive man who held complete control over her. Gouging at his wound could only result in terrible retribution, and still she could not stop herself from begging for the man she loved.

"Set him free, and I will deny you nothing."

"Not even your soul?"

"My soul is mine alone."

"Is it? Then why, when that outlaw scum has his hands upon you, does it seem your whole being, the essence that is you and you alone, belongs to him?"

Tears stung her eyes, for she knew he spoke the truth, and she knew it would never change. "Let him go," she whispered. "Please let him go."

"I'll see him dead first."

She made a move to run away from him, to return to the uncertain sanctuary of her room, but he caught her arm and would not let her get away.

"Have I not given you everything a woman craves? Why do you not love me?" He seemed puzzled, as if he expected love to occur as naturally as hens laid eggs after pecking their fill of their master's corn.

"You scorned me and made it abundantly clear you found me unsatisfactory," she cried. "How could you expect me to love you?" *Especially as you are not Michael,* she added silently.

"But all this!" He waved his hands to encompass the surroundings. "I have given you everything."

"I wanted respect. The right to hold my head high." She murmured the words to herself, knowing she had herself to blame for the drowning of those dreams. Pietr heard. He drew back, smiling a little, and she had the sick feeling that he somehow meant to use her modest ambitions against her.

"I will give both of you a chance, then. Providing . . ."

"Anything," she promised recklessly.

Triumph curled his lip while dread snaked through her.

"I demand your utter submission to my will. Honor your oath to me, your vows to me, by identifying him to the authorities."

"No," she whispered.

"We can use the excuse so handily provided by your precious pirate. We will tell the governor that you did not at first recognize the rogue, but during the ball you realized who he was—the man who on his own is responsible for smuggling nutmegs. Quite distraught, you waited until we were alone at home to ask my counsel about what you should do. I, of course, advised you to tell the truth at once."

She wanted to haul back and slap him until he admitted the truth. Yes, it would certainly suit her husband if she implicated Michael without revealing that Pietr himself was involved in nutmeg smuggling. She would never have understood the depths of Pietr's treachery if Michael hadn't risked everything to tell her. The knowledge would give her strength, Michael had said, and he was right.

The temptation to use that knowledge struck so hard that she had to press her lips together. Strength, she was learning, was a tenuous thing. Expending it too early, before it was fully developed, would render it useless. Michael had entrusted her with this information, confident that she would use it well. Nobody had ever credited her with so much ability, nobody had ever acknowledged that she held even a shred of competence.

"I am surprised, Pietr, that you give Michael credit for fashioning an explanation that could pass muster."

"I always admire courage, dear wife, especially

when it so unerringly betrays an opponent's weaknesses."

"You speak as though all of this heartache is part of some elaborate game."

"So it is, and I am the master player."

"Well, I will not play along. I cannot betray him. Ask anything else of me, Pietr, anything."

He seemed gratified by her defiance, and she wondered what it was about this small display of courage that he would be able to use against her.

"You will perform as required, Analisa. Turn him in, and you will redeem yourself of any hint of complicity in his original escape. The whispering about you will stop. The women will welcome you into their homes. You will gain that respect you crave."

He had unerringly homed in on one of her weaknesses. It took all her strength to spurn him. "I won't do it."

"He will die regardless. Your silly, womanish sacrifice will make you even more of a pariah than you are now, and this I cannot tolerate. I will have to protect myself. I'll be forced to admit to the officials that you knew this man's true identity and deliberately lied to save his skin yet again."

She knew how they would react. She could imagine the loathing, the accusations of traitor, that would be sent her way. And, by association, Pietr's way.

"You will have to set me aside," she said, unable to dim the spark of hope that flared at the thought. "My shame would reflect upon you."

"I will never set you aside." He gripped her other arm and held her before him, shaking her a little like a recalcitrant child that has refused to learn its lesson. "I could, you know, and everyone will be amazed that I do not, but I will make them understand that a Hootendorf doesn't turn his back on any vows, including marriage vows that bind him to an ungrateful, treasonous bitch. Everyone's sympathies will be with me. I shall not suffer the slurs, the insults, the ostracism. No, you—utterly isolated on this island, completely confined to the house, which I assure you *I can do*— you will be the only one who suffers."

She thought wildly of that room crammed with Hilde's frantic embroidery, of the loneliness and desperation implicit in each screaming stitch. She might as well dash herself off the cliff. The choices Pietr gave her were impossible. She could not betray her love. And she might as well be dead as to suffer the living hell Pietr predicted for her. She would have done it, would have flung herself off the cliff in an instant but for the child growing in her womb.

"I cannot betray him."

Pietr's grip tightened cruelly.

"You're hurting me."

"Soon you will know the true meaning of pain." And yet there was no threat in his voice, only an ineffable sadness as if he'd already plumbed the depth of her weaknesses and found them laughably easy to exploit. She could not fathom what sort of punishment he would have in store for her, for Michael.

She learned soon enough.

Of all the prisons Michael had occupied of late, this latest one wasn't so bad. The sturdy one-room cabin, built beyond the farthest edge of the nutmeg grove, lay nestled in a sheltered swell, where it could not be seen from the house, and yet it was open to cooling breezes from the sea. There was no doubt what it had been built for—it was the trysting place Michael's informant had told him about, the place where Analisa's husband had confined a young, pretty whore—a young, pretty girl who'd vanished after betraying one of Pietr Hootendorf's secrets.

And now Hootendorf had locked Michael there.

The secret Michael knew could cause far more damage to Hootendorf than a whore's ridiculing his manhood.

Analisa, too, knew Hootendorf's deepest secret. Somehow, Michael had to make sure that she would not find herself locked in this small prison, this hidden place that preceded a more final disappearance.

A set of manacles that had surely been built into this sumptuous bed for a different purpose bound Michael to the bedpost. Though he'd tested that deceptively light manacle again and again, it was as unbreakable as the thick iron restraints that had bound him on the *Island Treasure*.

He'd pitted his strength repeatedly against the massive mahogany bed, but hadn't been able to shift it by so much as an inch. He could stand, lie on the bed, take a few steps to his necessary bucket, no more. Even so, a bevy of servants arrived before noon and pounded narrow wooden slats over the windows, each a handspan apart from the other, so that Michael could not squeeze through even if he managed to shed the chain at his wrist.

He wondered why Hootendorf had been so solicitous of his comfort, for surely it would have been easier—and crueler—to seal the windows altogether rather than to leave him with a pleasant view and a comfortable breeze.

He found out soon enough.

Analisa, dressed in her wedding gown, with her hair loose and lifted by the wind, came with the wench who brought his morning meal and water. She stood cool and lovely far beyond Michael's reach, silent, staring at him with wide, agonized eyes while the serving girl, entrusted with the door key, brought him his food and drink.

She was back again late in the afternoon, with another serving girl. This time, Analisa held her right arm curved at her waist, with her left hand supporting the weight of the jeweled glove she wore. Though he'd never seen it, Michael knew it was her God-be-cursed marriage glove. The sun struck against the innumerable facets, virtually bathing Analisa in a dancing rainbow of color. Every inch of her glowed with a jeweled radiance proclaiming Pietr Hootendorf's wealth, Pietr Hootendorf's claim to everything the shimmering colors touched.

Michael understood—Hootendorf was taunting them both.

It was a masterfully designed torture meant to break her will as well as his. But either Analisa had not figured it out for herself, or she was too close to crumbling. No jewel sparkled more than the tears tracking down her cheeks as she stood staring at him.

She had obviously been placed under orders not to speak, and the vigilant serving wench was sure to report any breach on her part. But Michael had not been so restrained.

"Take heart, beloved," he called.

She made a move toward him, but was brought up short by a sharp reprimand from the servant. A servant, issuing orders to the lady of the manor. Michael's fist curled impotently.

"He means to impress upon you the helplessness of your situation, the hopelessness of mine," he cried to her. "You are not so weak-willed that you will buckle beneath such an assault. Your will and your pride have been honed and hardened. Where some women would bend, you stand tall. Where some would whimper and plead for forgiveness, you will never beg."

Her chin lifted. Her shoulders straightened. She dashed the tears from her cheeks and sent him a wavery smile.

She was back the next day, and then the next, always in the company of a different servant so that her humiliation should be fresh, so that more tongues could speculate. Each day she stood taller and stronger, unbowed. Michael's heart swelled with pride for her. It was not so bad, he thought, if he left this earth after accomplishing this one thing.

The next day, she came to him.

He was sitting on the bed, mindlessly working the hasp of his wrist manacle against the bedpost. He'd kept up the activity for virtually every waking moment with discouragingly poor results—he'd shaved only a few crumbs of the rock-hard, aged mahogany away from the inches-thick post. At such a rate, it would take him years to free himself. And yet he could not sit there, numbly accepting his fate, without making some effort, no matter how token, against his imprisonment.

Analisa had paused in her usual spot until that day's serving wench neared the cabin. And then summoning a deep breath and notching her chin high, she walked to the cabin. The servant, hearing the crunch of Analisa's footsteps, whirled about and spilled Michael's rations in her agitation. It mattered naught. The sight of Analisa smiling at him, being able to see the fine lines of exhaustion surrounding her eyes, the brave tremble of her lips, could sustain him for eternity.

The servant screeched warnings, threats, Michael couldn't tell which, only that Analisa silenced her with a well-honed sneer of disdain. The servant scurried away.

Analisa ran to his window, gripped the narrow wood slats between her hands. Her haughty manner vanished; she was once more the heartbreakingly gentle and loving woman who dared look beyond Michael's well-polished veneer. He moved as close to her as he could, cursing the manacle that bound him to the bed. For a moment they did naught but stare at each other. With no one to witness, there seemed to be no words powerful enough to express a lifetime of loving.

"She will fetch your husband," Michael said at length, his voice raspy with emotion.

"I do not care. I had to see you once more. Really see you. Each visit was timed so that this cabin was either cast in shadow or the sun was in my eyes."

"He is a devious and vindictive man."

"More than most people suspect. I am never quite certain what he plans to do. I am never sure whether I am obeying my own impulses, or jerking like a puppet in response to his will."

"I would spare you that if I could, beloved."

"I have a weapon against him, thanks to you. I am saving it for the right time."

It had been worth it, then. He would never go easy to his death, he would ever regret the adventures that had been denied him. . . but it had been worth it.

"I will never forget . . ." she began, and then a moist huskiness stilled her throat. She cleared it away. "You faced certain death, and yet you urged *me* to find my inner strength. You gave up your own dreams to help me fulfill mine."

"I love you, Analisa. I could not do less, and my only regret as I die shall be that I could not be the man to make your dreams come true."

"You gave me new and better dreams, my love. And they all came true, if only for a brief time."

She stretched her arm through the slats. Her hand, its long, graceful fingers, curved toward him. He had already gone as close to the window as his bound wrist would allow him, but he reached—and came up a good six inches short. She strained, her shoulder wedging between the slats, her face turned so that her cheek pressed tight against the bars. He strained as well, ignoring the burning in his manacled wrist, the bone-grinding protest of his shoulder as he pitted all his strength against the manacle holding him to the bed. It still wasn't enough. With a mighty lunge, and an involuntary roar against the agony at his wrist and shoulder, he managed to touch her. The lightest of touches, the briefest caress of fingertips against fingertips.

It was not enough. There would never be enough.

"I must go now," she whispered. "I will not come back."

He nodded, his teeth still clenched against the pain. Better she should go and stay away, far away, than endure this repeated agony of being so close and yet unable to touch.

He watched her until the swaying nutmeg trees enfolded her within their cool green shade. She was gone and there was no reason to keep watch, but he could not look away, fancying he could still see the air shifting around the space she had occupied. Then a movement caught his eye.

Pietr Hootendorf stepped from behind a tree. He had been watching, the whole time.

20

❧

Analisa heard the strong footfalls behind her and felt a tiny tingle of alarm.

"Analisa."

She came to a halt, her heart palpitating. "Pietr."

Her husband came up from behind her, *behind her,* so she knew he had watched while she spoke to Michael, while they'd managed that final, straining touch. The touch that had sparked her back into life, reminding her that her body was a living, breathing, *feeling* entity, reminding her that a proud spirit dwelled within.

Michael had sacrificed his dream in order that she might achieve hers. He could not know, she could not tell him, that his final touch had burned with the bitter knowledge that she could not live as this empty husk. She, too, must sacrifice everything if doing so would give him the smallest chance of survival.

"You disobeyed my order not to speak to him." Pietr caught up to her and gripped her by the elbow.

She jerked away from his hold, though she did not run, as she ached to do.

"You have no right to do this to him."

"I have every right."

"Please do not take that superior stance with me,

Pietr. I know your crimes equal his. I know that if he deserves to be executed for smuggling, you deserve the same."

He stood rigid for a moment, studying her. "What do you know?"

"Everything." She took a fortifying breath, praying her demeanor did not betray the raging fear battering away inside her. She had never imagined that using strength would require so much courage. Or perhaps she'd always known—why else had she bowed for so many years before the demands and sneers of those who considered themselves her betters? She had always possessed inner strength; it had taken Michael's love to ignite her courage. "I have proof that the smuggled nutmegs came from this *perken.* Witnesses are waiting to testify against you. One word from me and you will become a laughingstock."

She expected he might strike her, or look upon her with loathing, and she braced herself to accept that. She deserved no better, turning against the man who had offered her an honorable marriage, a life filled with luxuries. She did not expect the stark agony that whitened his features, the visible crumbling of the swaggering bravado that imbued Pietr Hootendorf's every movement.

"You would destroy me, for him."

"If you force me. I would hope that we could . . . come to another arrangement."

His lip curled. "You forget your place. You are thousands of miles from home, with none to care if you live or die. I could kill you here and now, and there would be no one to mourn you, no one to take me to account."

"You could," she agreed. She laid her hand protectively over her womb. "But I don't think you will."

The movement of her hand drew his gaze like a magnet.

"Damn you to hell and back," he whispered.

"Set him free."

"Never."

"Let him go, and I will play the role you created for me. I will present to the world the picture of loving contentment. I will produce all the heirs you want, and this island will blossom with Dutch mansions, all bearing the Hootendorf crest."

"You love him that much."

"Set him free."

"Go home, Analisa."

Fear shafted through her, but not for herself. She could not leave Pietr out here while rage simmered in his blood. He could so easily charge back through the groves and murder Michael while he was helpless. But a moment later, she realized she need not fear that— at least for now.

Pietr had gone wild-eyed. "No," he whispered, his gaze resting on a heavily laden nutmeg tree. "Mine." He swiveled toward the sea, and said it a little louder. "Mine, mine, *mine!*" He breathed deep of the nutmeg-scented air. Only a man totally consumed with passion for his holdings would behold them with such covetousness, would look so devastated to think others might laugh at him, and take it away.

"Why do you do it, Pietr?" She begged him to explain. "Why have you risked everything for the sake of a little extra profit?"

"You cannot possibly understand." He spoke remotely, as if some detached part of himself responded while the passionate part strove to cling to what was his. "You cannot know what it is like to be told what to do, to have your every movement monitored, your very wealth determined by some nameless, faceless person who rules from behind a desk. You cannot know what it means to succeed and have others whisper that your success would have fallen to you regardless, because of luck, lending no credit to the hard work and sweat and risks you have taken."

"I understand more than you might imagine," she said.

"Do you?" He had regained his composure and now seemed only mildly interested. "If you did, you would not have taken such pains to point out to me how easily it can all be taken away from me, based upon a woman's whim. A man must rule as a king, Analisa. He must circumvent his enemies and strengthen his fortifications. Nothing can destroy him save for rot from within."

He lifted his head high and drew a great breath. She breathed the same air, redolent of nutmeg and sea breeze. He said nothing more to her, but headed toward the house. He stumbled once, then twice, though not a single stone or hole marred the surface of the well-tended path.

She followed behind.

She sat in her room for hours, until she heard him in the adjoining bedroom.

He made no attempt to enter her room.

Her promise echoed in her mind. She'd promised to play the role of loving wife. She had asked much of him in return and dared insinuate she might destroy him. She had asked him to grant freedom to the man who had cuckolded him and stolen his wife's heart. Perhaps she ought to prove that she would honor her promise before expecting him to act on her requests.

She ventured into Pietr's room, the first time she had ever breached the connecting door on her own.

Pietr barked a curt order to the manservant helping him dress, and the frightened man scuttled from the room.

"To what do I owe this unexpected pleasure, my dear wife?" His earlier desperate uncertainty had vanished. He feigned confusion while triumph smoldered in his eyes. It was as though the frightened, wounded man who had confided his dream of ruling like a king over his groves had never existed, as though that role had been part of some elaborate ruse only he understood.

Perhaps that was for the best. If he could pretend his moment of weakness had never existed, she could pretend . . . for the rest of her life.

"You said I would be forced to admit you are the better man. Very well. He is but outlaw scum who cannot manage to hang on to freedom no matter how many chances he gets. You are superior to him in every way."

"Yes, I am. I do not need you to tell me so, and I don't think you believe it, though I must say you lie very prettily." He swept a tear from the corner of her eye, where it had leaked from the effort it had taken to denounce Michael. "Have you come to me now so you might play the willing wife?"

The afternoon sun shafted through the windows, illuminating everything. Analisa fumbled with the buttons at her collar, knowing the pitiless sun revealed how her fingers shook. She lowered her head to hide her revulsion.

Pietr's hand snaked out and caught her by the chin. He lifted her face to the merciless light, and his own countenance drained of color.

"Will it be this way for you every time?" he rasped.

She could not answer, and he did not need to hear the words to know the truth.

His lips trembled. That brief softening was not kind to a face more suited to hauteur, a face that had spent too many years frowning with discontent.

"Never mind about the dress. Get into the bed."

She moved like a puppet, obeying when he pushed her to the bed, and then tumbling into it when he pressed down on her shoulders. She lay there unblinking, watching, while he fumbled with his breeches. He caught her staring at him and cursed, and turned away from her. He tore his shirt free and fumbled a bit more, and cursed even more violently.

"This is the wrong place," he mumbled to himself. "Yes, that is it. I never take my wife in this room."

He pulled her from the bed and pushed her, prodded her, through the doorway to her own room. Hilde's old room. A square of dark paint marked the spot above the bed where Hilde's portrait had hung until so recently.

Analisa stumbled into the bed, then swiveled around to watch him. He paid her no heed. He stripped his breeches away, shucked away his shirt as well, and stood before her naked in the full light. She had never seen a man in the light of day, but she knew where he should have swelled, where he ought to quiver, and no such sight met her eyes. He stared down at himself, and then at her, and then at the square of dark paint.

"Curse you!" he spat at her. And then he left.

Four men came for Michael the next day.

Four muscular, unsmiling men with an oriental slant to their eyes and their heads shaved hairless save for swinging braids sprouting from their crowns. Four muscular, unsmiling men with the determined, businesslike air of hired mercenaries—Japanese, judging by the throaty, indecipherable words they used so sparingly with one another.

They fastened ropes to Michael's ankles, ropes to his wrists, and then controlling a rope apiece, wrestled him onto a *prahu* and rowed him through the predawn gloom to the base of the fire mountain, *Gunung Api.*

Dawn had broken, but the sun barely penetrated the fire mountain's smoldering crown. Michael splashed into the water when his keepers' tugs and grunts demanded he do so. The water lapped around his ankles and shins, surprisingly hot, and even through his breeches he felt the acid sting of the yellowish grit that billowed from the muck with every step he slogged.

A wide black trail snaked down the mountainside, remnant of a long-ago eruption that had sent the liquefied bowels of the earth cascading down *Gunung Api*'s sides. Greenstuff crowded the ragged edges of the trail: tangled thickets of small trees, tall grasses, and burgeoning shrubbery. A faint green haze drifted over the trail itself, and when he got close enough, he realized that nature had already begun the work of cracking and pulverizing the hardened lava. Determined shoots poked through tiny fissures, and vines ventured out from the trailside tangle to demand purchase with their blindly seeking roots. He took a step onto the lava and it crumbled beneath his feet into fragile layers, like shale.

"Up, up." One of his keepers shoved him in the small of the back and gestured toward the top of the trail.

Knowing he stood on enemy territory, Michael studied the terrain. *Gunung Api*'s summit seemed flat, lower than the surrounding mountains, testifying to the acres of boiling lava that had spewed from its heart. The verdant forest gave way to scorched earth there near the top, leaving the mountain banded with a ring of barren desolation.

The tiny figure of a man stood silhouetted against the steam roiling from the mountain's far off, flattened tip.

Hootendorf. There could be no other who could have summoned him here and awaited him at the literal mouth of destruction. Michael sent him an imaginary tip of the hat. The son of a bitch's strategy was

impeccable—one firm push into the volcano's simmering cauldron and there would be no Michael Rowland to threaten Hootendorf's good name, to tempt
his wife with forbidden passion. No body to embarrass
Hootendorf later, should the bones be unearthed or a
bloated carcass wash up on shore near his plantation.

It was an unexpectedly generous gesture as well.
Michael preferred a quick and silent swallowing by
this volcano, a tiny taste of hell's eternal burning,
against screaming in pain and begging for mercy at
the hands of the Dutch governor.

And, if God were with him, Michael might have the
chance to drag Hootendorf into the mountain's fire
along with him. Such an act would leave Analisa a
widow, which alone would be enough to keep Michael
smiling throughout eternity, no matter where his sins
landed him.

He swept his gaze along the boulder-strewn trail
and judged it to be only a little more than a quarter
mile to the top. No distance at all for a man who'd
once dreamed of crisscrossing every mile of the globe.

A low, involuntary moan commenced somewhere
down in his belly, burgeoning into a full-fledged roar
that startled his keepers into round-eyed fright. With
one quick swipe of his hand, he snagged all four ropes
free from his keepers and wound them round his fist
as he sprinted up the mountain to meet his fate.

The lava crunched beneath his feet, and he had the
fleeting notion that his passage made it easier for
those bold and determined plants to make inroads into
the hardened trail. Soon the forest would overtake it.
The rich ash and virgin earth would nurture a burst
of luxuriant growth. In no time at all, nature would
swallow every trace of Michael Rowland's last
journey.

21

~

Michael surged up the mountainside. The wind caught his hair and parted his shirt, revealing his straining muscles. His breeches stretched over thighs that bulged with effort. He moved like a magnificent wild creature, so bold, so bursting with life and raw male power, that Analisa's blood responded even now.

He slowed where the forest lost its battle against the poisons spewing from *Gunung Api*'s crater. The earth, from the tip of the mountain down to that stunted green edge, lay sere and sterile beneath drifts of noxious fumes. Plumes of yellowish, sulfur-laden steam smoked from cracks in the earth, turning the air heavy and acrid and difficult to breathe. She knew the change in the air must have affected Michael far more than herself, considering how he'd run so far.

He bent double, his hands gripping his ankles. His shoulders heaved, and she thought he might be finding it hard to draw breath, but then she saw him kick ropes away from his ankles, saw him strip ropes away from his wrists.

He stood erect, tall and proud and free. The wind lifted his hair away from his face, revealing the bold tilt of his jaw, the fierce narrowing of his eyes as he studied Pietr Hootendorf standing not more than a hundred feet away.

She knew Michael had not seen her, and she did not mean to call attention to herself and divert him from whatever concentration he needed to focus upon this game of Pietr's. But the part of her soul that was so attuned to him must have found its answering mate within him. He cocked his head ever so slightly and shifted his gaze just enough to spot her where she sat at the base of a rock. He froze in place, staring at her, just staring. Her heart thundered her love.

She did not think he could tell she had been tied. Or that she had been ordered to remain silent. Any lapse would be punished by a killing blast to Michael from the small Italian firearm shoved nose-first into the back waistband of Pietr's breeches. She channeled all her strength into sending him a smile, praying her eyes would not betray her terror.

Michael began moving toward Pietr.

Pietr's laughter ran out, swirling wicked and evil amid the steaming, stinging gloom.

"You must carry homing pigeon blood in your veins, Rowland. No matter how many chances you have to run free, you totter your way back to captivity."

Michael answered him with a faintly curving smile. He shifted his glance toward Analisa once more and the smile blossomed into full radiance. "Nonetheless, I always manage to end up exactly where I'd most like to be."

Pietr stiffened, and then he looked out to sea and visibly relaxed. "One small correction. Right now, you are exactly where *I* want you to be."

"Ah, yes, the master gamesman. Summoning people from all over to do your bidding where and when you see fit."

The words, clearly meant as an insult, seemed somehow to please Pietr. "Exactly so. You do me honor by recognizing my skill."

"Your skill, but not your intent. I admit I cannot fathom why we stand here, chatting about your play-making abilities."

"You'll learn soon enough." Pietr stared over Michael's shoulder, almost absently. The four burly men who had brought Michael in the *prahu* stood impassively at the forest edge. Pietr issued a sharp command in a strange tongue. They retreated a dozen paces but did not relax their vigilance.

Pietr squinted; Analisa thought he meant to make sure that the men remained within earshot, but no, it seemed he peered through the choking gloom toward the sea.

He pulled the firearm from his breeches.

Analisa gave a small cry; he shot her a withering stare and then looked back at Michael. "I am almost as good a marksman as I am a chess player. If you try to run away, I'll not miss a target so large as your back."

"I'd not choose to die that way. And yet I believe that running *toward* you would end in much the same way—there'd be a hole through my chest one way or another."

"Exactly so."

"Well, then." The situation, which strained Analisa's nerves, seemed to amuse Michael. "Are we to stand here insulting one another until we choke to death?"

"Not what I would choose," said Pietr, "but I am at somewhat of an impasse with my wife over there."

Michael's jaw tightened, and his chin shifted infinitesimally, so that it was difficult to tell whether Analisa had imagined it or whether it was the drifting, acrid steam that caused that minute waver.

"Women cause all manner of difficulties for men," he said, his voice gone hoarse.

But Pietr's had gone hoarse, too, no doubt from the effort of talking in that hot, stinking air. "At first glance, this would seem to be an untenable position for me. If I kill you, she will hate me forever. If I hand you over to the Dutch for what she deems such a minor indiscretion as a bit of smuggling, then she'll hate me as well."

"A predicament, to be sure. But then, you will still have her, no matter what she feels."

"Will I?" Pietr looked over at her almost curiously, as if surprised to find her still sitting there. "You do not know her as well as you think, Rowland, if you believe her mere physical presence grants ownership. No, she has traveled far beyond my reach, and you are to blame."

"So what is it to be—a fight to the death?"

"I would not call it a fight." Pietr peered toward the sea again, and a humorless smile tilted his lips. "Ah. We can begin now. I'll just fire this pistol so the fools will know where to find us."

Analisa struggled to see through the swirling mist. A stray breath of wind parted the haze, and to her horror she saw Governor Hoon's distinctive ketch disgorging uniformed soldiers at the base of *Gunung Api.* A warning cry began in her throat; it escalated into a full-blown scream when gunfire shattered the smoldering air.

She swiveled around, seeking Michael, and subsided with relief when she found him standing blessedly upright and unharmed. Pietr stood with his arm lifted toward the sky, the firearm smoking in his hand. He'd harmlessly discharged the weapon into the sky.

It was a trick; she just knew it.

Before she could cry out and urge him to be careful,

Michael bent double again. With a quick lunge, he rammed Pietr in the stomach.

Analisa felt mired in a nightmare as she fought ineffectually against her bonds. The steam and stinking sulfur cast an odorous pall over a scene straight from hell. Michael and Pietr wrestled to the ground. They twisted and writhed, coating themselves with ash while blood welled wherever their flesh scraped against razor-edged shards of cracked lava. Just beyond their straining figures, a line of soldiers streamed up the black-crusted trail. She could hear the soldiers shouting, calling reassurances to Pietr, promising to get there soon to help him.

Michael and Pietr clawed to their knees, grappling.

The first Dutch soldiers staggered beyond the forest's edge, then stepped back as if the noxious air had dealt them a blow.

Michael and Pietr had risen to their feet. Using each other for leverage, they inched their way to the yawning edge of the volcano.

Let him go. Stop fighting. Just run run run run run.

The refrain clamored in her head; she did not realize, until she found her throat rasping and burning, that she had been screaming it aloud. To Michael. Telling him to give up this pointless fight, to take whatever small chance he had and run, run now, before the soldiers shook off their breathlessness and lent their strength to Pietr's. Before Pietr's sounder physical condition prevailed, and Michael ended up pitched into the volcano's yawning mouth.

With a collective enraged roar, Michael and Pietr broke apart.

They circled each other like wolves arguing over a particularly tasty bone. Each time Michael neared the rim of the volcano, Analisa's heart lurched. But the circling ended with Pietr standing in the most vulnerable position, with his back to the smoldering pit and his boots braced uncertainly against the slipping, crumbling lava crust.

"Ram your head into me now," Pietr taunted. "The momentum would carry both of us into the inferno. You wouldn't have her—but neither would I."

"Michael, no!" Analisa screamed.

But he meant to do as Pietr suggested. She saw his intention in the way his stance shifted. Michael looked back at her, over his shoulder, and she read in those glorious golden eyes and the sad curve of his proud lips that he meant to do it.

I love you. He mouthed the words, and then he turned away from her and gathered himself to meet his doom.

"Michael, no!"

Her scream was drowned out by a sharp slap of flesh. Michael's hand caught Pietr's wrist as Pietr directed a wide-swinging blow straight at Michael's head.

And then Pietr did the strangest thing. While Michael still held to his wrist, he stepped *toward* Michael and gave him a mighty shove in the chest, pushing him away from the volcano's lip. As Michael staggered a few steps downhill, Pietr sent Analisa a mocking salute.

Pietr Hootendorf spun gracefully as a dancer, and with arms flailing, plunged into the smoldering abyss.

For a timeless moment, all the earth stood still. Analisa froze in place, her lips parted, her cry left unborn. Michael had fallen to one knee, one hand pressed against the ground. The swarming Dutch posed like toy soldiers, some with weapons held aloft, others leaning forward, still others with legs braced wide apart. Even the suffocating fog ceased its swirling to hang in an eerie pall above them all, while Pietr Hootendorf's trailing scream reverberated in their ears.

Michael was the first to break the unnatural stillness. He ran at once toward the crater. His feet crunched through the lava and sent showers of crust skidding down the trail. He gained the rim and stood there, rigid and disbelieving.

The soldiers jerked into motion. Swords clanked, boots scuffled, a few hoarse hacking coughs marked the effort of breathing the sulfurous fumes. Governor Hoon barked a command, and one of his captains broke into a stumbling run, going after Michael.

"You, there!" he cried, waving his saber menacingly.

Michael turned his head, looking back over his shoulder. The wind lifted his hair, and the choking mist framed his face. He tightened his jaw and narrowed his eyes.

"Michael Rowland?" thundered the Dutch captain. Michael nodded once, curtly accepting his identity. The captain pointed his saber toward Michael's heart. "Come away from there. You are under arrest for the murder of Mynheer Pietr Hootendorf."

Michael swatted away the saber tip that hovered before his nose like an annoying mosquito. He shouldered his way through the clump of Dutch soldiers, ignoring Governor Hoon, who demanded that he stop at once. He had to find Analisa. A sound roared in his ears—the reverberating echo of Pietr Hootendorf's chilling scream as he plummeted to his death. The sound overrode all others, so that while he could see the Dutch soldier's lips moving, he could not hear, and did not care, what was being said.

He had to find Analisa. He had to hold her, touch her, let her sweetness and purity wipe away the taint of death and disbelief that gripped him. And, God help him, the sense of triumph that surged through his very bones, shaming him with the urge to revel over the death of a man he despised.

He knelt at her side, pulling her into his arms and cursing inwardly when he felt the ropes securing her hands behind her back. He fumbled with the restraint and wished he had Hootendorf's throat between his hands, wished that he'd picked up the man by the scruff of his neck and the seat of his pants and deliberately pitched him straight into that glowing pit from hell.

Analisa trembled against him. He felt the warm brush of her lips against his throat. "You did not kill him," she whispered, absolving him. "I saw everything. He jumped."

"Aye. He planned this all along. He brought all of us here for this very reason."

Pietr, with all his talk of chess and gamesmanship, had performed the role of a lifetime.

"I threatened to reveal him as a traitor, Michael. He could not endure the humiliation."

"Nor could he endure knowing your heart belonged to another man," Michael said. He swallowed, knowing he should exult in the balance of what he must tell her, but his joy was dimmed by the bittersweet knowledge that Hootendorf had managed to outwit this ultimate triumph. Michael curved his hand over Analisa's belly. "Our child, Analisa, *ours*. If the rumors are to be believed, it cannot be his. In his soul, Pietr would know the truth about that—and perhaps he could not endure that, either."

"Oh, Michael, my heart told me so, but I dared not believe it!" With a rapturous cry, she hugged him round the shoulders and buried her face in his chest.

Hoon's second-in-command marched up to them and stood there rattling his saber and shouting some pompous-sounding orders at them. Michael swept up a handful of crushed lava and flung it at the man. "Away with you! Can't you see she's grieving?"

As am I, he added silently.

For Pietr Hootendorf's revenge had been well calculated and complete. Michael had stood between Hootendorf and the oncoming soldiers. The soldiers would have seen two men locked in mortal combat and watched one of them fall into the pit. To them, it had certainly looked as though Michael had thrown Hootendorf into the volcano.

And so it would appear to everyone that Pietr had been murdered, and not taken the cowardly escape of suicide. Any attempt to brand him as a traitor to the Company would be negated by skepticism, considering that the man doing the branding was the very man who'd apparently flung Pietr to his death.

Ironic. Of all the mistakes he had made, all the wrongs he had inflicted, Michael would be punished for the one crime he had not committed.

"Let me just hold you," he whispered against Analisa's hair, praying she would not sense the hopelessness in his grasp as he savored the feel of her heart beating against his.

"No, Michael. We must tell them the truth of what happened."

"Shh." He swallowed. "Let them think what they will about me. We must guard *your* reputation. They must never know why Hootendorf hated me so, or you could be implicated in all this." Her reputation meant nothing to her; he could tell from the way she struggled to escape his embrace. "Analisa, think of our child."

Think of our child. Michael's caution rang in her head, but Analisa shook her head against it. The certainty that it was Michael's child she carried imbued her with strength of purpose. She was finished with pretending, finished with caring about what others thought. She could not sit by, pretending to be the grieving widow, while the man she loved, the father of her child, paid with his life for a crime he had not committed—all so she might hold her head high, all so her child might avoid the taint of bastardy.

She could survive the slurs and innuendo; she had been doing so for all her life. Those survival instincts would be inbred in her child. And she would not make the same mistakes with her child her mother had with her—she would raise her child to be proud of its conception, to know that true and perfect love awaited those who never gave up hope or settled for second best.

Never give up hope. She would not give it up, ever again, beginning right now, when things admittedly looked desperate.

She broke away from Michael, remaining by his side, letting her hand rest on his shoulder. She challenged Governor Hoon. "What are you doing here, mynheer?"

"Why, Mynheer Hootendorf sent us a message." Hoon's soldier flapped a crumpled missive to punctuate the governor's words. Hoon snatched the document from the man's hand and waved it in front of Analisa's nose. "Your husband advised us that he'd trapped the notorious pirate Michael Rowland upon this mountain, and that you would be able to identify the man beyond a doubt."

"I see." Her brain worked frantically. She had spent all these weeks with Pietr; surely some of his skill at manipulation must have rubbed off on her. At the moment, matters seemed hopeless. Michael had already admitted his identity. The soldiers glowered at him, angry and almost visibly itching for Governor Hoon's order to clap Michael back in chains. She knew any protest would carry little weight.

They would incarcerate him and conduct investigations in a Dutchman's careful, methodical way. They would learn the truth about how he'd passed himself off as a British officer. They might learn he'd been caught in her bed, which would cast Pietr in the role of vengeful husband, Michael as despicable wife-seducer deserving of punishment. Everything Michael had done cast him in a guilty light, giving him strong motives for murder.

"Did my good partner Pietr's message tell you how he knew I would be here?" Michael broke in, in execrably bad Dutch. "Did he tell you that he arranged our . . . meeting?"

"Michael, no," she whispered through lips frozen with fear.

But he ignored her protest and stepped around her, shielding her with his body. "Ah, yes, Pietr and I knew each other well. I'll leave it to you gentlemen to determine why a British smuggler and a *perkenier* would find a friendship mutually profitable."

"Mynheer Hootendorf was no partner of yours!" Governor Hoon shouted. "I stood right next to Pietr when his wife denied you were the smuggler we sought."

Michael hooted with laughter. "Of course she denied my identity. Pietr Hootendorf ordered her to do so, for he knew that if I were discovered, I might well tell you fine gentlemen about him in order to save my own neck. A wife cannot go against her husband's commands. She is innocent of any crime against the Company."

His words were a jumble of English and Dutch, a mishmash of truth interspersed with fiction. She could see Governor Hoon struggling to sort it all out, and watched the dawning comprehension that made horror suffuse his face.

"You are admitting to being the smuggler, and you are accusing Mynheer Hootendorf of betraying the Company's trust by providing you with the fertile nutmegs."

Michael inclined his head. "Exactly. He's been

stealing from the Company and breaking the Company's laws for years. Years and years. I can prove it."

"Arrest him," Hoon ordered, and a half-dozen soldiers gripped Michael by the arms.

Analisa could not let this happen. "No, mynheer. You must proceed carefully, lest everything the Company stands for, everything our countrymen have worked for, comes crashing down."

"Explain yourself, mevrouw."

She had learned one thing from Pietr: that courage often sheltered weakness. There was nothing that spurred the Dutch East India Company's courage more than the thought of a threat to the monopoly they held on the spice trade.

"What this man says is true. Pietr Hootendorf was a traitor." She weighted her words with all the solemnity she could muster and stood unflinching before them as the soldiers hissed and protested their disbelief. Michael looked ready to interrupt her, to transfer the blame upon himself once more, but she stopped him with a light motion of her hand.

His eyes kindled, warming with intoxicating approval. She could almost hear his mind calling to hers: *There you are, my spirited lass.* His hand settled at the small of her back, lending her the strength to go on, placing his trust in her, for the words she chose would determine whether he lived or died.

"My husband deliberately jumped into that volcano." She challenged each of them with her stare. "There must be one man among you who saw the truth of what happened here today."

"I saw it, mevrouw," mumbled the soldier who had been the first to breach the forest.

"I saw him leap, as well," admitted another. "I could not credit what I saw, and believed it to be a trick of the fog."

"It was no trick, but the act of a desperate, guilty

man. I ask you, Governor, what other reason would Pietr Hootendorf have for committing suicide?"

"A man could have any number of reasons for taking his own life. It does not brand him a traitor to the Company."

"Then how will you explain his relationship with Michael Rowland? If you take Michael back to Banda Neira you will have to admit he was in collusion with my husband. Every Dutchman, every planter, will know that for years Pietr broke the Company's most inflexible rule with impunity. He aided smugglers and was not punished."

Hoon's eyes narrowed. "I am not some lackey who is forced to explain matters, mevrouw. I can order Rowland's execution without anyone questioning his connections.

"Then you'd best throw me into the volcano after my husband, Governor, for I shall tell anyone who will listen that the Company countenanced a traitor in its midst. I will tell them that *you* covered his tracks, and remind everyone that you called Pietr Hootendorf your friend. I would not be surprised if suspicion falls upon you as well."

She could tell by the quickly hidden smiles, the upraised brows, that Hoon's soldiers already entertained their suspicions. Hoon noticed. His complexion mottled. "Go back to the ketch," he ordered his men. "Take those Japanese hirelings along with you. Mevrouw Hootendorf and I have business matters to discuss."

"But this smuggler—" began one of the foot soldiers who had a fistful of Michael's shirt caught in his hand.

"How gratifying to know you fear for my safety," Hoon deliberately redirected the soldier's concern. "I assure you I am not so decrepit that I require an armed guard standing over me while I speak with a woman and an unarmed man."

Analisa felt a tiny bit of the stricture on her heart ease with each step the soldiers took. Hope, which had lain crushed and crippled for so long, stirred with new life.

Hoon spoke to her. "I wonder, mevrouw, whether you point out these potential problems from concern for my reputation—or concern for your own?"

"Perhaps a little of both, mynheer."

"I see." Hoon shot a covert glance toward his departing soldiers. "What might you suggest to solve this mutual dilemma?"

"Let him go. Let Michael Rowland go free." All of her aversion to begging, to pleading for favor, deserted her. "Everyone on the islands knows you have searched thoroughly without finding him. They no longer speak of the smuggler—he is forgotten. It would only embarrass you to bring him forward now and admit how thoroughly you'd been deceived. Let him go."

"I will take the mevrouw Analisa with me," Michael added. "We will go far away."

Hope burst into full and vibrant life within Analisa then. They could do this. She was a widow now, freed from her vows by the husband who had thought she lacked the strength to jeopardize her position for the sake of the man she loved.

"Hmm." Hoon studied them. "I cannot let you do that."

"Yes, you can," Michael cried.

"Why?" Analisa whispered.

"You carry Hootendorf's heir, mevrouw."

"No, you don't understand, I—"

Michael squeezed her hand, silencing her.

Hoon did not seem to have noticed how she'd nearly blurted the truth about her child's paternity.

"You cannot imagine the chaos, the bickering, the outright fighting that would ensue if you suddenly disappeared, leaving Pietr's holdings unclaimed. No, as an official of the Dutch East India Company, it is my duty to hold you and your child as wards to ensure the smooth continuation of nutmeg production from the Hootendorf *perken.*"

"You are saying you mean to hold me prisoner in my home?"

"A quaint way of putting matters, mevrouw. Especially since everyone will expect you to be overcome with grief for your husband. So long as you hold your tongue about your husband's crimes, you may live out your days with all the luxury and comfort that is your right as Hootendorf's wife. And you," he jutted his chin toward Michael, "you can be on your way, to wherever the seas may take you."

Pietr himself could not have fashioned a better compromise.

And it was truly a dazzling, generous offer. Hoon could not possibly know that the life he sketched for Analisa once comprised her most cherished dream. He could not have crafted better words to describe the adventurous future Michael cherished in his heart. And yet Analisa wanted to scream a denial, wanted to repudiate the bargain out of hand.

She would have, too, except that Michael's hand shot out like the tongue of a snake and gripped Hoon's, shaking to seal this devil's bargain.

She could not believe it.

"I will need a safe conduct for myself and all I carry," Michael said. "Now."

"Surely you can wait until we return to Banda Neira. I did not think it necessary to bring a clerk to this volcano," Hoon grumped.

"You will forgive me, mynheer, if I admit I am not eager to venture within ten feet of your fort, or to find myself outnumbered a hundred to one by Dutch soldiers. I won't require fancy new parchment. The back of the message that brought you here will do." He glanced toward the sweat-softened missive that Hoon had stuffed into his belt.

"I don't have pen and ink."

Michael turned his arm, baring a trail of blood trickling from a gouge near his shoulder. He must have gotten it during the fight with Pietr. "I'll provide the ink," Michael said.

Analisa swayed. She could not believe he was so eager to leave her, so insistent upon this safe conduct. He alternately winced and smiled as Hoon dragged a fire-hardened stick against the red wetness and then scribbled a few words on the back of Pietr's ill-fated message. Michael puckered his forehead over it in incomprehension. He flapped the safe conduct in the wind to dry, and then handed it to Analisa.

"Can't read Dutch," he said cheerfully. "What does it say?"

The missive read almost word for word what Michael had demanded. She read the roughly drawn phrases through lips gone numb with betrayal. "Do not hold this man. Grant safe conduct to him and all he carries." The governor's signature, bold and sure despite the primitive writing tools, streaked across the bottom, the red mottling into rusty brown.

"Well, then, there it is." Michael rolled it carefully and stuffed it into his shirt. He nodded toward the governor, and looked ready to bound away.

"Michael?" Analisa whispered. Her throat had gone so tight and achy that she couldn't squeak anything else past. Only his name, when her heart brimmed with a hundred questions, when her soul pleaded for just one explanation, anything, to tell her that his desertion was part of some far-reaching scheme. Since finding him, since loving him, she had felt connected to his thoughts, his feelings, drawing strength when she needed it, offering comfort when he felt despair.

Now, that magical connection had been severed. She felt nothing. She found nothing in those remarkable golden eyes save for a sparkling delight at finding himself free, a smoldering anticipation for adventures to come.

He sent her a slanted, distracted grin. "I must say it has been a singular privilege, mevrouw. Against all odds, we've each gotten what we wanted."

He bent in a quick bow from the waist, and then he left.

He worked his way down the lava-covered trail with lithe and supple ease. She watched, compelled by the sheer magnificence of him. She wished the volcano would blow just then, and coat her with a hard shell of rock. She did not know how she could endure this pain, this final betrayal. *Think of our child,* he had told her. Her hand fluttered over her belly. Michael's child. It would be born on Pietr Hootendorf's bed, and raised in Pietr Hootendorf's home, while Pietr Hootendorf's widow lived out the luxuriant, respect-filled life she'd always craved. And Michael . . . the man who had had his fill of caring for others, Michael would go to wherever the sea carried him.

And he would commence his adventures in Pietr's boat. She watched while he commandeered the *prahu* that had brought him to *Gunung Api,* and then watched while he expertly plied a paddle with a pirate's skill to send the small, light craft shooting out over the sparkling azure waters.

He was gone. This time, for good.

"Come, Mevrouw Hootendorf." The governor offered his arm for support. He avoided her eyes, but she read pity in his expression, and knew he considered her a foolish woman who had fallen for the wiles of a seducer. "I will take you home now. The Company will take care of you."

22

~

Maru tucked the end of Analisa's braid invisibly into the coil encircling her head. "Very nice, mevrouw. That mean old Mevrouw Pedersveldt, she can say nothing bad about your hair today, hmm?"

Analisa shook her head and tried to quell the shiver of distaste that racked through her. She had forgotten that today was Mevrouw Pedersveldt's turn to act as watchdog.

Analisa had not spent a moment alone since Governor Hoon had brought her back from *Gunung Api*. For every one of the past twenty-one days, one of the neighboring Dutch wives came to sit with her. She supposed their concern stemmed from kindness and genuine goodwill, but each time she saw one of them walking up the path, she remembered the island woman who had to be chained to a pole so she could not do such a foolish thing as plunge into the sea after the man she loved. Chains and poles came in a variety of forms, she had come to realize as she spent day after day beneath someone's watchful eye.

They never reproached her for remaining calm and dry-eyed, but with small telling comments they told her they found her lack of emotion incomprehensible.

"We'll spend the day sewing new clothes for Pietr's baby," Gerda Goenstedt always enthused.

"No needlework," Analisa always responded. She sat staring out the window while Gerda, her lips tightly compressed, plied her needle upon a steadily growing pile of tiny garments.

Trudy vanHelmer fussed over Analisa constantly, patting her hand, or filling her teacup, or tucking cushions behind her until Analisa wanted to scream. "Your strength is admirable, Mevrouw Hootendorf," Trudy said, "but one day you will realize how horrible it was that you could not even hold a funeral for your dear husband. You will break into healing tears." And then she would sit back expectantly, waiting for tears that never came, tears that would never come. . . .

Tali shook Analisa from her reverie by draping a dress over her knee. "This one for today, mevrouw?"

"That's a walking dress," Analisa said. "Choose another."

She had not ventured from the house since it had swallowed her up after Michael left.

"I was just thinking, mevrouw." Tali bit her lip. "That Mevrouw Pedersveldt, she has legs like big fat sausages. She puffs and turns red just walking to house from *prahu*. Maybe you tell Mevrouw Pedersveldt you wish to take walk today, and she say to you, 'go along Mevrouw Hootendorf and walk by yourself.' It is good for the baby."

Good for the baby. *Think of our child.*

Analisa nodded, though she had to admit the notion of escaping Marta Pedersveldt's disapproving presence swayed her as much as concern for the state of her health.

The plan worked exactly as Tali predicted, and Analisa stepped into the sunshine, leaving Mevrouw Pedersveldt dozing in a chair beneath a portrait of Hilde that Analisa had ordered rehung.

The grove seemed to welcome her within its leafy embrace. The shade cooled her skin. Doves cooed softly from the branches, fluttering as she passed beneath them. Their wings stirred the scent of nutmeg, perfuming every breath she drew.

She hesitated at a point where the path branched. The one to her left led to the *prahu* dock, which would bring a quick end to her walk. The one to her right marked the trail she had followed on those awful days when Pietr held Michael captive and taunted them both with his control. Her fingertips tingled, remembering Michael's featherlight brush, and her certainty that they shared a love to defy the ages. She could not follow that path just now.

She struck out on the middle path, which led to a commanding view of the sea. The sounds of the sea called to her. She hurried toward the rocky promontory with her hand pressed against her belly. Perhaps she'd take her child there now, and begin whispering tales of the brave and daring adventurer who traveled to wherever the sea would take him.

She had nearly reached the edge of the grove when she heard a snapping twig, the sound of boots crunching against dried leaves.

Something—or someone—was moving along the path behind her.

She paused, but could hear nothing over the hammering of her heart and the pounding of the surf. A dove squawked in alarm and rocketed from its perch, showering her with leaves. A plump ripe nutmeg fruit dropped at her toes.

"I'll take that," a man's low voice rumbled.

His voice held her in place. She couldn't breathe while his hand reached past her leg. A bracelet of scars banded his wrist. Strong, deft fingers squeezed the fruit and popped the nutmeg seed free.

"Want it?" he challenged her. He put one hand on

her shoulder and pressed gently, forcing her to turn around and look at him. "Want it?" he repeated with a grin, delight glowing from those remarkable ale-colored eyes. He tossed the nutmeg from hand to hand like a child teasing a playmate with a rubber ball.

Wordlessly, she held out her hand. Michael placed the nutmeg on her palm. It felt cool and sticky with juice, and looked different from the dried nutmegs she'd grown accustomed to seeing. This fresh-plucked seed looked smooth and golden brown, and a fine orange-red netting webbed over it.

Michael used the edge of his fingernail to pry a little of the orange-red netting away from the seed. "That's mace. You peel that off and grind it up once it dries. The mace is even more valuable than the nutmeg."

She found her voice, and it seemed safer to ignore the questions, wiser to tamp down the hope that burgeoned at his presence. "Did you come back here to impress me with your knowledge of nutmeg husbandry?' she asked.

"Ah, so you're admitting at last that I impress you." Satisfaction sparked from him, and the lips she knew so well, the lips she'd dreamed of kissing, curved to match the smile lines etched in his skin.

"Oh, Michael," she whispered.

"Don't start bawling on me," he cautioned. "You need to be clear-eyed to make an escape."

"Escape," she repeated. "You?"

"And you." He bent and brought his face close to her middle. "You, too," he called, and she fancied she could feel the vibration of his voice pass through her flesh into her child's.

"They won't let me leave," she said. If this were all a dream, it would end now, with the teasing, beguiling, dreamspun Michael admitting she was right—she was trapped here forever.

Instead, Michael shrugged, dismissing the will of the

Dutch East India Company. "I have a bit of experience in pirating fertile treasures from these islands. You see, I love you, Analisa, and I can't live without you. The Company will have to find itself another hostage."

"But . . ." Her voice trailed away. She didn't know why she felt compelled to contradict the evidence standing right before her, tall brawny evidence who still had his head cocked at her belly. "You don't believe in love," she said.

"Well, you must admit I put up a good fight against it. Had to be chained and shackled and hauled halfway round the world before I gave in."

"You left me. Governor Hoon said you could go, and so you left me."

"One thing I've learned is that when a Dutchman says 'go,' you ought to grab the opportunity and sneak back to settle the details after you've made good on your escape."

"Details."

"Aye. Passage. Provisions." He straightened and patted his shirt. A corner of parchment peeped from between his buttons; the document softened the sound of his slap. "Safe conduct, for me and all I carry. I've learned a thing or two since last I tried this."

"So I'm one of the details?"

"In truth, you're all of the details, Analisa." He pulled her into his arms. She could feel his heart thundering into her until all her shakiness, all her misgivings vanished beneath that strong, steady beat. "I need to know details, such as if I free your hair from all those cursed braids, how many shades of color does the sun strike from your curls? Such as the way your eyes change with your mood. I need to know all the sounds you make when I love you, and hear them again and again to make sure I get them straight. I need to know whether our child will be a boy or a

girl, and what the next one will be and the next after
that. All these details and countless more, and learning them all will be the grandest adventure of my life."

"Can we go to Virginia?' she asked. Excitement
surged through her, to imagine herself and Michael
and their children settling in that wild and free land.

"Aye. Though I must caution you about the society
there. Those hardy old matrons won't think much of
you, married to a rogue like me."

"Who cares what they think?" said Analisa. "When
can we go?"

"Now."

"Now?"

"Well, blast, woman, you've made me wait three
weeks as it is. I thought you'd never leave that house."

"You've been hiding out here in these groves the
whole time?"

"Every minute of every day."

"You could have been caught! Oh, Michael, Governor Hoon might have changed his mind about letting
you go—"

He stifled her remonstrations with a finger against
her lips.

"Yes, teacher. I doubt I'll ever get the hang of running away if you don't come along and help me. Once
we reach Virginia, I promise I'll write out 'I'm a poor
student when it comes to escaping' a hundred times
in my lesson book."

"You were here the whole time," she whispered.
All those awful, aching hours she'd spent staring at
nothing, when she could have been in Michael's arms.
She shook those regrets away. They faced a lifetime
of loving, beginning now.

"There might have been a moment or two when I
tended to some other matters," Michael said. "It's a
damn difficult business, snatching nutmegs from the
beaks of hungry doves."

"You're still worried about those starving colonists."

He gave an elaborate shrug. "There's room on the ship for a small sack of nutmegs, Analisa."

"A *sack?*"

"Those trees are cursed hard to grow. And weren't you the one who remarked I'd been a fool to risk my life for a *few* little nutmegs?"

"I'll have to get some spare clothes. And money. And—"

He stifled her protests with a kiss, one that she was sure he meant to be quick and quieting. The surf battered the rocks far below, and soon she could not differentiate that from the pounding of her pulse.

When his lips reluctantly left hers, he curved one arm around her waist and pressed his other hand against her belly.

"Let's be off now, beloved. You've brought everything we need."

Please turn the page
for a
sneak preview of

Captor of My Heart

Donna Valentino's
next historical romance
coming from Topaz
in the winter of 1998

1

Jillian Bowen dreaded confronting Death on moon-drenched nights.

She agonized over losing a patient at any time, but failure weighed particularly heavy when moonlight leached all color from the landscape and shadows swallowed all sound. The sky, the trees, the grooved ruts in the road—everything—lay bathed in shades of gray and black, silent and lifeless as the inside of a grave.

She shivered, though her cloak provided more warmth than required on this late September night. Her hands trembled, and her fingers cramped from gripping the reins so tightly. She could not loosen her hold, no matter how she scolded herself that she need not fear having herself and her father thrown from the wagon. Patient, plodding Queenie would never take the bit between her teeth and bolt.

Jillian had accompanied her father on similar midnight journeys a hundred times, a thousand times, before. What was so different about this night? She could not shake the sensation that unseen danger lurked under cover of moonshadows, watching her, waiting for the chance to destroy her world.

Ridiculous. The very notion brought a light sheen

of perspiration to her forehead. She'd woven a web of lies and deception to protect all she loved and valued. But no matter how she tried convincing herself she was safe, her nerves jangled, taunting her with the truth. It was only a matter of time before she lost everything, only a matter of time before forces she could not control stole it all away.

Her father sat half-slumped at the far corner of the bench seat snoring, blessedly oblivious to her apprehension. She craved the sounds of life, but rousing Wilton Bowen from his nap would only cause heartache rather than relief.

Queenie's hooves crushed through the fallen leaves that layered the road, sweetening the cool, crisp air with the scent of autumn. A nightingale's call rang out once in counterpoint to the wagon's squeaking wheels. Other than those heavy, muffled thuds, that brief trilling song, nothing stirred. There was no point in hoping she might come across a fellow traveler. Lord Protector Cromwell's iron-fisted restrictions made it virtually impossible to travel about without a permit. People spent the nights indoors now, with doors barred and windows shuttered against those who might spy on them from without.

But when the road curved, the moonlight revealed the silhouette of a mounted man sheltering beneath the shadow of a spreading elm. Queenie tossed her head, snorting nervously. Jillian's heartbeat quickened with fear and with an equal measure of relief. Her instincts had not been wrong after all—someone *had* been watching her, waiting for her.

And it was only Jenkins. She recognized the gaunt rider, aware of the irony. She was safe with Jenkins. She and her father might be the only two people in this part of England with the freedom to move about without traveling passes. And yet, much as she yearned for companionship, she would have preferred riding on alone over the company of the Lord Protector's henchman.

"Mistress Bowen. Doctor Bowen." The road rider's gravelly voice rang out harsh and loud against the quiet.

"Jenkins," she acknowledged.

Jillian's father stirred and mumbled something incomprehensible before lapsing once more into silence.

"A pleasant eve," Jenkins said as he guided his horse in a slow arc around the back of their wagon. Jillian knew his sharp eyes searched the empty space, the way he'd done countless times before without finding anything amiss.

"Not so pleasant."

Jenkins would expect her to explain why she and her father were riding out that night. She did not wait for him to ask. "Jamie Metcalf's dying."

He grunted with cursory sympathy. "Your father will set him right."

"Not this time."

Jenkins did not argue the point, but she saw his dismissal of her opinion in the way his mouth curled into a faint sneer, the quick shift of his eyes toward her father, as if he expected Doctor Bowen to leap up and declare her wrong. She could not take offense, because his attitude was exactly the one she strove so hard to foster. She wanted everyone to think that she merely assisted their beloved Doctor Wilton Bowen. But for three years now, *she* had been the one to analyze a patient's condition, to prescribe the proper course of treatment.

They would never forgive her once they found her out. They would drum her and her father out of the country, even if it meant depriving the area of a physician.

Nobody would accept treatment from a woman.

Jenkins's interest had strayed. He narrowed his gaze

toward the trees and then turned his head toward a field, seeking, searching. " 'Tis rumored Charles Stuart might sneak through these parts trying to get back to France. You didn't catch sight of any tall, dark-haired louts skulking about, did you?"

"Not tonight."

"You be sure to scream out good and loud if you do. The sound will travel far on a night like this."

"I will." Jillian hoped her insincerity didn't show, as she silently wished the king well. She never reported the frightened, wraithlike souls she sometimes spotted darting through the woods, doing their best to elude Cromwell's dreaded patrols. She would never betray the exiled king. She and Charles Stuart were kindred spirits, though she would never tell him so, even if she chanced to see him. He would certainly find it amusing to think that a woman who yearned to be acknowledged as a physician equated herself with a man who yearned to be acknowledged as king.

But at least Cromwell's forces were enemies Charles could see. At least a person knew that traveling without permission could incur Cromwell's wrath and punishment. Taking calculated risks wasn't like falling victim to Death and being struck down without warning or provocation. Or like the disease muddling her father's mind, gleefully eradicating his knowledge and memories, leaving him little more than an empty husk of flesh.

"I'll be riding this part of the country all night," Jenkins said.

"Then we shall see you later, once it's finished with Jamie Metcalf."

"I won't bother you then, mistress. I know such things weigh hard on your father."

"Thank you."

Jenkins touched his forehead and then reined his horse away.

Jillian clucked softly to Queenie, urging her to pick up their pace. The wagon jolted a little, and Jillian's father blinked awake.

"Jillian?" His voice quavered and he stared at her in shock. Jillian took heart. Uncertainty came upon him only during his most lucid moments, when he emerged from the fog numbing his wits and realized that he held but a tenuous grip on his sanity.

"Father." Hope surged through her. If he could cling to his sensibility for a little while, he might remember a treatment that could save Jamie Metcalf. She was all too chillingly aware that she'd learned only a small portion of the skill trapped in the lost depths of her father's ruined mind. "You remember Jamie Metcalf—you set his wife Mary's leg when she got kicked by a cow, and you delivered all four of their children. I have tried every remedy to ease breathing that you taught me, and nothing has worked."

Wilton Bowen blinked sleepily at her.

"Try to remember," she urged. "Jamie cannot sleep. When he tries, he feels as though a rock crushes his chest, and he must struggle upright, gasping for breath. He can no longer breathe without conscious effort. He is dying, father."

Wilton Bowen frowned. She wanted to burst into tears at the obvious effort he was making to think, to remember. And then his face cleared, turning as smooth and unaffected as a child's, and she knew she had lost him again.

He patted her arm. "Nonsense," her father blustered with the confident jocularity that always reassured their patients. "You're a fine, healthy young woman."

"Not me, Father. Jamie Metcalf. Try to concentrate."

"Try to concentrate." He echoed her words exactly, as he did when bending low over the sick and infirm and she fed him clues about what to say, guided him to prescribe the appropriate remedies. He fumbled with Jillian's hand, trying to disengage it from the reins. She allowed him, despair turning her muscles limp as he pressed her hand against his chest while he drew a great lungful of air. "This is how it feels when you breathe properly. In. Out. Breathe as I do."

"It is Jamie Metcalf, and not I, who has trouble breathing."

"Small wonder you cannot breathe, young lady," her father chided sternly. "You have a nervous temperament and an argumentative nature. I shall have my daughter mix a draught to calm your nerves."

"I am your daughter, Papa," Jillian whispered while anguish wracked her soul.

Her father was oblivious to her distress. "Do as I say. In. Out." he gave her hand a reassuring pat and settled once more into his corner. "Watch me now." He drew enormous, ostentatious breaths for her benefit, and then bewilderment settled over him, and she knew he had forgotten why he was breathing so hard. Within moments, he fell back into sleep.

It was no use. Jamie Metcalf would die on this moon-washed night.

And so might her dreams. Her father's condition had worsened. He could no longer make the mental leap required to discuss the condition of a person who did not actually sit right in front of him. The day would soon come when his hard-earned skill failed altogether, when they could no longer fool people into believing that Wilton Bowen could restore their health. Everything would end. Once everyone realized that her father was no longer competent to act as physician to them all, they would seek out another man. They would never let her go on as she had been doing these past years.

Death of another sort. The end. She wished suddenly that her formless, faceless enemies would take shape, so she could pummel them in her frustration.

The unfairness of it all coursed through her, pulsing and pounding while her mind screamed in denial. James Metcalf was too young to die. Her father was too precious and dear to lose in such a heart-wrenching way. And she had spent too many years learning a physician's art, set aside too many hopes, postponed too many dreams, to watch them all end so ignominiously. Death was a monster, she thought, whether it sucked the life and intelligence from a man, or modest dreams from a woman.

A monster.

She closed her eyes, wondering if her own sense might not be deserting her. Perhaps she ought to stop trying to hold on in the face of so much futility—abandon the patient horse clopping along the moon-washed road, forget all about carrying her father's insensate hulk to a dying man she could not save. But the sound of hoofbeats thudded on. Her father's indrawn grunts and whistling exhalations continued their steady rhythm. Sitting there wishing she could be spirited away would not solve anything. Reluctantly, she opened her eyes.

She slammed them shut at once, to dispel the disquieting vision that had taken shape before her.

But when she dared peek once more through the cover of her lashes, she found Death waiting for her, just as she had so recently and rashly wished.

Death stood in the middle of the road, an apparition in human form, but so huge and dark and formidable that it seemed they would be swallowed into his velvety blackness. Death wore a cloak that flapped in the night wind and a Druid-like hood that concealed his face, but there was no mistaking his menacing intent.

He had come for her. She knew it with a gut-deep certainty.

Her heartbeat faltered, and then she rallied. "Get up, Queenie," she cried. She meant to run straight through that nightmare standing on the road. She had been beset by doubts and fears the whole night long. This manifestation of Death was merely an hallucination. . . .

The horse shied.

Steady old Queenie would not shy away from an apparition that existed only in Jillian's head.

Before Jillian could react, before she could convince herself that perhaps the mare had sensed her fear, the monster's hand snaked out and grabbed the reins, bringing their wagon to a skittering halt. Jillian clutched for balance, flinging one arm over her father to keep him from tumbling headfirst out of the carriage.

And then Death vaulted himself onto the bench beside her.

He landed in place with the scrape of boot leather against wood, the hiss of wool sliding over the seat. He carried with him the scent of pine, as if he'd been hiding for so long in the road-hugging woods that his cloak had absorbed the odor of the trees. Warmth radiated from him. Heat, of a kind that drew her toward him the way a crackling fire did after a long night on the road. And though the moon did its best to silver everything it touched, Jillian caught the faintest shimmer of midnight blue in his eyes, and the barest glimmer of burnished gold threading through the dark hair that escaped his hood.

He leaned over her. The movement plucked his hood away. The wind whipped at his hair and sent strands stinging against her face. The moonlight darkened hollows below his cheekbones and eyes, enhancing the strong masculinity of a face that bore the fine, clean lines of noble breeding. He so pulsated with virility and vitality that she knew he was a living, breathing man.

A warm, living man frightened her far more than Death.

She whipped her head around, but Jenkins was gone. She was alone.

She cringed back until she was pillowed by her father's sleeping form. "Who . . ." she stammered. "What. . . ."

He placed a finger against her lips. "Shhh."

She froze, while his finger pulsed against her, and his whispered command washed over her like a caress.

Rabbits, she thought wildly, sometimes froze in terror when trapped by a hunter. She was no timid little rabbit, meekly accepting its fate. She screamed—or tried to. Drawing the required breath meant inhaling her captor's scent, and her scream came out sounding more like a yearning whimper.

"Shhh," he hushed her again. "Your father sleeps. You don't want to wake him."

She felt completely surrounded by him, by his warmth, by the elegant timbre of a voice that set the very air vibrating around her. She swallowed, and nodded her intention to obey his command. He did not move his finger away and so her lips stroked against him, up and down.

He smiled, slow and satisfied. A merry twinkle lit his eyes as the knave curled his finger and rubbed his knuckle lightly over her lower lip. No man had ever touched her so. Sensation rocked through her with the force of an explosion and roused an unexpected, pleasant ache low in her vitals, as if that place and her lips were somehow intimately connected.

The tingling that rushed through her restored her senses. Good God, she lay soft and yielding as a besotted schoolgirl while a giant of a man made sport with her in the moonlight!

Fury—and embarrassment—lent her strength. She slapped his hand away. "Who are you?" she demanded. And then she remembered Jenkins's warning. "You're not King Charles, are you?"

His demeanor shifted from merry and teasing into hard implacability. "Nay, I am not the king, Jillian Bowen."

Nothing had ever frightened her so much as the sound of her name coming from this stranger's lips. "How . . . how do you know my name?"

"I know everything about you."

"But why?"

"Because." He gathered the reins from her nerveless fingers and slapped them lightly against Queenie's rump. The mare obediently pulled against the traces. "I had to make sure you were the right one."

"Right for what?"

He stared straight ahead. "No more questions."

"I'll scream," she said. The warning restored a bit of her confidence. "Jenkins will hear and come rescue me."

He whipped around, and his piercing glare pinned her to her seat. His hand flashed out and caught her by the chin, not so tight that it hurt, but not so gentle that she dared hope for mercy. He tipped her face up to his, so she could read the determination written there.

"No one can help you now, Jillian. For the next three weeks of your life, you belong to me."

⟁ TOPAZ

ROMANTIC ESCAPES

☐ **SOMETHING WICKED by Jo Beverley.** Disguised as the mysterious beauty Lisette, Lady Elfled Malloren anticipates only fun and flirtation at the Vauxhall Gardens Masquerade. Instead, the dark walkways lead to an encounter with treason, a brush with death, and a night of riotous passion with her family's most dangerous enemy—the elusive Fortitude Ware, Earl of Walgrave.   (407806—$5.99)

☐ **DANGEROUS DECEITS by Barbara Hazard.** Miss Diana Travis would not be taken in by the tender words and teasing kisses of the charming, wealthy, renowned rake Duke of Clare. But still she faced the daunting task of outdoing this master deception, as she tried to resist her own undeniable desires.   (182022—$3.99)

☐ **SHADOW ON THE MOON by Connie Flynn.** When Morgan Wilder rescues Dana Gibbs, a biologist specializing in wolf behavior, he carries her into the circle of his desire—and his secrets. As passion sweeps Dana and Morgan into an affair neither can resist, Dana begins to see a threatening side of Morgan that disturbs her.   (407458—$5.99)

☐ **TRAIL TO FOREVER by Elizabeth Gregg.** Tormented by memories of war, Daniel Wolfe joined a wagon train headed for California's gold fields. In saving Rachel Keye, dark deeds that shamed him began to give way to unbidden longings in his soul. Now fate brought them together on this wagon train's perilous journey, the dangers of the past closing in from behind, and ahead, shining as high as heaven, a love to reach for and to keep.   (406370—$5.99)

*Prices slightly higher in Canada

Buy them at your local bookstore or use this convenient coupon for ordering.

PENGUIN USA
P.O. Box 999 — Dept. #17109
Bergenfield, New Jersey 07621

Please send me the books I have checked above.
I am enclosing $_____ (please add $2.00 to cover postage and handling). Send check or money order (no cash or C.O.D.'s) or charge by Mastercard or VISA (with a $15.00 minimum). Prices and numbers are subject to change without notice.

Card #_____ Exp. Date _____
Signature_____
Name_____
Address_____
City _____ State _____ Zip Code _____

For faster service when ordering by credit card call **1-800-253-6476**

Allow a minimum of 4-6 weeks for delivery. This offer is subject to change without notice.